The Salisbury Key

The Salisbury Key

Harper Fox

FoxTales

Dedication

To my lovely Jane, as always –
to Josh, who created order out of chaos –
and to KT, who chased away the wolf from my door.

FoxTales Publications
www.harperfox.net

The Salisbury Key
Copyright © June 2017 by Harper Fox
ISBN 978-1-910224-29-8

Prologue
Salisbury Plain, Wiltshire, June 2007

A big hand clasped round mine and dragged me up the last few yards of the embankment. "There," Jason said, pointing out across the plain. "The most beautiful place in the world. And the most dangerous."

I couldn't help but agree with him. Jason Ross, professor of archaeology, Wiltshire University. Forty-five years old, dynamically gorgeous, his thick grey hair showing traces of blond in the sunlight, brown eyes abstracted with the joy of far horizons. This was our first field trip together—the first alone together, anyway. We'd been coming out here onto Salisbury Plain with excavation groups for three years. He was my postgraduate supervisor and revered tutor. I was his student, twenty years his junior. And I wanted him so much I was just about ready to die of it.

I dragged my eyes off him and turned my attention to the vista before us. My feigned interest became real as I recognised shapes on the blue-hazed horizon. We'd walked for five hours, but the view was worth it. "God," I said, shading my eyes. "Is that Silbury Hill?"

"Yes. And there to the north, Avebury. You can almost see the West Kennet barrow. And behind us, of course…" We both turned, and there were the ancient trilithon of Stonehenge, dreaming their circle of unbroken dreams in the sun. A lark went up above our heads from the yarrow-starred turf. We noticed simultaneously that he hadn't let go of my hand, and he released it, smiling, colouring a bit, but not in any hurry. "Sorry."

My mouth went dry. I had to uncap the water bottle at my belt and drink before I could answer him, aware that my hand shook, aware that he was watching me. "Don't be," I said. I held out the bottle. "Here. Do you…"

"No, thank you. Are you all right today, Daniel? You seem a bit distracted."

I swallowed. It seemed like only yesterday that the *Mr. Logan* with which he addressed me in his lecture hall was sending shivers down my spine, racking up the pressure of what I had thought then was only a severe crush. But my first name in his mouth was much worse. Like an invisible touch, a caress from one of those broad, well-made hands. "I'm fine," I said. "Tired, maybe. I was up till all hours with my thesis."

"Did you get past your block about underlying geological structures?"

"Yes. Thanks for the Matfen study. But I still don't see how I can ever reconcile Devereux's theories—great as he is—with hard science…"

"Well, remember that solving the puzzle isn't the prime focus of your work. Devereux advances a step—in his case, the interaction of human consciousness with the stone circles—and you take another. Someone else somewhere uses your conclusions, and Devereux's, those of a hundred other writers, and makes the final leap."

I looked at Jason, who had straightened up and planted his hands on his hips. He was an inspiring teacher, and a good, kind heart, who somehow found the time to take warm interest in all his students' lives. I had adored him from first sight across the lecture hall, and had continued my worship—at, I had thought, a good safe distance—in tutorials and on field trips ever since. I couldn't work out for the life of me why things felt so different today. "All right," I said. "I'll try to keep it in mind."

"Good lad." Jason returned his attention to the view. I felt a mix of relief and disappointment as his focus lifted away from me. "I tell you what, though," he went on after a few seconds. "You'd stand a better chance without that lot down there. We all would."

Beautiful and dangerous. He meant the barricades. From this vantage point, they stretched as far as the eye could see—a thin line of crossed poles, strung together by barbed wire. Punctuated every few hundred yards by red and yellow notices familiar to everyone who walked or drove regularly across Salisbury Plain— *no public access, by order of the Ministry of Defence.* They had set up here in 1898 and now occupied more than half of the plain's three hundred square miles. Jason had campaigned tirelessly for archaeological access within the military zones, and I had joined his fight as soon as he had taught me how much Neolithic, Bronze Age and Roman culture lay there. I'd had reasons of my own too for taking up arms at his side. "Did you have any luck with that application to Colonel Bryan?"

"That pompous desk-pilot? You're joking. He had the nerve to tell me to reapply in ten years' time. They might have finished with it then. What a bloody travesty."

"I know. That was one of the things that drew me to you in the first place." I heard myself and tried to backtrack. "I mean to your course. The chance to fight for the plain."

Jason ran a hand into his hair. He was smiling, but he seemed troubled too. I thought how odd it was that such shadows could gather round so brilliant a man on a day like this. They were almost palpable. Then he shook himself back into the moment. "Is that what we're doing?"

"Among other things. Aren't we?"

"Perhaps, although I'd never described it to myself like that. Maybe I should put you in charge of the cavalry." He paused, and a second later gave me the tiniest, most undeniable once-over. "You look like a man in search of a good peacetime fight."

I blushed. I couldn't help it—it came burning up like sunrise. I wished I'd worn more than cut-off jeans and a T-shirt frayed half to cobwebs for this trip, and I wondered why the hell I hadn't, what fantasies had been idling round in the back of my mind

I knew I was in better shape than the general run of archaeology graduates. I loved my office, and I loved the detailed, backbreaking immobility imposed on me by a delicate excavation, but I had in me a restless need to be active as well. Not just active, if I thought about it. Pushed physically almost to the limit. In a different world, I supposed that I would simply have joined up and worked off the excess in the plentiful war zones available to young men of my generation. As it was, I spent most vacations white-water rafting or mountain hiking with Outward Bound, and during term time I was probably as often in the campus pool and gym as I was behind a desk. Probably it showed.

Shivering lightly, I glanced at the ground, and adjusted the straps of my rucksack to hide a sudden nipple erection. I said, awkwardly, "Maybe," no longer even quite sure what I was agreeing to.

Jason nodded. Briefly he looked like a man enjoying my discomfiture, or enjoying something about me. Then he sobered. "That's good. I could use an ally."

The word became seductive in his mouth, and I smiled. I didn't know what was going on between my tutor and me out here on the plain this afternoon—didn't even know for sure that Jason was gay. He lived alone. Someone that bloody beautiful must be doing so by choice, and we'd all just assumed that he preferred the ivory tower to a redbrick semi and domestic bliss. I took hold of his strong wrist, admiring the soft leather cuff that adorned it, wondering at my own daring. "Really, sir. It's okay. I like being rootless. Means I can wander about all day on field trips with you. Run off to Bali at a day's notice. That kind of thing."

"Bali," he repeated thoughtfully, not moving out from under my touch. "I did some near-infrared aerial photography work over the temples there."

"I know. I read your book. The wakeboarding's not bad, either."

"Not something I've ever tried."

"Well, it's never too late for first times."

"Isn't it? You know, I'd begun to think I...I'd had all of mine." He put a hand on top of mine and disengaged my grip, but unhurriedly. "Anyway. We didn't come all the way out here to talk about wakeboarding, did we?"

I wasn't sure. For once we hadn't discussed the objective of our field day at all, and I remembered that Jason sometimes did this with a student when he wanted him or her to find the point unprompted.

I thought that I'd succeeded. We'd passed by Stonehenge without more than the loving second, third and fourth glances the place called forth from all who came near enough to fall beneath her spell, and continued out for almost fifteen miles across the plain. I'd noticed how, very slowly, the ground beneath my feet was beginning to lift and lower, lift and lower, with a regularity that triggered all my instincts. It had been slight, but unmistakable. Archaeology, not natural history. Work of man. And, at last, we had climbed up onto this sunny embankment. Only five feet high, and possibly explained by an underlying geological feature, but I knew that it was not. Beyond it extended a pure, straight line, out past the barricades, through the golden gorse and into the distance.

I turned around and sketched with one finger the shapes I had seen in the earth, and then the far-flung line. "A settlement," I said. "Roman. Possibly earlier too, but definitely Roman at some point. There's the road. We're on the vallum line."

Jason looked at me. He wasn't one for extravagant outbursts of praise, but you knew when you'd got it right. He said, "The substrate is probably Neolithic. I got one near-infrared shot from a light plane last year before my pilot was chased off by RAF Lyneham. There are hut-circle marks in the vegetation beyond the barbed wire. Not bad work, Daniel. Not many people would have spotted it from the ground."

We made our way down the embankment's far side. Now that I knew what I was looking for, I could see twin parallels running a familiar eight feet apart—the road, nothing more than a shadow of a memory in the turf, but there, as all the wonderful untouched settlement was there, packed with artefacts, knowledge, evidence of all the thousands of human lives that had come and gone. I felt it all for myself—an itch in my palms, a prefiguring ache in my knees as my body anticipated the hours of excavation—but it was Jason's longing that transfixed me. Handsome under any circumstances, out in the field in pursuit of his life's purpose, he was bloody irresistible.

A fine tension animated every inch of his tall, strong frame. The wind seemed to feel his excitement and feed it back to him, moulding his clothes to his body. Unlike me, he was properly and classily dressed for the occasion: stone-grey North Face trousers and a dazzlingly white shirt whose high-tech fibre would protect him from the sun and dry out in the rain with equal efficiency. His leather kit bag, battered relic of a thousand field trips, swung gracefully from his broad shoulders. I followed him down the ancient trackway, mesmerised.

Just beyond the settlement's outskirts the road took a gentle curve. Not great fans of scenic diversions, these Roman road-builders whom I sometimes felt I knew better than I did my living colleagues. But they often built on top of existing Celtic tracks, and they had a healthy respect for the gods they encountered along their invasion routes. An interruption in one of their dead-straight lines often meant a temple.

Jason was seeing it too, and I came to a stop by his side. The curve was like an embracing arm, stilling the breeze, capturing sunlight to a golden quintessence, filled with lark song and the scent of warm turf. A cluster of gorse bushes flourished here, their flowers bright as the little Adonis butterflies that flickered among them. I looked at the shape of the outcrop. Vegetation over masonry often gave the game away. Jason's experiments with near-infrared photography had refined these signals to an exact science, drawing on elements of biochemistry and spectroscopy to analyse the differences between undisturbed plants and those which had grown back over ancient foundations. He said, "What do you reckon? Pre-Celtic?"

What I reckoned was that this was where I wanted to lie down in the sunlight with my tutor and die of the pleasure of his touch. I said, my voice catching huskily, "Or earlier. Is this where you'd start the dig?"

"I don't think so. Places like this deserve to be opened up the way they were put down." He rested a hand on my shoulder, turning me gently in the direction of the barricades, which were blissfully invisible from here. "I'd start from the beginning—over there, in the hut circles. This is close enough to Stonehenge to be one of the construction-workers' villages." He swallowed audibly, and the warmth of his hand slid down over my left shoulder blade, the touch at once distracted and intensely aware. "There's so much to learn, Daniel! Places like this, and all the others like them, buried behind barbed wire. I have to get access."

"You will. I'll help." I glanced at him, wondering at the note of anxiety in his voice. Passion, I could understand. But Jason at this moment sounded more as if he'd lost something personal and precious beyond the barbed-wire fence. Or maybe I was misreading the shivering tension that had sprung up in the bright air between us. "It'll be the battle for the plain, okay? And we'll win eventually."

"We will, eh?" He shook his head, passed a hand across his eyes as if brushing away cobwebs or the rags of bad dreams. Then he looked around the gorse-sheltered curve, with its inviting moss-and-turf floor, as if seeing it through new, non-archaeological eyes. As if abruptly seeing it through mine. "You know, you…you're a good lad," he said, then didn't seem to know where to take the observation. "A good student, and—well, it's nice to have someone around who could take over where I left off. Someone young and…and strong."

I allowed myself a faint glint of mischief. The front of his shirt had rucked up beneath his kit-bag strap. I reached out, just careful, unobtrusive fingertips, and pulled it smooth. "You're hardly past it, Prof."

"Well, I'm a hell of a lot older than you are." That was good—we were talking about something else now. I wasn't quite sure what, but the subject was a warmer one than his academic succession. "A lot older, and—you're my student."

"Postgrad," I reminded him. "Not a kid."

"No. Far from it. But I'm still damn well old enough to be your…"

He ground to a halt. I knew what he'd been going to say, and it was a thought I wanted nipped in the bud for both our sakes. "Listen," I said, taking hold of his hand and drawing it down. "You're not. I was a very late surprise to my mum and dad. I'm twenty-five years old. I've lived alone since I was eighteen. I've had three lovers, all men, one of them older than you." I swallowed. I was launched now. It was over the top or a lonely death in my self-dug trench. "I know exactly what I want, and…I know what you want too."

His grip clenched tight round mine. "Oh. Daniel."

We got as far as the nearest patch of sun and shade between gorse bushes. Jason folded down onto his knees, pulling me with him. A frantic rustling near at hand made me gasp—Christ, was nowhere safe, even in the middle of this wilderness?—and he shouted with laughter as two sheep and a rabbit shot out from a ditch between the roots. I'd never heard such an uninhibited sound from him, though he laughed readily and often, a welcome warmth on rainy digs when someone had punctured the strata and ruined a long week's work. He never got angry, not about stuff like that. He was a good teacher. He was a pillar of the Salisbury academic community. Everybody loved him—and, after three years of slowly increasing mutual respect and friendship, he was about to love me.

Disbelief hit me. I had dreams like this—of being alone with him in some vast, beautiful place, and suddenly out of the wild blue yonder he would make a pass at me. I hit the turf, laughing too, and dragged him down on top of me. "God, Jason! Yes.

Come here." He was solid—his weight knocked a breath from me and I sucked my next one from his lungs, reaching up to intercept his clumsy, shyly offered kiss. I tangled my fingers in his hair. Oh, I wasn't dreaming now. My subconscious had never provided me with the press of his rising cock against my thigh.

He moaned and tore back, catching his balance on his arms. "Oh, sorry."

"What the hell for?"

"I haven't done this in a while. I've thought about it, though—how it might be with you, I mean—and I meant to be so…"

I cupped his face in my hands. If I held him there, so his hair caught the sun, it was like looking into the face of a lion. "Subtle?" I suggested unsteadily. "Gentlemanly?"

"Mm."

"Be those things next time." I let him go, returning luxuriantly to the broken kiss. This time I opened my mouth for him, and when he shuddered, I pushed a hand down between our tight-pressed bodies and stroked his shaft over the fabric of his trousers, bringing him to full and impressive erection. His tongue flickered urgently against mine. Heat burned down through me, sweet as the sunlight all around us, the hot blue sky above. The scent of crushed cotton and fresh sweat filled my nostrils, and my cock surged hard against his. Our hands collided, fought for the privilege of undoing buttons and zips. He had the easier job—my cut-offs were so old that their silver buttons slid out of their holes almost of their own accord. His zip and kit belt gave me more trouble, and I swore softly, laughing against his mouth, feeling him moan and chuckle in return.

Then the underwear was out of the way, his pants round his thighs—mine too as he signalled me with a touch to lift up so he could tug my briefs down—and we both caught our breath, sobering. Flesh to flesh. Engorged shaft pressing hard and hot to kindred skin. "Daniel," he said huskily. "You're so beautiful."

I bit back a cry. I had no problems with self-image, but to hear it from him sent a wild ache of pleasure and longing through me. He made me want to display myself to him. I shifted awkwardly, grabbed the hem of my T-shirt and pulled it up and over my head, feeling the same urgency to bare my skin as seized me when I hit the beach somewhere foreign and hot. I wanted his sunlight. And his mouth on me—God, yes, after one long hungry stare, he had leaned to plant an almost reverent kiss to my breastbone.

"Are you sure?" he whispered, and I didn't know how he could think I had any doubts, flat on my back with my cock trapped and throbbing under his belly, but nevertheless I put a hand to the back of his neck and guided him down to suck my left nipple into his mouth. The flesh there had puckered almost too tight to endure a touch, and I flinched helplessly, then groaned, relaxing in jolts as his circling tongue undid me. It might have been a while for him but he was catching up fast. Made a brief, shattering dive for the other nipple—I arched up, gasping, trying to thrust myself into his mouth—then began to move, slowly, in big measured thrusts. His arms closed round me, driving off the trace of fright I had surprised myself by feeling when the powerful rhythm began. "Daniel," he whispered against my ear. "Dan, let me fuck you."

I would have. If he'd meant it like that, and we could have untangled me from my jeans, I'd have opened up and let him in, dry and unprotected. That was crazy, not like me at all. I looked after myself. Looked after my lovers. But a red-gold haze had entered my mind. Blood and sunlight... And mercifully all he meant was *let me have you, let me make you come*—it was just a good, wild thing to say, in the heat of it. I gave it back to him, bracing my bare feet—when had I kicked off my trainers?—against the turf, heaving up to meet his strokes. "Yes. Fuck me now. Come on!"

I felt it start. For both of us—his pace quickening, losing its beat. He was crying out on every breath, short, harsh sounds in which I suddenly heard a rasp of fear. It was going to be big for him. I thought I understood. I said, "It's all right, lover. Let me," and I took hold of his shoulders, pushed up and rolled him beneath me onto the turf.

He gasped as if punched. I looked down at him. His eyes were wide, his face a fierce, sunlit blank. He wasn't that much bigger than me, but at that instant I felt all his power—felt, almost, that there was a temerity in pinning him down. I shivered. I had always been an active lover, trading positions fearlessly enough. "Jason…?" I whispered uncertainly, a tiny cold taste in the back of my throat.

He didn't give me any more time to think about it. He seized my arms and dumped me straight back down. His cock rammed up hard against mine. I fought for a moment. God knew I didn't mind going under. It was wildly sexy to be overwhelmed, and if I could just lose the sense of not being properly there to him, as if for a second he'd lost track. Then he shifted. His grip on me became once more only the touch of a passionate lover, his voice in my ear reassuring, full of recognition and wonder, urging me on. The coldness vanished. I grabbed his backside. I tipped back my head and saw the stone-curlews circling blackly in the blue turn into streaks of gold as my vision blurred. "Jason! Make me come!"

"Yes. Come for me. Come for me, beautiful boy. Yes." He pounded down on me, knocking the wind out of my lungs, a second later rocketing me to a climax like nothing I'd ever felt before. I heard my own cry—Christ, almost a scream, shooting up to blend with the song of the wind—and threw my arms around his neck. Too much, too hard, and I squeezed my eyes shut against his shoulder, hearing with a desperate relief the crack of his own control, the moment when his heat shot out against my belly and his moans broke into deep sobs.

***

A long time since I'd been knocked into sleep by a fuck. When I finally raised my head, the sun was low in the sky, casting long shadows. I pushed myself up, grunting faintly. Jason's shoulder had been a beautiful cushion, but a cool breeze had sprung up, and my neck was aching. I took a moment out to examine his peaceful face. He looked like a savannah lion after a spectacularly successful hunt. Then I patted him on his broad chest, still rising and falling contentedly in sleep. "Jason. Jason, lover. Wake up."

His eyes flickered open. Yes, a lion, instantly alert, scanning first my face and then the space around us, as if he were expecting ambush. It only lasted for a second, then he focussed on me and smiled. "God. You're something, aren't you? What the hell time is it?"

"Nearly six." I shifted, groaning and laughing. I'd have been a sight for aerial photographers and Google Earthers this afternoon, my cut-offs still down round my thighs, my hip and backside grass-marked. As soon as I left the shelter of his body, I felt the cold and reached for my T-shirt. "We'd better move. You've got dinner with the dean tonight, haven't you?"

"Oh, bugger the dean," Jason said comfortably, reaching up a hand like a lazy paw to pull me back down. I grinned. He was one of the few men in Salisbury who could safely make the remark— he and Dean Anderson had been friends since childhood. I

Harper Fox

stretched myself out on top of him, cautiously this time, but he
didn't try to stop me. He closed his warm grip on my arse,
squeezing tight.

We were starting to soar again, well established for another
round, when I felt my brakes go on. I wasn't sure why. I wanted
him, could hear my own voice cracking with desire as we tussled
and rolled on the turf. But, I realised suddenly, I also wanted time
to think about this. About its intensity, about why the climax had
shattered me, snuffed me out into such deathlike sleep afterward.
"Jason," I moaned. I'd thought, when we had lain down together,
that this might be casual, just the culmination of a crush. "God's
sake. You won't have the strength to bugger anybody, if…"

A rumble of laughter went through his chest. I felt it, a sweet
vibration that almost melted me. "All right," he said, sitting up.
"You're right, I suppose. Come on." He kissed me once, only
tenderly this time, and we helped one another in a stiff-limbed
scramble to our feet. "Look at you," he murmured, and I had to
rest my brow on his shoulder, my eyes squeezing shut, while he
reached to fasten up my jeans.

***

Yes, long shadows. We stood together once more on top of
the earthwork. A hell of a lot had changed. This time Professor
Ross, head of department and senior tutor, had his arm around
my waist. A whole new perspective on the world. We had worked
and travelled together for so long that I knew what he was seeing,
just as he would know my own thoughts now—a landscape under
different light, slight differences in contour picked out by the
lowering sun. Sometimes an ancient foundation, or something as
ordinary but telling as fifteenth-century ridge-and-furrow
ploughing, would jump into clarity.

I followed the line of the wall I had noticed before. It was clearer now, its eastern boundary thrown into sharper relief. I thought that I could even see a ghost of Jason's stone-hut circles.

"Yes," he said, as if I'd spoken the thought. "It's all there. Come on. Let's go and have a look."

I glanced up at him in surprise. "What—from the barricade?"

"No. Up and over it."

"You're kidding. Won't we get shot for trespassing?"

"Would that bother you?"

I considered. We'd done plenty of this before, when Jason's idea of a boundary had not coincided with that of the landowner. We hadn't tried it with the army before. But I got a dark thrill out of entering our dragons' lairs, and Jason knew it. He held out his hand to me. I looked at his broad palm, waiting for mine. At his smile—the trace of uncertainty in brown eyes turning fox-coloured in the sunset light, as if his whole happiness depended on my consent. At that moment, I would have followed him straight into hell. I smiled, reaching out. "All right."

We made short, practised work of the barricade. Jason gave me a leg-up onto the supporting wooden cross post, and once I had my balance there I eased back enough of the wire to let him join me. Then it was his turn to hold back the wire, keeping the barbs carefully free of flesh and clothes. I leapt down on the far side, grabbed a fallen stick of gorse and wedged the gap open, reaching up to help him down. He grinned as he landed beside me, a familiar flash of complicity. Yes, everything was the same and utterly different. He did not let go of my hand. He led me, blinded by sunset light and half-hypnotised, into the forbidden zone.

We were almost within twenty yards of the stone-hut enclosure when we heard the first drone of a jeep. We'd been lucky so far, I supposed. Quarter of a mile to the west lay the road which led to the Fellworth military base. Jason drew me to a halt, scanning the horizon. "Damn."

"Reckon they'll see us?"

"Maybe not if they haven't seen us yet. Just keep very still."

It was a good trick, and one which had worked for us before. The instinct was to crouch, to seek cover, but a stand of trees or even open ground where nothing moved or changed was less likely to draw attention than one where something moved, even briefly. It took a bit of nerve. I waited, not shifting a muscle. Trying to let myself become part of my background, to merge with the earth and the sky. Easier than usual today, I found, immediately beginning to drift. Jason still had hold of my hand. His thumb was moving against my palm, a strong, soothing caress. Irresistibly it made me wonder how his cock would feel, pushing up inside me…

"So," I said quietly, not taking my eyes off the ground, "you think dinner with the dean will be a late job tonight?"

I heard him catch his breath. "Well, Malcolm needs his beauty sleep. I'll remind him of that if I have to. Why?"

"I'll be in the library for a few hours, but I should be home after eleven." I was fairly sure I would be finished with my thinking by then. I was pretty much through with it now. I wished I hadn't halted our second exchange back at the earthwork. I was aching and half-hard again inside my jeans. *Come for me, beautiful boy.* "If you felt like dropping by…"

He snorted faintly. "That's right, Daniel. I'll drop round late at night to the paper-walled flat you share with five other postgrads. We'll make out on the sofa while they watch TV."

"Stop," I choked. I clasped his hand, setting every muscle against the spasm of laughter. "All right. Bad idea."

"Only in terms of location. I tell you what—I'll be home after eleven, if *you* feel like dropping by."

The sound of the jeep was gone. I tried to recall, through clouds of surprise and desire, whether it had faded into distance or stopped, then I lost concentration. I thought about Jason's beautiful house, where he regularly invited his postgrads for friendly, shop-talking dinners. I'd passed the open door to his bedroom on my way to the bathroom upstairs. He was generous and hospitable, but I didn't think he made the hour-before-midnight invitations lightly or often. I thought about his wide double bed. "God, Jason. I…"

White light punched across the plain. It was sudden and real as a fist. We both swung round, shielding our eyes. Beneath it, faint in the glare, I made out a pair of headlights. "Christ almighty. What's that?"

"Our jeep, I think. That's his searchlight. He must have doubled round."

"Oh, great."

"I know. I'm sorry. Looks like we're busted." His hand closed on my shoulder. "It'll be okay. Just do as you're told, and let me do the talking."

I nodded. He'd taught me that surrender was the best policy when confronted with armed military, either here or abroad. I could see that it was appropriate too. Nine times out of ten we'd have been trespassing, obeying our own code as seekers after knowledge in preference to petty local law. Jason took such issues pretty seriously. In America, he'd told us, he'd been to visit an environmental campaigner called Starhawk, who had coached him in the art of passive resistance and calculated civil disobedience, everything from leaflet drops to lying in such a way that a police horse would step over rather than on you. Lifting his hands, staring boldly into the light, he took a step back in the direction we had come, and I followed him.

Perhaps we'd taken too long about it. The evening air split to the sound of a single gunshot. "Fuck!" I gasped, bumping into Jason as he crashed to a halt. "Did he just…"

"Shoot at us? Yes."

I wasn't so sure. I thought the sound had reverberated upward, not in our direction. Jason had started moving again— fast this time, in long, ground-eating strides. I ran to catch him up, grabbing at his shirt. "Hang on. I think it was a warning shot. He fired into the air."

"I don't care. What place do guns have out here? Daniel, I swear—these people will consume our whole bloody planet, with their wars and their compounds and their lines in the sand, if we don't…"

I didn't catch the rest. He tore away from me and set off at a run towards the fence, the lights and the bullets. On the whole, I tended to agree with him. I was dead set against the military too, disgusted with a brinksmanship patriarchy that dealt with the world by rocking it back and forth across a fulcrum of destruction. And my revulsion was a kind of birthright to me, though normally I pressed that dark thought down.

But Jason was going to get himself shot. I belted after him. He couldn't half shift, for a man of his size. What the hell was he going to do? "Jason! Jason, slow down." Running half-blind, seeing scarlet spider-veins in my own retinas from the light, I caught him up a few yards from the fence, grabbed his belt and tried to slow him up. "For God's sake! They're gonna fire on you."

"Too damn right we are," came a harsh, clipped voice from somewhere up ahead of us. "Freeze, both of you. Hands where I can see them."

"John Marsh?" Jason demanded. He had stopped at the foot of the barricade and was staring up at the soldier perched on the top of it, his expression fierce and imperious as a profile of a Caesar on a Roman coin. "Is that you, you puppy?"

"Captain Marsh, 3rd Brigade Anglian. And I told you to... Oh. My God, it's Professor Ross, isn't it?"

"Too damn right it is. I knew your father. I knew you, for that matter, when you were riding about in a pushchair, not a sodding armoured truck. Put that gun down."

I squinted up into the light. To my surprise, the tough-looking soldier was doing as he was bidden, holstering an automatic rifle back into his belt. Turning towards the truck I could now see was parked on the turf beyond the barbed wire, he made a gesture, and the blinding searchlight dimmed. "Stand down!" he barked to unseen comrades. "Situation under my control. Sorry, Prof," he continued, sounding more human. "But you know the rules. This area's been heavily mined."

"You think I don't know that?"

"I hope not, if you took a student in with you."

"This is a colleague. And he knows the risks."

Pride touched me—and then I lost a breath as if punched. For a moment I couldn't catch it again. Involuntarily I glanced back the way we'd come. It hit me that those red-and-yellow warning signs were more than boundary markers. I'd grown up, like most local kids, with their message in front of my eyes, limiting the scope of my wandering. The universal symbol for explosion, and an unfortunate stick man flying back from one. *Danger from unexploded shell and mortar bombs.* It was part of childhood's wallpaper for me. I'd never taken it seriously, eventually ceased to see it.

That was it. The breath came back. Those signs were like the bogeyman, the threat was enough. Half the wire strung out around this place was for the army's convenience, not public safety. Jason, who knew so much about this place, would know that. I didn't know what game he was playing with Marsh, but he would have his reasons.

I straightened my spine. *This is a colleague*, Jason had said. Coming from a man like him, that was a stunning compliment, and I tried to look professional, like I deserved the title and was clear and calm about the risks as well. Marsh put down a hand to help hoist us back over the fence, and Jason courteously gestured me ahead. I tried not to use Marsh's help getting up and over the wire. He'd holstered his rifle, but the proximity of all that death-laden hardware made my stomach heave. Once we were all down on the other side, he turned to us. "Sorry for the warning shot, Prof. Couldn't be sure of getting your attention otherwise."

"You could've shouted."

"Would you have listened?" He shook his head, not waiting for a reply. "Here's the situation, gentlemen. I've got a truckload of cadets over there, and I need to make a point to them—and maybe to you too—about peaceful arrest. No matter who's trespassing."

Jason shrugged. He glanced at me, his face calm again now, only wryly amused in the headlights. He held out his wrists. "Sorry, Daniel. Go ahead then, soldier."

***

I sat handcuffed in the back of the jouncing armoured truck, opposite a row of five grinning squaddies, and I wondered about my afternoon. Beside me, shoulder pressing unhidden against mine, Jason was calmly smiling back at the lads, as if all this was routine to him. Perhaps it was. He spent as much time in the field as he did in the office, and God knew how many lovers he'd laid down among the ruins.

I asked myself if I cared. Today it had been me. Tonight, unless we ended up in the holding cells at Fellworth, it would be me again. A strange euphoria began in me, starting in the pit of my stomach, blossoming outwards into the palms of my hands and down to my groin. I looked at the floor, afraid the excitement would shine from my eyes. I was pretty sure we were entertaining Marsh's cadets enough as it was.

Jason looked calm and tidy as ever, but I'd let my hair grow over summer, and I'd already surreptitiously picked out one crushed buttercup leaf from it. That, in combination with my grass-stained cut-offs, in which I now just felt half-naked rather than cool, probably shouted less colleague than toy boy.

But if Jason was happy with it, so was I. I resisted the temptation to dip my head down to his shoulder and let the boys think what they liked. I stretched out my foot luxuriantly, tried the grip of the handcuffs as if they'd been velvet-lined and hitched to a bedpost. *I'll be home after eleven, if you feel like dropping by.*

"Daniel? You all right?"

Lost in memories of the afternoon and anticipation of the night, it took me a moment to come back. Jason was looking at me in an odd mix of amusement and concern. His shoulder was rubbing against mine with the motion of the jeep. "Fine," I said, smiling up at him. "Why wouldn't I be?"

"Well, you're in military custody. Don't you mind?"

I snorted. Put like that, it did seem odd. But I didn't, not at all. Suddenly I wanted to prove it to Jason. I wanted to confide in him, give him something for everything he'd given to me. "Listen," I said. "I don't love the bloody military. My father worked for them—not as a soldier. In the military lab at Hartcliffe Dean. He wasn't anything special, just a technician. But he volunteered as a test subject back in the late seventies when they were working on some kind of nerve agent. Something like VX, although we never found out for sure."

Jason stiffened away from me. After a second, he struggled round a bit to face me. "*What?*"

"I know. I suppose you'd say he wasn't the brightest spark, but we were always short of cash, and they'd assured him the tests were harmless."

"But—they weren't?"

"No. Not at all, although no one knew until he and the other volunteers started getting ill years later. Not that anything was proven. He died when he was fifty. I was six."

Jason stared at me. This was why I usually kept my mouth shut. Nobody ever knew what to say. And Jason seemed more affected than anyone else among the handful of people I'd told. He'd gone pale under his tan.

"It's okay," I said. "It was a long time ago. I only mentioned it because... Well, any rings you want to run around this lot, any battles you want fought...I'm your man."

"Oh God, Daniel," he said. I frowned. I hadn't meant to freak him out. He was absolutely grey now, and suddenly looked his age. "Hartcliffe? The seventies?"

"Yes. Seriously—ancient history." That was godawful, coming from an archaeologist, and I grimaced. "I don't even remember."

He stretched his cuffed hands awkwardly towards me. Just as awkwardly, I reached back, only very distantly hearing one of the squaddies break into a laugh. Jason's fingers laced round mine. And although I hadn't meant to distress him like this, his look sent shivers through me. I didn't understand. We'd been so close that afternoon, and yet it was if he was seeing me properly for the first time. As if I was real to him. He cleared his throat and said roughly, "That must have been hard on your family."

"Briefly. They're all gone now." I squeezed his fingers tight. I wanted to pull us both out of these deep waters now. "I told you—I'm footloose. No ties, no worries. Don't look so serious. I'm okay."

Neither of us had noticed that the jeep had bounced to a halt. Jason sat very still. I fought the urge to blink, to try and hide from his regard. It wasn't that I wanted to, but his intense sable stare was almost too much for me. If I was inclined to believe for one instant what I was seeing there, I'd become something to him I couldn't yet be—something rare and of great value.

"Okay," he echoed faintly. "Okay. Good."

No ignoring the soldiers now. I sat up straight and offered them my best haughty look, but they only quieted when Marsh yanked open the rear door. "All right, you lot," he said. "And you two gentlemen—out, please."

Well, he had said something about making a point. I wondered distantly, clambering out of the back of the truck, what form it was going to take. Public execution, maybe.

Ah. Very public. The sides of the truck were canvas, and I hadn't been able to see much out the front. After a while I'd lost my bearings. But Marsh had elected to take us back to the Stonehenge car park, where, as he probably knew perfectly well, Jason had left his Citroën DS that morning. I could see it—the sleek old French model, one of Jason's few obvious extravagances—in the distance, conspicuous by its quiet glamour in the midst of the carnival parade of beat-up Deux Chevaux and vintage VW bugs and buses that had descended since we'd arrived at dawn. I'd forgotten. It was June the twenty-first. Summer solstice. I glanced back and saw Jason remembering too, looking out across the crowd, breaking into a broad grin as Marsh helped him, still handcuffed, down from the truck.

31

Mild pandemonium reigned. The car park, and all the meadows around the henge, were dotted with little groups of Wiccans, sun-worshippers, nutcases and the most passionate and genuine advocates of nature-based religion you could ever hope to meet. Campfires were on the blaze, a distinct smell of crisping veggie burgers filling the air. There was enough tie-dye fabric in enough colours to stretch a rainbow to the bloody moon, and, over by the chicken-wire fence that encircled the monument, the usual representatives of opposing Druidical orders were conducting the usual debate, amongst themselves and the attendant police and military, as to which of them was the real deal and therefore entitled to enter the circle and chant up the sunrise.

A few heads had turned at the arrival of the truck. The army weren't popular guests around Stonehenge at Solstice—they got the blame for the chicken wire and the limited access—unjustly, because all that was the work of English Heritage—and I heard scattered hoots and jeers rise up as Marsh led Jason and me away from the truck. Marsh, face impassive, shook his head. "Nice welcome."

"Well, I can't help but question your presence too," Jason said, scanning the crowd. He seemed to have recovered himself. "Do these people look as if they need martial law imposed on them?"

"Not at all. A giant butterfly net, I'd say. And I'd rather be home with my missus and kids, Professor Ross, but we're here by request of the police and the site managers. Crowd control only. Now…" He paused, and reached to unfasten a set of keys from his belt. "Now, gentlemen, if you could just listen for a moment, I have to tell you that you've been officially escorted out of a closed military area. The army won't be pressing charges, since you came with us peaceably, but I'm afraid you'll find a request for payment of a fine in your post within the next few days. Look, I know where you live, Prof, but I'm going to need to take down your..." another pause, and an amused, assessing glance at me, "...your young colleague's details."

"I'm sure he'll be happy to give them to you, if you'll just take off his cuffs. Though you might as well charge his fine to the university—that's where I'll be charging mine."

"I'm afraid that's not the point, sir. We need to keep on record the details of any potential, er, troublemakers."

I glanced up. The cuffs were chafing my wrist bones now, and I held out both hands, making sure I met Marsh's eyes. I wasn't sure about the nature of the trouble he thought I might be likely to cause, but I felt a mischievous impulse to let him wonder.

Then, suddenly, I lost interest. The sun was almost down, heavy bronze clouds piling high on the western horizon, but one last deep gold shaft had made its way through them, casting an unearthly glow on the henge and the eastern arc of its enclosure. Without it, I wouldn't have noticed the solitary soldier standing guard by the fence. He was young and very pale, as if this crowd-control duty was deadly serious for him. The unexpected light had cast him in ivory. His hair was sable, nearly black, beneath his moss-green beret.

For a moment I thought I was imagining him. Plenty of ghosts here on Salisbury Plain—tiny dark men in deerskins, who vanished off into the long-barrow mounds; and ghosts of soldiers too, victims of friendly fire shootings and tank accidents. But he was real. I could see the furrow of concentration between his shapely, strongly marked brows. I couldn't work out what it was that caught me about him, what made it hard for me to get the next breath into my lungs. He was, simply, the most beautiful thing I had ever laid eyes on.

Guilt went through me, that I could even glance at another man after the afternoon I'd just spent. But a glance was all it was. If he fascinated me, plainly for him I didn't exist. He was looking straight through me—through Jason, Marsh and the armoured truck, paying none of us any attention at all.

Not so the crowd. A ripple of laughter had gone through the little groups on the outskirts at the sight of me and Jason being unloaded, holding out our hands for Marsh's key. "Please don't do it again, sir," Marsh was saying. "I know you want access to the land, but there's proper channels." He undid Jason's cuffs, and a few cheers and a patter of applause rose up. Like attracted like, and by the time Marsh turned to me, I realised that half the gathered crowd was watching.

I couldn't resist. A bright bubble of elation was rising up in my chest. The evening, and the world, was wildly beautiful. Jason Ross was my lover, and my life was before me. The ancient rocks of Stonehenge, old bones of Earth, were calling people back to them—this crowd, now whooping and cheering as Marsh gestured to me to hold out my hands. I raised them so they could see. Marsh rolled his eyes but went with it, unlocking me with a wryly ceremonial gesture. Peripherally I noticed the grave young soldier shift and finally look at me. Yes.

The cuffs fell away. Grinning, I lifted both hands high, extending my fingers in peace signs. I remembered a dance move from my not-so-long-gone clubbing years, and briefly sashayed in the golden, laughter-filled light. My T-shirt rode up. I saw the young guardsman's dark gaze focus. I felt a flare of triumph, then, strangely, a sharp guilt, as if I had disturbed a priest at his prayers.

"That's right," Jason said, placing a gentle hand in the small of my back and propelling me off stage towards the car park. "You go ahead and antagonise the people we need to propitiate."

"What, the clockwork soldiers? That's rich coming from you, Indiana Jones."

He snorted faintly. "Fair point. But you nearly started a riot back there, and, well, I don't want us spending the night in separate cells."

We had reached the car. I sat down on the low, shark-nose bonnet of the DS, suddenly exhausted. We were still within earshot, and possibly sight, of the crowd around the enclosure, but I didn't care. When he leaned over me, I reached up and into his deep, shuddering kiss.

"Listen, Daniel," he said, when it was done. "You've had four lovers in your life. I've had…even fewer. I don't do one-night stands. And I couldn't bear to think of sharing you. I know that's repressive and old-fashioned. If you think so too, and you don't turn up tonight, I'll understand, all right? And we'll still be friends." He ran his fingers through my hair, or tried to—smiled when he hit the first tangle and pulled out another crushed leaf. "Either way, beautiful boy, I'll never forget you. And if you ever need anything…" He paused, the weird shadows flickering round him again, dimming his lights. "If you're in trouble, or you need help…you come to me. Come to me. Okay?"

Chapter One

"Sir? Will your companion be returning? May I get you something in the meantime?"

The waiter must be new, I thought. The regular staff here in Salisbury's most elegant restaurant came and went like well-trained ghosts. I returned him a blank stare for his own mildly suggestive glimmer—cute as hell though he was—and watched him take a backward step, discomfited. "He'll be back soon. I'd prefer to wait."

I'd been waiting quite a while. I hoped Jason was okay. I glanced at the stairs that led down to the men's room, and wondered why I hadn't gone to check. He didn't like to be fussed over when he was ill, and I'd probably have been sharply told to leave him alone, but that wouldn't have stopped me with anyone else. He'd been edgy and off-colour all day, as if tonight was going to be some kind of trial, not the marker of our third anniversary.

Le Boulevard was a beautiful place. A place for best behaviour. Nobody else, I had noticed, was leaning to gawp through the windows at the stream of life passing below. I sat up straight, folded my hands, and tried to affect an air of indifference to its sublime Deco architecture, slender pillars, ethereal glasswork ballooning out like sails over Kiln Street. I wished I could at least tug open the neck of my shirt.

I'd realised slowly that, in Jason's social circle at least, I was a bit of an urchin. His first serious present to me had been a trip to the Regency tailors and a baker's dozen of exquisite handmade shirts. Fun at the time, and I tried to wear them well, but restrictive collars had always driven me crazy, and as for the (very muted) rainbow of silk ties… Still, he liked me to look nice, and God knew I owed it to him.

I made myself taste the delicious, crisp Veuve Cliquot instead of just nervously knocking it back. He'd booked the best table in the best restaurant in town for our celebration dinner, and my tutor's wages weren't going to be covering the bill. Tonight was a treat, one I thought we'd both been looking forward to.

I glanced again at my Asprey cufflinks, then checked to see that I'd scrubbed out the last of the Neolithic mud from under the gold band he'd bought me at the end of year one. He'd been dead serious about the one-night stands, hadn't he? I'd dropped by his flat after eleven on that warm Solstice night, trying to look casual, shivering so hard inside that I'd almost dropped to my knees when he'd opened the door, shut it behind us and folded me into his arms. And that had been it. Three years of travel, learning, and the kind of love I'd never imagined could exist, either for me or in my own heart for somebody else. *Jason*, I thought, yearningly, setting my white linen napkin aside and starting to get up.

But he appeared on the stairs as if summoned, and I sat back down. He looked dreadful. No—magnificent as ever, in his charcoal fine-wool dinner suit, in the waistcoat whose two dozen tiny pearl buttons I'd painstakingly fastened for him on the way out. But pale to the gills, and shadowed in a way I'd noticed time and again over the past few months, as if hunted or haunted or…

Or permanently on the brink of delivering bad news. Okay. I straightened up and found a smile for him as he made his way between the tables. He was nearly fifty now, and I was twenty-eight. I knew I had my charms—he'd discovered most of them for me, rolling us around in that big double bed—and I'd been useful to him, scrambling about dangerous field sites, dealing with officials in the polyglot mix of languages I picked up with chameleon rapidity wherever we went. But I never had been, never could be, his peer. I was scruffy and disorganised, probably more akin to the New Age hordes who gathered at our megaliths than to Salisbury academia. I didn't shine during dinners with the dean. And although I was certain that he'd never so much as looked at another man during our three years together, there were times when I knew that something was missing for him when we hit the sack. He'd stare at me as if through me, into the eyes of someone older, stronger, more complete.

I kept the smile on as he pulled back the chair opposite me and sat down. Maybe we'd had our run. Odd time for him to tell me—odd place to bring me to do it—but...

"Danny, are you all right?"

I started a bit. *Danny* was for special occasions, and seldom public ones. I'd hated it like poison from anybody else, but from him it melted me. "Me?" I queried gracelessly, knocking over the flower vase and its single stem of heady-scented camellia. "I'm fine. I was just gonna come and check on you."

"Oh, Dan! Look at the state of—" Jase seized a napkin, reached over and pressed it to my wet sleeve. At the same moment, the maître d' appeared at my elbow, apparently plucking a fresh flower from thin air, and between these two civilising influences, I was put to rights.

"Sorry. It's okay, isn't it? It was just water."

"I know, but that beautiful silk…" He caught himself visibly, trying for a smile. "You just look so perfect tonight. Can't bear to see you messed up."

"Sorry. Thank you. There, it's fine. I was worried about you. Aren't you well?"

"Still regretting those king tiger prawns Ketut regaled us with in Padang, believe it or not."

I smiled in relief. His shadows vanished when he reached for humour, and I felt the sense that my life was about to end here recede. Because that was what it would be, if he was finished with me. I tried to push the cold thoughts aside. We'd just got back from Bali two nights before. He'd flown me out to the ruins of Pakerisan, newly discovered by his near-infrared aerial team, and I'd taken him kiteboarding. He'd loved that, beating me at my own game within a few hours of raising his sail, and we'd fallen together into the sands of the deserted beach afterwards, laughing at his bruises. Hardly the behaviour of a man getting ready to dump me.

"I did try to warn you," I said. "We don't have to eat here if you're not up for it."

"What? No, I'm perfectly all right." He looked it now, or better, anyway. Back in his debonair skin. He made the smallest gesture, and my waiter, eyes now demurely cast down, melted out of the gilded plasterwork. "We're ready to order, I think. Tell me, are the Provençale artichokes fresh on the menu tonight? We'll have those as a starter, and the confit fennel." He cast me a kindling glance. "You'll love those. The chef makes his own walnut oil. Then, for our main…"

I sat back. I was too happy to see him returning to his gourmet self to listen to what was being ordered for my dinner. And I wasn't exactly a hick, but growing up in a sleepy Wiltshire village hadn't prepared my tongue to pronounce the international menus in the kind of places Jason liked. I enjoyed what ended up in front of me. I didn't let it bother me either that he always picked up the bill, believing him when he assured me our funds came from the same joint pot.

Then the waiter was gone, and it was just the two of us once more. The hush that fell was not one of our comfortable at-home silences, and during it I realised I wasn't actually all that hungry. We'd both dropped some weight in the last year or so. Working and playing hard, I'd put it down to, but sometimes I wondered. Sometimes we were almost jumpy around one another, almost too anxious to please. A bit of an appetite-killer. Sometimes I wondered if I was really good for him.

"Daniel," he said suddenly. "I've got to talk to you." And my heart began a slow, cold slither down the inside of my ribs.

Weirdly, he was pulling a copy of the *Guardian*'s colour supplement out of his briefcase. My mind picked up and discarded absurd possibilities. If Jason had never so much as glanced at another man, I was acutely aware that I *had*. Soft-eyed Egyptian camel boys at Giza, tanned ripped lifeguards on the Turkish beaches... Never more than a glance, of course, but my paranoid fancy painted the society pages of the supplement with images stolen from my dreams. Why the hell I needed them, with Jason's handsome reality in the bed beside me, I didn't know, and I hated myself for letting them persist.

"Here," he said, opening the cultural section. "Look. They ran your article."

He spread the paper out on the table, shifting our wineglasses to make room. Somehow the action made me feel more comfortable, as if we were at home, shoving plates aside to accommodate our textbooks and laptops. I recognised one of the photos immediately—the snap I'd got from a low-flying helicopter out across the inundated temples of Kyon Kam. It had been a tourist flight, cameras strictly forbidden so close to the North Korean border, but I'd trotted out my decent impression of an upper-class English twit and they'd let me off, memory card intact. "Oh, Jase, it was hardly my article. I just spoke to the Guardian's Korea correspondent about it."

"Well, he quotes you at length. And this photo shows the problem far more clearly than any of the other images I've seen."

I shook my head. It was a good photo, but I'd got lucky. And Jason was normally unimpressed by this minor obsession of mine. "I thought you didn't like me buggering about with Kim Il-Sung's antiquities."

"Technically they're Kim Jong-il's now. I've been wondering—maybe I've been too rigid. Maybe there aren't diplomatic channels that will get archaeologists out there fast enough to save Kyon before it gets drowned or sucked into a war zone."

"What?" I could hardly believe what I was hearing. Jase knew my primary interest in Kyon Kam wasn't saving the temples but extracting from them the fabled artefacts their mythology promised, gilded-bronze sculptures of deities and lotus vases inlaid with turquoises and pearls. He thought of that as treasure hunting, not archaeology, and hadn't scrupled to tell me so. "Is this what you wanted to talk about?" I asked, puzzled.

"Oh. Er, no." He folded the newspaper up, but did not look at me. "At least… Well, it has bearing. You really think the temple hoards are significant, don't you?"

"Hell, yes. Doesn't everybody? I'd give anything to get my hands on them before North Korea decides they don't exist." I turned my glass between my hands, letting a small wicked grin surface. "Then nukes 'em to make sure it's true."

Jason failed to smile back. "That's just it. Everybody *doesn't* care about them, not the way you do. If you hadn't had a teaching schedule to come back to and a batch of Roman pottery shards to dig out of a midden, you'd have stayed out there and kept trying for them, wouldn't you?"

I stared at him, bewildered. I'd given it thought, but it had never been a serious option for me. "God, I don't know. Anyway…" I paused. His shadows were back, all around him, flickering between the rags of the candlelight. "Anyway, love, it's not the bloody teaching and middens I come back for, is it? You know that."

"Yes. Yes, I suppose I do, and it never ceases to astonish me. You're young, hungry, resourceful. You could do so much out there as an activist, rescuing places like those. Every time I see you walk through my front door, I ask myself why you still want to tie your world to mine."

I thought it was our *front door.* A childish, unworthy thought, but it carried a sting. I paid my way—probably nowhere near what the place was worth, but we split all the bills and expenses. Even if I hadn't, Jason had assured me, with a sincerity that had made me believe him, that his gorgeous house was my home. "It isn't a tie," I said uncomfortably. "Jesus, Jase. Don't we *share* a world?"

"Yes. Yes, we do." He pulled out an immaculate white cotton handkerchief—the scent of vetivert wafted across to me—and dabbed it to his forehead. God, he *was* nervous, wasn't he? I'd never seen him like this. "Think about it, though. I'm not saying you wouldn't make the greatest career academic in the world, but before you come to any big decisions regarding your future…"

I frowned. I wasn't aware that I had been on the verge of making any. Of having one made *for* me, catastrophically perhaps, but I didn't see how that tied in to my extracurricular activities. I said, uncertainly, "I don't understand."

"I know. I know. I don't mean to be vague. But… Salisbury is a small town, and the university is a smaller town within it. And the academic community, as you'll find, can be a series of tiny, suffocating villages within that town. Especially in archaeology." He paused, smiled. "Dan Brown can sex it up as much as he likes, but we're still men who spend our best years staring into the mud."

"Okay. Okay, I'll bear that in mind." By now I was thoroughly bemused. If some kind of axe was about to come down, why was his ankle gently pressing mine, his haughty face softening in the way it sometimes did in bed when he'd pushed me too far or too fast and was sorry? "Jase, come on. Whatever it is can't be as bad as the hot tin roof you're on now."

"Ah. It shows, does it? I don't know. I'm almost scared to jump down. I need you to try and forgive me."

I always had forgiven him. It hadn't been much of an effort, his misdemeanours so few and far between. All right, he could be overbearing. But how was he supposed to know that, if I never fought back or objected? And I never did. He conducted himself at all times with such gentle power that I just went under. Often quite literally. He never had learned to enjoy being topped, and occasionally failed to notice that the energies he was unleashing on or into me were leaving bruises. But, Christ, he was so kind. And even if it wasn't perfect, he loved me. Where again would I ever find such a love as that? I'd forgive him anything.

"I'm sure I will," I said. "Tell me, love. It'll be all right."

He sat back a little, then he reached into the inner pocket of his jacket. I recognised the envelope he withdrew from it— university issue, with our archaic heraldry woven into the logo. Dean Anderson resisted all attempts at modernisation. And the letter was from the dean's office, I saw, as Jason laid the envelope cautiously down on the table between us.

I saw that it was addressed to me. I glanced up in confusion. "I don't understand. Did…did the dean give you this to pass on to me?"

"No. I'm sorry. It came through the post yesterday morning, and I…I kept it."

All right. Something real for me to forgive, this time. It was almost a relief to me. I was so far from perfect, and he was so damn close to it. But nevertheless I was shaken. "Kept it? Why?"

"Because I'm nearly certain of what's in there, and…I wanted to talk to you before you saw it."

I looked at him enquiringly. If he knew why the dean might be writing to me, I hadn't a clue. I cast back urgently over the last few weeks for anything I might have done to bring the college into disrepute. I could see Jason holding back the notification that I was about to be sacked. "And did we? Talk, I mean?"

"A little. Not very effectively, I suspect. Open it, Dan."

I shook my head, aware that I had been awaiting his permission to open my own damn mail. I unfolded Dean Anderson's creamy parchment—a single sheet, announcing that he'd selected me from a strong field of other candidates to take the assistant department head's chair.

I'd forgotten all about it. I'd gone through the application process automatically, because staff were expected to show an interest in the grades above them, even though my preference was for fieldwork, not the higher posts that would lead me increasingly towards admin. Jason had wanted me to progress my career too. My interview with the dean had been professional enough, but more in the nature of a friendly talk and, after I'd met and chatted with the outside applicants, I'd assumed the post would to go one of them and thought no more about it. I spread my hands. "This…this is good. Isn't it?"

"Yes. I'm so proud of you."

Then why try to hide it from me? I let the thought go. It *was* good. If nothing else, it would help redress the balance of seniority between me and Jason. If I felt less junior, less of a student, maybe he could relax a bit and let me become more of a real, adult partner to him. "I can't believe it," I said, folding up the letter. My hands were shaking a little. "I…I'd be pretty young for the post."

"Yes." Jason shot me a small, wry smile. "It's almost unheard of. But the dean is impressed with your work, and you're good with students. You've earned it."

Something in the way he said it touched a warning bell in my head. "Oh, Jase. None of this had better be down to you."

"I was afraid you would think that. That others would too. That's why I stayed clear of your application process. But in fact, when Malcolm talked to me about this, I…I opposed it."

"You…" I stared at him. I felt genuinely, stupidly hurt. "God. Why?"

"It's a heavy weight for young shoulders. That's what I was trying to tell you, my love. So much responsibility, and deskwork too, admin and grading…"

"I know. I know about all that. But I think I want this."

"Of course you do." For a moment he sat watching me in silence. I saw how pale he was beneath his Bali tan. Then, suddenly, he reached out and closed one hand on mine. "But what if I didn't want it *for* you? What if I wanted something else?"

My throat went dry. He was never this demonstrative in public. Times were changing, but Salisbury was an old-fashioned town, and a few heads were turning, a few startled gazes coming to focus on the place where this man's hand was clasped around another's. Well, fuck them. Carefully, tenderly, I reached out my other hand and cradled his grip. "Well, I…I'd listen."

"Oh God. You're such a perfect… You always were such a perfect boy. All right. Come away with me."

His skin went hot and then cold under mine, and I felt dampness break on it. "What," I said, "for a…a holiday, or…"

"No. No, not at all. I've poured out my whole life here. I don't want to see you doing the same. Let's just—go. Go to one of the amazing places we've seen together, and leave all this behind."

"Leave Salisbury?"

"England. I don't—I don't want to stay here anymore. I don't want you to stay."

I wondered briefly if my sober, dignified professor had scored something off one of the chemistry students. If, more likely, he had picked up a bug and started a fever. His eyes were bright enough for it, his grasp one shade off desperate. "But what would we do that for, love? Everything we've worked for is here, and this…" I glanced down at the envelope still on the table. "This makes it perfect."

"Oh, Dan. You'd be perfect anywhere. We don't have to stay on the tracks, in this Camberwick Green little world where the bloody puppets at the other tables are staring at us right now because I'm holding your hand!" His voice was rising. Automatically I disengaged my grip far enough to stroke his wrist, trying to soothe him. "I want us to have more, to be committed to one another…"

"Christ. You think I'm not *committed* to you?"

"No. I've been the one who's been scared, who's tried to hide, for the sake of my fucking career. I'm sick of all that. Let's… Oh, I don't know. Let's go the hell back to Bali, and have some absurd civil ceremony on that heaven of a beach you showed me, and let's just…never come back."

"*Jason!*" There went my voice too. Okay, now people were really having a gawp. In a way I didn't care. I'd honestly thought that this man, this unlikely lover who had given me three years of

46

his life, had come to the end of what he could share with me. I'd thought we were over. Instead he'd more or less asked me to marry him.

No. To elope. Something was very wrong with Jason Ross tonight. My heart was pounding hotly, but I drew a couple of deep breaths and tried to raise the barricades around it. If he was upset about something, or sick, I mustn't take him literally. I had to wait for some calmer moment, get him home and find out what he really meant. And although I didn't mind the curious eyes upon us on my own account, I didn't want him exposed, not fever-bright and off-centre like this.

I said, quietly, "I don't need a ceremony to know how you feel about me. If it's what you want, we'll do it, but…"

"But you want to stay here."

"I just hadn't thought about doing anything else. And now this post has come up…"

The waiter appeared out of nowhere. Jason dropped my hand. Somehow I'd managed to forget that we were there to eat, and the gentle touchdown of the confit he'd ordered, along with the walnut-oil artichokes, startled me. It did look beautiful. But my stomach was describing slow arcs inside me, after this last roller-coaster half hour, and when I glanced at Jason, he was grey. I paused until the waiter was out of earshot. "Jase. You all right?"

"Actually, no. I don't feel well at all. Do you mind? Will you take me home?"

It was so unlike him to be ill—or, when he was, to ask for my help—that I almost leapt to meet his request. I ran outside and hailed a taxi, then ducked back in and grabbed the bill. An assistant department-head could afford it, after all, couldn't he? I reassured the anxious maître d' that we didn't have a problem with the food, and then I went back to our table, where Jason was sitting as if cast in stone, resting his brow on his hands. I didn't know what the hell was going on here tonight. All I knew was that I loved him, so much that my heart felt ready to crack my rib cage apart.

I crouched down beside him. "All right," I said. "Come home. Come with me."

Chapter Two

He went straight upstairs when we got in. I hung back in the hallway, watching him go, then turned away to give him the privacy of the bathroom if he needed it. Once in the taxi, he had transformed once more into his independent self, deflecting my concern with his usual kindly detachment. Yes, he was fine. It was nothing. He was only sorry for spoiling our night out.

I went down the steps into the living room and poured myself a brandy from the decanter shimmering gently among its glasses on the cabinet, for once feeling as if I really needed a drink. I pulled the scratchy shirt collar wide, undid my tie and tossed it onto the sofa, following it there a moment later myself, cradling the glass between my hands. Then I sat staring into the room's rich shadows, as if they could give me my answers.

The house was one of Salisbury's oldest, an immaculately restored Elizabethan three-storey, redolent with history and with ghosts. This room was set a few feet below street level, or rather the street, over the centuries, had been layered up slowly outside of it. Despite his policy of leaving ancient treasures strictly in their country of origin, Jason had collected over the years a few magnificent pieces, bowls made out of gold-streaked turquoise Macedonian glass, goddesses and emperors in marble and bronze. The room in the firelight looked like a magical cave, a burrow where he and I had taken refuge time and time again, delighting in fucking in broad daylight on the sofa while the world passed, oblivious to us, on the pavement outside.

How could he think about leaving? I sipped the brandy's mellow fire and wondered, trying to calm the still-disturbed rhythm of my heart. This place was Jason's treasure house, every room either lovingly stripped back to its Elizabethan charm or subtly transformed, like the bathroom and the huge, well-equipped kitchen, to a modern purpose. He'd never shown the least sign of wanting to be free of it—or, for that matter, of his academic chains, where if he was trammelled he also thrived, teaching and researching with enormous enthusiasm, turning out book after acclaimed book on the pre-Roman world.

Yet when I thought about it, tonight had been a culmination of something, hadn't it? Now the crisis seemed to have peaked and passed, I could allow myself to look at my own worst fear— that it had been me, and not his world, that had been becoming too small for him. I should have had more faith. That idea was crazier than the notion I could ever tire of him, start chafing at the restrictions of my beautiful tailor-made world, and…

I shivered, sending concentric ripples through the brandy. Where the hell had *that* thought come from? One of those morbid impulses, I supposed, like poking at a rotten tooth, or imagining yourself in a car crash and how your friends would react when they heard you had died. I shoved the insane fantasy aside. I had better things to consider. Now that I had time to take in what he'd said, what he'd invited me to do, I was almost dizzy with it. Our first year had been one blaze of happiness. During the second, it was as if the passage of our first milestone had reminded him of troubles he'd been diligently setting aside, and over the past few months at least, he'd been an anxious man, as if sands were running out for him somewhere beyond his control. Paranoid of me, and egotistical too, to assume that the problem had been me.

I unfolded the letter from my pocket and read through it again with a new pleasure. I didn't think of myself as an ambitious man, but, having chosen my field, I had wanted to do well in it. Far more for Jason's sake than my own, since moving in with him. He'd ploughed so much time and energy into my studies, encouraged my progress beyond articles and journals to the first draft of a book of my own. I wanted to be a rich harvest to him. When he'd said that he was proud of me, my heart had almost climbed out onto the restaurant table. Becoming his assistant, I had thought, would have crowned for him my achievements, given back to him some of his light.

But, if he was serious about Bali and the beach wedding, stuff all that. I would run away with him—follow him to the ends of the earth. All I wished was that I had said so at once, as soon as he asked. I felt my hesitation to do so as a sudden, bitter regret. What must it have cost him to make such a request? And what must he have thought when I gave him my half-assent, my talk of careers and local adventures?

I heard the shower running upstairs, and then a silence. God, had he gone straight to bed? I uncoiled from the sofa, abruptly too sick at myself to stay still. I was an idiot. I'd let my fears about his commitment to me erode my own to him until I couldn't even talk straight to him, tell him what was in my heart. Setting down my glass, automatically careful by now not to leave it on anything priceless, I headed for the living-room door.

But I didn't have to find him. He was halfway down the stairs on his way to find me. When he saw me he came to a halt, and so did I, transfixed, throwing out a hand to the doorframe to steady myself. The old copper lantern in the hallway was shedding a warm glow from its amber panes. Jason, gripping the banister, looked as I might have imagined his ancient Greek namesake to do, after dealing with his golden fleece and dark-eyed exotic witches and his last Argonaut—descending slowly into his kingdom, his princely hall. Tired, with the salt of his voyages still tangled in his wet hair... So beautiful that my eyes stung, his summer silk robe clinging damply to the contours of his shoulders and back. He was naked underneath it. Its front hung open, exposing him from the hollow of his throat to the place where his half-erect cock was rising from the shadows of his groin.

He was looking down at me in silence, his brown eyes tawny in the light. Carefully, getting my balance, I pushed off from the doorframe and went slowly to stand at the foot of the stairs. The view was even better from here. I hardly ever got to see him like this. We undressed one another in bed, or in the dark. Lovely as he was, he had none of my generation's penchant for flaunting, and would no more have stripped off his shirt on a hot excavation site than he would in the dean's office. He would even go from his bath to the bedroom wrapped in a concealing robe.

Not this one, which concealed nothing. I recalled the last couple of times when I had seen it, and I smiled, beginning a slow climb towards him up the stairs. "God," I breathed. "Look at you."

"I came down to see if...if you were coming to bed."

"Yes. I definitely am." Shocks of excitement were rippling through me. He had his own subtle signalling system, my Jason. I wasn't sure if he was even aware of it himself. If he didn't like to be topped, still something in him seemed to need it—to demand it, from time to time, and then he would give himself over entirely, shuddering frantically all the way through, coming in silent, grinding spasm when I had fucked him long enough and hard enough to set him free. He never told me when he wanted it. I remembered only a handful of times across our three-year history when he had. But, I realised, on each occasion, the cream silk robe had been his flag of surrender.

With another man, I might have made a joke of it. *My God, it's the fuck-me robe.* But for Jason, these rare nights of barely voluntary receptivity seemed deadly serious, and I'd never have teased him. I closed up the last couple of steps between us, and took him in my arms, crushing the fabric in my grasp. "Listen. Back in the restaurant, I should have said—"

"No. Hush." He seized my shoulders, pulling the beautifully tailored jacket off them and dumping it over the banister. "Don't talk. Just take me to bed."

I stopped off in the bathroom, to clean my teeth and run my fingers through my hair. I glanced at my own pale reflection. The trouble with the long intervals was that I sometimes worried I'd forget how. I was good at everything else he liked, but this… This just didn't get an airing often enough to let me be sure of myself. I undid my shirt, sniffing discreetly. No time now to stop for a shower, and I'd had one before I came out, but the trench-and-midden smells could linger. No, fine. Just the Patou cologne he liked me to wear, and warm, excited flesh. I'd leave the rest of the undressing to him.

Setting my cufflinks down by the sink, I finally noticed the round glass tub on the cabinet beside it. Oh God. The second signal. Jason didn't care for proprietary brands of lubricant, and either discreetly bought or had made up for him these fat, intriguing little jars, which turned up in handy grabbing range in all parts of the house where passion might spring up between us. I had never asked him about it. It was part of his mystery, and it was very efficient. And, if it was left out plainly on a surface for me to find, he wanted to be fucked.

I shuddered, unscrewing the lid, letting the scent of crushed leaves and warm earth rise up to wrap me round. My half-hard cock, which had quailed a bit at the thought of the task before it, stretched and stiffened in primal response to the smell. Laughter shook me too—silent, mercifully, quenched on the back of my hand. For a moment I thought about it. Camping my way into the bedroom, as I would have with any previous boyfriend, the jar held aloft. *Man, I am so in there tonight...!*

No. Not with Jase. His sense of humour, though rich, erred more on the side of cerebral than slapstick. He put up with my occasional clowning—as a patient puppy-trainer might, God knew—but that would never do. I composed myself. He wanted me. His desire had turned out to be, for me, the most powerful aphrodisiac in the world. My mouth dried out with hunger.

Bad enough, when he would wait for me lying on his front, spreading his beautiful thighs a little as if in fear and helpless anticipation of the act. He was complex and tough to undo on these nights, and no matter how bloody thrilling I found it to push into his body, I had to hang on until he was ready. Tonight I was afraid he might sabotage my self-control before I even got to him. He had stripped off the robe and was sitting up naked in the wide oak-carved bed, his face flushed, his cock big and taut, almost flat to his belly.

"Danny," he rasped, stretching out a hand. "Come here, for God's sake. What the hell were you doing in there?"

"Just making sure I was nice for you." I seized his hand and came to kneel between his thighs. "And...getting this." I fished the jar out of my trouser pocket. It was as much of an acknowledgement of the way he did things as either of us could bear, and I watched while the colour in his lovely face deepened and a small, wry smile tugged the corners of his mouth. "You sure?"

"You bloody know I am."

He took off my shirt with gentle passion while I knelt kissing him, pushing my tongue rhythmically into his mouth in response to the firm press of his. His hands closed briefly on my waist, then my hips, then went expertly to work on my belt, buttons and zip.

"God," I whispered against his mouth as he reached in and took hold of my shaft. "Don't, love. Not if you want me to hang on. How do you want it?"

"Can we... Can we do it so that I can see you?"

"Mm." Heat shot through me, and I knocked away his hand. "Hell, yes." Then it struck me—did he mean was I willing, or was he unsure of the practicalities? He liked to fuck me from behind. I'd thought it just a preference, but... "Any way you like," I whispered. "Just lie back."

He took hold of the waistband of my trousers and pushed them down as I leaned over him. I would have liked to be free of them, but didn't want to take the awkward, scrambling moment. He had obeyed me, pulling out the pillows from behind his back and subsiding slowly flat, the muscles in his chest and stomach rippling. This would do. I put one hand to the insides of his knees and pushed gently outward, gasping at the corded strength of his resistance, finely calculated to give at my touch, but slowly, slowly, so it was like tearing into some coarse-fibred fruit.

"Dan, I'm sorry."

I stopped, disappointed but not surprised. Too much for him? When I eased my grip on him though, his hands came down on top of mine, restoring the outward pressure.

"What for, love?"

"I haven't... I've hardly ever let you do this."

I shivered. If he stopped to analyse, I was lost. A sweet, deadly heat was beginning in the root of my cock. I tried for a smile, and said unsteadily, "All the more incredibly bloody hot when you do."

"Is it? Have I been good for you?"

I put the jar of lube into his hands. These were *my* fears surely, not his, a long-term doubt of coming up to scratch. I told him, as I would have liked to hear but had never dared ask, "You've been beautiful. Perfect. Every time."

"Oh, Dan. I'm glad."

At last he was uncapping the jar. At last his strong fingers were on me, coating me from shaft to tip, expert but quick, avoiding caress, reading how close I was. He grunted in assent when I increased the pressure on his legs, transferring my grip to the back of his knees, exposing him, and I closed my eyes while he dipped into the lube again, knowing that the sight of him touching himself, fingertips disappearing into his own body, would certainly be my undoing. My cock was leaking thin, clear fluid as it was. When I dared to look again, I saw that his was too.

"Come on, beautiful boy," he whispered. "Time to get us both off this hook."

I did my best. I leaned into him, propping my weight on stiff arms, moving carefully. He winced and said *no* as the head of my shaft broached his entrance, and I considered the sound of it, decided it wasn't a complaint and pushed on. A moment later his thighs closed warmly on my waist, and he continued a soft, half-wailed litany—*ah, God, no, no, no!*—all the way through my slow slide up into his body, his head arching back, his legs wrapping strongly around me.

My head spun and I fought for control. His sounds of ecstatic denial were too much, and I knew suddenly that if I stayed here, buried deep and motionless at the end of this first long stroke, we both would come over, jerk to climax without another touch. One more cry from him would do it for me, and I could feel the frantic pulse of his cock, wetly trapped against my belly.

No. I wanted more for both of us. I sat up, the movement and the slight withdrawal it caused making his eyes fly open. I put both my hands to the backs of his thighs, my grip slippery and damp on his hot skin. "Lift your legs over my shoulders."

"What? Christ, I can't…"

"You can. I'll fuck you so deep. Make it so good."

He groaned. There was a kind of despair in the sound. But he shifted, his back arching, obeying my guiding touch. I gasped as he curled up and suddenly draped his knees over my shoulders, and our voices rang out together, one harsh, startled cry. The movement had let me drive one last inch farther, laying him open to the core. "Daniel! Dan!"

"Yes. I love you." God, I was so deep inside him, curled round, over and into him, the intimacy shattering, almost unbearable. I dipped down to his mouth, snatching brief kisses. Then his hands slipped warmly down inside my pants, clasping at my backside, urging me up and forward. "Yes! Come on!"

I wanted to hold him, to bury my hands in his hair, cup his face tenderly while we ploughed through to the end of this. But I couldn't keep my balance, not with him surging and bucking beneath me, and I flung out a grip to the carved bedhead, grasping tight. My arms locked convulsively, and, anchored in place, I began to piston into him, again and again in an increasing rhythm until his face contorted and his grasp on me became a vice.

"Ah, Danny. Make me forget. Make it… Make it all go away!"

All what, love? I couldn't say it, or even think it in anything clearer than a hot red blur. I was beginning to come, seismically. My mind wiped clear of everything but skyrocket ecstasy, and the relief, at last, of feeling him jolt and explode to orgasm beneath me. I lost my hold on the bedhead—I bore the bruises of its carvings on my palms for days—and fell into his arms, finishing in long, hard strokes, groaning against his neck.

When at length I could get my head up, I did try to ask. We were still locked together, in a sticky, exhausted embrace. "Make all what go away, love?" But his gaze was soft and far away, focussed on some point far, far beyond me. His face was streaked with tears, and he didn't respond.

A little while later, when I'd carefully pulled out of him and we were lying entangled, still breathing raggedly, he shifted away. The mattress dipped and lifted. I heard him pad off, I thought in the direction of the bathroom. I tried to stay awake, to make sure that he came back. That he was all right, after such a surrender. I waited, and my darkening mind marked off the point at which he had been gone too long. But I'd been up since dawn, arranging a practice dig for a bunch of freshers, and out in the sunny air all day after that. I felt my limbs go slack, stretched out on my front with a shuddery moan, and fell fast asleep.

***

He must have got up early. His half of the bed was not only vacant but cool. He often surfaced first, though, for a run or a trip to the gym, and I wasn't concerned. A bit disappointed, maybe. I'd had nice dreams. A reassuring scent of *l'Occitane* sandalwood drifted from the bathroom, and the cashmere jumper, which he'd got back from the drycleaners and folded over a chair, was gone.

I showered and made my way downstairs, yawning, pushing my hands back through my damp hair. Brilliant June light was painting the hallway. It caught on a tiny, gilt-framed picture he'd bought me in Florence last year, an overlooked relic of the Medicis left gathering dust in an antique shop until his appreciative eye fell upon it. We'd had it cleaned up, but it was still a dark little scene, almost overwhelmed and at the same time enhanced by its massive surround. I stopped on the stairs, extending a finger to brush its patinaed surface. I smiled. The sunlight had brought out the heaven-blue of St Cecilia's robes, where she sat at her spinet. For the first time I saw that she wasn't alone, that behind her, ethereal in shadows, stood a stern, sable-haired angel.

I must tell Jason. Straightening up, I vaulted the end of the banister and landed on the hallway's soft runner, whose colours were also glowing like jewels in the sun. It was a morning for noticing such things. I felt amazing. If Jason still wanted to run off to Bali, I would go with him, marry him, no question. But in the meantime I was assistant department head of archaeology at the university of Wiltshire. I was also the man who could make Jason Ross open up to the core and sob his way to climax in my arms.

It shouldn't have made a difference, but it did. A big one. I felt as if my veins were filled with light. Jogging down the steps into the kitchen, I looked around. The coffee percolator was silent and shining on its granite worktop. Good—Jason hadn't got here before me. Must have gone out for the paper. I liked my coffee a lot stronger than he did, and he, like the sweet soul he was, would invariably do it for me my way if he got down here first, then sit opposite me with his cup, uncomplaining but visibly twitching from the caffeine rush. I pulled out the glass beaker, filled the well and spooned about half my normal amount of Brazilian into the filter.

I scanned the bright room. The kitchen was an extension to the mediaeval body of the house, but beautifully done, incorporating the old rear yard, over which the builders had thrown spiral panes of glass in shades of pale blue and sea green. Jason had redecorated since I'd moved in, letting me choose the surfaces, the tough, warm parquet flooring. Or had he? I had a vague memory of being shown brochures, like complex foreign menus, agreeing to wonderful things, and being told that my taste was excellent. It didn't matter. I loved the place. The light was incredible, dancing off the rack of copper pans, the spotless worktops.

It didn't look like he'd been down here at all this morning— not so much as a teaspoon in the drying rack. Deciding that I'd get breakfast on the go for him in just a minute, I snagged the last issue of *The Archaeological Review* out of the rack and sat down at the gorgeous ironwood table with its inlay of hand-painted tiles.

Got straight back up again. It was nice to have the place to myself for a few minutes, wasn't it? Against the far wall, our high-end speaker system was rigged to play CDs, my iPod or the radio throughout the whole house. I padded across and popped up my last playlist. A firestorm of Pendulum promptly swept over me. Lovely, and I could easily flip it back to Radio 3 when I heard Jason's key in the door.

There was another sound. It didn't stand much of a chance against the pounding of *Propane Nightmares*, but it was familiar to me, and I listened for a few seconds, picking it out of the off-beat. Then I switched the music off. Yes. A faint, well-known purr. Jason's old Citroën DS, ticking over in the garage which, as well as the kitchen, had been adroitly tucked into the space behind the house. One kitchen door opened straight into it. The sound was a frequent backdrop to our early breakfasts—on cold mornings, the old girl needed a good few minutes with her engine running before she'd consent to sail forth. I smiled. She was fantastic. I'd lost track of the places we'd taken her to. Jason preferred to roll her onto a ferry and drive to our destination than to fly.

But it wasn't a cold morning, was it? I leaned my elbows on the granite worktop, distractedly watching how the brilliant mica chips in it made rainbows of the sun. Sunshine was pouring through the little mullioned window, dappling between the leaves of the clematis that flourished all around it.

The coffee whispered in the percolator, beginning its slow boil. In the hallway, the post slithered through the letterbox onto the rug. The engine purred on.

I stood in front of the door to the garage, looking at it. Just now I was only puzzled, trying to backtrack in my mind if I'd heard the car start up on my way down the stairs. Jase might be tinkering with her, I supposed, though it was hard for me to imagine him with his head under the bonnet, up to his rolled-back cashmere sleeves in oil. The door was nicely fitted to exclude draughts from the garage. But now, beneath the perking coffee, I could smell fumes.

I yanked the door open. Involuntarily I fell back a step or two. The kitchen instantly flooded with exhaust, the sunlight turning oily and grey. Christ almighty, what had he done— switched her on, then absentmindedly gone off for his walk, or his trip to the shop, or…

The garage was in darkness, a miasma. I snatched a breath, then ran down the concrete steps and felt my way to the control panel on the rollover door. I missed the switch on the first try, and by the time I found it and the door had completed enough of its slow, stately rise to let in the morning air, I was coughing and choking. All the time my mind said to itself, and to him, wherever he was, *what the fuck, Jason?* He loved the car. He loved the house to smell airy and nice. He'd be mortified by this lapse. I'd better get her turned off and all the windows open before he came home. Because, despite everything, I still was expecting him to appear from round the corner, paper in hand, or through the front door. Not to be sitting, when I turned around, propped behind the fucking wheel, his eyes shut, face a hellish shade of cherry red in the sunlight streaming through the garage door.

I'd read about—I supposed it was a topic that fascinated most people—the adrenal surge that allows panicked mothers to lift cars off their trapped children. I don't think I had one then, or, if I did, mine was a poor relation and didn't last long. But something happened, other than a jolt of horror so intense that my bladder tried to give. I ripped open the car door, barely noticing the rubber hose that dropped out and onto the garage floor. I wouldn't have thought that I could have lifted him deadweight, but I got him beneath the armpits as he slumped sideways towards me. The concentrated fumes inside the car were unbreathable. I was gagging, my eyes streaming, before I could haul him clear. Then, somehow, I had an arm under his knees as well, cradling him, beginning to carry him out into the light.

I was bearing more than my own weight, and that couldn't last. The supernatural rush of adrenaline ran out, and my knees buckled, dropping us both to the floor. I scrambled round him and made an undignified job of the rest of our exit, hauling him by the armpits out onto the drive.

Christ, that whooshing, hollowed-out sound was me, trying to breathe. No. Crying. I knelt for a second on the driveway, for a moment unable to take in anything more than the sunlight and the song of summer blackbirds in the hedge and my own ragged sobs. Then, oddly, it was my mother's voice that I heard inside my pounding head. I hadn't thought about her in years. *Daniel, you stop this at once.*

Well, she was right. I knew how to revive an unconscious man. I'd done courses. Christ, I'd *taught* courses, before setting off on mountain trips with climbers. I had better things to do than sit here sobbing like a frightened six-year-old. I lurched up and leaned over Jason, not permitting myself to see again the colour of his skin. I felt at his throat for a pulse, helplessly snatching my hand away as soon as I'd established that there wasn't one, because he was... God, he was...

No. I wouldn't take that in. I had to breathe for him. I tipped his head back. I opened his mouth. His airway was clear—oh, clear of everything but cold dank fumes—and I gently closed his nose off and leaned down to him. Gave him one breath and another, then sat back, my motion away from him almost a jump, a recoil, because he was...

No. No, not that. All right. What next? I braced my hands to his breastbone, pushing down hard with both palms, one on top of the other. Counted out from one to thirty, pumping firmly, ignoring the sweet familiar feel of cashmere on his beautiful broad chest. A check at his silent throat, and then two more breaths, another thirty compressions. Nothing. Okay—next cycle. I knew my CPR. I had saved an old man on the bus like this once, when everyone had given up on him. I'd started up stalled jeeps out in the desert. If Jason wasn't much of a mechanic, I was. Nothing stayed dead under my fucking hands.

It was hard work, hard. I jolted up from my next set of mouth-to-mouth, seeing red mist. All I was getting from him— from his beautiful mouth, which I'd bitten and sucked the night before, vividly hot beneath my own—was a taste of petrol, as if his lungs had been stilled and soaked for hours in carbon monoxide.

Through crimson sparks I saw our neighbour from a few doors down, Elsa Reid, out for her morning jog. A no-nonsense doctor in her fifties, she nevertheless put her hair up in an absurd grey-white ponytail on top of her head for her run. The incongruous flag, whipping past our windows in all weathers, had often made me and Jason laugh. In later days, that was what I would remember more clearly than any other physical detail from that morning—Elsa's flying hair, jouncing to a stop a few yards away from us, wiping her face with her hand. "Jesus fucking Christ, Daniel! What's happened?"

I'd never heard her swear, or call me anything other than Dr. Logan. On reflection, I was wildly glad to see her. My CPR was good, but she worked in the Salisbury A&E—hers had to be better. I tried to speak, coughed violently, and found my voice. "Found him…in the car. In the garage. Help me, Elsa."

She dropped to her knees at Jason's side. I saw her do all the things I had done—or begin them, anyway. She felt for a pulse at his carotid, then at his wrist. Her hands were tanned and fine. Tough, capable little hands. She would make it right. But then I watched her sit back on her heels. She dragged sweat-damp strands back off her brow and kept her hands there, as if she couldn't believe what she was seeing or wanted to shield herself.

"Daniel," she said. "Go and switch off the car."

I glanced back towards the garage. I hadn't thought to do that. Yes, the DS was still rumbling in the shadows. What the hell did that matter? "I…I will. Just…"

"Daniel, go and switch off the damn car."

I obeyed helplessly. I supposed it was the sound of an adult voice. But I was an adult, wasn't I? Leaning in, turning the keys and pulling them out, I stood in the sudden, absolute silence, wondering what the fuck was going on. I was an adult, and my partner—my lover—was lying on the driveway, while I messed about with the car.

Lying alone, because Elsa Reid sure as fuck wasn't helping him. She was on her feet again. She was pacing up and down at the end of the drive, her mobile phone tucked beneath one ear, arms folded tight over her chest. When I had slammed the car door shut, stumbled out of the garage and intercepted her, my hands closing far harder than I'd meant on her thin shoulders, she said to me faintly, "Daniel, I'm so sorry."

"What for? Elsa… Help him."

I couldn't wait for whatever insanity had seized her to pass. Jason couldn't be left without breath for this long, he'd brain damage. I shot back to his side, and after a moment felt her come and lean over me, trying to pull me away. "Daniel, stop. It's no use. I think he must have been dead for hours. He's stone cold."

***

There were sirens, and voices. Others of our neighbours had come out of their houses. The driveway was busy with them. Elsa had asked one of them—Michael, I think he was called, a burly security guard—to keep hold of Daniel, to hold him back from the body. Daniel had been trying CPR for ages. He was exhausted and in shock and wouldn't quit. And Jason's lungs were full of toxins. *Just hold Daniel back until the coroner gets here.*

Daniel. The coroner. I crash-landed back into my body. I was Daniel, lunging frantically against the grip of our poor neighbour, who had my arm up my back in what I thought must be his gentlest, but still very professional, half nelson. All I wanted was to get through the forest of uniformed legs—some green, some blue, paramedics and police—surrounding Jason. It was hard on Michael though. I stopped fighting him and felt his restraining grasp quickly lock on to me in support as the driveway tried to lurch up at me. "Let me… Let me go."

"Doctor says you've got to stay out of the way."

"I will, but…" I shut up. There was someone in front of me, solid and broad. Dark blue jacket, epaulettes, cap. Our local police inspector. I knew him too, now I came to think about it. He'd been there on that Solstice night three years ago at Stonehenge, and I'd seen him many times since, when Jason and I had been at one of our endless meetings with the military brass and constabulary over access to the plain. His lips were moving. I forced myself to focus past the static in my ears. He was asking me if Jason had had any reason to want to take his own life.

The question was meaningless to me. I'd have helped him if I could. But now instead of fizzing and a kind of feedback shriek in my head, all I could hear was Elsa's voice, echoing. *Dead for hours. Stone cold.* Yes. That was why I had flinched back from my efforts to revive him. He had been like marble, even in the places where warmth should have lingered: his throat, his handsome, eloquently sculpted mouth. Even in his armpits, when I'd hauled him out of the car. I'd known. The scent of him in the bathroom had been faint, the shower base and the towel he'd hung over the rail almost dry. *Dead for hours.*

"To take his own *life?*" I heard myself rasp out, a stranger suddenly catching up on a debate in a foreign language. "Don't be so bloody ridiculous. You need to be out there finding who did this to him."

"Oh, Daniel."

A fourth voice. Not Elsa's or Michael's or the blank-faced copper's. I jerked around in Michael's grip and saw, to my huge relief, Dean Anderson straightening up from beside Jason's body. I hadn't seen him arrive, but glancing through the crowd I saw his Rover pulled up by the kerb, half on and half off the drive, as if he'd come here full pelt and screeched to a halt at random.

"Dean," I whispered. "Thank God. Can you tell these people…"

What? I couldn't even remember. Something urgent, about Jason. I remembered how long he and the dean had known one another, and stretched out a hand to him, which he took in both his own.

"Yes," he said, and another shock of relief went through me, that at least he knew what I was talking about, even if I'd lost track myself. "I'll tell them. I will, but for now I want you to come with me into the house, and let them do their jobs."

***

It was the same sunny, beautiful place I had walked out of half an hour before. Someone had pushed the kitchen windows wide, and the air was clear again. The coffee had perked and was ready on the hob. *The Archaeological Review* was still open on the ironwood table. Dean Anderson pulled out a chair for me, and I sank into it. I was aware that he went away from me, and ran water at the sink, and came back. "Daniel."

I looked up. He was very pale, and his composed, patrician face was wet with tears. "Dean," I whispered. "He didn't kill himself. He wouldn't…"

"All right. We'll talk about it all later. In the meantime though, I want you to take these. The police doctor gave them to me. He thinks you should probably go to hospital, but—"

"No." I shuddered. I wasn't going anywhere, not without Jason.

"Okay. You've had a horrible, horrible shock, and you're not quite making sense." He unscrewed the top of a small brown plastic bottle and shook out two tablets onto his palm. "Can you get these down? Here's some water."

I took the pills without even looking at them. The action seemed pointless, irrelevant, not worth arguing. What wasn't I making sense about? I felt fairly clear, fairly logical. I felt as if I could have taken my thoughts and laid them end to end in a neat, clean path into deep space.

I put my elbows on the table and rested my brow on the heel of one hand. I tried to, at least. After a moment or so, the muscles in my arm seemed to dissolve, and my suddenly lead-weighted skull dropped forward. I heard a door bang, and footsteps. Dean Anderson was patting my shoulder, as if I'd done something right. Well, I had, hadn't I? I'd have liked to thank him for my new appointment, now that I remembered it.

I heard a new male voice say, "How's he doing? Did you get those into him?"

"Yes, Doctor. I think he's on his way out, from the look of him."

"Good. Right. Well, they'll knock him out pretty hard, so…"

"I don't think he'll make it upstairs. But there's a sofa just through here…"

Just through here. Yes, up the steps out of the kitchen, into the high-ceilinged hallway, where the great copper lamp was now gleaming bright in the sun. The light had passed from the little mediaeval painting, the dark-eyed angel vanished. I'd never got to tell him about it, had I? I would, though, when I woke up.

A shiver of something like laughter went through me. I wasn't accomplishing any part of this journey through into the living room under my own steam, and that was pretty embarrassing. Being propped and half-carried towards the big leather sofa by the dean of my university was actually mortifying. He was setting me down onto it with great care, so I trusted that I hadn't in some way disgraced him.

"All right," the other man—the police doctor?—was saying. "We're going to clear up out there, get Professor Ross taken in. Can somebody stay here with…"

"With Daniel. Yes. I will."

"Okay, but the police will probably want to see you at some point."

"Yes. All right. My wife's on her way."

The conversation spiralled out and away from me. I was floating, serene and calm, somewhere between the point at which I'd woken up that morning and the first sound of the Citroën's engine. Maybe I was a mote of dust in the sunlight, poised above the stairs. I subsided flat onto the sofa and rolled onto my stomach, burying my face in the crook of one arm. Yes—from here I could see my way into the painting, and I drifted fearlessly into the frame, to see if I could find again the strange winged figure I thought I had noticed there.

Chapter Three

The sense of waking up on the set of a tame domestic soap...

The room was very quiet. The blinds were down and only a gentle bronze light making its way through their fabric, enough to illuminate the sedate little figure of a woman in a corner armchair. The faint clicking sounds which had called me up from grey limbo were the rhythmic contact of knitting needles. I lay for a while, watching her through my eyelashes. A lot seemed to depend upon my working out the pattern and colours of the spreading garment laid out across her lap. Very nice, I thought. Not a grandma's Christmas jumper effort at all. Just a few shades of grey, dove and charcoal. Oh, I had it. The dean would appear for lectures in nice subtle hand-knitted sweaters like that.

I had no idea what Mrs. Dean was doing in my living room, but clearly I was being very rude. I sat up, wondering at the leaden clouds in my head and on my tongue. My mouth was dry as dust. I'd been lying on my front. As I moved, a blanket from the upstairs linen box fell back from my shoulders. "Oh. Hello, Mrs. Dea— Mrs. Anderson."

Poor thing, she jumped, and although I was no expert I could see she'd lost a row of stitches. "Daniel!" she said, as if she somehow hadn't expected to encounter me here on my own sofa. She got up, pushing needles, wool and work aside in a tangle. "All right, dear. Now..." Leaning over the coffee table, she poured water from a jug into a glass. I heard ice cubes chink and jangle. "The doctor said you'd be very thirsty when you woke up, so have some of this, and..." She held out the glass, and I automatically reached to take it. I was puzzled. Everything around me—the blanket, the jug, the glass—were familiar yet strange objects belonging to Jason and me, of course, but not the ones we'd use ourselves. It was as if kindly strangers had been through the house, picking things from cupboards. I tried to formulate some sort of question. She was right, though—my throat was arid, and I broke into a fit of coughing. "Oh, dear," she said, awkwardly patting my back. "Malcolm's just back from... He's in the kitchen. I'll go and get him."

I watched her neat, Jaeger-clad little figure disappear up the living-room steps. Then my throat seized so hard that I couldn't do anything but clutch the edge of the table to stay upright while the bout of coughing shook me. It was uncontrollable. To my shame, I choked and threw up a mouthful of water onto the carpet. *Shit*, I thought, reaching blindly around me for anything Jase or I might have left lying about to mop it up.

Christ. I could taste petrol. Gasping, I heaved to stillness, pressing both hands to my mouth. Memory flew in like a fucking meteorite and made fireball impact in my sleepy brain. Something horrible had happened. Ah, something unbearable. I couldn't bear it, and the only answer—the only comfort, hope, refuge—was

Jason. I had to find him and tell him that he'd died. I bolted up off the sofa, knocking glass and jug aside, and I ran.

Dean Anderson intercepted me on the stairs. He wasn't tall, but he was stocky, and he stopped me with sheer bulk. I heard his winded grunt, and then my own voice, twisted up with fear and barely recognisable. "Let me go. Where's Jason? Where's… Where's Jase?"

"He's not here." He fixed both hands on my shoulders and met my eyes with a kind of brutal sanity that insisted I find my own. "They had to take him away."

"But I've got to talk to him. I've—"

"Dan." He detached one hand and cuffed me around the face, hard enough to make me catch my breath. "Listen to yourself. You know that Jase is dead. And… And I've lost him too, so…*please*, son, try to calm down."

I stared at him. His handprint stung on my cheek. It was a distraction, almost a relief, from the blunt iron spear someone was ramming slowly through my solar plexus, twisting it as they went. I found myself thinking about Jason and the dean. Childhood friends and colleagues for two decades. Malcolm was far more closely his peer than I could ever hope to have been. Certainly more powerfully and lastingly his friend. An old, barely acknowledged jealousy died in me. "God," I choked out. "I'm so sorry."

And that was it. I'd let myself know that Jase was gone. I'd had to in order to feel through my own panic and fugue that bright splash of compassion for somebody else. A second later the enormity of it hit me. My legs gave. Malcolm grabbed hold of me and marched me back to the sofa. "Down," he ordered. "Sit down. Put your head down."

"But how the hell… Why the hell would anybody do that to…"

He sat down beside me. His arm went round me shoulders, but hard, almost cruel. "Now, you listen," he said, his voice cracking painfully over the words. "I don't know why—but, for whatever bloody incomprehensible reason, Jason went to the garage last night, ran a tube from the exhaust of his car, put the tube through the window and shut himself in. There isn't a mark on his body. All your doors and windows are intact. Nobody killed him. He did it to himself."

I locked both hands round the back of my head. I could shield my ears a bit that way, but it didn't make much difference. I was seeing again, through the water-stained rug, the concrete garage floor and a length of rubber hose falling flaccidly out onto it, like a dead snake. Everything else neat and tidy, the way he always kept it. Just this one point of disorder. "I don't understand," I said dully. "How could he just... How would he even know how?"

"I spoke to the inspector. He had his scene-of-crime officers go over the garage and the house, even though... Well. He said that Jason did a good job of it. That it probably wasn't as spontaneous as it seems. He had a hose which fitted the car exhaust perfectly and didn't look like it had been used for anything else. Listen. Not today, of course, but—some time soon, when you feel better, they're going to want to talk to you."

"To me?" My skull was once more full of petrol-soaked cotton wool. "Who will? About what?"

"Ah... Daniel..." He made a sound between a chuckle and a sob, as if after all it might prove to be my shell-shocked idiocy that undid him. "The police, son. About why Jason did this."

I swallowed. All my little fears and guilts, the biting small worries of three years, came boiling up out of the depths, a school of piranha, glittering and diamond-bright with fangs.

I don't think I ever was smart enough for him. I let a cute Moroccan boy rub sun oil into my back in Riu Tikida last August. Last night Jason and I fucked, and that sometimes upsets him, even though he wanted it, and I didn't stay awake long enough to make sure he was all right.

The iron spear moved again, taking what felt like a gigantic twist through my liver. "I don't know," I said. "I don't know."

"Of course not. It's far too soon. You don't have to do anything at all, apart from... Well, Mrs. Dea— That is, Diane and I would like you to come home with us for the night. You shouldn't be here by yourself."

I tried to take this in, but my thoughts kept fragmenting. Every time I got hold of something—this invitation, for instance—the reason for it gaped underneath it, and it slithered out of my grasp.

"Then tomorrow," the dean was continuing, "or whenever you're ready, we can talk about Jason's will, and—and the arrangements."

I lifted my head. I knew what *the arrangements* meant, of course. He meant the bloody funeral. Jason's funeral—as if the man who had stood in this room with me less than twenty-four hours ago, smiling gently at me while he fastened my tie, was no more than a corpse to be dealt with. I glanced at the ormolu clock on the mantelpiece. It was nearly seven o'clock. Oh, God—a whole world's turn now separated me from that moment, a whole stretch of that time stolen from me, drowned in sleep. I said, involuntarily, "You doped me."

"Oh, Daniel. I had to. You were in a hell of a state."

I got up. He put up a hand, to restrain or steady me, but I found that I didn't need either. Absently pulling the blanket up after me and wrapping it round my shoulders, I went to the window. I didn't need a dim-lit room. I opened the blind, letting in the rich evening light. I turned and looked back. Mrs. Dean had returned and was perched nervously on the arm of the sofa, watching me as if I might explode.

They were good, kind people, both of them. But they didn't understand. And if I wasn't very careful, they would pull me down with them, into their world of wills and arrangements and *dealing with it*. When the truth was that I didn't need any of it. All I needed was solitude, the easy silence of the house I shared with Jason. I said dryly, and far more harshly than I'd meant, "You have to go."

"Ah, Daniel."

"Yes. Sorry." I cleared my throat. I had to sound more convincingly sane if I was going to win this point. "I know you're worried about me, about what I'll do, but...I promise you, I couldn't be further from wanting to hurt myself." It was true. I could feel my pulse beating strongly, in my wrists and the base of my throat, the ancient drum of life in my ears. I was clothed in living flesh. "I just want... I'm asking you, please, just to leave me alone for a bit."

He got up. I saw Mrs. Dean flash him an incredulous look, but he waved her down. "All right," he said. "No, Diane, we have to respect him. But if that changes—the not wanting to hurt yourself—you have to promise me something."

I nodded. At that moment I'd have promised him anything, to get the weight of him off my skin and my soul.

"Give me the chance Jason didn't give you. Phone me and tell me."

That almost cracked me. I heard my own soft inhalation. But my new shield, whatever it was—and I hadn't had time yet to heft it, examine it in the light—was good. It held true. "Okay," I said. "I promise."

"In fact, phone me anyway. Before you go to bed, and first thing in the morning. If I don't hear, I'll..."

"You'll be at my door with a battering ram," I finished for him, managing a smile. "Yes. I'll phone."

***

I did better than that. I walked into the dean's office at nine the following morning, said hello to his secretary and sat down, when he invited me to do so, in my usual chair on the far side of his desk. I was clean, well slept and sensibly dressed for the day that lay ahead of me, no easy feat when that involved a lecture followed by supervision on one of the muddier midden digs.

He said hollowly, "My God, Daniel. I had no thought of seeing you here today. You're not planning on teaching, are you?"

"I'd rather. If you'll allow me."

"Well—of course, but... You're entitled to some compassionate leave."

I ran my hands over the fine leather satchel Jason had bought me in Budapest. The feel and the scent of it suddenly filled the dean's quiet office with voices, a dashing babble of Hungarian, side-street hustle, wet pavements and elegant old lanterns. With Jason's look of smiling concentration as he lifted the strap over my shoulder, to check for weight, fit, suitability for classroom and field.

Carefully, deliberately, I brought myself back. It was the dean who looked as if he needed leave. He was white and unshaven, shadowed hollows underneath his eyes. "I think I'm better keeping busy," I said. "But I've come here to say—if you don't mind, sir—at the moment I'd rather not take up the assistant's post. It was a great honour, and I hope you won't think..."

"*Sir?*" he echoed. Something like laughter shook him briefly. "Don't call me that. And as regards your post—at the moment I've got to find a new department head, let alone..." He paused and ran a hand through his hair. "Sorry. No, I don't mind. But I don't see how you can just go out there and pick up where you left off."

Of course he didn't. He didn't have my shield. Once he'd finally left me alone the night before, I'd had time to look at it. It wasn't perfect, but it was so much better than I'd hoped—and so much better than standing, as I had, stark fucking naked in the middle of the war zone. Probably he thought me callous. "I'm better keeping busy," I repeated, unable to think of any other way to convey what I needed.

"All right. All right, I understand." He picked up his attaché from the floor by his desk and flipped up its catches. "Look. You should know that Jason appointed me one of his executors. Of course he lodged a will with his solicitor too, but I have that, and some other paperwork too, and—"

"Sorry." I cut him off, getting to my feet. I'd never mastered an air of academic importance, of having urgent business to attend to. It was a tough trick in archaeology, where most matters of interest had lain buried for centuries and would certainly get by without you for another half an hour or so. But I'd seen Jason pull it off when he didn't want to be bothered with red tape or student queries. It couldn't be too hard to do. "Sorry, Dean." I looked at my watch. "I'm due in the lecture halls." Jason would do this with a certain charm, leaving whoever he'd brushed off unoffended. I flashed him what I'd been reliably informed was a lovely and disarming smile, saw it fail to alter his wondering, grief-shadowed face. "I'll see you later, all right? We'll talk later."

***

But we didn't. I taught and supervised all that day, and at the end of it sidestepped him and went home. Once there, I locked the doors, made myself a cup of tea and sat down to look at my shield.

Of course I couldn't look at it for long. The point of it was a calculated indifference, only the most peripheral awareness of its existence at all. It relied upon the realisation, which had struck me so beautifully hard the night before, that a difference which makes no difference is no difference. And I had to do my part by playing along.

Because I'd been alone in this house before. Jase and I had swung as many field trips together as we could, but there had still been times—conferences, book signings—when he'd had to head off on his own. His last book had been such a hit that he'd been away for nearly a month, touring the American universities, lecturing, sexing up archaeology for a whole generation of students who took his handsome face and his brilliant delivery as an advert for their chosen field. I missed him, of course, but I didn't...I didn't *grieve* for him.

A difference which makes no difference is no difference. His books were still on the shelves, his contact lenses in neatly stacked boxes in the bathroom cabinet. His crumpled shirts and some underwear, when I came to look, tangled with mine in the snake basket. I'd get round to sorting that out, but it was the sameness of routine where I had my sanity currently invested, and since I never usually threw myself at such tasks in his absence, I didn't hurry now. Mail continued to arrive for him. As always when he was away, I waited until the door was getting hard to open, then piled it up for him on the table in the hall.

I spent a rational enough evening—going through lecture notes for the next day, grading papers, staring vacuously at some American TV drama—*24* or *CSI* or *Lost*, all guilty pleasures for me because Jason would automatically reach for classical music in his downtime, and I never wanted to seem to him childish or lacking in culture. Then, tired, I went to bed, just before midnight. The usual time. Routine. Only a pang in my gut reminded me that I hadn't bothered to eat. That didn't matter. I'd had sandwiches with the kids on the dig at lunchtime. They'd been pretty subdued, not at all their raucous selves. It had taken me a while to work out why, and then I'd been distantly touched and had tried to jolly them along.

I stretched out on my stomach, enjoying the chance, as I always did, to sprawl out on Jason's side a bit. Sleep took longer to find me than I'd expected—certainly longer than last night, when the remains of whatever mickey the dean had slipped me had wiped me out straight away—and for an instant I panicked, my mouth opening wide against the pillow in a sudden, soundless wail. Then my mind blanked itself quietly out, and I burrowed down between the pillows and into the dark.

***

In this way I navigated the next three days. The silent phone, my empty inbox, were a problem for me, until I thought of unplugging the one from the wall, and only checking my professional account on the other. Even this wasn't too false, too much of a manoeuvre. Jason and I didn't call or mail each other every day, did we? Both of us were long past that stage. We weren't romantic, although he could be, devastatingly so, when the mood took him. We were solid. I worked, slept, even ate, and if I saw Dean Anderson around the corridors of the department, I diverted.

My mistake was in allowing myself to get buried in the part. I sat calmly in my office after hours on Friday night, so absorbed in a promising student's essay on carbon dating that I failed to hear the footsteps on the tiled floor outside and barely looked up when the door swung open.

"Daniel," the dean said, coming uninvited to sit down among my plants, piles of papers and files that defied categorisation. "Jason Ross—your partner, and my dearest bloody friend—is lying in a metal drawer in the Salisbury District Hospital morgue. Now I understand that you can't face seeing his will yet. But you will damn well read the instructions he left for his funeral and make the arrangements, or I'll open up the personal correspondence he left you and do it myself."

For one dreadful moment I was on the brink of saying, like a thwarted child, *Fine. Go ahead.* Better that than look properly at the image he had just thrust into my head. *Jason. In a metal drawer.* I hallucinated my living flesh into it with him. I suffered badly from claustrophobia, always had, though I'd overcome it to follow Jason down dark passages and into tombs. Six walls of steel, waking inside them in the pitch-black, with no room even for panicked convulsion.

The dean had his attaché with him again. This time when he pulled out an envelope and thrust it across the desk towards me, I took it. "Isn't there... Doesn't there have to be an inquest?"

"No. There was an autopsy, because he died suddenly. But only suspicious circumstances would warrant an inquest, and, as we both know, Jason took his own life."

Autopsy. Metal drawer. I'd watched too much fucking *CSI* this week. I saw in my head the Y-incision, heard the whine of bone saws. A heaving grey wave of sickness took me, and I mentally hurled myself—leaping for my life—onto the high ground of my fantasy, where Jason was only away. Maybe packing up now for his return trip home, running out to the local antiquarian dealer to buy for me whatever book he thought best expressed the history and culture of the place he had been staying. Jason's version of a holiday present. Not much of a one for straw donkeys.

I caught myself on the edge of a smile and desperately erased it. The dean was saying, "We have to bury our friend. If you loved him, then honour him now. Do your duty by him."

"I will," I said. I sounded to myself as flat as a punctured balloon, but I was okay again, I thought, far enough back from the cliff edge to function. "I'll look at this at home tonight, and I'll talk to you."

"Good. And before you do that, you'll talk to the policewoman waiting outside in the corridor right now, the one who's been calling your house for days and getting a dead line. Plug your phone back in."

***

I opened Jason's envelope sitting on the carpet in the hallway, my back up against the front door. I'd gone to scoop up the drift of mail that had just begun to block it, and it seemed a sensible time.

And, after all, it wasn't such a big deal. The letter was very impersonal, as if he'd written it before he knew me. It could have been addressed to any partner, to a generic ideal partner who dealt easily and maturely with life-and-death issues. Well, I could try.

On some level, the letter pleased me. It was very him. If I hadn't already thought of him as among the best of men, this would have done it. He carried his gentle, dignified principles through even here, not stuttering on the brink as so many self-declared atheists did and lapsing suddenly into flowery Catholic funerals and *The Lord Is My Shepherd*. He wanted his friends to come to the Ingersoll humanist chapel where the minister, another friend of his, would take a short, secular service. He wanted John

Donne's "Death, Be Not Proud" read, and, incongruously, Dylan Thomas's "Fern Hill". After that, I would find that he'd set aside a sufficient sum from his estate for everyone to go to the Rose & Crown riverside pub for a good feed and a few pints. No flowers, please. Donations, if we liked, to a hospice whose name rang a faint bell with me but didn't mean anything beyond that. He would prefer cremation.

He would. No graveside scenes for Jase. I imagined myself, the pale bereaved young lover, fainting onto his coffin, and how pissed off with me he would be. I burst out laughing, the sound of it echoing through the empty hall.

All right. That was done. I could certainly sort all that out for him. While I was here, I might as well look through the post. Everything addressed to him could wait—*till he came back*, the tiny drowning voice in my head told me insistently, though it was getting fainter and weaker by the hour—but I had to look at my own damn mail.

Except that, after cracking the first envelope, I couldn't. It was ridiculous. They were all the same. Stiff, smart envelopes, more social, decorative, than functional. I got assailed by envelopes like these on birthdays and at Christmas. Nice, expensive, full of love and best wishes—and, this time around, *deepest sympathy for your loss*. Christ, there were about two dozen of them. I couldn't even remember off-hand having that many friends. I'd more or less dropped my own circle of acquaintance after moving in with Jase. Jase and rowdy postgrads hadn't mixed, and who could need more or better company than my beautiful professor? I'd been wildly in love. I'd man-dumped a whole bunch of mates. This first card, the one I'd been fooled into opening, came from Mike, with whom I'd shared my postgrad flat until Solstice 2007.

Well, it was nice of him. I didn't deserve it, but I was grateful. Everyone, I could distantly appreciate, was being very kind. Even the WPC who'd come to my office had been nice, almost tender, in her dealings with me. Probably she was the one they sent round to deal with their basket cases. *Just a few questions, Dr. Logan.* About financial troubles, professional worries. I'd answered automatically, no, and no. He had been wealthy, academically respected. The third question she'd tiptoed up to, as if perhaps I might not have realised, despite living with and most sincerely fucking another man for three years, that I might be gay. Clearly Professor Ross cared for me a great deal—there was no possibility that he might have been concerned about my fidelity, there being such a gap in our ages? That one I had rejected with a vehemence that had startled both of us. If I had an eye for male beauty, I was certain I had never let Jason see me seeing. Dear God, if that wasn't true, if he *had* noticed and it had grieved him… I sidestepped the thought as if had been a school of piranha. No, and no, and no, and the police officer seemed happy with that, closing up her notebook and telling me, like all these cards in their sealed envelopes, *sorry for your loss.*

So I couldn't open Jason's mail or my own. That left only one envelope. I was tired now, and my head was aching, but I picked it up and turned it over, looking with mild curiosity at its machine frank. Not Royal Mail—military. MoD Fellworth, to be exact, and it was addressed to both of us. *Professor J Ross and Dr. D Logan.* I liked the look of our names linked like that, in stark, undeniable typeface. We looked good together, didn't we? We always had.

That morning, I suddenly recalled, I had padded quietly into the staff coffee room and overheard Rachel Keats, a colleague I'd liked and trusted, saying to the assistant head of European history, *I never thought it was a good idea, you know. Daniel was so young for him—*

practically a toy-boy. Still, maybe Dan needed a father figure... I'd turned and padded just as silently out. The words hadn't penetrated my shield. I was certain—almost absolutely certain—that our partnership had been as good, as satisfying and nourishing to him, as it had been to me.

I ran my fingers over the label, as if it held some power of reunion, to bring together what had been put asunder, then ripped the envelope open, being careful not to tear that part with our joined names. I was shaking a little bit. My brain had started to give me thoughts of Jase, of our relationship, in the past tense. I'd plugged the phone back in, obedient to the dean's orders, and its reverberant silence was getting to me. Feverishly, praying for distraction, I pulled the letter out and unfolded it.

Prayer answered. Not just distraction—sheer bloody disbelief. Colonel Roy McCade courteously requested our presence at a meeting with himself, delegates from Wiltshire County Council and English Heritage. He was pleased to announce that one of the areas of the Salisbury Plain Training Area in which Professor Ross had expressed a longstanding interest was due for demilitarisation. Unexploded ordnance remained on the site, but if the professor and his colleague Dr. Logan would attend and indicate their priority excavation targets, bomb-disposal personnel would be assigned to them. The meeting was provisionally scheduled for 1100hrs on Friday, 26 June, at the Fellworth base.

Friday. Tomorrow. I scrambled for the phone, suddenly oblivious to weariness and headache. To everything, in fact, beyond the necessity of dialling Colonel McCade's assistant on the number indicated. It was after seven o'clock, but I supposed the military didn't observe normal knocking-off times—the line picked up on the second ring. McCade's assistant, though perfectly polite, sounded surprised when I identified myself, then more so at my eager acceptance of the meeting. He tried a sentence which began with, *in the circumstances, we'd assumed*, but I cut him off. No, I would be glad to attend. I thought it essential that my colleague's work be honoured and continued in this way. I would be there.

I hung up before he had a chance to tell me he'd cancelled the councillors and EH reps. He'd just have to damn well un-cancel them. Then I scrambled to my feet, re-energised. The letter containing Jason's funeral instructions fluttered to the carpet, and I picked it up, because I would never disrespect anything of his, but I folded it and tucked it carefully into the table's top drawer, the one we used for matters that needed our attention soon but not immediately. Because, dear God, what would Jase think of me if I spent the evening now moping around, ringing his friends and calling up the Ingersoll minister? He'd be disgusted. If he were here, he would by now be scouring his bookshelves and filing cabinets for every scrap of information he had gathered on the land inside the MoD's barbed-wire fence.

And in his absence I could do that. I knew where he kept everything. We had travelled far and wide, but he had never lost his interest—his near obsession—with the military zone. He'd refined his ideas about it over the years, believed passionately that the Neolithic and Bronze Age builders of the circles had never erected their strange, numinous structures randomly—that they had been actuated by a profound understanding of how their world and its energies worked, a comprehension that had been as universal as it was now universally lost. Even I couldn't follow his reasoning sometimes. With any other man, I'd have called his evidence patchy, insufficient to fuel his desire to get past the MoD's fence. Not Jason, though. Jason had just been drawing strands together. And if he believed it, I did too. He had been going to publish a career-crowning book called *The Salisbury Key*.

That could be my task now. I drew a huge breath of relief. I would be fine. I knew what he wanted me to do.

***

That night I slept the instant my exhausted head hit the pillow, and I had a strange dream. I was at Stonehenge. I had, outrageously, driven Jason's DS right into the middle of it and parked, which was allowed because the car was loaded with books, papers and tiny, beautifully wrought little keys, all pertaining to something desperately important which for now I couldn't remember. The day was sunny, a sweet brisk breeze romping over the plain. I went to one of the trilithons and stood stroking its flank, which was warm as something living. I became aware that I was distracting myself, trying to give myself a reason not to look back at the car.

But when I did, my father was there, smiling at me from behind the wheel. This was odd in several ways. I hadn't lied to Jason, all that time back, when I'd said I had few memories of him, but now it seemed I could, after all, recall every detail of his face. I could remember, too, that as far as my six-year-old cognition went back, he had been confined to a wheelchair, and now he was unfolding himself from the car, looking fit and well, bizarrely wearing Jason's favourite North Face trousers and all-weather shirt. I was so bloody pleased to see him.

I ran across the circle, feeling it stretch big as if I had shrunk six-year-old small. I shouted out, *Dad, Dad,* and he reached down from a towering height to scoop me up. *My son,* he said against my ear. *My boy. My beautiful boy.*

Chapter Four

Colonel McCade, who from his name sounded as if he should just have ridden in from Fort Laramie, turned out to be a neat, dapper Wiltshireman without a trace of tumbleweed about him. I liked him at once. He was clearly very busy and anxious to turn all his focus on the matter in hand. That suited me perfectly. I liked to have around me people who were single-minded. I thought at first that perhaps he hadn't even heard about Jason. Then he asked me curtly if I wished to appoint another colleague, and I replied equally coolly that, for the present at least, I'd be working on my own, and then that was over.

I sat for almost an hour in the MoD Fellworth briefing room, trying to stay awake. Now that I had this new focus, a lot of the barbed-wired tensions in me had dissolved, and, unless frenetically occupied, I seemed to be sleepy all the time. The English Heritage rep, who had known Jason well and whose look of profound condolence I'd had to deflect, was explaining to McCade the groundbreaking importance of his decision to let researchers onto the Salisbury Plain military sites, and McCade was nodding brusquely and reminding him of how limited and thoroughly supervised all such access would be. They were like two men very politely and elaborately telling one another to fuck off, and I repressed a smile, letting the rhythm of their undeclared argument soothe me.

The morning was glorious, even behind the barricades of the military compound. Somebody somewhere was mowing grass, and the scent of it drifted through the cracked-open windows, together with lark song. Impossible to forget that this stronghold was a superficial blot on a landscape so ancient and vast that, drowsing in its summer silences, it could wipe out all human concerns and...

"Dr. Logan?"

I jerked upright in my seat. It was a bit too comfortable. Jason and I had been in this room before, and I knew it was the interface between army inscrutability and the public domain—a few concessions had been made, in its décor and furnishings, to civilian life. There were chairs in which you could, just about, drift off into sleep. Colonel McCade was looking at me curiously, the EH rep with frowning concern.

"Sorry," I said, aware that I'd missed my cue. "Would you mind going over that point again?"

Not a bad try for a cover, but it had been McCade's invitation to come forward and look at a map that I'd missed, not a point, and my inattention must have been plain. Courteously he repeated, "If you'd just like to step up and indicate for us the areas you're most interested in."

I thought I was safe, but then Basil Hunt from EH pushed up from his seat and came towards me, holding out a hand as if to an endangered toddler. "Really," he said, "Dr. Logan, you shouldn't be here. Will you let me give you a lift home? I can easily phone the university and have them send someone else out."

That wouldn't suit me at all. The fact was that the university, and, in particular, its dean, didn't know I was here in the first place. Technically speaking, I required the department's authorisation to be out here acting in its name, and I couldn't have risked not getting it. So, that morning, I had called the dean's office and told him, in a husky, tired voice it hadn't been hard to fake, that I would need a few days' compassionate leave after all. He had been very kind. Relieved too, from the sound of it.

I straightened my shoulders. Out of the corner of my eye I could see McCade, and I let myself pick up some signals from his posture, his imperturbable gaze. I said to poor Basil, "I appreciate your concern. But you must understand that I need to continue to act professionally with regard to Professor Ross's projects."

I wasn't even quite sure what that meant, but it worked. Basil nodded, stepping back. "Yes. Yes, of course. But I want you to know, Daniel, that you have the condolences of everyone at Heritage. He was a marvellous man."

I skipped over the last part. I was caught by the idea of having my grief endorsed by the whole of English Heritage. Like being declared a national monument, or an area of outstanding natural beauty.

"Thank you," I said gravely, impressed with my own tone, which was just right, tinged neither with tears nor the sudden unsettling laughter that inappropriately dogged my more serious moments these days. "All right, Colonel. If I could take a look at the map…"

Rapidly I checked and discarded about ninety percent of the land the army was preparing to demilitarise. I was surprised by the amount they were willing to let go, and I heard, distantly, Basil Hunt's excited chatter to the councilman. The Wildlife Trust would want to step in here and here, wouldn't they? And this part, to link up two areas of special scientific interest…

"Here," I said, cutting across them, planting a finger on my target as if by doing so I could claim it straight away. "This is what he wants. Where Professor Ross and I had hoped to gain access, that is."

McCade came round the table to look over my shoulder. "Well, that's very definite."

I supposed that it was. Over the years, Jason's interest in a wide number of potential sites seemed to have narrowed itself down, and although of late he hadn't talked to me much about the reasons why, I no longer cared about them. He had wanted it, and now I could get it for him. That was enough. The area stretched from the Bronze Age hut circles we had noticed three years ago, and for about a mile from there northwest across the plain. I would start my dig from the bottom, as he had taught me—from the oldest part of the site I could identify, and work upwards and forwards from there.

McCade made notes of a few coordinates, then went to fetch a file from the stack on his desk. "Fair enough, Dr. Logan." "But you've chosen a site of heavy artillery use. You'll need expert help to locate and disable buried explosives."

"And will I get it?" That had been too sharp, almost a demand, and I immediately regretted it. *Don't antagonise them*, Jason whispered in my ear. I frowned. I was being tactful, wasn't I? But Jase would have found a way to be gracious about this, not jeopardise the one precious step forward we'd made. "Any assistance you can give us would be greatly appreciated."

McCade nodded, one eyebrow on the rise. Probably perfectly aware that my manners were the icing on the cake. "Well, I'm not about to allow you to blunder around in there on your own, Dr. Logan. Sergeant Phillips, if you would fetch Lieutenant Rayne and tell my aide to bring in coffee and sandwiches for the gentlemen…"

***

I didn't want lunch. I wanted whoever it was that could get me out with the sunshine and the larks and blow enough unexploded crap out of my way to let me start my work. I stood impatiently by the window, nursing a coffee, while English Heritage and Salisbury CC converged on the sandwiches.

When, after what seemed like an unforgiveable stretch of time, a firm knock sounded on the briefing-room door, I turned around sharply.

"Ah, Rayne," McCade said to the new arrival. "This is Dr. Daniel Logan, the archaeologist from Professor Ross's department. Dr. Logan, Lieutenant Rayne, our EOD man. Explosive ordnance disposal," he clarified. "We used to call them UXBs. Am I right in thinking, Doctor, that you'd like to drive out to the site you've selected now, so that Rayne can assess it for you?"

I nodded. I couldn't take my eyes off the upright young soldier who had come to stand by McCade's desk. Distant bells were ringing in my head. I could smell, for some reason, soya bacon burning on a wood-smoke fire. I remembered a sable-haired angel in a mediaeval painting, there one minute, gone beyond redemption the next time I looked. A nervous squaddie standing guard outside the Stonehenge barricade...

If the sight of me was raising any corresponding memories in Lieutenant Rayne, he wasn't letting them show. His dark gaze was perfectly expressionless. It rested on me like obsidian, like cool water. It was exquisite and maddening—summed me up in one long look and dismissed me as irrelevant. A task to be dealt with and forgotten.

"Very well," McCade was saying. "This will just be a preliminary survey, Doctor. It may not be viable for you to start work out there straight away. My final permission will depend upon the lieutenant's assessment. Rayne, if you take Dr. Logan out to the south gate, I'll have a jeep sent round for you."

At last the cool-water gaze left mine. Rayne turned to the colonel. "Yes, sir."

***

I was surprised, once out in the sunshine, that I'd recognised him. He had altered enormously, from my one glimpse of him on that Solstice night, which when I thought about it now seemed at once a century ago and only yesterday. I studied him, subtly as I could, as he steered the jeep out past the barricade and onto the plain. He was leaner—less obviously, boyishly handsome. He seemed to have come into a kind of tighter focus. To have burned something off. He still reminded me somehow of a priest, in his intent, unfaltering attention to the road ahead, his stern profile. He had a deep-laid scar across one cheekbone, and some grazing that looked recent. The sculpted mouth was the same, though, tense in its corners as if constantly forbidding itself a smile.

Okay, I was staring at him. I was astonished that anything beyond the basics of my mission could interest me, and I turned my gaze front. He drove with an odd technique, now I came to look, deftly whipping the jeep round the edges of potholes I was sure its sturdy frame could handle. I watched that for a while. The silence between us wasn't yet awkward, because neither of us had tried to start a conversation, but it had potential. Deciding I wouldn't be the first to break it, I unfolded the map. Six or seven miles to our destination. They were going to be long ones, at this rate.

I didn't care. It was quite liberating. All the tiny things that normally bothered me had dropped away. I had liked to be liked,

liked to flex a little seductive muscle even from the harbour of my partnership with Jase. To make sure I still had it. But today I didn't give a damn if we travelled the length and breadth of Salisbury Plain without a sodding word.

The road became monotonous. Even a week ago, I would have loved to be driving out here, watching how the summer was baking the vast stretch of country to its pitch of saffron and gold, but now that remembered beauty was oppressive to me. Almost frightening. Helplessly I returned to my covert study of Lieutenant Rayne's face. Dark fringe, cut short in spikes beneath his beret. Heavy-duty insignia on the sleeves of his fatigues. He'd done well for himself over the past three years. In weird contrast, that generous mouth, and eyelashes so long they split the sunlight into beautiful brushstroke shadows across his face...

He reached for a pair of sunglasses from the dashboard, and I flinched inwardly. Then I took a breath. He couldn't have seen me.

"Not far now," I said, losing my nerve and the game, and he replied, in a distinct, soft Hampshire accent I hadn't caught back in the briefing room, "Yeah. You've changed a lot, as well."

I stared out through the shield. For a moment I forgot that I didn't care about anything anymore and contemplated a rolling dive out the door and onto the turf. Then it occurred to me that he might not mean the night when I had performed my impromptu dance in front of the Stonehenge crowds. Perhaps he had seen me on a more dignified occasion, supervising a group of students or laying out the lines for a dig.

The jeep shot down a couple of hundred more yards of road, her driver still adroitly evading the potholes. Then he continued, "Cut-off jeans, spray-on T-shirt. Oh, and a pair of Captain Marsh's handcuffs."

"Jesus." I folded the map up. I knew where we were now, and I felt an uncontrollable urge to wrap my arms round my chest. I'd have drawn a knee up too, if this had been three years ago and I'd been wearing kick-off trainers, not sensible boots laced tight, the better to impress McCade with my professional demeanour. I was tightly done up inside all my clothes, I realised. Tie, belt, a jacket Jase had given me almost as a joke, for those occasions when only a smart tweed with actual leather elbow patches would do. It was my attract-the-sponsors coat, when we were schmoozing for funding for a dig, something I was very good at. Way too hot for today. I said dryly, "I can't believe you remember that."

"It was hard to forget. You had a colleague with you that day. I heard he died."

I waited for more. *I'm sorry*, perhaps, or *what happened*. But he left it as baldly stated as that—no more than an observation. And for once I didn't reach reflexively for my shield. It was getting damn threadbare now anyway, as the days went by and the differences which made no difference began to wreak transformational havoc on my world. For a moment I was outraged, that he had dared to make such casual reference, where others had tiptoed, used every word but the right one. *Loss. Bereavement. This sad time.* Never, simply, *he died.* There was nothing there for me to fight. The words dropped inside of me like two stones down a well.

God. It was real. Nausea washed through me, and I said, "Yeah, he did. What the hell are you driving like that for? You're making me travel-sick."

"Like what?"

"Dodging every bloody pothole."

He hadn't been aware of it. I saw that, saw him glance at his hands as if they didn't belong to him. A moment later a very faint flush appeared on the cheekbone I could see. He said icily, "Perhaps that's because I spent the last three years avoiding mines in Iraq, Dr. Logan. The ones I didn't have to stop and detonate. That's my job—not nursemaiding academics with more brains than sense around some imaginary bloody Roman town."

Well, that was real too. And plain enough. "Okay," I said. "No problem. Turn around and I'll get McCade to find somebody else to nursemaid me."

He snorted. The faint, angry colour was still there. "Chances. I already tried to ditch you. You're my assignment, for as long as you need me, and if you've any bloody decency you'll keep it short."

I sat back. I felt, for some reason, vaguely satisfied. Secure too for the first time in days. Partly it was because I had managed to get under his military hide—partly simple pleasure in being so roundly disliked. I didn't know where I was anymore with the rest of my acquaintances. Friends had become kid-gloved ghosts, padding around me. Professional rivals—the nearest thing I had to enemies—smiled at me gently in corridors. This was better. And now we were speeding in an arrow-straight line down the centre of the single-track road. Rayne had put his sunglasses on, and his face was a marble-carved mask. I fished out my own pair from an inner pocket. They were aviators, just as cool as his, and probably ten times more expensive. I delicately put them on and schooled my own face to expressionlessness as the jeep hit every single bump and hole in its track for the next five miles.

And so it was that when we reached the open stretch of moor Jason and I had come to on that day three years ago—when I scrambled down out of the jeep and stared off towards the earthwork and the flowering gorse where he had laid me down—I was only irritated. Not crushed with flashbacks and grief, my shield evaporating under this last proof that everything had changed. That was all I had dreaded today, seeing this landscape and falling apart. No chance of that now. Annoyance flickered in me, and that buzzing, persistent satisfaction.

I slung my satchel over my shoulder and set off, not really caring if Rayne followed me or not. I hauled in deep breaths of the beautiful air, ripping the neck of my shirt open. Gorse flowers, thyme, the weird tang of pineapple mayweed which only grew for the pleasure of being trampled underfoot and giving off its hot, slightly sickening scent. Thank God, I was out under the sky, untouched and untouchable. If the wind blew just a little harder up from the wide slope below me, I would walk up on its wings and leave this incomprehensible bastard of a world behind me.

"Hoi! You! Logan!"

I jerked to a halt. It wasn't voluntary—I felt as if my leash had been snapped tight. My preflight sensation evaporated. Slowly I turned around, irritation resolving itself into anger. That had been the yell of a drill sergeant to a recalcitrant squaddie across a parade ground. How did he dare talk to me like that?

He was standing behind the jeep, leaning a hand on its open back door. To my surprise, he was smiling. I had no intention of staying around him long enough to discover if his bark was worse than his bite, but that was a hell of a smile, even mitigated by his reflective shades. I saw that he had unloaded three black cases from the back. They looked heavy.

"What?" I shouted back at him, already knowing.

"Your party, Doc. You help carry the cake."

"Oh. Sorry." Immediately I hoped the wind had snatched the words. Wherever I had been, I didn't want to back down from it, not yet. But—at least until five days ago—I'd never been the surly, uncooperative git I was channelling now. I instinctively shouldered my part of whatever load it was. I strode back over the fifty yards or so of ground I'd managed to cover, trying to make it look as if I'd meant to take a short detour. Once at the jeep, I pulled off my tie and stuffed it into a pocket. I took off the hot, heavy jacket and slung it into the back, and I rolled up the sleeves of my shirt, wishing I'd left behind the beautiful but none-too-macho silver cuff bracelet Jase had bought me in Mexico.

He was watching me attentively. I thought about apologising again, and then about reminding him I wasn't a recruit. But his stance, his silver-shaded gaze on me, didn't seem to require defence or defiance. I picked up the two smaller cases and walked off.

I realised my mistake soon enough. I thought he might leave me to struggle, but he ran to catch me up, his hand closing over my wrist. "No. Put it down." I obeyed, carefully, sure he was less concerned about me than whatever delicate item I'd been just about to drop. "That's a magnetometer," he said, extracting the handle from my grip. "Heavy. In your other hand…" He dodged behind me, helping me lower the second case onto the turf. "Computer and scanner, also heavy. The big case is my protective gear—awkward but light, if you don't mind."

"Your gear? I thought this was just a preliminary survey."

"It is. But if it takes us over some old Howitzer shells, we won't be coming back for the real thing. I clear up as I go along, Doc. Let's get on with it."

I followed him. Now I wasn't quite so confident of his dislike. His manner varied from brusque to a kind of restrained friendliness, as if I'd been a comrade. A low-ranking one, I told myself, biting back a grin, but a comrade nonetheless. I couldn't figure him out, and the effort of trying, and my surprise at wanting to make it, carried me once more across dangerous ground. It wasn't exactly wind-wings underfoot, but it worked. That, and the powerful, rhythmic movement ahead of me of his khaki-clad…

I swore silently and tore my gaze down. Christ, would nothing stop me? This was automatic, surely. Some kind of death throe. Or would it take my own death, not just that of the man I'd loved more than sunlight, to still the reflex? I marched on in silence, watching my feet and the turf, wondering what the hell was the matter with me. Okay, Rayne was lovely. Not the unmarred boy I'd seen three years ago, but still bloody stunning. I didn't know how he got by in the military with that kind of fine-wrought, unmissable beauty—unless, I thought bitterly, his fellow soldiers had some kind of decency and restraint and didn't feel a morbid need to stare at anything male, shapely and unique, stare hungrily until the image was imprinted, consumed…

Because that was all I wanted. I didn't want to fuck him, any more than I'd wanted to fuck the lifeguards or hotel pool boys I'd encountered on my trips with Jase. Promptly, helplessly, I imagined fucking him. An impossible scenario in a military locker room—*nice, Daniel,* I told myself, *classy*—where he dropped the towel he was wearing and turned from me, bracing for me up against the wall. *Quick, quick, before we get caught.*

"Oh God," I said aloud, and saw him stop a few yards ahead of me. The sun was beating down. I couldn't remember the last time I'd eaten. Jason was dead, and I had no idea, none at all, of what the hell I was doing out here.

Rayne put his cases down and gazed at me. He had left his sunglasses behind in the jeep and I noticed, irrelevantly, that his clear grey eyes had a deep charcoal ring round the iris. "What?" he said. "Are you not well?"

I scrabbled for some inner handhold. "No. I mean… I'm fine."

"You look like shit. I've got water, if you need—"

"No. I just need… I just want to get on with this."

"Well, be my guest." He turned away and shaded his eyes to look northwest across the plain. "This is it, isn't it?"

I looked around. I saw, with faint shocks of recognition, each of the landmarks I had picked out for Jase all that time back. The barely visible ridges in the turf that marked the Roman settlement, and the track of its ancient road, the ditch and the vallum. We were on the earthwork. Today I hadn't even noticed the rise in the land. In fact, if I glanced back and down to my right, I would see the sheltered patch of gorse where...

"Listen, Logan. If you're sick or getting sunstroke or something, tell me, and we can do this some other time."

We were back to brusque. His fists were balled on his hips, a tense impatience clear in the set of his shoulders.

"I'm not," I said tiredly. "It's just that... Well, these remains are hard to spot, unless you know what you're looking for. Do you have some archaeological training?"

"Not a day of it," he said, crouching down beside one of the cases. "What remains?"

I frowned. "You must be able to see them, or you wouldn't have stopped here. This earthwork, the ridge that runs off north there. The line of the road, and off over there, the remains of a Bronze Age village. Hut circles."

"Oh, is that what those are? Sorry, Doc. I know this place from an MoD map, that's all. Your hut circles are target 37SW, I think. We use 'em to practise cargo drops from the Globemasters." He paused and looked at me assessingly. "As for this ridge... We took potshots at it from Copehill when we were testing the new Sherman cannon."

I undid the strap of the bulky pack I'd been carting around for him and let it drop onto the grass. He talked pretty casually about all that hardware, didn't he? Targets, cannons, old Howitzer shells. McCade had done it too. What had he said, back in the sunny, sleepy briefing room? *You've chosen a site of heavy artillery use.* I'd barely taken any notice of it at the time, except as something I needed getting out of my way.

But the land McCade had been talking about—the land I'd earmarked—was the exact same stretch where Jason had led me out that night to see the Bronze Age huts. Where I'd followed him, because even then my trust in him had been absolute. Something clenched in my throat. I'd had a weird, persistent catch there since last Sunday. If I thought too hard about it, or the taste it still brought to my mouth, I would throw up.

If I thought too hard about anything, I fought for control. And then it was easier to veer off into anger. Apparently I had a nice big button on the front of my shirt which Rayne knew how to push. Had I seen a tiny flash of mischief in those serious grey eyes? My temper came up, a hot, bright flag in the wind. I welcomed it. It sent blood beating back into my limbs, burned off my encroaching sense of panic.

"Jason was right. You're all the bloody same. That road—this settlement—was laid down two thousand years ago, by engineers and architects whose techniques you couldn't hope to understand. That none of us ever will, because you lot bomb the shit out of places like this before we get the chance to excavate…"

He was watching me again in that unfathomable mix of detachment and concern. After I'd caught my breath, but before I could continue my diatribe, he said mildly, "Roads and ruins laid down by a warrior nation that had annexed and occupied this one pretty much because it could. Maybe I understand your Romans better than you think. Come on, Doc. Help me unpack and set up."

Damned if I'd do either. I stood there, still gasping for breath. I had great counterarguments for his point of view. Jase and I rehearsed them all the time. We'd been to Whitehall and presented them to government, during our battle for Salisbury Plain. I couldn't believe his cool disregard of me. He was on his knees now, unfastening catches, his dark head bent gravely over his task, as if I didn't exist. Well, bollocks to that—he could listen to me, respect my position, or…

"Oh, is that the magnetometer?"

My own sudden question surprised me. Aggression dropped away in favour of curiosity. I didn't want to let it go, but I sounded like myself for the first time in days. Rayne glanced up, one brow quirking. Carefully he finished lifting out the device from its foam-rubber housing. "Yep," he said. "Used one before?"

"Yes. We've got one in the field department, but…" I knelt beside him, instinctively reaching to help. "It's nothing like this."

"Well, you need a defence budget to have one like this. I *know*," he added, after a moment, a little wearily. "But don't rip another strip off me, Doc. I don't choose the rules."

"You chose to serve."

Up close that long-lashed gaze was a devastating challenge. I fought not to blink first. More urgently, not to be afraid of him. He said, so softly that I could barely hear him over the wind, "Back off, Logan. You don't know anything about me, and you don't need to. I'm just here to help you with this bloody job."

Together we set the magnetometer up. I could see that although some of the components were similar to those in the machine I'd been loaned from time to time by the field department, the principle of it was quite alien to me, and I confessed as much, sitting back on my heels after hooking up a series of wires and components on the do-as-you're-told method.

"Was the one you used before a fluxgate?" he asked, lifting the lid on what I recognised as a high-spec Toughbook computer.

"Yes. A pair, actually, to get a gradient between readings."

He nodded tersely. I reckoned we would get on fine, if all we ever talked about was machinery. "Right. This is a CVM, a caesium-vapour model. Wish I could say it was basically the same, but fluxgates run on electricity and magnetism, and this relies on…"

"Quantum mechanics," I finished for him, smiling. I let my bulls-and-barley Wiltshire accent, which normally lay buried deep unless I was drunk or exhausted, lumber up to the surface. "We don't have one, but they do let us…*talk* about 'un, down on the farm."

"Oh, funny. Yes. Quantum mechanics. Its photon emitter pulses at the same frequency as the Earth's magnetic field, and any variations in that field will indicate metal sources—improvised explosives by the roadsides in Iraq, or leftover Howitzer shells here in our sunny back garden. There's virtually no noise. It's highly efficient. And, unfortunately, we don't need to split up to use it. Here. Grab your end, and be *fucking* careful."

I walked at his side along the line of the ridge, balancing the device on the two rubber grips of its tray. After the first five minutes, the muscles of my arms were on fire, but Rayne wasn't complaining, and so I kept my mouth shut too. About that, anyway. Like his machine, he seemed to want to go about his work in silence, and I wasn't sure why I couldn't let him. I imagined unimaginable interactions of light and electrons going on in the enigmatic beast we were carrying, and said, "How come a poor archaeologist gets time with this miracle of science, anyway? If it's more at home sniffing out bombs in Iraq?"

"You wouldn't, ordinarily," he returned flatly, squinting at a readout. "This is a new model. McCade wants it tested, and this is a good way of tuning it in."

I gave this thought. Somehow it made me feel more secure—a good, selfish military answer. No favours conferred. "And what about its operator? He must be pretty high-spec too. Are *you* getting tuned up for something?"

"Logan." This time he just sounded tired, not dangerous. "Tell me. Am I prodding *you* with questions you don't damn well want to answer? Because there's plenty of scope for that, isn't there?"

I caught my breath. I supposed there was. Starting with *why are you here on your own.* Maybe *what happened to Professor Ross* as a main course, and *does anyone in your department know what you're up to* as the cake with the cherry on top. I couldn't go near any of it. Jason's name, or even the thought of it, was like a loose end of wool in my mind—pull it, and the whole fucking tangle which was all that was keeping me together would dissolve. He would have loved this machine, for example. Would have charmed Rayne into telling him how it worked, and understood the explanation too. He'd have asked questions, but intelligent ones, not irritating little grabs for information Rayne clearly didn't want to give, and which were irrelevant anyway to our work out here.

Something occurred to me, a silver thread of rationality, and I seized it. "So this—the CVM—it can distinguish between, say, the shape of an IED and a shell?"

"Yes." What was in the look he shot me? Gratitude that I'd laid off, or amusement, maybe, at how easy I was to shepherd. "No bother at all. If we get any good readings here, I can show you on the monitor once we're done."

"Then it could pick up buried spearheads. Armour, coin hoards, that kind of thing?"

"Warts on the emperor's nose, if you want. Right. That should be enough. Let's have a look."

We sat down together in the lee of the ridge. I was bloody glad to set the CVM down and surreptitiously rubbed at the tops of my arms while Rayne flipped open the Toughbook box. It had snap-out sunscreens that blocked the westering light. I came to kneel close to him as the monitor activated. For one instant I was acutely aware of him—just the shape of his shoulder brushing mine, his intense warmth—and then the screen lit up. "Bloody hell."

He grinned. "Yeah. It's a bit good, this, mind. Hang on. I can enhance it… There." He indicated a contour line towards the bottom of the screen. "We're here on the ridge, and…"

He didn't need to say more. I could read the rest of it for myself. The image was GPS and magnetic variation combined, and I was used to interpreting satellite views. Silently I traced the line of the road, the beautiful grouping of the huts, Neolithic circles quietly countering the linear Roman mindset. And the scene was starred all over with tiny, glowing shapes, lovely, really, constellations in pale green light.

Rayne flipped a switch, and each of the luminescent stars was overlain by a red spot, a code I didn't recognise. I said faintly, "Are those…"

"Shells, mostly. Howitzers, hand grenades, artillery. Place is loaded." He sat back a little and gave a low whistle, shaking his head. "You choose your spots, Doc. We might not be able to do this—not here, anyway. Weren't there other areas you and the department were—?"

"No. Nn-nn. It has to be here. Look, can you zoom in a bit, on this part?" I extended a fingertip towards the screen, barely noticing when Rayne pushed it aside before it could make contact. "Look, your machine can't be accurate." That was the answer, the firm ground in the mire that had almost swallowed me up a few minutes before. Machines lied. So could men, and no doubt Rayne, McCade and their kind made a practice of mythologising the dangers of the Plain. "Jason and I came here. Jason—

Professor Ross—took me over the barricade at this point, and we got nearly halfway to the huts and back. We were fine."

"What—here?" He tapped at the keyboard, drawing the mouse pointer down in a circle like the view through a rifle's sights. Once the crosshairs were over their target, he flicked deftly through a series of drop-down menus and dialogue boxes, zooming the image, tightening it up. "You and Ross crossed this terrain?"

"Yeah, before one of your heavy mob interrupted us. It must be clear. We…"

I shut up. My mouth had gone dry. I was quick enough at picking up new methods, new tools for assessing the land where I plied my trade. I'd seen, on the area overview, how each numbered code represented one of the buried monsters listed down the side of the screen. And Rayne was right—at this resolution, you could see individual shapes. I said dully, "Those can't be live."

"No," he agreed. "Not all of them. But intact like this— ninety percent or so would blow up at a touch. A footstep."

The panic I'd managed to burn off in anger surged back again. "He couldn't have… We didn't know."

I'd started the lie reflexively but finished it consciously enough. Hiding myself in solidarity with Jase. *We didn't know.* But Rayne just looked puzzled. "Seriously?" he said. "He studied and fought for that bit of land for years and missed that one detail? Jesus—was he just trying to kill himself, or did he want to take you too?"

No. He was a good man. He would never, never have done anything to endanger me. I couldn't seem to get the words out. I stood up, taking a couple of steps backward, having to steady myself as my foot caught in a hollow. Blindly I watched as Rayne folded down the monitor screen. He unhooked a couple of connections, calmly, as if having completed his job he had forgotten my existence.

"Well," he said, "either he had the luck of the devil, or he was too mad to care."

"Shut up," I whispered. I wasn't even sure he heard. He was busy unhitching the various parts of the delicate mechanism, saving the scan onto the Toughbook's hard drive.

After a moment, though, he paused and looked up at me directly. "Well, it pisses me off," he went on, almost conversationally. "You and your professor come out here and jump the barricades. This time God isn't looking after kids and idiots, and he gets blown to tatters, or you do. And for the next ten years, the army has to live down the rep of having killed this brilliant academic light. Despite the fact that he was on our land, behind our bloody barbed wire. Did you say he was your friend?"

I shook my head. I hadn't said anything to Rayne of what Jason had been to me, and I didn't intend to. I had only one intention. But for that, Rayne had to be on his feet and facing me. I watched, mute, barely breathing, while he finished powering down the equipment and levered himself upright.

"Colonel McCade knew Ross well," he said, dusting windblown seed-fluff off the sleeves of his camos. "That's why he kept pushing to grant his requests to dig here. And I'm pretty sure Ross knew how heavily this whole section of the plain is mined. Did he tell you? Because if he did, more fool you for running after him. And if he didn't, he was a dangerous bastard who—"

That would do. The heat-flash engulfed me. He was looking straight at me—it was fair. I drew back, let all the rage coiling up and down my spine find a focal point in my clenched right fist, and I swung for him.

He caught my punch in midair. It was instinct—he hadn't even looked. His eyes were still on mine. His hand closed round my fist, warm, absolute. Absolutely forbidding. I saw the muscles of his arm absorb the blow. I gasped as the momentum of it recoiled into my shoulder—I hadn't been playing around. To my cold mortification, he reached to steady me. "All right," he said. He sounded more amused than angry, and his face was calm. "All right, Doc. Made your point."

"Professor," I grated out. His hand was still wrapped tight round mine. It was unbearable to be touched by anyone else, the more so because his clasp was so steady and sweet. I snatched my hand away. "*Professor.*"

"What? I thought you were..."

"Not me. Him. Professor Jason Ross. You don't go around calling him Ross, like he was one of your barrack mates, or..."

"Or somebody I could ever be good enough to know?"

That was exactly it. I didn't need to agree. He shrugged and flickered me another of his enigmatic half-smiles. If he'd been a different man, I'd have said he was hiding a trace of hurt, but that couldn't be true—how could I ever hurt this armour-plated military drone? I couldn't explain to him that, as far as I was concerned, *nobody* was good enough to have known Jason, or to use his name without the deepest respect.

He wasn't about to give me time. He had crouched down beside the CVM's cradle. After a moment he gestured at the other end. "Well," he said, "if you're finished chucking punches, you can help me cart this home."

***

I hadn't thought the trip back to Fellworth could be any more awkward than the way out. Of course, I hadn't calculated on making such an arse of myself in-between times. My shoulder still ached—partly from lugging the CVM, more particularly from having the force of my own blind attack turned so neatly against me. For Christ's sake, I'd tried to hit him. I'd lost all control and tried to sock a soldier round the face. I was meant to be a professional. I was meant to be out here representing Jason Ross, and if his memory meant so little to me that I was willing to belt someone for dropping his title, I damn well needed to do better.

I wanted to apologise, but not to Rayne. He seemed quite unconcerned anyway. His hands were steady on the wheel, and he'd dropped the evasive manoeuvres in favour of a law-abiding straight line home. *I'm sorry, Jase*, I thought, leaning my brow against the passenger window's glass, feeling a grief I couldn't even begin to handle or contain boil up in me. It wasn't about my conduct now, not really. It was about every other time in the past when I'd been—oh, stupid, ungrateful, looking about me and scenting the air for other things, other men, when I'd had my beautiful Jason right there beside me. Christ, I'd lifted my arms and danced for Rayne not three hours after Jase and I had first made love. My shield was gone. I was screwed, about to burst into tears in a military jeep in the middle of nowhere.

"So is that why you were in handcuffs the first time I clapped eyes on you?"

I jolted back to surface. Rayne hadn't taken his eyes off the road. He was gazing calmly ahead. He didn't look like a mind reader, or a man coming back for another go at me, and I wondered if this was just his effort to make conversation. I decided I appreciated it. Having to think back, to respond to him, had yanked me out of an avalanche. I realised suddenly that, in fact, he had been distracting me all afternoon.

"Yeah," I said roughly, and cleared my throat. "The bloke who pulled us in—Captain Marsh, I think it was—wanted to make an example of us for his cadets. He was pretty decent, otherwise." I thought about what Rayne had said, about bombs and barricades and the apportionment of blame. "In the circumstances."

"Captain John Marsh? Yeah, he was decent. He died last year in Mosul."

I blinked. Rayne had delivered this as calmly as news of a change of address. I had seen Marsh through shadows, from behind Jason's shoulder. Briefly taking part in my charade before the Stonehenge crowds. Remorse, and the beginnings of a return to reality, hit me like a brick.

"All right, Rayne," I said, shaking my head. "I'm sorry. We live in different bloody worlds—I know that. And I shouldn't expect you to risk your neck, helping me bugger around in mine. I *don't* expect it."

He absorbed this, still expressionless. Then, quite suddenly, pulling up to the Fellworth gatehouses, he turned to me and smiled. "So. Not gonna come back tomorrow then?"

"What? What for?"

"To start your dig."

"There's no way McCade's gonna let me work in there now. And you wouldn't want to help, would you?"

He pulled up at the barrier, lifting a casual salute to the guard on duty. "Did I say that? Anyway, McCade lets me make my own calls." Steering cautiously through the crisscross of other vehicles and soldiers on foot, he brought the jeep to rest a courteous two feet away from the DS, where I'd left it in the base car park. Looking at its sleek dark lines—distinct against all the blue-grey and khaki paint jobs surrounding it—it struck me for the first time as a little odd that I was still driving it around.

But I couldn't seem to finish the thought. I was too caught up on the possibility of continuing Jason's work, despite what I'd seen out there today. "But we can't... It's too dangerous, isn't it?"

"I've dealt with worse. We'll just have to go careful." He switched the jeep off and turned round in his seat, slinging one arm over the back. The sun had caught his cheekbones. He was lovely. I tried not to stare at him—or at least, since in these close quarters I couldn't avoid it, to throw some intelligence into my regard. "Look, it's up to you, Doc," he said after a moment. A smile lit his face—challenging, questioning in a way I couldn't define. "But I bet I'll be seeing you again."

Chapter Five

Of course I went back the next day. I didn't have a lot of choice. The house, when I had returned to it last night, had for the first time howled at me with its emptiness, and I hadn't been able to sleep—not in the bed, not on the sofa, and ultimately not at all, and I'd sat at the kitchen table from two in the morning till five, staring at the clock. Then I'd gone for a bone-jarring run. I'd run—dodging down a side street when I saw Elsa Reid, grey-white ponytail flying high—until I was sure the gym would be open, and I'd stopped off there to shower. The bathroom—the entire house—was transforming from a refuge to a horror, some kind of cheap fairground haunted castle. I felt that kind of child's absurd, half-laughing terror in its shadows. I had to get out and stay out, and Rayne had offered me a way of doing that.

Anyway, I was committed. Even if I didn't tell Dean Anderson what I'd been up to, somebody would—Salisbury, despite its big plain, was a bloody small town—and, when he found out, I had to have something good to show him, to make him forgive my disobedience and allow me to go on.

Already I was doubting very much that I would find it. I was puzzled. Jason had been so sure. But there had been nothing on the magnetometer survey to indicate anything unusual in the area. I stopped off at home long enough to pick up my gear, then I drove out to the site.

Rayne was already there. I saw him from a long distance out, leaning on the bonnet of his jeep. Something about him—his solid, elegant slouch—set a warmth inside me, and I tried not to acknowledge it, pulling up onto the verge nearby. No, not a warmth exactly. Just an easing of the chilly sickness that dogged me, a shaft of sunlight through fog.

He pushed gracefully upright and came to meet me halfway between the vehicles. "Morning, Doc," he greeted me, a bit cautiously, I thought, and no wonder, after yesterday. "No offence, but you look like crap."

I shrugged. I'd hoped my morning's exertions and a hot shower might have livened up the unshaven ghost I'd seen in the mirror first thing. "None taken. I didn't sleep, that's all."

"Oh good. I love hitting enemy ground with half-asleep squaddies in tow."

"I'm not one of your..." I began, and then let it go. I found a reluctant smile rising to match the wry, teasing one he was bestowing upon me. I couldn't think what I'd done to deserve its kindness. "Well, I've got some coffee," I said, hitching my rucksack off my shoulder. "Have one with me? It might make me fit for duty."

We sat on the turf in the lee of the jeep. The plain stretched out before us, verdant, keeping its secrets to itself. Perversely, as soon as I cracked open the coffee flask, I felt the tug of sleep that seemed to come down with the sunlight and the aromatic breeze on June days here. Rayne had settled beside me, just close enough that I could have put out a hand to touch him. He was

112

unfastening a black MoD-stamped file. "Here," he said. "I printed off those scans we were looking at yesterday. We might be able to find a safe way in."

A real safe way in, he'd had the grace not to say, and I wished I'd had the grace not to think it. "Okay. Thanks." I grabbed a couple of nearby stones and put them on the top corners of the scans to stop them flipping up in the wind. The flask was the type with two cups in the lid, and I absently handed one to Rayne, who took it just as distractedly, giving me a nod of thanks. "Pretty detailed, aren't they?"

"Not bad. Could really use some aerial shots to back them up. You can read a lot from the way vegetation grows back over bomb sites."

I felt, just for an instant, like the stewardess in *Airplane* who pulls a bobby pin out of her hair at the crucial moment when only a small piece of metal will save the day. I bit back a snort of laughter. Rayne probably thought I was unhinged as it was, and as for Jase—well, although we shared a lot of cinematic tastes, I'd never even tried to turn him on to that one. "Can help you there, oddly enough," I said, reaching into my satchel.

I carried Jason's aerial photos around with me almost by habit. I knew that they were central to his work wherever he was, and to me they were his signature, his trademark. When I looked at them, I felt as if I was seeing through his eyes. I set them out on the turf, aligning them so they matched the scans.

Rayne glanced up at me. I told myself I didn't give a toss what he thought of me, but there was nothing I disliked in that brief glimmer of surprise and respect. "Where did you get these?"

"Jason took them. Professor Ross," I amended, aware that for the first time I'd got the name out without half choking on it. "It's one of his primary research methods."

"Well, he probably shouldn't have," Rayne said, and I thought about telling him not to worry, that an RAF jet pilot had been big and brave enough to scare away the frail little Cessna, but I shut myself up. I'd lost the strange urge to gibe at him that had possessed me yesterday. "Still, these aren't half bad. Near-infrared, are they?"

"Yes. If you look here—and here, and down this line—you can see where the earth's been torn up and resettled."

"Right. Yeah, that's a good way in for us. It backs up the scans. I reckon everything that can blow up around there already has done. Okay, Doc, grab your kit."

"Daniel," I told him suddenly. He looked at me, eyebrows on the rise. "Not Doc or Logan. My name's Daniel."

"All right," he said, after watching me for a moment. I noticed that the circle of black round his irises seemed to have increased, soaking into their silvery grey. "That's nice. But for you, it's still just Rayne."

I didn't care. I was mildly surprised that he wasn't insisting on *lieutenant*. And once we got beyond the barricades and into the danger zone, I had enough to occupy me. As well as my field kit, he had made me lug a metal detector over the fence. He had gone to work with that, while I followed with compass, scans and detailed OS map, giving him directions. Every time the damn thing squealed, he stopped dead, even though nine times out of ten it had found nothing more than a concentration of iron in the soil, and I found his insistence on a halt frustrating until, the tenth time, I saw the curve of a Howitzer shell rising under the turf, like a dolphin breaching surface.

That one—too small to show up on the scans—was only a fragment, but it changed my view of my surroundings, and I trailed him with a bit more patience. Once we'd cleared enough of a safe trail, he made me go carefully back along it, marking its boundaries with what looked like pointy-handled ping-pong bats, the paddle of each of which was coated both sides in fluorescent plastic. I drove the points into the turf, marking us a safe retreat.

Glancing up from my work at one point, I found him watching me, expressionless as usual, and I called out, pushing back imaginary locks of long hair, "I feel like Ariadne!"—patronisingly expecting him not to get it—and he shook his head and returned, deadpan, "You look more like the bloody Minotaur to me," and I burst out laughing, forgetting for whole seconds that my world had crashed and burned.

We worked all that day, and on the second we got far enough into the hut-circle enclosure that I thought it was worth my sinking a trench. By then I was a bit delirious with sleep deprivation, but I didn't mind the sensation—it was like a mild fever, the slight high of flu before the symptoms kick in. Now it was his turn to do the grunt work.

I marked out a two-by-five in pegs and tape just on the edge of the settlement where the aerials showed disturbed ground, and I set him to dig, watching and making notes as the edge of the shovel turned over first topsoil, then deeper sedimentary layers I knew from experience had last seen light of day about five thousand years before. I was hoping for a dump site, a depository of broken flint arrowheads or axes, or pieces of the deer-horn spades with which the Neolithic communities here had dug out everything from their own homes' foundations to the stupendous ditch surrounding Stonehenge. These began to turn up soon enough, and I stopped him with a touch to his arm. "Here we go. Look."

He crouched beside me, turning over the collection of objects I'd gathered onto a tray. Surreptitiously watching his face, I saw there the alteration I'd seen happen time and time again with indifferent students, the ones who were there because they hadn't looked past "A" in the prospectus. Textbooks and lecture halls were one thing, quite another to get a piece of the past raw from the earth and hold it in your hands. Gently he blew clinging soil from an arrowhead, and I smiled and handed him the right brush for the job. He looked very different with that in his strong grasp from the way he had while holding the heavy detector or the wheel of the jeep.

"So," he said, feeling the finely worked edge with his thumb. "This lot is pretty unusual then?"

I shook my head. The afternoon was cooling a bit, heavy clouds massing up to the south, as if a storm might blow in from the Channel later on. "That's just it," I said. "It's not. They're beauties, but you could find them on almost any site from this era if you knew where to dig. I can't work out what Jason was looking for here."

Rayne set the arrowhead down and looked around him. "Well, we've just started, haven't we?"

"I guess. It's hard to know what direction to take, though, if nothing much is showing up here." I opened the file with the aerial shots carefully sheathed in their plastic covers. Rayne leaned close to me, looking over my shoulder. I noted, automatically damping down each new sensation as it came, that he smelled good, of soil and fresh sweat from digging. That I had chilled down in the breeze, and he was radiating warmth. "Here to the north might be good. And I wouldn't mind taking up a few layers in the centre, where they might have had a communal fire."

"What—to look for bones, evidence of diet, that kind of thing?"

"Yeah. Yes, exactly. You sure you've got no archaeological leanings?"

"Not a single one." He grinned and looked more like himself, or more like my preconceptions of him. "And interesting though all this is, Doc, if you want to go in either of those directions, I'm gonna have to blow something up."

I watched while he set out his gear. Now the sky was overcast, the wind turning cold. I sat on a grassy hillock just inside the safe zone, drawing my knees to my chest. I'd offered to help, and he'd dismissed me—not unkindly, but with gruff military thoroughness. He could play at being an archaeologist, I supposed, but I couldn't play at bomb disposal.

He was laying out what looked like small charges of dynamite on the turf and lengths of wire. Suddenly, looking at these brutal practicalities, I felt sweep over me a sense of the preposterousness of what I was asking him to do. I didn't know why it hadn't struck me before, except perhaps that it had been sunny, and the plain was a place of broad and magical possibilities under blue skies. Now a cold scatter of rain, sharp as gravel, was hitting my face. I was tired, nervous energy draining from me as the weather changed.

"Hoi," I called, standing up. "Can I come over there a second?"

He thrust a hand towards me, palm out. "Not a chance. I told you—safe distance."

"You haven't even plugged anything in yet."

"That's right. And before I do, I'll send you twice as far away."

"Rayne, please. Just for a minute."

He sighed, perceptible even across the distance between us. "Stay put. I'll come to you."

He trudged back towards me, movements hampered by the Kevlar shielding he'd strapped on over his fatigues, still somehow graceful. I could see him walking, lonely and purposeful, along the edge of a dusty desert road. When he was near enough to me that

I didn't have to shout, I said, "How did you get those cuts on your face?"

He frowned. For a moment I thought he wasn't going to answer. Then he came to a halt, bending down to fix a piece of armour that was coming adrift at his knee. "Iraq," he said, shortly, not looking up at me. "Got too close to a culvert bomb. Why?"

"Because I can understand—almost—how you'd risk your neck out there, with lives depending on you. But here? For the sake of a few shards of bone?"

He shrugged. "It's what you wanted. Not me."

"Yeah, I know. I did. To be honest, I…I'm not sure what I was thinking. Come on. Forget about it. I'll work in the zone we've already cleared safe."

"Logan, you blew into Fellworth like a bloody hot wind the other day. You practically gave McCade your orders, not the other way round. What's the matter?"

"I'm not sure. Maybe I just don't want you on my conscience. I'm serious. Put your gear away and let's go home."

Let's go home. The words hung oddly in the cooling air between us. When I said them to Jase, they contained a promise, a magic. They were for the end of boring cocktail parties, for moments of mutual weariness when we looked into one another's eyes and decided, silently, to make our escape. They meant journeys home late at night in the purring DS, closed doors behind us, lights shining warmly. Skin on warm skin… I didn't have any of those things with Rayne. I wasn't even sure I had a home anymore, not one I could bear to go back to. I didn't know why I'd said it.

He watched me in silence. "Well, if it helps, I'm not just here to cater to your whims. The army's not that generous. McCade wants all this ground cleared off eventually anyway. Some of the demolition gear he's given me is experimental, like the magnetometer. So, if I do blow myself to buggery, it would be on him, not on you."

"Technically. Not much consolation."

"Ah, come on. Let's get on with it. If you want to make yourself useful, help fasten me into this damn Kevlar."

***

And, after all the preparation and drama, there wasn't that much to it. I felt numbed out. I'd told Rayne my objections, and watched them bounce off him like the droplets of the sudden cold shower that had begun as I pulled Velcro patch to Velcro patch and buckled nylon straps into place. I'd have enjoyed the task, a week or so ago—snapping the tough, body-contoured shields around this man's strong frame. Now I did so only with dispassion, and a sense of inner retreat from the scene, so that it hardly seemed to matter when he packed me off bodily too.

I retreated without further protest to the hundred-yard range he'd ordered, and took shelter as he'd told me beyond a small rise in the turf. I didn't even watch. It seemed more important then to watch the pair of stone-curlews lifting off against the grey sky. They were rare, scarcer by far than archaeologists or soldiers. A breeding pair—and they were flying wing-to-wing—was good news for the plain.

The sight of them was trying to trigger something in my head. Before I could track down the memory, a dull, thudding explosion rocked the afternoon. It was smaller than I'd expected, barely making me jump. It rolled away down the flanks of the great space around me without finding echo and was gone. The curlews had veered off a bit. Everything else was the same.

I turned and saw Rayne walking back towards the safe trail. That had gone well, I supposed. He was taking off his visored helmet, giving me a wave. Trying to recapture the feverish interest that had buoyed me up until lethal explosives came into the deal, I got up and began to jog towards him.

He tripped and fell. It was so unexpected that I almost laughed. That was my style of performance—to pull off some impressive feat or other, identify perhaps the exact place where a valuable find would turn up, extract it in front of a bunch of admiring students, then fall into the ditch. I'd never have predicted it from Rayne, model of military competence as he was, from the top of his close-cropped head to his sturdy desert boots. He did exactly what I'd have done in the circumstances too—tried to lurch straight to his feet, as if it hadn't happened.

Something was holding him down. I thought for a second he was only struggling against the weight of the Kevlar, but that was less heavy than awkward. Then I saw that he was tangled, though in what I couldn't tell. Suddenly he jerked up his head, holding out a hand to me. There was a bright-red stripe across its palm. "Stop!"

There it was again, his shout to the squaddies. I'd obey that when I packed away my trowels and joined the fuck up, and not before. I belted across the scrubby grass and crouched by his side. "What happened? Did you cut yourself?"

His Kevlar knee-plate was snagged on something. I could see it now, when I came to look. A thin, fine wire, barely visible till you got it broadside on. When I reached to help, he slapped my hand away. "Leave it. Jesus. Do you not think that—just for sodding once—if I tell you to do something, I might have a good reason?"

"Probably. You're bleeding, though. What is this crap?"

"Wire from an antitank missile. I thought they… We always clear this stuff up."

"An antitank missile?" The edges of the wire were razor sharp—his palms and wrists were crisscrossed with fine lacerations. Grabbing a dusting cloth from my pocket, I wrapped it round the strand that was fouling the plate and held it back. "There. Pull now. Why does a missile need wires?"

"For guidance. The operator shoots them, and... Look, I'll give you the ordnance lecture later, okay? Jesus, I should have seen it. Get out of here, Logan."

"Why? We cleared this area, didn't we?"

"Yeah, and there's nothing on the scans, but..." He detached the last piece of his Kevlar from the wires. "I'm not happy. Fuck it, Logan, will you just go?"

"I will if you will." The cuts weren't deep, but the sight of his blood sent a pang through me.

I put down a hand to help him up, and after a moment he took it, shaking his head. "All right, all right. I'm coming. You've got some big balls on you for an archaeologist, I'll say that for you."

I was still turning over this observation thirty or so seconds later, as we made our way back into the safe zone. I supposed it was a compliment. His opinion still meant nothing to me, or so I told myself, steadying him over a tussocky patch of ground where grazing cows had mired up the mud. And that was a point... "What if sheep or cattle stray into that rubbish?"

"They get tangled and cut up, just like—"

"Like you did. Great. It's bloody lethal."

"I told you—we tidy it up after an exercise. That piece was a freak. And it's harmless enough if you handle it right. I shouldn't have grabbed it."

"It's always same story with you lot, isn't it? Everything's harmless—old warhead silos, depleted uranium..."

I stopped short. There were several more global outrages I wanted to list for him, but behind us, back in the direction we'd come from, a weird dull thump had just resounded. A kind of popping noise. Beside me, I saw Rayne wheel around too, whatever retort he'd been preparing dying on his lips. "What was that?"

"An explosion."

"Not much of a one. It sounded like…"

"Like something popping. Yeah. A priming charge for something a fuck of a lot bigger. Daniel, run."

The first time he'd used my name. It was that I was thinking about, when the turf behind us heaved itself up into a sudden weird dome, the brown soil beneath it bursting richly up and out. That, and the fact that we were well matched for a sprint. I only had a half dozen strides to reflect on it. We ran as one. I did not have the cold despairing moment of three years ago, when, blind though I'd been to the danger around me, I had felt Jason leaving me behind.

***

I lay on my back, and I watched the unfolding drama of the Wiltshire sky. The curlews were at the height of their arc. From here, the sun caught their undersides, turning them into heraldic devices on a grey flag of cloud, or Celtic brooches, to fasten a chieftain's cloak…

I was so fucking relieved. So happy that I was laughing, though for some reason I couldn't hear myself, only feel the convulsive emptying and filling of my lungs. Finally, finally, I had worked out where I was, and I had woken up. The curlews—black shapes on blue when Jason had lain me down here—had blurred and streaked to gold when he had made me come. And I'd fallen asleep, and the weather had changed. The place and the view were so perfect that I could take the two loose ends of time and dovetail them together, dismissing the gap as a dream.

The cloudscape flickered. Something had passed over it. Only for a moment though, and I resumed my memories, feeling the weird, silent respiration shaking me still. A warm grip was coming and going on my limbs, like someone patting, squeezing. Checking I was unbroken, or still all there...

Then the clouds and the curlews eclipsed again, replaced inexplicably by the face of that mediaeval angel neither Jason nor I knew was there in the painting he'd bought me in Florence. Pale, and gravely beautiful. Severe, as all such depictions should be, the seraphs belonging as much to Lucifer as to God, messengers between the worlds, not feathered escorts for idiot humans. This one was talking to me, slate-grey eyes intent, their iris hooped round in jet black, but I couldn't hear him. Finally my brain sorted itself out, dismissing the illusion for what must be the truth—not some half-memory from a painting, but Jason, warm and real. Trying to wake me up. Calling out his name—I heard it only as a hazy echo, far off in the distance—I bolted upright and into his arms.

The wrong arms. I was holding on to the wrong body. Everything was off—the scent flooding into my nostrils, the fabric under my hands. Jason washed in sandalwood, not a mass-produced soap you would probably find in half the bathrooms and barracks of England. He would never wear thick, stiff drill cotton like this. All wrong. Nevertheless, whatever I had here was all I had, and I clung on to it, fighting to catch my breath. Maybe if I called it by the right name often enough... My own voice was beginning to filter back through to me. "Jason. *Jason*!"

"I'm not Jason. Let me go."

I heard that too. Deep and rich against my ear. Instantly I obeyed. The grip on me didn't immediately vanish—closed a little tighter round me, as if in kindness or regret—then eased, letting me back down onto the turf. "Jason…"

"No. You're shell-shocked."

I raised both my hands to cover my face. When I did that, I could taste blood, so I lifted them off, examining them. The palms were cut and grazed, as if I'd thrown them out to cushion a fall. But there was more to it than that, wasn't there? Yes, blood in bright wire streaks on another man's hands as I'd reached to help him up. My ears popped, and my head cleared painfully. "Fuck. What happened?"

"Antitank missile went up. It was live."

"What? Why can't I hear properly?"

"Blast deafness. It'll pass. The fucking missile blew. Are you all right?"

I could remember who he was now. Not an angel—Rayne, the soldier. *An angel in the rain*, I thought distractedly, watching the shower that was beginning to thicken to a downpour slicking his black hair, making his camo gear cling to him. Rayne. Not Jason. A fucking stranger, when I thought I'd come back to life in my lover's arms.

But, yes, I was all right. If I wasn't, it was more than I could afford to let anyone else know or to tell myself. I scrambled to my feet, grabbing instinctively for the stranger's arm when the sky and earth heaved round me. "Fine," I said. "Why didn't it show up on the scans?"

"Too new. More plastic than metal. But I should've… I should've seen it."

I could still barely hear him. But I caught with surprise, through the staticky roar in my head, this new note. I hadn't thought him capable of sounding—what? Uncertain? Ashamed?

124

Then I lost interest. It seemed hard to hold any concept in my head for more than a few seconds, much more effort than anything could be worth. "Never mind," I said tiredly. "Let's just go, before anything else blows up."

"Are you all right to walk?"

"Course. Why wouldn't I be?"

"Logan, we got a few yards away, but the blast edge… You went about ten foot. That's why—don't you see? That's why civilians can't come here."

I tried to give it thought. I was sore, now he came to mention it, as if I'd been picked up and casually chucked back down onto the turf. He'd said something else too—about civilians, and not coming here, but I'd been hearing that for years. I didn't have to take it in. I looked at him. In addition to his bloodstains, he was now quaintly marked with grass and mud across such bits of his fine white skin I could see past his Kevlar. "Whereas you," I said, "simply absorbed the shock into your manly frame."

"*No.*" Again, that flicker of unwilling amusement in the corner of his mouth. "It threw me too. But…"

"But you're a hard-arsed soldier, not some academic poof who can't function if his specs get broken. Okay."

"That's not what I…"

I turned and walked away from him. That seemed the best way of proving I could walk. I headed back up the trail we'd laid out, between the markers that glowed oddly in the rainy light. I was almost impressed with myself. I'd lived through a bomb blast. Jason would love this story, when he got home, I thought, and then immediately after, *Jason would love this, if he was alive to hear it.*

The two thoughts ran parallel in my mind. Unconsciously I assigned one to each set of fluorescent markers, a handy external structure. One running ahead forever to my left, the other to my right, commanded by the laws of geometry never to meet. I could live with that, probably.

If my stupid, lawless, non-geometric brain would let me. In there, in that flickering darkness, the lines *could* meet. I could feel them now, grinding flank to flank like icebergs in a frozen sea. My vision blurred, turning the markers to streaks that converged at the barbed-wire fence a few yards away. Impatiently I rubbed the rainwater out of my eyes. It tasted of salt. Behind me I heard footsteps, running. Felt a warm grasp close on my shoulder. I was almost at the barricade. I shook him off. "Leave me be. I'm fine."

"Let me give you a hand over here."

"I told you, I…"

The lines met. Rainwater somehow in my throat too, rising and hot. Jason was dead. He should have died three years ago, and so should I—on the night when he'd led me, like a stunned bloody sacrificial lamb, into a minefield. The lines of truth, black and sharp as the missile guide wires, met and severed the fantasy thread I'd been weaving, day in, day out, for the best part of my life's worst week. I jolted to a halt by the great wooden support posts we'd scrambled over to get in here. My lungs were full of this terrible salt rain, which now tasted of petrol too. This time when they seized up with coughing, I stood no chance. I doubled up, flailing out blindly for support.

I was distantly aware that Rayne grabbed my hand one inch shy of a strand of barbed wire, guiding it to the wooden post instead. I clamped the other to my knee. Christ, *had* Jase been trying to kill himself back then? Trying to take me with him? The coughing turned to retching and I twisted away, ashamed—but that wasn't going to be the worst of it, I knew, trying to flinch out from under his grip on my shoulder. My stomach wrung itself violently empty. "Oh, *fuck*!"

"Jesus, Logan."

"Let me alone." I dragged a hand across my mouth. The imprint of Jason's was on it, cold and terrible. Christ, I would have given anything for our last kiss to have been the hot, exhausted one we had exchanged before I had fallen asleep on Saturday night. I would have given anything not to have found him dead. An absolute loneliness seized me. I wished he had blown us both to hell three years ago. I'd have traded that for this, with all my heart. I could've been at peace for all that time. I could've been gone.

I folded down onto my knees on the wet turf. The next in-breath was a sob, and the next. I couldn't bear the sound, and I clamped my hands over my ears.

Rayne touched my shoulder. Briefly he laid one hand to the back of my head. I couldn't assign more importance to these sensations than to any of the others assaulting my senses—the scraping pain in my lungs, or the patter of raindrops, like cold little feet on the nape of my neck, exposed by my short crop. Jase had liked my hair to be tidy. I had liked to please him. Something came down over my shoulders, stiff drill cotton that smelled of soil and sunlight. Rayne said, "I'll wait for you at the jeep." And then I was alone.

***

"What happened to him, then?"

I sat in the jeep's passenger seat, a cup of tepid coffee from Rayne's flask cupped between my hands. I didn't want to be there. I didn't want the coffee, but I knew that without it I wasn't going to have the strength to get away and drive home. Most particularly, I didn't want to answer any questions. I was aching from head to foot. My eyes were swollen, and my sinuses felt finely sandpapered.

"To who?" I said dully, deliberately obtuse. I had folded Rayne's jacket up and given it back to him. I didn't know what else he wanted of me.

"To your friend. Jason."

"It doesn't matter. Thanks for the coffee. I...I'm gonna go now."

A sigh, deep and weary. "At least let me run you home. I'll have someone come and get your car."

I sat up. Through the rain-streaked windshield, I could see the DS sitting patiently by the roadside. "No," I said. "I'm fine to drive. Will you be here tomorrow?"

"Tomorrow?"

He sounded incredulous. Turning round stiffly in the seat, I looked at him. He was a handsome mess, daubed in mud, his hair damp and spiking. I wondered if the military didn't work Saturdays anymore. Well, he was entitled to a weekend. "Monday, then?"

"Logan, we're not gonna be doing this anymore, for God's sake."

I frowned. "Why not?"

"Because I nearly killed us both. I have to report back to McCade what happened, and...you will too."

"What? I thought you said there was no way to check for that missile. It was an accident."

"I should've refined the magnetometer scans. I missed it. I missed one just like it in fucking Iraq last month and someone died. That's why I'm home."

My mouth opened. I was lost so deep down inside myself that it took me long seconds to surface. Rayne's tone had barely changed—his expression less so. He was a fraction paler under his mud, that was all. "Bloody hell," I managed.

"Yeah. So add this in, Doc, and I'm screwed. I'm sorry. Field trip's over."

I ran a hand over my face. My head was pounding. I assumed I looked as much of a wreck as I felt. "Look," I said unsteadily. "Leaving aside fucking Iraq… What the hell would I be doing, running to McCade with stories? What you do is your own business. I'm not part of your sacred bloody army machine."

A silence descended, broken only by the staccato of raindrops driven against the jeep's glass and metal by the wind. After a while I realised I wanted to tell him I was sorry about what had happened in Iraq, but I had no idea how. He was staring off up the road, patting his fingers on the wheel. Suddenly he said, "I heard he killed himself. I heard it was in a car. Please tell me that it wasn't that one."

He was looking at the DS. The last couple of times I'd got into it and started it up, it had struck me that I was doing something very strange indeed, but I hadn't been able to get past that point in my thinking. I wanted to lie to him. But all that came out of my mouth, lamely, hopelessly, was, "So?"

"*So?*" He turned back to face me. "So put it on eBay, or…park it by the road with a sale price in the window, but don't drive around in it torturing yourself, you moron. What the hell are you thinking?"

I drained the coffee cup and screwed it back onto the flask so hard that the plastic cracked. "Right," I said. "Here's the deal. I'm not gonna fuck up your life, so as far as I'm concerned, this afternoon never happened. You're safe with McCade." I grabbed my satchel and shoved at the jeep's door, giving it a kick when it didn't open. "And you stay the fuck out of my head too. Leave me alone."

Finally the damn door gave. I slithered out into the rain. The drop from the passenger seat was always further than I anticipated, and I stumbled, catching the wing mirror to pull myself upright. Jerking my head up, holding my spine straight, I walked away.

Chapter Six

At about eight that night someone knocked on the door. It was a big house, and we could have used a doorbell, but Jason had disliked the sound of them, so the original Elizabethan iron ring remained in place, clutched in the jaws of a grinning demon. The sound of that would roll through the hall like something out of *Macbeth*, sending me halfway out of my skin between kitchen and living room. Somehow over the last week I had learned to ignore it. I'd plugged the phone back in, hadn't I? Anyone who wanted me could use that or stick a note through the door.

I wouldn't have answered this time, either, but I was drunk. Flying, actually. I seldom indulged these days—I'd been a typical student, but with Jase it had been little, occasionally, and very, very good—so the quart of vodka I'd got through since my return to the house had hit me full force. On reflection, I couldn't imagine why I hadn't thought of this obvious solution before. It was so bloody easy. If I couldn't sustain a self-imposed mental numbness, all I had had to do was reach for the chemical sort. I pushed up off the sofa, where I had been sitting watching the rain for the last three hours or so. My legs still worked. I felt fine. Sociable, almost.

I thought it might have been the dean, or Mike, my old flatmate, who had left a few messages on the machine. I could have coped with either. As far as the dean knew, I was only enjoying the privilege of my compassionate leave, and Mike—well, Mike had made sporadic efforts to hit on me for as long as I'd known him. I wondered, vaguely, pulling back the bolts and locks which Jason seldom fastened and which I had never opened since his death, how I would respond to that tonight. I was prepared for pretty much anyone.

Except for Rayne. I stood in the open doorway, leaning on the jamb, staring at him blankly. For a long moment, I hadn't recognised him. I don't know what I'd thought—that his uniform was grafted onto him, or he had to wear it for social calls too—but his civvies came as a mild shock to me. I wasn't sure why. They were very nice. Very ordinary. A T-shirt and jeans, and a worn, soft leather jacket. It was as if, until now, I had only seen him in a shell. He looked at once accessible and harder still to reach than before.

While I was still trying to puzzle that one out, he said, "I came round to see if you were okay after this afternoon. Christ almighty, Logan. Haven't you even had a shower?"

I didn't reply. I was too busy taking him in—him, and the battered little Audi parked on the kerb. Then, slowly, I became aware of my own state, which hadn't bothered me or even occurred until then. I was still coated in mud. Still damp, streaked with grass stains. Seeing the direction of my gaze, he glanced back over his shoulder. "Well, what did you think? They don't make me drive around in a Snatch the entire time. Can I come in? It's pouring."

I stepped aside and let him past me. He stopped in the hallway to wipe his feet, a gesture I appreciated—the hall carpet was priceless. What I couldn't work out was why, until now, I'd forgotten. Jase would have been horrified.

Leaning on the post table, I kicked off my muddy boots. "Er, yeah. No, I haven't had time yet. I've been busy." I didn't think I sounded drunk. But Rayne gave me a quick, dark glance, in which there was a mix of compassion and amusement, as if he knew exactly how I'd been employing my time, and I blushed. Then the pressure of my unbalanced lean on the table made it rock. It creaked and deposited an avalanche of unopened mail on the carpet at my feet.

Those nice expensive envelopes had just kept on coming. There were other types, too—official ones, with utility-company logos on them. But all of those were addressed to Jason, and I'd piled them up neatly, separately from the rest. I had been mildly pleased with myself, actually, for not just leaving them on the floor. Well, they were back there now. I needn't have bothered.

"Fuck," I whispered, and crouched down to pick them up.

My fingers were numb and unsteady. I wasn't doing a very good job. Detachedly I observed the other, more competent pair of hands down there with mine, gathering up the snowdrift. One of them was bandaged round the palm. Yes, I remembered—that one had been cut up by the wire. Bright scratches still showed across the back of the other. I asked faintly, "You okay?"

"What? Oh, yeah. Got patched up, and I've stopped hearing bells. You?"

"Er, yes. More or less."

"Good." He turned over a couple of the envelopes, then handed them to me. "Looks as if you've got some bills here. Want me to…"

"To what?"

"Well—I'll have a look, if you want. It isn't easy—"

Cold fire leapt up in my stomach. My temper snapped, brittle as a twig. "What—you think I can't pay a fucking bill on my own?"

He heaped up the remaining post and shoved it back onto the table. "I'm sure you can," he said, getting up. "But first you have to fucking open them. What I was going to say was, it's hard when someone dies. And it won't get any easier if they cut your gas and electricity off."

I straightened up too. I couldn't stay on my knees on the floor in front of him. I supposed that he did have a point. I wasn't sure that I had one, in my defensive backlash. *Could* I still independently settle a bill? Part of my salary went, on automatic direct debit, into Jason's account, but everything was in his name. I swore softly under my breath and grabbed a handful of envelopes, picking out the business ones. This was stupid. I'd lived on my own for seven years before I'd met Jason.

"All right," I returned angrily. "Christ, no, I don't want you to look at them. I will."

I turned my back on him. I got halfway down the hall before it occurred to me that I was being abysmally rude. Through mists, I remembered that afternoon, the terms on which we'd parted. I'd more or less told him to fuck off, hadn't I? In the circumstances, it was decent of him to make a house call.

"Sorry," I said, not looking back. "Do you... Do you want a cup of tea or something?"

A brief silence. I wondered if he was about to let himself straight back out into the street. That wouldn't matter to me at all, I told myself, and I couldn't understand the bitter tang of fear that rose in my throat at the thought. Then he said, with just that faint smile audible in his voice once more, "A cup of tea or something would be nice."

"Right. Kitchen's through here. Come on."

I put the kettle on, banged a mug onto the surface for him, then applied myself to the brown paper bag I'd brought home from the off-licence, double-parking the DS on my way home. Stupidly, or optimistically, I'd bought two small quart bottles instead of one large one, but the first was empty, and clearly I wasn't about to stop there. I'd had to bring in my own supplies. Jase never drank to anaesthetise himself—all we had in the house were fine wines and exquisite vintages of brandy and single malt.

Rayne watched me unpack my second quart, try and fail to locate a glass, and slosh a measure into another mug. Well, it was one better than drinking from the bottle. He said, "Is that helping?"

"As a matter of fact, it is."

He nodded. "Fair enough. Tell you what." He went over to the sink, which was where all the glasses were because I hadn't washed up in six days. He extracted one, rinsed it and filled it with cold water. "Have that with it. You'll last longer. Better still…" He held the glass out to me, and I took it from him on reflex. "Take that, your mug, and your filthy, sweaty self upstairs and have a shower. I'm telling you seriously to do this, Logan. Cats are gathering."

I stared at him. Superficially, I was outraged. I had a good right to be. What was he doing, ordering me round in my own home? But a bubble of laughter had somehow found its way into my chest. I snorted to hide it. "You're kidding me, aren't you?"

"Not in the slightest. I'll make my own tea. Go on, sunbeam. I'll still be here when you get back."

Why would he imagine I cared about that? I did, as it happened—even through the numbing cotton wool of vodka, I cared quite urgently that I wouldn't come back downstairs into an empty house. But did it show? I stared at myself in the bathroom mirror. No, there was no lonely beacon flashing there, no outward sign of my conviction that, if I'd been left to my own devices tonight, I might have followed Jason down a self-wrought path into the dark. Not in the bloody garage—no way was I methodical, determined enough to organise all that. More likely I'd get rat-arsed and fall down the stairs, or set the house on fire whilst attempting to cook chips.

I saw my own ghost of a smile and winced. I looked like hell. I had hollows under my eyes you could collect rainwater in, and my guest was right—I was filthy. I couldn't understand how I'd sat around Jason's beautiful house for hours in this condition with, as far as I remembered, my muddy boots propped on a Renaissance-tapestried footstool. Most archaeologists enjoyed getting knee-deep in muck, and I was no exception, but I had loved getting clean again afterwards, emerging steaming from the shower and putting on fresh clothes, so I could go downstairs and see Jason glance up at me, his eyes kindling…

Fuck. I doubled over, burying my face in my hands. This was no damn good. Every thought led to him. When I stripped out of my dirty clothes, I would put them in the basket and remember yet again that his were in there too, that I hadn't yet done a wash. Or made the bed, or washed a dish, or opened the bloody post. I couldn't bear it. Being trapped here in my own skull was suddenly unbearable. I stumbled a step or two back from the mirror, as if by losing my image I would disappear.

I switched the shower on full and got in still dressed. Everything I wore was filthy—it made no odds. I stood with my eyes closed, dragging the clothes off me like heavy skins, letting them fall.

***

Rayne sat opposite me at the kitchen table. He was calmly making his way through a cheese and pickle sandwich of his own construction. Outrageous, to have helped himself, except that he'd made me one too. It had been sitting on a plate waiting when I came down.

I couldn't eat. My stomach was a dully aching knot. I sat huddled in the outsize jumper, relic of undergrad days, that I'd found in the bottom of a wardrobe. Rayne wasn't looking at me. He was leafing through the archaeology magazine I'd been reading on the previous Sunday morning. I remembered the page I'd been on, the article I'd been reading. Before I'd got up to switch the music on. Before I'd heard the sound of the car.

But it was as if I couldn't sustain another shock. Couldn't respond, as if I'd been electrocuted again and again until the muscle was burnt out, my reactions exhausted. Everything in this house was and always would be a relic. So Rayne had touched the magazine. So I'd washed away, unthinking, any trace of Jason's hair or skin that might have lingered in the shower. I just couldn't feel it anymore.

In the time it took me to make this realisation, I had apparently reached for the sandwich and gone automatically halfway through it. It was good, and now I came to think about it, I was fucking hungry. I picked up the mug which I'd brought down from the bathroom with me, and choked as the unexpected taste of raw vodka met the cheese and pickle.

Rayne glanced up from the magazine. "Here," he said, pushing his own mug across the table to me. "That might be better."

It was, though he took his tea just as strong and laced with sugar as his flask coffee. "Make you one?" he offered casually.

"I'll get my own."

I got up and switched on the kettle. It seemed weird, to thank him for a sandwich made with my own ingredients, but also it felt rude not to. A silence had fallen. If he was finding it awkward, he didn't let it show. He'd propped his chin on one hand and returned to what looked like a genuinely interested perusal of the *Review*. I, on the other hand, was starting to hear my heartbeat in my ears. I said, after a moment, "Ta for making that. Did you, er... Did you talk to McCade about this afternoon?"

He sighed and set the magazine down. I was immediately sorry to have disturbed him. Spreading its pages absently flat with both hands, he replied, "No. But I'm going to have to. And you should too."

"What if I don't feel inclined?"

"Well, you've got a perfect right. You were a civilian under my supervision, on official business."

"Ah. Official business." I stood by the counter, looking into the swirl of my tea. I was too tired, and there was too much alcohol still washing around in my system, for me to hold that one up anymore. If I wasn't already rumbled, I would be soon enough. "I wouldn't call it exactly that."

He raised his head. I didn't turn round wholly to face him, but I sensed him watching me with a kind of bright interest. "You're kidding me."

"Unfortunately not." I sat back down. "Unfortunately McCade's letter arrived a couple of days too late, and I wasn't sure my department would let me take up the project. God knows it's probably not in the best taste, but..."

"But Jason—Professor Ross—had been gunning for it for years, and you weren't going to risk a refusal."

"Yeah." I was distantly touched that he hadn't lapsed back into *Ross*, after my outburst the other day. "So I'm kind of out there on my own recognisance. Jason was so keen."

"Do you know what he was after?"

"Not specifically. Which is odd, because he talked the hind legs off me about all his other stuff. He thought there was something that united all the stone circles, a function, like…a grand theory of everything for them." I was way too drunk to explain this. "Do you know what I mean?"

"Not even slightly. Do you?"

I snorted. I hated that he could pull a laugh out of me. I was meant to be grieving. "Actually, no." I hated that he made me tell the truth. "I thought I'd just find something straight away, something important enough to justify to the university what I've been doing."

"Okay." He ran one finger round the edge of his plate, sucked butter off it in a gesture I would have found distracting at any other moment. That bloody lovely mouth. Curling up now in a smile of irrepressible amusement at my extracurricular activities. "Interesting, Logan."

"Yeah, I know. The thing is—I'm not ready to pack it in yet. I want to carry on, at least until I've established there's nothing significant there. And to do that, I need you."

"Even after today?"

"Even after today. Come on. I fuck up all the time."

"Not with plastic explosives, you don't. So you don't want me running off to commit career suicide with McCade, because…"

"I need your help." *God*, I thought. *In vino veritas*. I struggled to articulate a less brutally honest reason. "And…I'm just a bit opposed to suicide in general at the moment. Why should you lose everything, just because…" I paused and thought about it. "Jesus. Is that what it would boil down to? What the hell happened in Iraq?"

He groaned. "Oh, man. I wish I'd never let that slip." To my surprise, he snaked an arm over the table and picked up my first mug, the one with the vodka in it. "Mind if I…"

"Be my guest."

"Ta." He drank, then continued, a little roughly, "No, it wouldn't amount to that. The army's been bloody good to me, which is one reason why I don't want to argue the rights and wrongs of it with you. Two little accidents with unexploded bombs, they'd still look after me, but it'd be a desk job at Fellworth, probably. Making McCade's tea and welcoming visitors. I'd rather…"

"You'd rather get blown up by the third one."

"Absolutely. I need to get sorted out over here, and then I need to do another tour. It's the only way I can prove myself."

"What—by going back?" My head was clearing. That was no good. I finished my tea and sloshed a good measure of vodka into the still-warm mug, reaching over the table to top Rayne off too before he could protest. "God, Rayne. Every week on the news I see them unloading the coffins from the planes. They're kids. I don't think we should even be out there."

"Well, *we* aren't. I didn't spot you in the hangar at Baghdad last time I landed."

"What—I'm not a soldier, so I can't have an opinion?"

"Have one by all means. I'd just be happier if you kept it to yourself—you and every other woolly liberal, politician and unmarried marriage-guidance counsellor out there."

I raised my eyebrows, not quite sure what I'd just been called. Truth to tell, I hadn't been thinking much about the politics. Even my knee-jerk hostility to military solution seemed to be in abeyance. I just couldn't bear to think of one of those flag-draped steel coffins ever being his. "Okay. Okay, sorry. You've got to do your third tour, and to be honest, I'd rather step on a fucking land mine than give up on Jason's last wish. I don't want to stop, either. I don't think I can."

He held the mug between his hands, watching me over the rim. "His last wish?"

I blinked. I wasn't aware that I'd formulated it as such in my own head, but there it was. "Yes. I don't understand it yet, but I'm sure of it."

"Why? Was it in a note he left you?"

"No. But he fought so hard for access to that land, and..." I stopped. *A note.* Rayne had said it as if he expected there to have been one. And, if I thought about it—wasn't it common practice for a suicide to leave one behind? It had never occurred to me. Just as, until now, it had never occurred to me to think of Jason as a suicide. The label, the process of using it, tore him and his memory another step further away from me, and I inhaled roughly. "He didn't... He didn't leave me a note. I don't know why he did it."

A silence fell. It was a deep, cold one, and I realised that I was missing the central heating's barely audible whisper. I hadn't switched it on. I sat staring at the tabletop. Then, after a moment, I heard Rayne shift. "Look," he said awkwardly. "Do you want to have a look at these bloody bills while I'm here? I know you don't care. It would just be a step."

Towards what, I couldn't imagine. But it was better than the newborn desolation, the gap in the world where Jason's letter to me should have been. The letter that said *why*. Blindly I reached out and pulled over the stack of envelopes. I tore them open, one by one, and spread their contents flat on the table in front of me. "Okay," I said, at length. "They're nothing. They're routine."

"Two of them are red." Rayne leaned forward on his elbows, but I wouldn't meet his eyes. "Can you pay them?"

"Of course. There's plenty in the account."

"A joint account?"

"No. His. I…"

"Then you'll need access to it. Didn't his will give you instructions on how to—"

"Rayne. Shut up." I grabbed the mug full of vodka, clutching it hard. I needed him to be quiet. His questions were like stones dropping into a bucket of water already full to the brim—I was spilling coldly over, mouth filling with words I didn't want to say but suddenly couldn't contain. "I haven't looked at his will, all right?" I got up. Maybe if I paced the length of the kitchen, pressing the soles of my bare feet to the cool wooden floor, I would regain my poise, or at least the gift of evasive silence that had got me this far. I set off, slowly, cradling the mug. "I haven't done anything. I haven't arranged for his funeral."

"What? Where is he?"

In a metal drawer. I got to the far end of the kitchen, the beautiful high-tech Aga, and jolted to a halt, slamming the mug down, clutching at the bar of the stove. "He's in the… He's still in the fucking morgue."

"Oh, Jesus, Logan."

I rounded on him. The rage I wanted to feel would have come easier if there had been a shadow of reproof in Rayne's grey eyes, but he just looked shocked. I tried for it anyway. "It's none of your damn business. You don't even know me. I—"

"Were you lovers?"

Brief laughter scraped out of me. "Christ… What about it? Are you homophobic? Or just opposed to human relationships in general?"

"I'm opposed to anything that screws someone over this bad. Are you just gonna *leave* him there?"

I ran both hands into my hair. I could no longer fight the overpowering urge to curl up. I let my knees give, and my spine slid bruisingly down the front of the cold Aga, handles, knobs and all. I sat down hard on the tiles and closed my eyes.

I sensed Rayne close to me. An instant later, closer than I thought, one hand closing on my hip. I sucked in a breath—but the gesture was only businesslike, a frisking. Rayne said, "Okay, there it is," and pulled out my mobile from my trouser pocket. "Now… What else are you gonna need?"

The phone book, the address book from the hall, and the pile of unopened sympathy cards. I told him so. Still collapsed by the stove, I watched while he set these things down in front of me. "I can't."

"I'm sorry. You have to. Never mind the bills for now." He crouched down on the parquet, putting the phone book into my hands. "This is the one thing you have to do. Start with a funeral home. Stellon's is good—we…we recommend it to the families. While you do that, I'm gonna open these cards, okay? From those and your address book, you'll know who to invite."

I swallowed. "But how do I…"

"You phone them. One by one, while you're still sober enough to talk. And after that, you can finish drinking yourself into a coma." He tore open the first card and read it, his brow furrowing. "Because you'll fucking well need it by then."

***

I lay on my back, looking up at the dark-beamed old ceiling. A full moon had risen over the rooftops, her light mixing weirdly with the street lamps. I had hoped for the coma. I had got it for a while, but then it had dissolved into ordinary sleep and dreams of the kind I now had all the time and could not begin to deal with, dreams where Jason and my dad were one person, benign and loving but an absolute and total headfuck. I had surfaced, sweating coldly.

Alcohol seldom let me rest. My limbs felt full of aching bones and maggots. I had a headache you wouldn't wish on a dog, and my stomach was roiling. This was why I hadn't missed partying when I'd moved into Jason's more temperate, civilised world.

Still, it had got the job done. Watching the eerie mix of light, I tried to piece the last part of the night together. I'd made my calls. I only remembered the first few. After that, the various tones of surprise and awkward sympathy coming back down the line at me had all merged into one. I remembered that I'd started shaking, finely but unstoppably. Rayne had refilled both our mugs with vodka and handed mine down to me.

After that there was a blur. I didn't think he'd helped me upstairs. Maybe followed me, a safety net in case my grip on the banister slipped. Maybe he had stood in the doorway, watching dispassionately while I stripped and fell into bed. I did seem to remember that. I hadn't cared at the time, and now I wasn't sure how it made me feel.

It hardly mattered. Probably he had gone home. I lay listening to the house. It was whispering again—he must have put the heating on, or maybe I'd done it myself. But there was some other quality to the quiet, something that told me the place wasn't empty. For a moment I thought I was irritated. What the hell did he want—breakfast?

But then I got stiffly out of bed. I made my way to the window. There was a relief I couldn't describe, in seeing the space outside the house still occupied by his Audi. I leaned on the window frame, feeling my heartbeat shake me. I didn't want to be alone.

I wasn't being a good host. If he'd decided to stay over, I hoped he'd found somewhere comfortable to sleep. We had a spare room, but over the years its token bed had disappeared under an avalanche of my books and clothes. I was profoundly, inherently untidy, and Jase had always kindly ignored the chaos I created there, as if he knew I needed a safety valve for keeping order in the rest of the house.

That left the sofa, or face-down on the kitchen table. I'd tried both recently, and neither was very restful. It was good of Rayne, I decided, to have come here tonight, and to have stuck around. I'd hated him for making me do it, but something in me felt marginally less dreadful for having made those phone calls. Pushing away from the window frame, I grabbed my crumpled dressing gown off the bed and went to see if he was okay.

I moved quietly on instinct. You didn't run around in a mausoleum, did you? And the house had a deep-night, underwater feel to it. If ghosts were going to walk, now was the time. It struck me, with hollow amusement, that maybe I was the ghost. I felt more like a haunting, like someone's fading memory, than flesh and blood. My bare feet fell silent on the thick carpets. And I heard—briefly, barely more than the scrape of a moth's wing— the unique sound of someone turning over a page.

It came from Jason's study. I stopped dead, breath catching in my throat. Soft lamplight was falling onto the landing through the half-open door. I hadn't registered it. It was such a normal sight to me, on a small-hours trip to the bathroom. Often—more so over recent months—Jase had found it hard to sleep, and on those nights I was used to his caress of my hair, the retreating sound of his footsteps and the faint click of the study door.

The room was peculiarly his. I'd always treated it as sacrosanct. For myself, I could work anywhere, sprawled on sofas or the rug in front of the fire. He needed formal space, though, and I'd always liked the nights when he retreated to his study, finding them oddly reassuring. It was nice to be living with such a man, to be near to the forge where yet another brilliant creation was being hammered out.

And I'd liked it, hadn't I, when my dad had gone into the box room he laughingly called his study in our tiny village house, because that meant that for once he felt well enough to work. A sob shook me. I clamped a hand to my mouth. *What the fuck?* For a man with no memories, that one had come back crystal bloody clear, hadn't it? And—oh, God, why was my brain trying to overlap my every thought of Jase across dreams and visions of the father I'd lost when I was six? I'd never grieved for him. I'd never given him another thought. *You don't take it in at that age*, my mam had said to a neighbour, sitting in a shaded room on the morning of the funeral. And she'd been right—apparently I'd had to wait until I was twenty-eight and standing in a hallway watching light from a room which contained the ghost of my lover, unable to hear any voice in my head but my own, saying, over and over again, *I miss my dad. Oh, I miss my dad.*

I was still pissed. That was the beginning and the end of it. I'd slept, but there was still plenty of active booze in my system, enough to account for this latest bout of insanity. And as for ghosts—well, I'd seen too many strange things at twilight on archaeological sites to say I didn't believe in them, but there sure as fuck wasn't one in Jason's study now.

Which only left Rayne.

I shoved the study door wide. He was standing behind Jason's desk, turning over the pages of a file. His jump, when he saw me, was the hard-trained one of a soldier, and his right hand blurred across his body for a weapon I was glad he didn't have. His pale skin turned to ivory in the desk-lamp's light, and I knew a brief pleasure in having scared the crap out him.

"You bastard," I rasped, striding over to the desk. I grabbed the file and snapped it shut. I didn't care what it was—I just wanted his hands off it. Wanted to wipe the trace of his vision off its pages, reach into his handsome bloody skull and tear out whatever he'd read. "What the *fuck* are you doing in here?"

I watched him preparing his lie. After that instant of fright, his face had resumed its haughty, seraphic blank. He was looking at me as if I were the intruder. As if he'd been rudely interrupted. My blood came to a half-enjoyable boil. *The arrogant bastard.* Then he frowned and looked human again. "Logan, why are you crying?"

I wasn't. He'd got *crying* mixed up somehow with white-hot rage. With my being about to kill him. But when I raised a hand to check, it came down from my face soaked. My breath was being hacked up into irrepressible sobs. *I miss Jase. I miss my dad.*

And that, finally, tripped me over the edge, fury at myself mixing into the cauldron. I lurched over to him. I seized him by the arm and the back of his T-shirt and dragged him out from behind the desk. "Get the fuck out of here."

"Logan. Wait." After one unresisting moment—surprise, I thought, at being manhandled—he was stiffening under my grasp. I could feel the muscles bunching in his shoulder, in the arm I held. It was like holding an angry rock. "I'm sorry about this, okay? I'm sorry. But I need to talk to you."

"To *talk*?" I could barely get the words out. Suddenly I was seeing everything he'd done since he arrived in a hellish new light. "About what? You conning your way in here, making sure you saw his bills, his private—"

"Oh, God, no." He sounded genuinely repulsed. "Listen to me…"

"No. Get out." I tried to shift him, but now he was set like concrete. "I said—"

Abruptly he tore out of my grip. That was fine by me. That would start the fight I'd been dying to have with somebody for days. We faced off, both breathing hard. He said warningly, "We've done this dance before, sunbeam. Don't try it on with me."

I remembered. That time, though, I'd been caught short, unready to follow up the wild punch I'd thrown. I didn't have military combat skills, but I hadn't spent my life in a damn library, either. I climbed mountains. I white-water rafted. In build and weight, we were roughly matched. And—best of all—I hated him, with an incandescent purity I hadn't thought I could feel. I repeated, brokenly, "You bastard," and threw myself at him.

I didn't do bad. I caught him off-balance—or maybe his heart wasn't in it—and we fell through the study door onto the landing. He went down hard. I heard the breath knocked out of him by the impact. This time I was ready for his block and snaked a hand past it, landing one cracking blow to his jaw.

"Ow! You little shit!" He jerked out from under me so fast that I lost my balance and slammed down flat, burning the skin off one arm on the carpet. Before I could regroup, he was scrambling up onto his knees. I knew that if he got me straddled and pinned, the game was over, so I jackknifed up as hard as I could, driving all my weight and rage up and forward...

Forgetting the flight of six stairs that led down to the next landing. I knocked him past his centre of gravity and felt his automatic grab for me. But I wasn't anchored, either. I was in mid-pounce—blind, blank, crazy. I went straight over the top of him, and we crashed in a flail of arms and legs down the short flight. I landed on my back at the bottom, whacking my skull on the skirting board. Through blood-haze I saw Rayne twist in midair like a cat to avoid using me as a crash-mat, and almost succeed. I cried out as he thudded down into my arms.

"You stupid fuck!" he yelled, nose an inch from mine. I could have fallen into his eyes. I would have liked to—to fall, and burn to nonexistence in those cold fires. "I might have broken your stupid fucking neck. Jesus, Logan!"

"Shut up." I was winded. It came out inaudible. I tried again, locking my hands onto his shoulders. "Shut up. You treacherous shit, Rayne. Get out of my house."

"With pleasure. Can't get away from you fast enough, you nutcase. Let me go."

I did. At least—at least I let go of one of his shoulders. Then, inexplicably, what I did with my free hand was cup the back of his head—seize him, careful and fierce—and pull his mouth down to mine.

I felt his lips part. I could taste his shock. Blood, too, from where I'd walloped him. His ribs were heaving. He was warm and alive. I couldn't think of anything else, and when he tore up from me, I cried out as if we'd been grafted together and he'd had to rip skin. He stared down at me, pupils dilated all the way, only a flicker of wolf-silver iris at their rims. Briefly I wondered if he was going to hit me. Then he made a faint sound—something between a gasp and a moan—and plunged back down to my mouth.

I wasn't sure which of us was fighting harder. After a moment I didn't even know what we were fighting *for*—to get away from one another or to close the gap. His knee drove hard between my thighs. I was naked under the dressing gown and his jeans burned my skin. My cock surged up rigid at the pain, shaming me until his next struggling thrust rammed us together tight enough for me to feel that he'd got hard too. Our mouths ground together, a bruising kiss that felt more like a battle to steal the last breath from one another's lungs. I surged to be up, to be on top, and he grunted and let me, thumping down onto his back on the beautiful Persian runner. There was barely room for us to measure our length—his skull was over the edge of the next flight's top step. His palms flattened on my chest and he shoved me back. "Don't," he snarled, the cords in his neck standing taut. "Don't, you bastard. I'm not even—"

"What?" I knelt over him. I ran one hand hard over the swell of his shaft, feeling it lengthen and leap. "Gay? Queer?" Getting balance, I tore open the front of his jeans. Underneath he wore black cotton briefs, damping already with pre-come.

He gave me a look that should have dropped me in my tracks, then perversely lifted his hips for me, making me gasp. His hands were still propped against my chest. I hauled jeans and briefs down his thighs, exposing his cock, so long and thick and yearning that my throat seized.

"Christ," I whispered. "You've got to be fucking kidding me, soldier boy."

He moaned explosively, the tight-locked resistance of his arm muscles melting, and I rammed my hips forward, bringing us into touch. I felt his length against mine, rigid and scalding against the chill of my belly.

"God," he ground out suddenly. "All right. Move."

I did. I braced my grip on the top step on either side of his head, and I began to drive against him with a force I had never unleashed on any lover in my life before. The bastard could take it. He was tough as fucking whipcord, crying out on each impact but bucking up to find the next, and his gaze never left mine. His hands clamped on my arse. "Harder," he commanded, his voice cracking over the word. "God! Harder!"

I tipped my head back, groaning. Starting to come. We'd wound up just beneath the mediaeval St Cecilia. I couldn't see her angel now, not in the weird mix of moon and lamplight. I saw Rayne instead. He looked like something chucked out of heaven, survivor of a drop through infinity and shattering impact with earth. A climactic ecstasy was gathering on his face. His shaft was throbbing so hard against mine that I couldn't tell the two sensations apart, and I let go, yelling, pounding down onto him with all my strength.

***

I crawled away from him. The second the maelstrom of hormones and endorphins reached its peak and died back in my blood, the second I'd spent myself against his belly, feeling at the same instant the answering rush of his coming, I couldn't bear to be near him. I could hardly stand to be in my own skin. Subsiding into a breathless heap against the wall, I watched him. He didn't look any happier than I felt. He flipped lithely onto his front, then surged upright, dragging up his jeans. I noticed, with a detached pity, that he was shaking.

He ran his hands over his hair. "Logan," he said unsteadily. "What the fuck was that?"

"I don't know." My voice sounded like rust and cobwebs. "Nothing. It's over. Will you... Please just go now."

He turned away and set off down the stairs. As I'd asked him to do, and what the hell had I expected? I heard myself ask, low and urgent, as if I could throw the words out like a line and stop him, "Did you find what you were looking for? In Jason's study?"

He halted at the foot of the stairs. His fine-boned hand, whose print I could still feel on my backside, clenched tight around the newel post, but he didn't look back at me. "Do want me to tell you?"

I thought about it. But the curiosity died between one breath and the next, a cold, dead passivity taking hold. I couldn't imagine Rayne telling me anything I could possibly give a damn about. "No," I said. "Just go."

I closed my eyes. A moment later the door clicked, and I was alone—just my own cooling flesh, in the house where I had betrayed my beloved Jason. It was Saturday, near dawn. If I'd hung on another twelve hours, I could have comforted myself with the thought that I'd held his memory sacred a whole week.

Chapter Seven

The next time the demon's knock resounded, I went down numbly. I didn't really care who was out there now. I opened up and stood blinking in the sunlight, slowly distinguishing the face of Dean Anderson. That was all right. I could cope with him. Then I noticed a stranger beside him, a neat, small man in a fashionable beard and severe-looking casuals. His face was rather carefully blank. "Oh," I said, and fastened my dressing gown.

"Daniel. Hello, son." The dean put out a hand, which I took on reflex, though we met each other five times a week and I didn't really know what was going on. He clasped it warmly. "It was good of you to do all that. Very brave. But I'd have helped you, you know."

I swallowed and managed a smile. "Yes. I...I know." Then my talent for theatre failed me, and I added in bewilderment, "All what?"

His face creased in sympathy. "Poor Dan. We've just woken you up, haven't we? Arranging the funeral. You phoned me about it last night."

Of course I had. I remembered, but only because as an "A" he'd got done early, second to Dr. Abrams, Jason's friend and long-term chess partner from the medical school. I'd reeled him off the same short speech as I had for everyone else.

"And I thought," he was continuing, "that if you were ready for that, we should really get Jason's will sorted out for you. You must be needing a bit of help by now, with the house and everything. So I asked Jason's solicitor if he would come round here with me today. We thought it would be easier for you than dragging you into his office." He gestured to his companion. "Daniel, this is Geoffrey Taylor, from Taylor Long Associates. Geoff—Dr. Daniel Logan."

I shook his hand. So this was what solicitors looked like on Sunday. I could see the corresponding wonder in his eyes at the off-duty appearance of university doctors, and I almost laughed. "All right. Yes. I'm sorry. Come in, please."

In the hallway, the dean murmured something to Taylor, who nodded and continued towards the kitchen. He turned to me, his face gentle. I supposed that, unshaven and bloodshot, I finally looked like his preconception of a grieving man. He seemed to find it reassuring. "Ah, Dan," he said. "I'm so sorry. But it's better this way. You have to mourn for him. You were scaring me before." He hesitated. "Having said that…you might want to go and just get dressed. Don't hurry. I'll make some coffee for Geoff."

***

I came back slowly down the stairs, setting my feet carefully. I knew that if I glanced off to my left at the turn, I would see a patch on the carpet where the pile was rucked up the wrong way, and one faint but utterly distinctive stain. I couldn't afford to look.

I'd crawled back up to bed after Rayne had left me bruised and aching but so wrung out that I had been asleep before I hit the mattress, and so spared the necessity of thought. Since the dean's knock had dragged me up out of the pit, however, the sheer bloody enormity of what I had done had been sailing in like well-aimed rocks, making me wince with each memory. What in the name of hell had happened to me? I'd found Rayne going through Jason's papers. I'd have been within my rights to call the police. And instead I'd...

"Daniel? You okay up there?"

I'd taken too long over finding some clothes. Yesterday's were still in the shower, steeping in their mud, and I couldn't bear to touch anything I'd worn the night before. And there were wardrobes I had to go into with fingertip delicacy, eyes half shut, because although I'd now violated most of what Jase had left behind, his clothes were still too intimate, too immediate to touch. I negotiated the landing and jogged down the rest of the stairs, tucking whichever shirt I'd finally grabbed into my jeans. "Yes. Sorry. I'm here."

The dean was standing in the kitchen doorway. My blood chilled. You'd have to know the stain on the carpet was there in order to notice it, but no one could miss the bomb site I'd made of the kitchen. Piled-up plates and glasses. All those kindly sent cards, the dean's included, ripped open and dumped with no trace of appreciation or respect on the floor, a drift of bills across the table...

Suddenly I remembered what I'd said to Rayne about those. That had been pretty rotten. Whatever he'd been doing, I was fairly sure it had been nothing little or mean. That he hadn't wormed his way in here to steal Jason's identity. I wished I hadn't said it. I would never see him again, so it scarcely mattered. But I wished that, and also, fervently, that I could forget the feel of his

155

cock, rising hot against mine. Bracing myself, preparing a smile and an apology for my guests, I joined the dean in the hall.

But the kitchen was fine. The glasses and crockery had been washed, dried and neatly arranged on the worktop. All signs of my binge-drink approach to admin had been cleared away—the mugs and vodka bottle, the scattered paperwork. A familiar hum from the utility room told me that the washing machine was turning itself over on a holding cycle. And, now I came to think about it, my dirty clothes hadn't been lying round in the bottom of the shower, had they? That, and the rest of the bathroom, had been tidy.

"Daniel?"

I swung round. The dean and the solicitor were sitting at the kitchen table, watching me curiously. I tore myself out of abstracted wonder, at a man who would spend time bringing comfort and order to the grim mess of my life, then coolly settle down to read my dead lover's private papers. "Sorry," I said. "Yes. What do you need me to do?"

"Nothing. That is… We're here to help you. Sit down." The dean indicated the chair beside him. "Because Geoff is a lawyer, and I'm Jason's named executor, this can constitute a formal reading of the will. We'll get it all over with, and then you'll know where you stand. I know it hasn't been your priority, but Jason would have hated for you to be struggling, when… Anyway. Geoff, will you go ahead?"

"Wait," I said. "I don't understand." Taylor, who had been taking out a file from his briefcase, looked at me patiently. "Jason and I helped each other out with everything. Why wouldn't he appoint me as executor?" I was suddenly, ridiculously hurt. I knew it was only a whole mess of large griefs finding focus in a small one, but it didn't seem to make any difference. Had he thought that I would screw it up—that I couldn't act for him? *Well, you've made a lovely job of it so far*, my own mocking voice said to me, but I thrust it aside. "I could have...I could have done this."

Taylor nodded at me. He looked pleased to have a legal question to deal with, although really it hadn't been one at all. "Yes. Technically speaking, you could. Though it's a common misconception that you can't appoint executors who are also your main—"

"Geoffrey, please." The dean reached over to lay a hand on Taylor's arm. "This is going to come as enough of a shock as it is. Just open the will."

I looked from one to the other of them. The dean was wrong, of course. Nothing could come as a shock to me now. I wondered if he thought I'd mind, if Jason had decided to leave everything he possessed to a cat-and-dog shelter, or some illegitimate child conceived somewhere back down the line. I thought of being thus stripped of everything but my own earnings, thrown back naked into the world, and I felt a wild, almost dangerous sense of freedom. If Jason was gone, all the weights of society—home ownership, academic progress, all the things I'd loved because they were part of him—should be cut away from me too.

The surface of the table had blurred out. I was seeing bleak wide landscapes through the woodwork. Taylor had started reading. I forced myself to attend. And, after all, it was very simple. *All my assets, including my property and funds in the following accounts, being the sum of...* I lost track at that point. Numbers had never been my thing. After a moment, during which the dean and the solicitor were clearly watching me for a reaction, Taylor laid the document down on the table and turned it towards me so that I could see for myself.

It didn't make much difference to me, in terms of comprehending the figure. There were a hell of a lot of zeroes. I swallowed convulsively. Then I shoved away from the table, almost upsetting my chair. I scrambled onto my feet and backed away. "No. No, I don't want it."

"Daniel." The dean sounded weirdly relieved. To my bewilderment, he leaned forward and glanced at the paper as if checking its contents for himself. "This is good. This is all as it should be. Just calm down for a second."

"No. Christ! Did you know about this?"

"Yes. Jason altered his will in your favour a long time ago."

I threw out a hand to steady myself on the edge of a cabinet. "But I…I can give it away, can't I, if it's mine? This bloody lawyer can be my witness. I hereby bequeath it to the university. There, Dean—build a new department, or a lab, or—"

"*Daniel.*" I could hear laughter in the dean's voice and didn't blame him, though I still didn't understand the shiver of elation, as if something he'd been scared of had just gone away. "Take a breath. You can't do anything with Jason's estate until this will goes to probate, apart from a sum which he's set aside to defray your immediate expenses. So—thank you for the lab, but cool your jets for the moment. Sit down, and let's just get through to the end of this, shall we?"

Taylor was gathering papers together, fishing some other ones out of his case. "Quite right too," he said, with a prim emphasis that made me want to slap him. I supposed that grieving gay lovers were out of his field, especially ones who didn't want their inheritance. "We're not finished here."

"Oh, there's more? Great." I sank back down and ran distracted fingers into my hair.

"What more can there be, Geoffrey?"

If I still had curiosity left in me, I'd have looked up to see the dean's face. His voice had altered completely. It was taut and strained. But I felt like a shuttlecock between two big professional badminton racquets, and I didn't really care.

"I have a further document to give Dr. Logan," the bloody lawyer announced with dignity. "Professor Ross placed it with his will package."

"The professor didn't mention any additional…"

"No, Malcolm," the lawyer said, leaning the faintest emphasis on the first name, as if he didn't particularly like being *Geoffrey*'d even by a dean, and this was a tiny revenge for him. "The professor gave me specific instructions not to discuss it with anyone, and to put it personally into Dr. Logan's hands. Dean Anderson, please witness that I am doing so now."

An envelope. It was plain, businesslike, thin. It looked like nothing much, and I put out my hands—both of them, formally, as if to play along with Taylor's little ritual—calmly enough. Automatically I began to open it.

Then my heart turned over. What had Rayne said, last night, between the vodka and the funeral arrangements and the wild sex on the landing? We'd been talking about the excavation, and Jason's last wish. *Was it in a note he left you?* And telling him no— that I'd had to make his last wish up for myself, together with every other comfortless scrap of self-comfort, because he hadn't left me a damn thing. Nothing I could use, anyhow. Not until now.

This was my letter. I jammed the seal back down. My hand convulsed around the envelope, crushing it, but I found that I couldn't let go. I lifted my hand, pressing the back of it to my mouth. I heard the dean say, from a crackling distance, "What is it? Don't you want to know what it is?"

You want to know. The conviction of that swept through me. That was why he'd brought this Sunday lawyer here the second he'd thought I would consent to look at the will. Why the hell should this letter matter to him? It was nothing to him. Everything to me.

"He wants to open that on his own, Malcolm."

"Well, I don't think he should be left on his own. He's clearly distraught."

"We should go. He'll be all right."

I tried to lift my head. I was fine. But when I drew a breath to say so, a terrible hard cramp seized my lungs, making my rib cage buck. My hand was still clamped to my mouth—blocking what, I now didn't know, and didn't dare move it to find out. A wail? A sob, or a cry of rage and relief, that even if Jason had left me, here at last was his word, my reason why?

They were leaving. I saw peripherally that Taylor closed his briefcase and unhooked his jacket from the back of his chair. Then I saw the dean come quietly round the table. He drew out the chair beside me and sat down. He was very close to me. To my absolute surprise, he leaned closer still and actually brushed a rough kiss to my temple. "Dan," he said. "Promise you'll call me any time, if you need me?"

I nodded mutely, speechless. Tears were starting to spill over my tight-clenched knuckles—real ones at last, not shocked out of me by rage, drink or bomb detonation. Already the relief of them was exquisite. But I needed desperately to be left alone.

"I knew Jason for most of his life. I'm going to tell you now—he did some things that made him unhappy later. That made him ashamed. They preyed on his mind. He might have said things, confessed to things, that aren't even true. Do you understand?"

I ducked my head again. I didn't. And if he didn't go now, I wasn't going to be able to hang on. As if sensing the end of my tether, he got up quickly, and I heard him shepherding Taylor down the hallway and out of the front door. It creaked, and I heard briefly sounds from outside—a murmur of traffic, and birdsong. Then the familiar clunk of the heavy old oak going into its frame, and the thud, like a coda, of the demon's brass ring against the wood. I was alone.

I took my hand down. A half-drowned, half-suffocated sob tore out of me. It was stupid. I'd held out for solitude, and now—perversely, stupidly—I didn't want to be alone. Unforgivably, what I wanted was Rayne. He was nothing to me. I barely knew him. I couldn't trust him. But something in me remembered and craved his touch, and the penetrating kindness of his gaze.

Shuddering, I ripped the envelope open. Christ, surely I would find in here my sanity, the foundation I needed to go on with some kind of rational life. I stared at my name on the envelope, in Jason's beautiful hand. Promptly a huge, scalding tear landed on it, blurring the ink. "Fuck!" I snarled at myself, dabbing it away with my sleeve. This was a good thing. Salvation. Jase had written to me.

There was one sheet in the envelope. I unfolded it carefully, no longer trying to fight the sobs tearing through me. He was gone. His message to me, whatever it was, would bring down the reality of that, allow my mind at last to accept it because there would be at last a reason. I should have known…

A map.

I sat, my elbows propped on the table, resting my brow on one hand. For a long time I was aware of—well, nothing, really. That a sob had died in my throat. That I had stopped crying as if unplugged at the mains and was staring at the single sheet through eyes that slowly became sore and arid. A fucking map. There was nothing in me that cared enough to investigate it further or to wonder about it, and I just sat there, feeling all the grief in me shrivel to dust.

And yet it was familiar to me. Very. I'd seen so many versions of it lately that I could have walked the place at night, land mines and all. McCade's detailed military OS. Images on a computer screen, magnetometry overlaying geophysical. Jason's own near-infrared aerial shots. This was barely a sketch. That same damned piece of land again—a mile northwest of the barricade, encompassing the Roman road and the Bronze Age huts, though neither of these were shown. Just an outline—the limit of the military land, and the enclosure of fields beyond it. A scale and compass cardinals. Nothing else.

The corners were yellowed with age. It looked less like an original than a poorly done photocopy or a blueprint. It was shadows and angles and nothing.

Nothing. No message. And no reasons, because there weren't any. Jason had become obsessed and died by his own hand, and that was all.

***

The next three days slipped by almost without pain for me because I was hardly there to feel it. I'd accepted that I had to dispose of my lover's body. After swallowing such an enormity, arranging his funeral hardly seemed like a big deal at all. The minister at the humanist chapel knew who I was and what I needed the moment I identified myself to him on the phone, and quietly took the matter out of my hands.

I took Rayne's suggestion about the funeral directors. They too were gentle ghosts, making impossibilities like choice of casket and transportation of the remains happen with scarcely any input from me. I wondered at their calm efficiency, until I reflected that dealing with the dead was as routine to them as marking an essay or delivering a lecture would have been for me. Anyway, they were kind. I recalled Rayne's advice—*try Stellon's, we recommend it to the families*—and I could imagine them quietly intervening after the loss of a son or a daughter, making one part of the unbearable at least pass by and be done,

Rayne cared about such things. Rayne, faceless instrument of war as I'd tried to make him, was concerned about the fallout of death, the collateral damage. Had been concerned about me, before I fucked everything up—brainlessly fucked *him*, then threw him out of the house like an unwanted cat. I doubted I'd see him again. Weirdly, that loss, the absence of something I'd never really had in the first place, was the one feeling that made it through the fog of my solitary hours.

I didn't think about the map anymore. It lay on the table where I'd left it. Such a sorry end to all Jase's work, all his belief. His convictions regarding the megaliths and circles had been the one academic field where anyone had dared question him. He'd been derided for New Age sympathies by a few of his hardliner scientist colleagues. But Jason Ross had not been a man you could easily dismiss. Backed by degrees in human biochemistry and physics as well as his own teaching subjects, he had produced such solid evidence for worldwide links between megalith-building cultures that even the hidebound Salisbury archaeological community had been beginning to see by his light.

All gone now. I moved carefully around the ashes, keeping the kitchen tidy as Rayne had left it. I answered the phone and spoke efficiently to the Stellon's staff and even to the dean when he called, sounding distant and odd, to ask how I was getting on. Otherwise I just sat curled on the sofa in the living room, wrapped in the blanket I'd never bothered to take back upstairs, waking up there on the morning of the funeral with a sense of utter disbelief.

The humanist chapel, though conscientiously free of all religious symbolism or trappings, was nevertheless housed within the precincts of St Magnus Martyr, one of Salisbury's loveliest Catholic churches. The stained glass—whether removed by a hurled Reformation brick or careful twentieth-century hands—was gone, and the light, on this hot first of July, fell with a silver purity onto Jason's gathered friends. No statues or crucifixes, of course, but the place wasn't bare—the minister, taking inspiration from the Damanhur temples in Italy, had commissioned each wall to be painted with representations of humanity interacting with the four elements. Exultant young farmers strode after the plough to the north. To the east, a wind turbine was going up, centuries of fossil-fuel cloud being blown away in the clean air. To see the other two, I would have had to look behind me, or to my right across the heads of the rest of the congregation, and I'd already caused enough whispered commentary by the coolness with which I was taking this whole affair. *He doesn't seem all that bothered.* That had been my friend Rachel Keats again. I wondered what I'd done to piss her off. Then her companion: *don't be so cruel. He's in shock, that's all.*

Neither of them was right. Looking back over my actions of the past ten days, I could see that all of them had been the flailing knee-jerks of a man half-drowned in shock, but that part of my reaction was definitely over. The denial phase was long gone too. I could not sit here in the front-row pew, six foot away from the plain wooden coffin on the cremation platform, and kid myself that Jase was coming home.

As for *all that bothered*—I was, I supposed, unforgivably calm. Not numb and self-protecting anymore. Just empty. I lifted my head at the sound of my name. The minister was asking me if I could come up and read Jason's favourite work by John Donne. I stood up. Yes, I could. I had with me Jason's own near-priceless seventeenth-century edition of the collected works—mine now, I supposed, although nothing could have felt less so, and I wondered if laying it on top of the coffin afterwards would be considered bad form.

I read well. Without much emphasis, but composedly. I knew parts of it by heart and during these I looked out across the chapel at Jason's friends, who had come here for him and deserved to be seen. I got through it all, even the last couplet, which had always before made my agnostic heart ring like a bell and stung tears to my eyes. *One short sleep past, we wake eternally. And Death shall be no more...*

The dean, up next with "Fern Hill", had a harder job of it. He got as far as *the birth of the simple light*, then stopped, voice breaking, hands clenching tight on the lectern. A kind of silent moan of empathy went through the congregation, and Mrs. Dean, holding my hand to comfort me, broke into tears of such noisy freshness that I felt at that moment that I loved her. I didn't really care about her husband or his struggles, watched him with an almost clinical interest while the minister went up to him and whispered an offer to take over. But the dean straightened up and finished bravely, his voice steady, tears rolling down his face.

A perfect ripple of Bach began from the choir. That was the Sarum string quartet, striking up the *Suite 1 for Cello*. I'd forgotten them—forgotten that they'd asked me, as Jason's friends and favourite performers, if they could attend and play. Of course I'd said yes. They'd asked me for a piece, and I hadn't been able to think of one, except this, which sounded regularly from Jason's study when he was feeling particularly inspired. It was hardly funereal. It sounded to me like a satisfied deity putting the finishing touches to a world in which all was and always would be well, but that seemed very Jason. It was lovely. I'd forgotten the quartet, and I'd forgotten that I'd agreed with the minister that this would be the signal for the cremation to begin.

I watched the coffin begin to roll. It seemed to take the unforgivable hell of a time, and I lifted my head instead and looked at the perfect Gothic arch that divided the nave from the chancel. Really, I thought, the humanists ought to have their own purpose-built place, and not house their services like hermit crabs inside a borrowed shell whose every line of architecture aspired up and up to a far-off Catholic god—who would, now I came to think about it, have condemned Jase to a suicide's burial, hushed up and hugger-mugger, well away from sacred ground. I looked again. I had missed it. The coffin was gone.

I got up. I think at that instant I might have achieved a moment of—well, not popularity, but acceptance at least, on this day, among Jason's friends. The young lover, about to throw a scene—faint, maybe, or burst into tears, or behave in some other way as expected. But all I wanted to do was walk quietly out into the air.

I was desperate for air. For sunlight too, as if I'd been buried alive. I pushed the chapel door wide and strode out into the brilliant July sun. St. Magnus was fronted by a beautiful green quad. I gazed out across its flat bright space, letting my mind go blank. My lungs were working overtime to get the oxygen and light inside. Briefly I was dizzy and came to a halt on the path. Then, when I thought I could walk a straight line, I set off again.

The dean caught up with me before I could reach the lychgate. He was panting, from emotion and his run. "Oh, Dan," he said, laying a hand on my arm. "Dear boy. I know. That was so hard."

Had it been? I looked at him, pushing my fringe out of my eyes, trying to see through the dazzle. I had expected it to be much, much worse. That morning, getting up and dressing, I hadn't been able to imagine myself living through it. And yet here I was. "Er, yeah," I heard myself say. "Look, I…I just need a walk. Will you…"

"Ah, Daniel. I do understand. But the worst's over now, and it would be better if you came back and—"

"No. I can't." I schooled the snap out of my tone. "Ten minutes, that's all. I've got the cars booked for three, to come round and pick everybody up for the Rose. I'll be back by then. If I'm not, will you just make sure they all get there?"

"For God's sake…"

"I know. I'm sorry." Running dry on excuses and explanations, I began to turn away—then froze. The dean had grabbed my coat sleeve. I couldn't imagine him ever having made such a gesture in his life before. I wondered if he'd ever been punched in the face. "Please let me go."

"Dan, I've got to ask you. Wasn't there anything at all in the letter he left you, to…to explain why he might have—"

"There was no letter. There was just a map."

The dean's face clouded. "A map?"

"Yes. Of that same bloody piece of Salisbury Plain he'd been trying to get access to for years. I didn't understand. I still don't." I waited for a few seconds. Then the same wave of tired indifference that had broken over me in the chapel stirred again, currents dragging. I'd had enough energy to answer the question, but not to care about the effects of it on this tearstained old man who now for some reason looked ready to faint. His mouth was hanging open. "Never mind," I said. "I'm sorry, Dean Anderson. I know what Jason was to me, and that's enough. I've got… I've just got to get out of here for a while."

I didn't get far. I was exhausted, and if I'd had any breakfast, I didn't remember it. I threaded my way through the traffic on Southhill Street, none too carefully. I wasn't sure that anything as empty and unreal as myself had the power to impact on a car bonnet. On the far side of the road there was a little square, with obedient civic trees growing neatly from their concrete circles, and a few benches. That would do. I chose one that would be out of sight of the party exiting the chapel, and I sank down. I didn't hide my face in my hands. I didn't want to be conspicuous, though I longed to blot out the light. Contrary today, wasn't I? Five minutes ago I'd been craving sunshine, and now all I wanted was a dark hole. I settled for leaning my elbows on my knees and staring at the pavement, as if someone had carved an intriguing message down there, between the cracks and the patches of chewing gum.

Almost immediately, the bench creaked, its slats shifting under me. *For Christ's sake*, I thought, almost saying it aloud. There were six benches set around the perimeter of the square, all of them empty when I had sat down. What possessed people to clump up like cooling bloody porridge, violating the space of others, especially those signalling as clearly as I was that I wanted to be left the fuck alone? I swore if the new arrival made a conversational gambit, I would tell him or her to piss off so far and fast they'd bounce off the walls of the square as they left.

But my companion remained silent. And it was odd, what you learned about a person without realising, wasn't it? If you'd asked me, I would have denied absolutely that I could have picked out Lieutenant Rayne's sweet, earthy, subliminal scent from every other human body in the city. He cast a kind of heat-shadow. I didn't possess a black jacket—the dean had turned up with one belonging to his son to loan me that morning. Through its fabric, I could feel my left shoulder and arm warming.

Not looking up, I said, very politely, "And just what the fuck are you doing here?"

"I knew the service was today. And, as I said to you the other day—a couple of times, I think—I need to talk to you."

I sat up. He had observed of me, sometime between our first meeting and an explosion, that I had some pretty big balls on me for an archaeologist. Well, his were no baby peas either, considering the terms on which we'd parted. Even for a soldier. I thought about telling him so, or the simplified version. *You've got a bloody nerve.* But he gestured across the road towards the church. From here I could see that the eight big black limos I'd ordered—since I was a wealthy man and had no need to skimp, and there was certainly nothing else I could possibly imagine to spend the money on—pulling up, causing mild chaos amongst the other traffic.

"Is that cavalcade for you?"

"Yes. I…didn't actually realise how big they'd be."

"I suppose you have to go. Are they all going back to your house?"

It's not mine. I looked at Rayne, distractedly taking him in. He was out of uniform again, and this time he'd left his jacket behind. His close-fitting black T-shirt left nothing to the imagination. He had one arm slung along the back of the bench. With the other hand he was lightly clasping the ankle he had crossed over his knee. He looked utterly serene. I wondered if I'd hallucinated knocking him flat on his back and fucking him on the landing carpet.

"No," I said. "Jason put some money aside for us all to go to the pub and have a bit of a party."

"Really?" Rayne gazed out across the road for a moment. Then he smiled. "He must have been quite something."

I thought about this. "Yes." Somehow, between his death, his inexplicable will and the grim necessities of his funeral, I had forgotten. "Yes, he was."

"End of the world, if you don't join them now?"

I shrugged. "Probably not. They all think I'm some inconsequential little jerk who was never good enough for Jason in the first place."

He turned on the bench and eyed me with amusement. "That's their undivided opinion?"

"Well," I amended, "maybe a couple of them do. The rest of them… They're good friends. I really should go."

"Or come with me and have lunch. I won't keep you long. You look like shit, Logan. You could use a break."

I drew a deep breath. I couldn't decide which one of us was the more bloody outrageous—Rayne, for suggesting the abandonment of my guests, or me, for giving it consideration. And I was. Somehow, in his T-shirt and jeans, sprawled casually on this ordinary city bench, he looked like sacred, God-given life. I didn't want to leave him.

"Okay," I said, at length. "Half an hour. Although why you think you'd be light relief, I can't imagine."

Chapter Eight

"Thanks for tidying up after me the other night."

It was a poor conversational opener. Rayne and I had way bigger fish to fry than that. But instead of laughing, he looked at me over the restaurant table, one eyebrow winging up as if in acknowledgement of the inadequacy, and its reasons. "Army habits," he said. "Do you know what you want yet?"

I glanced back down at the menu. I was more or less able to see it now the green flashes were clearing. Rayne had led me from the square and down a cobbled side street I hadn't known existed. We had left the glaring day, where the sun had begun to hit me on the back of the head like a brick, and gone down stone steps into a barrel-vaulted cellar, dim and cool. I'd followed him blindly to a table. I could see now that the long, low room opened onto the Avon at the back. A glimmering light from the river made scallop patterns on the old stone overhead. My head was spinning. "A pint. No, just a half. I can't stay."

"Eat, or you'll faint into the cucumber sandwiches. The shepherd's pie is good."

I considered this. It was almost as good as being out with Jason, being told what to eat and when. It was also so completely different that my tongue loosened up and I said, "Okay. I might as well. God knows, we screwed on his staircase before he'd been dead for a week. I might as well hang out with you on the day of his funeral."

Rayne sat back from the table. He folded his arms over his chest and let go a long, soft whistle. "Wow. You sound like anything but a doctor of archaeology right now."

"Well, I left my tweeds at home."

"Looks that way, doesn't it? And as for the screwing…" He paused, dark brows contracting ominously. "Up until the moment you knocked me down the stairs and landed on me cock-first, it never crossed my mind."

"Yeah. I think you were about to utter the immortal words *I'm not gay* just before you let me rip your pants off."

"Well, I'm not. I haven't been anything in particular so far." He rested his hands on the tabletop. "I'm not in denial. Not that it's any of your business, but I've had a few meaningless girlfriends—enough to keep the shithead jocks off my back at Fellworth—and I've had you."

I stared at him. One free speech had deserved another, I supposed. Then I heard what he'd said. "And—and me? Christ, that can't have been—"

"A first for me, yes. Thank you. It was beautiful."

I put a hand to my mouth in consternation. The waiter drifted up to the table. Rayne ordered shepherd's pie twice and two pints of Wessex, and sent him on his way. God. I remembered my first time. Clumsy and awkward, in a disused barn with my best mate from school, but so tearingly, unforgettably sweet that I had nearly died of it. I said hoarsely, hearing the dangerous rattle of laughter in my voice, "Shit. I'm so sorry."

"Don't be. You're right—I wanted it."

And that, even now, could send a deep, hot shiver through me. I pushed it carefully aside. Then, in merciful distraction, it struck me that he was right too. It *wasn't* any of my damn business who Rayne had slept with and when. He was about as far from garrulous as it was possible to imagine. "I don't understand. Why are you telling me this?"

"Because I owe you. That's why I wanted to talk to you. I lied to you, at your house the other night, and then I did something pretty despicable. So now I'm telling you the truth."

The truth. I thought that would be nice. When I looked back over the past ten days, I seemed to have been struggling to see through mist. "Okay," I said. "I appreciate the biography, but for me, you can start with your despicable thing. Which I hope was going through Jason's papers. What the hell were you looking for?"

"McCade asked me to have a look around. He doesn't understand any more than you do why Professor Ross was so anxious to excavate that land."

"McCade told you to search the house? For God's sake, what interest could the army possibly have in Jason's research? He was chasing motivations for Neolithic stone-circle construction, not splitting the bloody atom."

"I don't know."

The waiter arrived with our drinks, and Rayne took his blindly, staring straight at me. "I just had my orders. We were both trying to do what someone we respected asked of us. Weren't we?"

I snorted. "There's no comparison. Tell me—is that why you came over that night?"

"No. I came to see if you were okay. But when I was there, I…used my opportunity."

Jesus. I should have got up and walked away from him. There wasn't a flicker of remorse in his steady grey gaze. I realised that, in the same circumstances, he'd do the same again.

"You bastard," I said calmly, wishing the brutal quality of his honesty wasn't having the effect of making me believe the good in what he said, as well as the outrageous. I believed that he was an unscrupulous tool of the military—and also that his concern for me after the explosion had been genuine. "You were in my home as a guest. You don't follow orders that far."

He shrugged. It was a strong, sensual movement, one shoulder lifting powerfully under its fine cotton. "I do," he said simply. "I'll do what McCade tells me as long as I'm able to, as long as I'm an officer in the armed forces. There's no point otherwise."

"In being a soldier? Yeah, I can see that, but what the hell makes someone like you settle for that? For blind bloody obedience?"

"It isn't blind. Don't worry, I'm not gonna trot out the Nuremberg defence for you." He took a long pull on his pint, and I tried not to watch the movement of his fine-skinned throat. All of this would have been so much easier had I not been so ripplingly aware of his every shift, every action. "McCade's a good commander. His reasons for asking me to do what I did must have been good ones."

"But he didn't confide them to you?"

"No, of course not."

"Then it *was* blind obedience. God. How could you?"

"I'll tell you how, if you really want to know. If you can stop sitting there like the Last bloody Judgement and listen."

I felt my mouth open slightly. I wasn't, was I? Not that I didn't have the right. Slowly I realised that I was bolt upright in my chair, my spine so stiff it was aching. That I'd actually taken my knife in a white-knuckled grasp. I let it go and very carefully and deliberately lifted my pint. The one that ought to have been a half, as I now recalled, but that would have been a waste of time, given the inroads I now made into my full measure. I was painfully thirsty, though I hadn't known it until now. Hot. Thirsty, confused and bloody furious, if only I had the strength to sustain it. The chill of the beer scratched my trachea, and I swallowed hard, setting my glass down.

"Go on," I said roughly. "I'd love to hear."

"I don't know. Is there much point, trying to explain to someone like you what it means to find—a place, a brotherhood, when the rest of the world's doing its best to piss on you? I joined up when I was sixteen, and I'd done a cadet year before that. I was nothing. No qualifications, no family. And McCade, and other men like him, took me on anyway. Just as I was."

"What—*the army was my family*?" As soon as the words were out, I hated the cruel little rasp that had altered my voice as I said them. "You know, if we're down to shitty childhoods, I lost my dad to the Hartcliffe Dean bioweaponry tests when I was six. I didn't feel the need to replace him with some military uber-father who was gonna tell me what to do for the rest of my life."

"No," Rayne said calmly. "You replaced him with a lover twice your age, who's still telling you what to do now, a week and a half after he died."

I got up. I did so very quietly. I hadn't actually realised that I was going to move at all, and I wasn't offended. I just felt as if I'd been punched in the gut, and I needed to be away from the table to deal with the blow.

Behind me I heard Rayne say, "*Logan*," but it didn't seem to matter. My head was full of breaking dreams. They created a sensation like pressure change, of coming in to land on a sharp descent, my ears popping painfully. While Jason, who was never troubled, smiled at me affectionately and passed me airline mints.

I reached the door and pushed it open, palms sliding on sweat. The steps back up to the alley looked steep, but I began them, clutching at the iron handrail for support. Dreams of Ilfracombe beach, where I'd never been with Jase and didn't think I could remember being with my dad. But there we all were, only there weren't three of us. Just me, at indeterminate age, and a tall, smiling shadow, whose presence meant that I was safe. And those dreams were the benign ones. I did not think I could wake up beside the shadow in bed many more times and stay fucking sane. I reached the top step and lurched out into the light as if surfacing.

And now, bizarrely, my mind was full of "Fern Hill". I loved that poem. I couldn't think how I had more or less blotted it out during the service. I didn't wholly understand it, but its cadences and images rocked me, lit up the inside of my head with weird water-light. Jase and I had discovered early on that it was a favourite in common. I knew it well because my dad had been a massive Dylan Thomas fan. My mum had given me the copy he had kept by his bed, and I'd kept it by mine for a few years, then forgot where it came from and gave it away to charity when she had died too and I'd had to clear the house. *Nothing I cared*, I thought, walking slowly down the alley, away from the main street, *that time would take me / Up to the swallow thronged loft by the shadow of my hand...* It was cool and quiet here. *Oh as I was young and easy in the mercy of his means...* Mosses and lichens grew on the damp walls. God knew how much of a mess they made of the back of my borrowed jacket as I slid down to sit on the cobbles, but that couldn't be helped. *Time held me green and dying, though I sang in my chains like the sea.*

Soft footsteps. I knew Rayne's tread by now, as well as his scent. I sensed him come to a halt beside me, though I couldn't look up. He said, "Logan, why do I turn into such an arsehole when I'm with you?"

Probably because I'm unbearably bloody provoking. I couldn't tell him so. I was crying helplessly—and, mercifully, in silence—balled up at the foot of the alley wall.

"That was a dirty crack about your dad. I'm sorry."

I'm sorry I earned it with the crack about yours. I really wished I could get my head up, if only to tell him I wasn't damn well crying over that. But there was no chance. I was one stone in a landslide, going down. I felt him come to sit beside me, and I shuddered. There was nothing in this pounding hell of release that would let me endure being touched. But he didn't try. First he gave me his handkerchief, which I snatched blindly, burying my face in it. Then, when I'd destroyed that, he handed me some paper napkins from the restaurant. And after that he just sat in silence and waited.

"Come on back inside."

"Oh, you're kidding, aren't you? I look like I've been hit in the face with a pan."

"You're not too bad. Oh, except for… Yeah. That's got it." A pause, while he surveyed me, and I wondered how being the focus of that wry, grey-eyed attention could set a warmth in me I had thought lost forever. "You need hot food. I told them to hold the order until we got back. Come on."

So we went back indoors and ate shepherd's pie. Neither of us talked until we'd finished. The silence should have been awkward, and it was a little, but not as bad as it could have been. It seemed to me that we had each worked out our ability to detonate the other's temper with a few well chosen words, and so we shut up, long enough at least to let one another eat. I'd forgotten the simple benefit of that. It didn't heal grief, but it eased the plummeting sensations of grieving whilst at the same time feeling physically drained and incapable. Laying down my knife and fork, I watched Rayne carefully for a few seconds. He had his imperturbable soldier's mask back in place, but it wasn't hostile. Something in his dark eyes was receptive.

I broke the silence at last. "I meant to say out there. I'm sorry too."

"That's okay. Maybe we should stop chucking rocks at one another."

"I wasn't…" I paused. *Crying* seemed too pathetic, even though he'd sat and watched me do it. "I wasn't upset over that."

"I didn't think you were. I thought you were probably doing what you couldn't do in front of half Salisbury's academic community."

I was impressed. My throat was still raw, my sinuses aching. No way I could have let that lot loose with the dean and the minister looking pityingly on, and Mrs. Dean patting my head. And I did feel better now, if appallingly tired. My head was clearing. I could think about what had brought Rayne and me here.

"You know," I began cautiously, "I can't imagine what McCade thought you would find in Jason's things, but if you'd asked, I'd have let you look."

"On that night? Really?"

I thought back. I saw a possessive, super-sensitised monster wearing my skin, ready to rip out the throat of anyone trespassing on my lover's turf. "Well, maybe not then," I admitted. "But I think I would now."

"Because you've come to the same conclusion I have. That…"

"Yeah. That there's nothing there. That Jase just got caught up on something and began to obsess about it. I think it was driving him crazy. I don't know how the hell I didn't notice." Articulating this for someone else was painful. There was more to it than that too—my conviction, growing daily, rank and sharp as nettles, that in some way I must have been part of the problem myself. Not good enough. Too young, too unappreciative. But Rayne, when not snarling back at me, was a good audience, his gaze attentive but undemanding. Letting me get there in my own time. "I'm not sure if he was completely sane when he died. He left me an envelope in with his will. I thought it was a letter, but it was just a map of the same bloody place."

"Oh. Ouch."

I glanced up in time to see his brief flicker of empathy. No more than a wrinkle of his nose, a contraction of his brow, but it looked real, and it went inside me. "Yeah. Didn't help. I don't get it. It wasn't even… It looked more like the type of map your lot would produce than anything archaeological."

"Well, I'll have a look at it sometime. If you want."

"And if it meant anything to you, you'd tell McCade." I kept my tone neutral. It wasn't a challenge. I was just getting a feel of his boundaries.

"Yes. But I'd tell you too."

The silence that fell then was a strange one. Again, not awkward, but full of a prickling tension. Now we'd got this big stumbling block out of the way, I was remembering the other major feature of our night together in Jason's house. The moment when he'd stopped holding me back from him, his faint consenting moan…

I found myself tracing idle pentagrams within the circle of moisture my pint glass had left on the table. "Okay," I said. "Fair enough."

"You don't need worry about McCade. If he's concerned about any of this, it'll be for a good reason. He's a good man. He'd help us out, if we needed it."

I nodded. I privately thought that if McCade gave a stuff about me personally, he wouldn't have told Rayne to search my house, but I decided to keep that to myself. Clearly Rayne trusted him. With good reason, I thought, remembering one of our conversations prior to our cataclysmic parting. "He helped you out, after what happened in Iraq, didn't he?"

"Yes. Any other CO would have busted me straight down. Instead he told the enquiry panel I had combat stress and flew me home to Fellworth."

I frowned. "But I should think you did."

"What?"

"Have combat stress. I don't know what it's like out there, but..."

"It's no excuse." He shifted, clenching his hands together on the table. "Look, can we leave it? I'll go and pay for this, and then we'd better make a move."

"Oh. Yes. No, I'll get it. I...I can certainly afford it. I could buy the fucking restaurant."

He stood up, smiling. "No. My treat. You have to admit it's been a treat, Logan."

I shrugged in surrender. "It has that."

He must have left his credit card at the bar. I saw him head off towards the men's room and put down impossible, automatic thoughts of following him there. The usual guilt ripped through me, but it seemed to have fewer claws. Maybe I wasn't a treacherous bastard for having a high-pitched libido and a strong appreciation of male flesh. Maybe it was just who I was. And the only person that could have injured wasn't alive to be hurt by it anymore. I rested my chin on my hands, my mind in a whirl.

The waiter brought Rayne's card back on a little tray. He left it on the table in front of me. That kind of mistake was a bit of a first for me. Restaurant staff had always unerringly brought the bill to Jason, but Rayne and I were of similar age. Probably did make it hard to work out who was being the gentleman on this occasion. Idly I glanced down. I didn't mean to look at the card, but his name was there. His full name.

When he came back to the table, I was laughing. I couldn't help myself. It was proper, unforced laughter, such as I thought I'd never experience again. He sat down opposite me, eyebrows on the rise. I said unsteadily, "*Summer*? Your parents called you Summer Rayne? What... What kind of hippies were they?"

"The kind who left my brother and me in foster care, got into their Volksie bus and fucked off over the far horizon, never to be seen again. That kind."

"Oh. Shit." I clamped a hand to my mouth. His expression was calm, but with him that could mean anything, and I didn't want to have pissed him off again. *I was nothing. No qualifications, no family.* Christ, no wonder he'd turned into such a perfect army boy. I said, dead sober now, "I'm sorry."

"It's okay. But I'm telling you now, you ever call me that, and I'll rip off your bollocks and feed them to you. Nothing personal. Same rule for everyone."

"Er... Okay. Fair enough."

"And having said all that, I..." He leaned forward on his elbows, for once not meeting my eyes. "I don't feel like fighting with you anymore. I've thought about what happened the other night and... Well, sometimes I can't think about much else. I suppose you've got to be getting back to your guests, right?"

I went still in surprise. "I suppose so. Yes. I'm not sure."

"Okay. I'll give you a lift. Come on."

Out on the road in the sunlight, the sight of Rayne's Audi—a small, tough, practical shape, crouched low to the tarmac—triggered a series of shivery thoughts in my mind. I stopped by his side on the kerb, waking up, breaching surface, letting go. "I don't suppose you know anyone who wants to buy a car."

"Not off-hand. I'll ask around." He looked at me, and I felt for the first time that day as if I had done something right. "It'll be like pulling teeth, you know. But it'll help. It's a start."

***

The Audi's interior was boiling. Scents of hot leather and vinyl assailed me, and I helped Rayne wind down the windows and push up the rusted sunroof. I reached to turn the heater dial to blue as he started the engine, and he said to me, "We'll have to be going somewhere for that to do us any good."

I nodded. Anywhere other than the Rose & Crown would mean something pretty significant. I took out my mobile phone and flipped its lid up, holding it thoughtfully between my hands. Jason's speed-dial option appeared on the screen, hard to read in the sunlight. I shivered. So that was why I'd deliberately been leaving the damn thing at home.

The dean's number was there too. After almost a minute, I dialled it. It took him a while to answer, and when he did, the background was discreetly noisy, just the kind of sound you'd expect a bunch of senior academics to be making in a pub on a solemn occasion.

I told the dean that I was ill and had gone home. That I was terribly, terribly sorry. I asked him if he could look after everyone at the Rose in my place, and not to mind if they went over Jason's budget, just to send me the bill. The dean said that of course he could. His tone was almost perfect—concerned and reassuring. If he was irritated at me for flaking out on him, he was keeping it to himself. And yet I felt at the same time almost as if he were perfectly capable of peering down our satellite connection and seeing me in the passenger seat of a strange car, with a handsome soldier sitting beside me.

"You're a pretty crap liar," Rayne observed as I hung up. "You do still look rough, though. Want me to take you home and make the rest of it true?"

I thought about the house, which was mine now and may as well have been a tomb. I thought about its silences. It was Jason who always had wound up the ormolu clock in the living room. He did it lovingly, big hands delicate on its key. I could see him so clearly, in the red and gold behind my eyelids now. When it had stopped last Sunday, I had left it alone. "No," I said. "I don't know where."

"All right." Rayne put the car into gear. We slid out into the flow of traffic, and I tipped my head back, letting it happen. Down the western road, and then left, out towards the water meadows. He said, slowing up for the next roundabout, "That was nice of you. About the bill at the pub."

I shook my head. "Not really. Not my money." He glanced at me enquiringly, and I went on, bitterly, "Jason left me everything. House, car, whacking great bank balance about three digits longer than I've ever had in my life."

He absorbed this in silence. I wondered for a wild moment if he was going to take me back to his barracks. This road, narrow and full of sunlight, dancing on either side with cow parsley, would lead out to Fellworth eventually. Then he flipped his indicator and turned left onto a single track, narrower and brighter still. "That's...a good thing, isn't it?"

"No. No, it's bloody not." My hands were twisting in my lap, hard enough to hurt. Deliberately I undid them and breathed deep. Scents of hay and fresh-cut grass were blowing in through the open window. "What am I supposed to do with it?"

"Are you seriously asking me?"

I looked over at him. His attention was on the road ahead. I saw that he drove this car like a civilian, not a traumatised war vet. One hand on the wheel, the other resting loosely on the gear stick. I would have given a world for him to reach across and rest it on my thigh, the way Jase did sometimes. I'd have given a world to be touched. "Yeah," I said hoarsely. "I think I am."

"Okay. You need to think about what you want to do with the rest of your life, or the next few years of it, anyway. Take the money you need to finance that, and, if the rest of it bothers you, give it away."

I drew a breath to reply, to protest maybe, because it was outrageous, wasn't it, to throw away something bequeathed to me with such end-of-life passion. Then I shut up. It also made simple and perfect sense. I didn't have to drown with the weights that had been fastened to me. I could keep them or release them as I chose.

The car was slowing down. I saw on my left a track leading off into woodland. "Where are we?"

"About a mile outside Ashvale. Used to be a picnic area, woodland walks and that kind of thing, but some of the tracks got flooded out last year and they closed it. It's quiet."

It was. A green shade closed overhead as the Audi bumped down the track to the small car park, sweet and relieving after the sun. When I thought about Rayne's reasons for pointing out its quietness, my heart pounded. There were a couple of dilapidated picnic benches. Behind a screen of tangled elder and brambles, I could see the glitter of a stream.

He pulled up and switched the engine off. In the silence that followed, I became hyper-aware of him, and wondered if he too could sense the heat envelope that surrounded each of our bodies, merging in the narrow space that divided us. The car wasn't large, and now that we were motionless, there was nothing to distract from our proximity. His hands were on the wheel. His profile was still, but I thought he was breathing more quickly.

I said softly, "I didn't know this place was here. Or the restaurant, for that matter. Seems odd, to find out about them from someone who's come here from..." I paused, and he turned to see if I would get it right. I was quite good with accents. "From...Andover? Via Iraq."

He smiled. It was the smile with down-turned corners that meant he was trying not to look too interested or impressed, and it brought his generous, fine-cut mouth into such a perfect shape that my own lips prickled. "Not bad. St Mary Bourne, to be exact. Yeah, I've found a lot of odd corners around Salisbury. I like to get off the base when I can."

"Is it..." I hardly knew what I was asking. "Is it difficult there?"

"No. Not at all. I'm as used to that as you are to your library. It's home. But it's rowdy sometimes, and..." He paused, smile creasing to a deeper irony. "If you mean, would it be difficult there if I was gay—hell, yes. I've seen a couple of lads try that one. A dog's life doesn't even cover it."

"I thought the army was meant to be an equal-opps employer these days."

"In theory. In practice, that's so much propaganda. Maybe your CO will nod and smile understandingly. Then you find yourself locked overnight in a barrack with fifty crew-cut enlisted men, and... Well. Not for me. I might've looked over to your side of the fence, but believe me, it's not worth it."

I could imagine. I was also aware that the bit of greener grass I'd shown him the other night would hardly change his opinion, not with that much stacked against it. "Rayne," I said, surprising myself with the note of rough yearning in my voice. He lifted his head, turning to me. "If that was really your first time with another bloke—that bloody smackdown with carpet burns the other night—I'm sorry, okay? Really sorry."

"What? Why?"

"Because it should've been... You deserved better." I put out a hand. He watched it come gently to rest on the side of his face, then returned a wide-eyed gaze to me. He didn't resist when I put the other hand to his shoulder and drew him forward.

As different from our first kiss as I could have imagined. A different world. He tasted of after-lunch coffee now, not blood, and I didn't have rage to fuel me. I could feel him breathing, fast and shallow, his mouth like cool satin on mine. Probably as awkward for him as it was for me. I eased my grip on his shoulder, so he wouldn't feel restrained. So he could end it if he wanted, pull back and...

He cupped both hands gently round the back of my skull. Shuddering, he opened his mouth for me. My tongue slipped between his lips, wringing from me a faint, explosive grunt. *God!* Heat shot down my throat and up my spine. He was letting me dictate the pace but holding me to make damn sure I did. The cool satin warmed suddenly, and I felt his moan as a vibration as his tongue met mine.

"Nn-nn. Rayne. No. Wait."

"What?" He eased back in response to my brief, frantic shove to his shoulders. He was flushed, his eyes brilliant. "Why?"

"Because I don't want your second time to be more of a disaster than your first."

His reddened mouth quirked in mischief. "Would that be possible?"

"Yes, if you make me come in my pants like a randy teenager now."

"Oh." He glanced down and centre. "Yeah. I see the problem."

"So will any innocent picnickers who happen to turn up. You're gonna have to give me a minute."

I fell back in the passenger seat. Plenty of things I could think about right now to quench even the sturdiest erection, and my mind seized on a good one. Too good. The concept of conscious betrayal—not a heat-of-the-moment scuffle, but a cool, premeditated journey to the place where I was going have some form of sex with this new man.

"Logan."

I jumped. Rayne had got quietly out of the car and come round to open the passenger door. He was observing me closely, his gaze diagnostic. "I want you," he said. "But not if it's gonna fuck with your head, okay? Do you want me to just drive you home?"

I looked up at him. He was in a fair way to scare the picnickers himself. Did it make it worse or better to be left with this much choice? Temporarily worse, I decided, getting out of the car. It felt like using a muscle I'd allowed to atrophy. Rayne had been wrong. Jason wasn't telling me what to do even now. He never had. But he'd been strong, and loving, and for three years I'd allowed myself to lie back and be a kid again. I looked beyond the bridge over the stream to where the woodland track forked. "Which way?"

"They're both good. After you."

Chapter Nine

My choice took us to a clearing about half a mile into the woods. The track we'd been following ended there, by a waterfall that had carved for itself over time a crescent-shaped basin, overhung with birch and frondy ash. The water was almost deep enough for a swim. If I'd been filming this, that was how I would start—me and my illicit lover, washing away guilt and care, emerging from the water with our clothes clinging to us...

I glanced back and saw Rayne looking around him, hands on his hips. For once he wasn't hard to read. He was checking out the height of the crag behind the waterfall, the clear line of sight back down the path. A narrow defile. A defensible position. I smiled a bit grimly. I wished I had one.

"Come on," he called, eyes still on the track. "This place is quiet, but it's not bloody deserted. We won't have much time."

The crag was crumbling into boulders, cool grey shapes painted with moss and startling orange lichen. Rayne, following me a few yards deeper into the trees, briefly leaned on a rock, and before he could push up I stopped him, laying a hand to his chest. "No. You look perfect there."

He frowned, and I thought he was going to argue. Wondered, briefly too, if I was going to have to face a takeover bid, and how that would make me feel. But after a moment he subsided, pressing his spine up against the rock. It braced him beautifully. Supported him but pushed his hips forward. He got hard under his denims as I watched, then groaned as if the position aroused him and shamed him at once. "Oh, God," he said roughly. "Whatever you're gonna do, will you get on with it?"

I nodded. All right. Lack of time to think was my greatest luxury at the moment. I dropped to my knees in front of him, glad that I'd possessed my own pair of black trousers and wasn't going down here in a pair borrowed from the dean's son. Rayne was gasping by the time I'd unbuttoned his jeans—a task I'd have taken more slowly with such lovely old Levis as these, one delicious silver button after another, but I could smell fear and need coming off him, and I knew I had to work fast. I hauled his jeans and his white boxers—laundered to dazzling military standard—down around his thighs, and there he was, in daylight before me at last.

God. I held his hips, caressing, trying not to lose my poise. The skin under my hands was pale and rich, fitted round deep-sculpted muscle with a loving accuracy that made me want to follow every inch of it, with my fingers, my tongue... He was ivory-cream in the sunlight, warm, free of the faint note of blue that chilled some fair-skinned men. And his rising cock was of a piece with it all. Straight and big, flushing rose all down its shaft.

I said, unable to help myself, "Beautiful," and heard his ragged breathing shake into laughter.

"Thank you, Logan. But I'm not a bloody installation at the Tate."

No. He was real, and alive, and about a minute off coming. For the first thirty seconds of it I grabbed his backside and just let him have it. He was big, but I was in plenty of practice, and I listened to his choked-off cries as I opened up for him, sliding him in and in and over the back of my tongue. I felt his hands in my hair—a fierce pressure as his grip closed round my skull—and got ready for deep-dive manoeuvres, for breathing through my nose for the short time it would take to hot-throat him over...

"God! Sorry!"

The pressure vanished. I glanced up in time to see him clamp his hands to the rock instead. Their knuckles were white. Carefully I disengaged, coughing as his swollen tip left my airway. "What? It's okay."

"It's not okay to fucking choke you."

"You weren't." I wrapped a grip round the base of his shaft, stroking firmly up and down in case his conscience took him off the boil. "What?" I teased softly. "Did none of the meaningless girlfriends do this for you?"

"Yeah, but..." He was looking down at me with peculiar intensity. "I didn't pay much attention. There was never any possibility of me wanting to do it back to them." He shivered and gave me a lopsided grin. "Odd as some of them were."

Oh. That was the nature of the look. Whoever had trained him to disarm bombs had probably seen it too. He was watching and learning, with the hunger of a bright, disciplined mind ready to seize on new knowledge and use it as if his life depended on it. Then I heard him properly. *He wants to do it back to me...* Why this hadn't occurred to me, I didn't know, but it sent a bone-deep shudder of arousal through me.

"Oh, okay," I said. "Well, next time you're up against a *very* odd one, just hold her here..." I stopped my caress and let my grasp close on him, tight enough to elicit an explosive groan. "Then she can't drop down your throat like a shark after a baby seal."

A snort of laughter. "Ah, Logan..."

"And while I'm handing out advice..." I didn't really care, but if he was taking notes, learning his lesson... "Tell me when you're gonna come."

"Wh— Why?"

"It's safer, you idiot. And sexy as fuck, I promise you. You talk to me, you hear yourself say it. Then I jerk you off. I watch you while you come off for me. You'll be so bloody beautiful."

I held him tight. His head was tipped back, both hands spread flat on the rock. I sucked and tongued at the length of his shaft in my mouth, and then—yes, almost thirty more seconds after our instructional hiatus—I heard him say to me, or to the sunlight and the sky, "I'm there. Christ! Gonna...gonna come."

I eased back. I could hardly see through cobwebby mists of arousal, but I did as I had promised, bracing hard on my knees, working my grip savage and fast until he let go one shout, drove his hips forward and came, a wild white jet that made hot impact on my neck, on my chest in the opening of my shirt. God, so much, and so hard, as if he'd been waiting forever.

"All right," I gasped, reaching up to grab him as his knees buckled. He didn't look like a man who went down easy. I felt a mix of pride and fear. "You're okay."

"Oh, you reckon? God, Logan..."

He subsided to his knees beside me. For one instant he clung to me. My heart was pounding, my breath in rags, but in that second I forgot everything, even the hungry ache between my legs. "Rayne," I whispered. But his weight was shifting already. Before I could move to return his embrace, his hands were on my shoulders, pushing me powerfully back over into the leaves. "Jesus," I managed, laughing. "It's okay to catch your breath."

"Catch it later. I'll catch yours too. Just lie down and shut up."

I obeyed, mesmerised. Rayne parted me from my funeral trousers and the respectable underwear I'd chosen—Christ, had it only been that morning?—with brisk efficiency, making a small sound of impatience when the zip caught. Then he knelt between my thighs, and he looked at me—not down at my straining shaft, but straight into my eyes. Too much.

I lifted my wrists, crossing them over my brow, obliterating vision. "Please," I heard myself say, like a parched desert wanderer begging for water. "Please."

He learned fast. He locked a sweet and satisfying grip round the base of my cock, and a moment later the wet heat of his mouth enclosed me. A stillness, and a brief retreat, making me flash back vividly to my own first time, when the reality of sucking off my best friend Davie had hit me, forcing a thousand shocked revisions on my fantasy. Then the happy acceptance of the beast for what it was, with its scent and taste and throbbing veins... Rayne moaned as he dipped back down to work, and fought not to push up as he took me in, careful and calm, all the way.

I thought I would die of it. My climax halfway up the stairs of Jason's house had been sheer fury, a kind of whole-body howl, at fate and injustice, and—yes—abandonment, by the one man in my life I had trusted to stay and take care of me, though up until today I'd have sworn I needed no such thing. I hadn't touched myself since. I was ready, surging up on wave after wave of pleasure that I realised he was stopping with his grip, holding tighter each time I arched and cried out to go over.

For a second I thought he was drawing it out on purpose, and disbelieved his story of virginity. Then it occurred to me that he was scared, for all his valiant and continued rhythm down there. He hardly knew me. Couldn't trust me, could he, to warn him when I was going to...

I almost didn't. Almost wasn't in time. A terrible seizure took me, a rush that would breach the barricade of his hand. I hauled a breath, but my throat closed, and all that came out was a wail. Jerking desperately up—feeling a stomach muscle tear—I grabbed his shoulders and shoved him back. "C'mere," I snarled, and after a moment when he stared at me in flushed and total confusion, he launched himself at me, powering me down into the leaves.

***

A fretwork of branches on sky, more beautiful even than the leaping Gothic arches of Salisbury cathedral, and probably the inspiration behind them. Jase and I had talked about that. Early churches built to reproduce the groves of Pagan worship and ease the transition… My drifting thoughts sought focus, and I slowly let them. Church, trees, sky. Jason in free possession of them all, no longer sealed in a metal box in the morgue.

He never had been. This truth came to me, suddenly and without drama. That had been my own fear, the cringing of all mortal flesh from its ending. Jase had been free, everywhere and nowhere in the universe, since that moment ten days ago when he had severed himself from what I'd found behind the wheel of the DS. I surfaced from the warm, shallow waters of sleep, and felt Rayne's fingers gently draw my fringe back from my brow. His voice came out of the earth and the breeze. "All right then, Briar bloody Rose?"

Briar Rose… I smiled. How long had I lain in my glass coffin this time? My neck was cushioned on his thigh. He must have sat up from our tangle in the leaves and made me as comfortable as he could. Well, what had I expected—that he'd have got up, driven off and left me in the woods? Still, I was surprised. I was surprised at the continued movement of his fingers in my hair. "Sorry," I said. "Did I sleep a long time?"

"About an hour. You went out like a light almost the second you were done."

I groaned. "Oh, great. I'm such a perfect lover at the moment."

"You're a caveman, Doc," he informed me. "But that's okay." I looked up at him and found his upside-down face as forgiving as his tone, and just as wryly amused. "You looked like you needed it, so I let you alone."

"Ta. You must have pins and needles, though."

"It's gone past that. Numb from the waist down. Full epidural."

Laughter shook me. He wasn't showing any signs of wanting me to move, and I stretched lazily, arching my neck over his thigh. I lifted a hand and reached back, tangling my fingers with his. Somehow it seemed a more intimate touch even than the passage of his cock between my lips. I half-expected him to pull back, but instead his clasp tightened, and I shivered in pleasure. I wanted his touch. Wanted to stay here, in this shelter we had built that kept out pain.

Sleep, and the beginnings of a new arousal, tugged at me in equal measure. When I shifted my head, I felt against my cheek the stir of his erection. "Rayne…"

"Nn-nn. No. Absolutely not. I'm due back on duty in forty-five minutes, and I have to drop you off, so…"

"I'll thumb a ride."

"Stop it."

That sounded serious. But he hadn't let go of my hand, and I'd heard the under-note of desire in his voice. I lay gazing up into the sun, sleepily trying to think of ways to distract him. Sunlight through leaves. It was perfect here, I thought, a perfect moment in my life that had come to me on one of its worst days. A sudden renewal of summer.

Summer. I rubbed my thumb over the back of his hand assessingly. We'd come a long way since our meeting in the square off Southhill Street, but I was fairly sure I wouldn't get away with that. Then one thought led to another, and I asked cautiously, "What happened, then—to you and your brother, after your parents shipped out?"

I felt a tiny quiver in the strong muscle under my neck. "Way to throw cold water on it," he growled. And now that sweet firm grasp round my fingers did slacken. "Probably just as well. Come on."

I twisted onto my side and pushed myself clumsily up off his lap. "Shit. I'm sorry."

"No need. It's not a deal. I've just got to get going. You too, or your mate the dean is gonna have paramedics knocking your front door down." He scrambled upright, using the tree behind him for support, brushing leaves off his jeans. Then he stopped. He put down a hand for me, frowning thoughtfully as he hoisted me onto my feet. "Actually, it… It *isn't* a deal. What do you want to know?"

"Absolutely nothing you don't want to tell me." My head was spinning from the sudden move, and I could have bitten my tongue out. The shelter was gone. I'd tumbled it down with one inadvertent kick. "Forget it."

We set off back down the track. I wondered how we'd have made the return trip if I hadn't opened my big mouth—if he would have walked beside me, not kept half a pace ahead, so that I could see more of his lovely moss-stained shoulder than his face. If he'd have put an arm around my waist, or let me… No, I decided. He wasn't that type, in any circumstances. I wondered if he'd at least have talked to me.

"It's not much of a story," he said suddenly, not changing his pace or looking back. "No sadistic foster parents. Nice ones, actually—just too many of them."

"Oh." I pushed my hands into my pockets, trying not to sound relieved. "Why... Why were there so many?"

"My brother. He didn't take as kindly to being dumped as I did. Social services were trying to keep us together, and the families would put up with him for a few months then give up, and we'd get moved on."

I looked at him—at the man who *had* taken kindly to being dumped. Or adapted to it, anyway. His quietly ferocious air of independence made more sense to me now. "What happened to him?"

"Don't know. At least not details. I kept an eye on him—out of habit, I suppose, just to know if he was dead or alive. But I haven't been near him since we were sixteen."

"Does he live around here?"

"Yes, like some sort of wild man in a cabin in the woods. Living on pinecones and sheep shit, for all I know or care."

"Don't you..." I hesitated. I was regretting even more my crack about his army family now, and didn't want to step on any more of his corns. "Don't you miss him?"

"No. Why should I?" It came out brusque, and I eased a step or so back from him, ready to let it go. Then he sighed, and to my surprise slowed up, waiting till I fell into pace at his side. "Sorry. I raised the subject, didn't I? No, I hated the little bastard, to be honest. And the feeling was mutual."

"Why? You must have been through hell together."

"We'd have been better off apart. But I was meant to be the responsible one, the saviour who was gonna pull him back from the wild side. Screw that, though. I had my own shit to deal with."

"So you joined up."

"Yeah. I wanted order, brothers I chose. He never forgave me."

"What—for enlisting?"

"For joining that sacred bloody military machine you were telling me about the other week. For choosing the other side. He was just like our parents—I mean exactly like them, down to the dope habit and the dreadlocks. A perfect fucking hippie, head to foot. We couldn't have been more different." He paused, and now I could see his face. To my surprise, a glimmering amusement was gathering there. "Do you... Do you want to guess his name?"

"No way."

"Yeah. He always used to say our mam and dad had got it the wrong way round. Being as I was such a miserable bastard."

I broke into shocked laughter. I tried to stop it, remembering how well that had gone down back at the restaurant.

But then—silencing me anyway, on one astounded breath— he reached out and slipped one arm around my waist. We walked that way for the quarter mile or so of the distance that remained. I hardly dared breathe for fear of disturbing him. I couldn't even return the gesture, beyond a short, shy caress of his back. Odd, when I'd happily knelt to suck his cock, but without passion's impulse I felt awkward with him as a teenager. As soon as we came within sight of the car park, where a couple of other vehicles had now arrived, he let me go.

Believe me, Logan. It's not worth it.

I did believe him. I sat beside him in the hot little Audi, thinking about the barracks room, the fifty crew-cut squaddies, and I wondered how he had dared this much. As if to answer the unspoken question, he said, "The fucked-up thing about it is, it was...the best."

I snorted faintly. "It didn't start off great. Got better, I'll grant you that."

"If I'm honest with you…" He sighed and leaned an elbow on the window ledge. "Even your smackdown on the landing was better than most things I've come across in my life. But…"

"It's okay. You don't have to say it."

Because it wasn't worth it for me, either. Ten days after the death of my lover, I'd stumbled across someone I not only wanted to fuck but take home with me afterwards—someone I didn't want to let out of my sight—and in almost every way, that was appalling. If we both backed off now, I'd be spared the landslide of guilt my own heart would ensure descended on me, with every one of Jason's friends adding stones to the pile. I could be, for a dignified while at least, the grieving partner the world had a right to expect.

The grieving partner I was. Rayne, now watching me quietly, didn't look as if he expected his attentions to have cancelled out my pain. But nevertheless it was best this way. "It's okay," I repeated. "You're right, it was great. So let's not screw one another up with it."

"I don't mean I don't want to be your friend. When you're not picking fights, you're decent company."

He started up the car. As we pulled out onto the long sunny road that had brought us here, now glowing copper in the dusk, I became slowly aware of my own disarray. We'd brushed each other down, but there were still leaves in my hair. Soil scratching gently in the crease of my backside. There were, for God's sake, stains of his come on my shirt. *Well, there goes the presidency, Monica.* I smelled of him.

I leaned forward and picked up the iPod jacked into his car radio, more to have something to do with my hands than anything else. "Can I?"

"Yeah, go ahead. Knock yourself out."

Arcade Fire, Mumford & Sons. Some banging rock—the Strokes and the Charlatans. Pendulum, *Propane Nightmares* included. I shuddered, and stopped dialling through the tracks, suddenly stone-cold in the sweet evening warmth.

He glanced across at me. "Wow. My taste that bad?"

"No. No—based on this, I think we might actually share some common ground, which sure as fuck hasn't been apparent so far." I set the iPod down and ran my hands into my hair. "Listen, Rayne… I don't want to not be your friend, either. If you know what I mean."

"Just barely."

"If you get the chance, do you want to come over and look at that map for me sometime? Then we could—I dunno, go for a pint or something, like…"

"Like friends?"

"Exactly." In a way I knew it was absurd. I couldn't even hear my own voice asking him out for a drink without a twitch at the root of my cock. He would be so lovely, hitched on a barstool, his powerful hand wrapped round a glass. But I told myself I could do it. Better than losing him outright or pulling down the walls on top of both of us. "Like friends. I think I remember how."

"Okay. Well, I'm on duty for the next long shift, but I could call in late tomorrow afternoon, if you'll be around."

"I will. I'm going to start sorting through Jason's stuff." God, was I? I hadn't realised it myself until that moment. I looked at Rayne and wished I hadn't. His brow had contracted in that elegant scowl I now knew signalled sympathy, grave and severe but very real. His hand came out towards me. I caught it and planted it gently on the knob of the Audi's gear stick. *We're going to be friends, that's all.* "Got to do it sometime. I'll be okay."

Chapter Ten

I was sure as hell looking forward to a pint with my friend Rayne. The places where I'd been working today generated dust, even in the cleanest of houses, and my throat felt like a desert. Books and papers, and after that always more books.

I'd decided to start with the study. It was only now, eight hours into the task, that I was beginning to ask myself why. Jason's library was, after all, the least of my problems. If I was going to be a career archaeologist, I'd need most of his texts. I was fairly certain now I had to sell the house—or go slowly, inevitably mad, pinballing about between one relic and the next—but wherever I lived, it would have enough room for the books.

If I was going to be a career archaeologist… Kneeling on the floor by Jason's desk, I let the heavy tome on prehistoric cave paintings fall from my hands. There had never before been a question over that, not even for a second. What the hell else would I do? Jason and I had been going to be partners. Downstairs on my laptop was a near-finished study on Saxon burial hoards. I'd been busy revising it in the light of the amazing find Terry Herbert had made in Staffordshire with his metal detector the year before. Jase had been my mentor and critic; had spoken to his publishers, and it was almost a done deal. Historia Clio only printed the very academic best. It was one of the cornerstones Jase had encouraged me to lay down, the building blocks of a job for life.

For life. I hadn't heard undertones of prison sentencing in those words while Jason had been alive. Now he was gone, I knew that I had started to ask myself how much of my future plans had been built on the love of my subject, and how much on pure love for him.

Yet Rayne hadn't taken anything for granted, had he? *Decide what you're going to do for the rest of your life*, he had said, as if there were options, possibilities. He'd said more than that. *For the next few years, anyway.* As if nothing was set in stone and even heavy choices like careers in academia, where you started as a postgrad and ploughed onward and upward until you got tenure, need not be final.

A car engine purred in the street outside, and I lifted my head, listening. I thought I might be able to pick out the Audi's note by now. It had been, after all, the prelude and the coda to a pretty intense afternoon. But the sound passed on, and I forced my thoughts to segue to their next task too. That was over. If my heart had leapt, that was only because I'd had a rotten lonely day of it—because, over the last three years, I'd become very short of friends of my own, and it was nice to know that one would soon call round, that we would say hello like ordinary, civilised men, and go down to the pub for a pint.

Yet how my whole soul had yearned up and out through the treetops when he stretched out his length on me, thrusting me to climax with great powerful movements of his hips—how it had tried to unmoor itself, from my flesh and burning marrow… I'd flung my head back, loosing sounds I hardly recognised, until he had put a hand over my mouth to hush me, then laughingly replaced the hand with his mouth, kissing me to silence, and barely twenty seconds later to sleep.

Shit. No. Books—I had books to sort out, and papers, and of course that was the reason I'd been up here all bloody day, leafing through text after text. Because Jase was all about the books, and although I thought I'd accepted that his final message to me was a meaningless map, a symptom of whatever delirium had shaken his wits at the end of his life, something equally delirious inside me was still hoping. It would be very like him to have left me a note inside a book.

Another purr of engine noise. That *was* the Audi, slowing down and stopping. I recognised the squeak as her handbrake went on. I got up, taking my time. I'd wait until he knocked before I even started down the stairs. No need to rush, was there? Not for a friend and a pint.

Rayne looked the same and yet subtly altered. There was a tension in him I hadn't seen before, a faint rosy colour under his skin. Any other man standing on my doorstep with such symptoms, with such dark dilated pupils, I'd have said was both nervous and aroused. But this was Rayne, my hard-arsed soldier, who had said to me yesterday—and I had agreed—that enough was enough.

"Hi," he said, and even that was different. A little rough, as if his throat was dry too. "You all right?"

"Yeah. Are you?"

He frowned, a *why wouldn't I be* effort that miscarried and left him rosier than before. A different man would be on the edge of a blush. "Fine. Do you want to go straight out, then, or…"

"Come in for a second, till I get changed. I'm up to the armpits in dust. And…I put that map out, if you really don't mind having a look."

***

We were doing quite well, me and my new friend. When I came downstairs, fastening up a fresh shirt, he had been leaning with both hands on the kitchen table, conscientiously looking over the map spread out there, and I came round to face him on the opposite side before his posture could spark in me thoughts unsuited to our fledgling alliance.

"Well," I said. "What do you think?"

Whatever had been troubling him when he arrived, he seemed to have dismissed it. When he looked up, he was all business. My ideas of modern combat were a bit woolly and influenced by *Ross Kemp in Afghanistan*, but I could envisage him in a field tent, dust-covered, working out strategy with McCade. "You're right," he said. "Looks more like a blueprint or a plan."

"Not much to it, is there? I don't get it. Jase produced better maps of the area himself."

"Thing is, this is a copy. An old one." He lifted the sheet to the light. Yesterday's outdoor-sex weather had broken, and only a rainy silver was making its way through the kitchen window. It was enough, though, to make the map slightly transparent. "Look. There's some kind of numbering up the side here, in the margin."

I couldn't see it. Letting go my slightly too-tight hold on the back of one chair, I came to stand beside him. "Oh. Yes, I've got it. Looks more like a watermark than something printed on."

"Exactly. Something in the paper, not picked up off the copy. That's weird. It looks a bit like the numbering we'd use to identify documents, where they were produced, but—not quite."

He shut up suddenly. Too late, we both had heard it, the spasm in his throat he'd had to swallow hard to try and conceal. We both had seen the tremor in his hands. I was too close to miss it. The numbers were almost a line-of-sight phenomenon.

Instinctively I'd tried to see them from his angle. My cheek was an inch from his.

"Rayne," I said. "Are you all right?"

"Oh, fine," he told me hoarsely. "I slept for about two hours last night. I spent the rest of the time reminding myself I could never have you again and desperately trying to work out ways to get round that. I can't stop thinking about you."

I didn't move. Nor did he, except to lay the map flat on the table again. We both continued to stare at that, as if it was still our point of focus. As if it still existed. "Okay," I said at length. I sounded quite steady to myself, in the circumstances. I'd wondered briefly if I ought to apologise, for obtruding myself on his thoughts. "Well, here it is. I know you can't have me as in civil partnership on the steps of City Hall. I can't have *you*, not that way. Not and live with myself. We... We don't have to go on Gay Pride marches, or tell McCade. We could just have the sex."

I felt his shoulder quiver with silent laughter. "Oh, the sex, eh?"

"Yeah. If you want."

"Jesus. Is that not a bit shallow?"

"Yes. Can *you* afford to go any deeper? Shallow, casual sex, no strings, no damage, until we work off whatever this is and we can think straight again, because..." I stopped for breath, giving up. I didn't know if I'd have held off, if he'd arrived in purely friendly guise and never raised the subject, but as things were... I turned to face him. I couldn't put my arms round him, that gesture too lover-like, too much the way I'd have started off with Jase. But when he turned there was barely an inch of space between us, and I looked straight at him. "Because I can't stop thinking about you either. And I need to."

"No strings?"

I bit back a sigh. "Rayne, do I look like I've got a string left to me? My partner just died. I loved... I *adored* him. And all I can think about it screwing you. No strings, no damage to the army career. Nothing goes outside this house, for both our sakes."

"Oh, God." His intent wolf's gaze suddenly altered. I couldn't read it—couldn't have predicted that a second later he would put his arms around me. He was hard, and I felt it, but despite that there was barely a trace of sexuality in the embrace. It was only kind. Private Logan, getting picked up off the battlefield. "I'm sorry," he said against my ear. "I'm so sorry about Jason."

I had tensed up momentarily, almost unable to bear this new touch. Now, having let go and leaned briefly into it, I could hardly bear the thought of it stopping. I eased back, ending it myself. I wanted his passion, didn't I? That was all. "I know," I said. "I know. Thank you. Now come to... Come with me."

Because *come to bed* was a problem. I was still sleeping on my own side of the double up there, and what I should have spent today doing was clearing out Jason's clothes, which I didn't need, not pretending to sort through his books, which I did. I tried to envisage rolling around in the sheets I still hadn't changed, the wardrobes looking on in silent witness. I came to a halt in the hallway and felt Rayne gently collide with me. We both looked through the open living-room door at the sofa.

I said faintly, "What do you... What do you want?"

"Christ, Logan. I think I want you to fuck me, and I'm not even sure what that entails."

I felt my eyes widen. "Not seriously."

"What—about the fucking...?"

"No, you idiot—about the not *knowing*. I can't—"

He cut me off impatiently. "No, for God's sake. I know the—biological details. I just can't imagine it being good."

"Well, I'll attempt to show you, but…" The sofa wouldn't do for that. Quite apart from recent memories of Jase ploughing me down onto it—he loved that, to consummate passion while people went about their ordinary business, back and forth on the pavement outside—I needed space, or the demo would end up just as uncomfortable and awkward as Rayne probably feared.

I saw him seeing my problem. He was so alert. I could imagine being in a relationship with him, enjoying his delicious quickness, the sense of his being in pace at my side. No. Just a fuck. A good one, for preference, but that would be all. He glanced upstairs and made a wry face at me. "I get it. Want to go to a hotel?"

Now there was a certain seedy, dreadful charm in that. Salisbury wasn't long on establishments where you could book an afternoon room, but maybe we could find somewhere. Stay overnight to make it look good, screw each other blind and stupid and maybe get all this out of our systems in one fell swoop.

I swallowed, feeling faintly sick. That prospect felt worse—by just one shade, but definitely—than doing it in Jason's bed on the day after his funeral. "Nn-nn. No."

"Okay. Well—don't you have a spare room up there?"

I thought about it. *Dan's rumpus room*, Jase had once called it, in affectionate disgust, passing by its open door. "Yes," I said. "Of sorts."

"Neutral ground?"

"Just about." It would have to be. Apparently there wasn't enough guilt in the world to stop me starting my slow burn. Heat like summer lightning, flickering all over the surface of my skin… He saw that problem too, and this time he didn't say anything. He just took my hand.

So we each took up a position on either side of the bed, and between us we cleared it, in painful silence. I would have felt much better if he'd laughed at me for my untidiness or for the range of my taste in books. I hadn't always been a serious-minded student, and there were layers of history here—Frederick Forsyth novels and training manuals from the short time in my life when I'd wanted to be a commercial airline pilot.

But Rayne had thoughts of his own to occupy him. His hands moved efficiently, lifting off one stack after another. Eventually the mattress appeared. There was a pale blue undersheet on it, but that was all. I reached to brush dust off this and to tug it straight.

"God," I said. "That looks a bit clinical. I'll go and get a duvet."

"No," he said. I looked up at him. He was standing with his hands on his hips, surveying the mattress in much the same way as I'd seen him assess our next bit of dangerous ground on the plain. "Don't. Putting a duvet over this isn't gonna make it any better."

I straightened up. Leaning on the wall, I folded my arms. "Better?" I echoed. There were things that I could tackle in a lover—initial shyness, mistaken ideas about anatomy—and things that I could not. Things that people had to straighten out for themselves. "Do you think what we're going to do is bad?"

"What—morally? God, no. It just doesn't fit...what I thought I was. What I thought I was going to be."

"Which is?"

He shrugged. "Very boring. Wife and kids."

With anyone else, I'd have laughed. I wondered what he thought was going to happen to him here on the spare-room mattress that would deprive him of the power to marry and reproduce. But he was pale, the rainy light and the expanse of sheet setting tired, nervous shadows under his cheekbones and eyes.

I said, "You can still have those things, can't you? Did it ever occur to you that not getting killed in Iraq might be a better idea, if that's what you really want?"

"Oh, I don't really want them. I just…" He went to the window and carefully pulled at the cords of the blind until the slats were almost closed. Then he turned to face me. "Do you know what I wanted? I wanted to find some poor woman, marry her and squeeze a handful of kids out of her. Then be a perfect husband and father for the rest of my life, so I could shove my perfect fucking family in the face of…something that I don't think even exists anymore."

I repressed a whistle. His eyes were blazing. "Okay," I said. "You can still have *that,* I suppose. But those are some bitter bloody reasons, Rayne."

"You think I don't know?"

I dropped a last handful of books and came towards him. We met in the narrow space at the foot of the bed. He went into my arms with a faint noise of surrender, and for a moment I held him there, tight as I could. He was shaking.

"C'mon, soldier," I whispered to him. "You'll be all right."

I left him unsteadily beginning to unfasten his shirt and went into the bathroom, my heart beating so hard I could feel it in my fingertips. They fumbled at the door of the cabinet, and I stopped for a minute, trying to calm myself. There were considerations, weren't there? Things I hadn't had to think about in years. Jason and I had stopped using condoms almost immediately, once I'd moved in. I'd had my blood test, just in case, and it never crossed my mind to question him. He was my professor. He was Jason. I supposed, staring at my hollow-eyed self in the bathroom mirror now, that that might have been stupid. That I might have told my younger self to act different.

Did we even have any? I started pulling things out of the cabinet to see. Oh, Christ—there was one of Jason's exquisite little jars of lubricant. I set it aside, shuddering. I'd need something—lots of it, with a first-timer—but even the scent of that stuff would make the introductory session a short and disappointing one. My cock was softening now at the sight of the bloody jar. Thank God—farther back, a tube of the KY we had used for less ceremonial occasions. That would do, but still didn't solve the problem of the—

"Logan?"

I started, dropping the tube into the sink. Turning round, I saw Rayne leaning in the bedroom door. He was stark naked, and even with the light behind him, that was a sight to stop my breath. He had something in his hand. "Bringing condoms seemed presumptuous," he said, thoughtfully, giving the packet a chuck and catching it. "But then *not* bringing them seemed a bit presumptuous too, so…"

***

I lay curled round his back, kissing him, trying to distract him. He was having a desperately hard time of it, a battle raging inside him that I thought had only a little to do with my lube-coated finger holding open his entrance. His eyes were squeezed tight shut, his face half hidden against the mattress. The veins on his neck were standing. He'd gone down so fast and sweet, ripping my clothes off, tumbling me down with him onto the bed, that I'd thought we might fly through this on the strength of his enthusiasm, but the moment we'd stopped tussling and settled to business, he'd tensed. I hadn't had to guide him to roll away, to lie on his side with his back to me. It was as if he'd read a book and learned that that was what you did, and suddenly there was no more passion to it than that.

"Rayne," I whispered to him. "Rayne, we don't have to do this." I couldn't read his soft grunt of response. I moved my finger gently, and heard him gasp. "Maybe we're rushing it." Glancing down along the length of him, laid out in my arms like a beautiful, hard-hunted panther, I shivered. "I never even saw you like this before. We've never just...been to bed together. Rolled around with our kit off and humped."

A convulsion went through him that I realised with relief was laughter, and the tight-clamped muscle round my finger gave a bit.

"We can do that," I said, pressing the advantage home. A bit higher, a bit deeper, and I'd find...

"Ah—Jesus!"

"Sorry. God, sorry. Here, I'll stop."

"Don't you fucking dare." He lifted his face from the mattress. He was breathing hard, his fists clenched on the sheet. "Is that my prostate?"

"Oh, God. You *did* read a book."

"What?" He threw me one dark, puzzled glance over his shoulder. "No. Looked at a website."

I snorted. "Not on an army computer, I hope."

"Fuck, no. Internet cafe. Touch there again."

I obeyed, feeling for the little bump that marked the gland. After a moment he shuddered, and a long, grating moan tore from him. "Yeah, that's it," I said, carefully working the spot. "Better?"

"Marginally less—*bastard* unbearable, yes."

"Okay. That's good. Now roll onto your front—slowly—and get up on your knees a little bit." These orders sounded suddenly strange to me, coming from my own lips. To teach someone, to guide instead of being guided... Disorientation shook me, and I realised that I was remembering being in Jason's good hands. I didn't have time to react. I just had to do what he had shown me, didn't I, pass that strength and kindness on... I heard some muffled comment from Rayne on the lines of not being a performing fucking seal, and smiled. "I know. It's okay. It'll help."

He obeyed me, moving to my touch, and it was all I could do to cope with the sight of his taut arse rising up, my finger disappearing inside of him. Plenty of light in the room, despite the blinds. Silver light, daubing his pale skin, picking out our act in clinical detail. Probably he should have let me get that duvet, given us both somewhere to hide. I knelt behind him, trying to shield him myself, and reached under this belly to jerk him off, a touch of simple pleasure in the midst of tough new developments.

"No. Don't." He tried to flinch away from me. "Hurt too much at first. I...I lost it."

I ignored him. He was holding on to the edge of the mattress now, too tight to spare a hand to stop me, so I took firm grip on his softened cock and used his distraction to ease another finger inside him—slick and careful but merciless, straight up to join the first at the sweet spot. He bucked and swore, but the movement only thrust him harder into my hand, and he stiffened immediately.

"Well, don't worry," I told him hoarsely. "The beast is coming back."

"Fuck you, Logan—wait till I get you on *your* bloody knees..."

"Yeah. Take it all out on me then." I could see it. My own erection, quelled by my fear of hurting him, resurrected itself. It would feel so much easier, so much more familiar, than having to be in charge. He'd be beautiful, wouldn't he, pounding into my flesh, making me feel safe...

"Logan!"

It was a raw shout. I jumped. "What?"

"I am *not* bloody doing this if you aren't bloody *concentrating!*"

Shit! I jerked back to the moment. He had twisted round far enough to gaze at me fiercely. The hollow of his spine was beginning to bead up with sweat. How the hell had he known? I hadn't faltered or broken my caress of his shaft, now thick and heavy in my hand. "Sorry," I whispered. "What did I…"

"Nothing. Can always tell when some bloody squaddie hasn't got his eye on the ball. Look, sunbeam—I know this is weird for you too. Are we done with the foreplay?"

"I…I don't know. You could probably use…"

"I could use a fuck. Let's get on with it."

So I sheathed my aching cock in one of his condoms, relieved to find them of the plain-and-basic kind. I couldn't have handled any sudden discoveries about him at that point, any penchants for ribbing or fruit flavours. I ran lube from my tip to halfway up my belly, decided it wasn't enough and added more, until my hands were too slippery to put the cap back on and the tube dropped out of my grasp. Plain, scentless KY. I knelt behind him on the bed, on the stripped-down mattress. He had come up without a word from me to brace on his hands and knees. Yes, braced was the word—as if for a bomb blast. As if for impact. His head was down.

I took his hips between my hands. For a moment I felt clinical. The bare bed, the chilly light; Rayne's position, as if we'd posed for a biological-textbook shot on what one gay man does to another. Then he whispered, *"Daniel,"* and my heart burst back into life.

I'd prepared him almost well enough. The sounds he made as I entered him were still as much pain as excitement, and I stopped halfway, stroking his heaving ribs. I couldn't speak. Tears hot as blood were blurring my vision, clamping my throat tight. I'd thought I would never do this with another man. I heard Rayne say my name again, questioningly, and a third time with a faintest rasp of fear.

"Oh, God. It's all right." I steadied him, leaned warmly over him and kissed his shoulders. Finding the angle I knew would carry my thrust up against his prostate, I moved, once and again, and again until I felt him clenching tight at the base of my cock. His moans had turned to fractured gasps. "You okay?"

"What a stupid *bloody* question!"

"Want me to stop?"

"Nn-nn. Not—not ever to stop." He met my next thrust with a move of his own. "Not ever. God!"

I unleashed myself slowly. I could have given it all up and pounded straight through to completion—something bestial in me wanted that—but Rayne was like a dream becoming real beneath my hands. His struggle was turning to welcome. I drew back and pressed in again, a little harder, a little deeper than before.

He writhed and whispered, "Yes," and I began a pulsing motion, reaching under him to clasp his shaft. He was at full erection, stiff and hot in my grip. My control began to unravel.

"Rayne, are you... Can you come over for me?"

"Yeah. I'm there. But I can't... Let me lie flat. Lay me down."

So I did. I half-pushed, half-cradled him flat onto his stomach, following his movement so we didn't miss a beat. I laid him down, stretched out on top of him. I called him *Summer*, and he didn't rip my balls off and feed them to me, or whatever that threat had been. He shuddered and purred, made a move like a swimmer thrusting up for surface, and came, driving his hips again and again against my hand. The mattress muffled his cries. My own rang out unstoppably, one on the tail of the next. I couldn't get a breath between. Anguished pleasure seized me, the harsh rejoicing of the flesh that comes of its own will, serves its own purpose, makes no account of life or death, love, loss or decency. I needed Rayne, and I spilled myself into him, sobbing hard against his shoulder.

My withdrawal wrung a wail from him, though he promptly bit it off, burying his face in the crook of his arm.

"Sorry," I whispered, easing out as gently as I could. "I know. Not good."

He lifted his head. "Worth it," he rasped, and struggled wearily over onto his back. "Worth it. Fucking hell, Dan. Come here."

***

It was getting dark when I next opened my eyes, the distinction between the strips of the blinds and the cloud-filled sky behind them almost gone. I lay on the bare mattress, my head pillowed on Rayne's shoulder. I let time slip by me, drowsily watching the shapes of our entwined limbs. How my arm looked, draped across his chest. The beautiful spent innocence of his cock, and my thigh crossing his, tanned skin on pale...

Slowly it occurred to me that I didn't know how long he had planned this visit to be. He was still sleeping deeply, and I tried to imagine his reaction if he woke up an hour late for his duty shift. Reluctantly I pushed up in the bed, disengaging the arm he had round me, and I sat cross-legged, watching him. I could indulge myself in a lot of that, given time. I decided to compromise by going down and making us a pot of tea and a sandwich, and I got up gingerly, pulling on my shirt—damn him, a couple of the buttons were gone—and my crumpled jeans.

My bare feet felt strange on the carpet. Light, as if they weren't really making an impression. Padding down the stairs, I saw that St Cecilia's angel was back, and I wondered how I could ever have missed it. It was obvious, really, even in this light. You just had to know how to look. I brushed an affectionate fingertip touch to the painting as I passed.

And I stopped. Walking on air, seeing angels. Symptoms of a dangerous and undeserved euphoria, surely. I shouldn't be feeling like this. Clutching the banister, I looked around me. I could see through open doors into all the downstairs rooms from here. Every shape of their furniture, every line of their construction, even their damn light switches, had until now given me a barely realised sense of pain, as if seen through a headache. Now they just looked like rooms again. Not like home, but ordinary. Harmless. My blood was singing. I thought of Rayne, stretched out and sleeping upstairs, and it sang louder. *What the hell, Daniel?*

A scrape of footsteps on the path outside recalled me. Through the slender glass panels to either side of the door I could see someone approaching, indistinct through the rich floral engraving. Any second now a hand would close on the knocker and send its boom through the whole house. I jumped to forestall it. Didn't want him woken up like that, late for duty shift or not.

The dean. I should have known. Stupidly, I hadn't given him a second thought since extricating myself from my social obligations the day before. Guilt tried to sting me but didn't get far through the layers of bright pleasure that seemed to be wrapping me round. At the very least, I'd owed him a phone call. I wondered how many times he'd tried to call me. I pulled the door wide. "Hello, sir. I'm sorry I…"

"Dan, please." He looked as concerned and paternal as ever. Something was different, though—a faint, faint chill, which increased just perceptibly as he took me in. "Nobody expects you to be behaving normally at the moment. I was just worried about you."

I ran a hand over my hair. Untidy. Very. Slowly it dawned on me that ingenuously pulling the door wide might not have been the best idea. Which buttons had Rayne popped off? I didn't want to draw attention to them by checking. "Thank you," I said. "I know I ditched out on you yesterday."

"It's all right. Everyone was fine. I..." He paused, frowning. "You know, son, I hadn't thought to see that lovely smile of yours again for a hell of a long time." My hand flew up to hide it. "Don't do that," he went on mildly. "I'm glad to see you looking better. May I please come in for a moment?"

Christ, no. I swallowed that reflex down. *It's not a good time* might have worked—or, more likely, given away a game I already suspected was crumbling around me. Instead I stood back from the door. "Of course. Please."

The hall was quiet. I reckoned that, even if Rayne had woken up, he would probably be discreet enough not to tramp around up there until I'd got rid of my visitor. I wished that I cared more. The silver-wrought mirror by the door confirmed that I'd rearranged my face to pale gravity, but I was still warm all over, my bones deliciously loose in their sockets. I was, apparently, lost to all propriety, like a Jane Austen wild-child, Lydia Bennet maybe, gone forever off the rails.

I gestured the dean ahead of me into the living room, where, as he took a seat, tugging his trousers up at the knee like the neat middle-aged gentleman he was, he said, with absolute civility, "I hear you got a lift home from the Ingersoll yesterday."

I leaned in the doorway. Fucking Salisbury—eyes in every statue, carving and gargoyle. Still the implications of his quiet statement weren't getting through to me. I only knew that I didn't want to start lying to him. "Yes," I said. "A friend picked me up."

"I thought I knew most of your friends. I knew one of them..." He paused, seeming to struggle with some emotion. "I

216

knew one of them so well that no one will ever fill the hole he's left in my life. I don't think I know the attractive dark-haired boy who picked you up yesterday."

A thin red needle made its way through the haze around me. It wasn't outrage at having been watched and reported on, although I did vaguely wonder if I had Rachel Keats to thank for it. And it wasn't guilt, not yet. It was a sting of fear, that any part of what I had shared with Rayne yesterday might have come under hostile scrutiny. I hadn't realised that over the past twenty-four hours I had become so protective of the memory.

I'd have killed anyone who tried to get past me and upstairs.

I had to say something. My pulse was slowly rising from its slow postcoital rhythm to a thud I could feel in my neck and hear in my skull. In a way, I was just incredulous that the dean would come here—God, had that been the sole point of his visit?—and say this. I had never known him to stoop to notice a colleague's personal crimes before. But clearly this one was special to him. And, if I was honest with myself, could I blame him?

"I needed to talk to someone," I began, as calmly as I could. "He met me, and—"

"I don't need to know anything about him, do I? If he's just your friend."

Okay. The dean was glaring at me. The academic veneer I had taken for the whole man was stripped away. I barely recognised what was left. I didn't know why I couldn't just agree with him. *Yes, just a friend.* It wouldn't have mattered. And yet somehow, powerfully, it did. I didn't want to deny Rayne. I sighed. "What *do* you want to know?"

"I want to know… The other day, when you said Jason had left you a map…what the hell did you mean?"

"What?" I frowned. Hadn't we been in the process of exposing my treachery? "Just… Just that. I told you, didn't I? A map of the area he'd been campaigning to get access to. It didn't mean anything to me."

"Nor to me, when you first mentioned it. But I've been thinking. I'd like to see it."

I shrugged. I didn't understand, but if that was my way out of this horrible encounter, I would take it. His words—the look in his eyes—were sending cold trickles down my spine. Somewhere under the aftermath of loving Rayne was my own fear, rising up by the second, that I deserved every bit of his condemnation. "Okay. Of course. It's in the kitchen—I'll get it for you."

"No. I'll come through." He was already pushing up off the sofa. I wondered if he didn't trust me as far as the next room. He almost hustled me up the stairs from the living room, and followed at my shoulder all the way down the hall. The map was where Rayne had left it, and I remembered that he had seen something in it that I hadn't, something he'd been trying to explain.

"Is that it?"

"Yes. God, Dean Anderson, I know I've pissed you off, but..."

"Please be quiet." He shouldered me aside and planted his hands where Rayne's had been. I saw him go pale. "He left you *this*?"

"What is it? I've told you, it doesn't mean anything to—"

"No. Nothing does, does it?" He straightened up and swung on me. His cultured county accent had roughened to a bark. "Nothing Jason is or was apparently means anything to you. And yet he left you... He *trusted* you, with something that should've gone with him to his bloody grave!"

I took a couple of steps back. I didn't want to, but I felt so sick and lost that I couldn't square up to him. "Please," I said. "Stop this. He meant everything."

"Bollocks, Daniel. You've no right—to his memory, to his house—and certainly not to this." He grabbed the map off the tabletop, and before I could move to stop him, had crumpled it and shoved it into his jacket's inside pocket. His voice rose to a raw yell. "He didn't know what you were. You bloody little puppy, you couldn't even keep it in your pants on the day you cremated him! Could you?"

"Hoi."

The dean and I both spun around. Up until that moment—of turning, and seeing Rayne halfway down the stairs, leaning over the banister—I wouldn't have believed that anything could happen to make this encounter worse. But there he was. He had got dressed, which was something for me to be grateful for. Undermining that was the just-woken flush on his cheeks. The spikes in his close-cropped hair, and his general air—indefinable and undeniable—of having been recently fucked. He was so lovely, gazing down at me. I didn't want anyone else to see him.

"Rayne," I said hoarsely. "No. Go back up."

"I will, if you're all right."

I tried to tell him I was. But the words wouldn't come. Rayne locked one hand round the banister, tensed his arm and vaulted the rail, jumping silently down onto the hall carpet. It was like watching a panther drop from a tree. He steadied himself and stood up straight. His hands were loose by his sides, his gaze assessing.

"This is the dean," I managed, then added, like a society hostess making one last stab at saving her party, "Dean Anderson, from the university. He... He was just leaving."

The dean looked at Rayne, then back to me. I wondered if it was in any way nice for him to have his suspicions turned into handsome, hard-toned fact. Simpler, certainly.

"All right," he said. His voice was shaking slightly and laden with so much disgust I thought he would spit. "You know—when Rachel told me you'd left with someone else, I didn't believe her. I told her not to insult you, because you would never insult Jason in that way. I've defended you, over the years, from all kinds of people with opinions like hers. I didn't mind. I thought you were worth it."

All kinds of people. I'd never thought about public opinion. I'd been good enough for Jason, and I'd never looked further. I'd minded sometimes being taken for his son or some kind of bloody escort, but how had he felt at being taken for the father? The respected older man, who'd risked so much to set up home with a lover half his age. "Don't," I said. "I know I deserve it. But…please don't."

"Did he ever tell you how he used to worry that you'd find someone younger and leave him? Did you think he didn't see you looking?"

"I didn't leave him. He left me."

"Oh, don't you dare try to defend yourself like that. God knows how far you drove him into it. My God, when I think about somebody like him—one of the greatest minds of his generation—fretting himself to death over a toy-boy brat like—"

"Okay. That's enough."

I blinked, half-blinded by tears. Rayne had left his observation post in the hallway and was in motion. I tried to get between him and the dean, but he put me aside, his gesture gently absolute. He said, "That's more than enough, old man," and took hold of my esteemed employer by one shoulder and the collar of his jacket. I could imagine him marching dissidents off the streets of Basra in that grip. It wouldn't hurt, but it wouldn't leave a choice.

"Rayne, for God's sake. Leave him be."

"If you're gonna let someone into your house to shout at you and make you miserable, sunbeam, you'd better wait till I'm not here. Didn't Dan say that you were just leaving, sir?"

The dean tore out of his grasp. He was colourless, face frozen in a place beyond outrage. I guessed that he had never been manhandled before in his life. "I am," he gasped out. "This isn't my friend's home anymore. Live with yourself if you can, Dr. Logan. Thank God you were too damn dense to understand what he tried to tell you at the end."

Rayne walked him out. He opened the door for him, politely held it, quietly closed it afterwards. There was no sarcasm, no mockery, in his gestures. It was as if, now he'd gained his point, he was willing to be courteous again. But the dean had been seen off the premises.

I watched this much. Then I couldn't see anything. I couldn't keep my head up or get air into my lungs. My rib cage was caving in at the front. Blindly, clamping my hands over my face, I began to fall into the pain.

"Daniel."

Swift footsteps on the parquet. He caught me. His arms went round me, a warm vise. I fought for a moment, but there was no point. I buried my face in his shoulder. "All right," he said. "Shush. Shush."

I breathed him in. The only way I was going to get breath at all, my frantic, unmanned sobs muffled so I wouldn't have to hear them. Hot scents of sex and salt flooded my head. I choked, and his grip round me tightened.

"Breathe, you fucking pillock," he ordered me. "It's all right. He's gone." He hoisted me up to sit on the edge of the kitchen unit behind me, and even now I could feel that in other circumstances that would have been the sexiest move in the world. Only functional at this moment, so he wouldn't have to hold me up. So he could hold me better, more deeply.

I wrapped my arms around his neck. I opened my thighs so he could lean between them, pressing our bodies together, and I clung to him, finally put beyond shame.

I felt something tear in my chest. This pain was new, so physical that I tasted blood. Rayne was wrong. I wanted him— Christ, at that moment I was pretty sure I loved him—but nothing would ever be all right again. The dean—the words he had put into my mind and my heart—would never be gone. Because he'd been right. When I looked at men of my own age, it had stopped being innocent admiration. I didn't know when, but I'd begun to use them as comparisons between the safe, tight-buckled world all around me and the whole wild universe I'd sacrificed to live in it. I'd begun to use them to try and look into my own future. If Jason had lived, I wouldn't have stayed his beautiful boy forever, would I? I'd have grown up. Though I might have torn off my own wings to try and stop it, one day I would have understood and broken from my cage.

***

"Daniel. Here. Drink this."

The scent of brandy reached me. I lifted my pounding head from my hands. Rayne was settling into a chair beside me at the kitchen table. I said, as about the least relevant thing that came to mind at that moment, "You do realise you're calling me by my first name, don't you?"

He shrugged. "Looks like. Doesn't mean you get to call me by mine. Unless you've got your cock up my arse, when for some reason I seem to quite like it. That was your boss, then?"

"*Was* is probably right."

"You're kidding. Not because of what I did?"

"Oh, yeah." I picked up the glass and unthinkingly drained the generous measure of brandy in one. I barely noticed its fire going down, but my hands stopped their tremor. "Because we were doing so well, until you came down and went all *Dog Soldiers* on him. No. I don't think he can actually sack me for…"

"For screwing someone ahead of his schedule?"

I looked up. Rayne was sitting, arms folded, expression impassive as ever. I must have imagined the touch of uncertainty in his voice. "Because that's all it was. Remember that. I can see you're dying of guilt over there, and there's no need. It wasn't love, or any of the stuff you had with Jason. Just a fuck. And, if you want, that can have been the end of it."

There it was again—the trace of doubt. For a moment I stopped thinking about myself and remembered the proud, stiff-necked man who had laid himself down for me barely an hour ago.

"No," I said. "I don't want. Are you okay?"

"Yeah. Why wouldn't I… Oh." His puzzled frown cleared. "I can still sit down, if that's what you mean." He smiled. "You were very good, Doc. Very gentle. And…it was bloody amazing. But I mean it—I can see what you're up against now. I'm not gonna make things worse for you."

I pulled my chair over so it was right next to his. I reached to touch his face, and he unfolded with a little start of surprise from his defensive posture and leaned towards me so that our foreheads were almost in contact. Our hands met clumsily. We had scarcely touched, outside of sex. *Not love, or any of the stuff I had with Jason.* Thinking about it like that might keep me sane, but it was no longer true.

I closed my fingers round his hand, and after a second felt the grip fiercely returned. "You don't make things worse. Do you know how it felt, to have you come jumping down the bloody stairs to bail me out? He was killing me. And I bloody deserved it."

"Nobody deserves that."

We sat for a long time. He had curled one hand round the back of my neck. To my surprise, he was pressing occasional kisses to the side of my face—awkward, and of surpassing tenderness, each one sending its own set of shivers down my spine.

Eventually he said, "I do know, actually. How it feels to be bailed out—by your mates, by your brothers. It's part of why I do what I do. It's why I have to get back out to the desert. Can you understand that a bit better now?"

I eased back to look at him. I hadn't known it mattered to him in the least, what I thought of his choice of career. I wanted to tell him there were ways of finding that kind of love without carrying a gun to pay for it, but I was turning out to be so much less adept than I had thought, at navigating my way through my free world. "Yeah," I said. "I understand."

"Speaking of which…" Another kiss, this one finding the corner of my mouth, making me gasp. "If I bust every speed limit between here and Fellworth, I might make it back in time for my shift. I've got to go. Look, do you want me to take that map with me, see if McCade or any of the lads in the offices can make anything of it?"

The map. I sat up, mists in my head clearing. "Sorry. It's… Er, it's gone. The dean took it."

"The dean?"

"Yeah. He was really freaked out by it. Grabbed it and shoved it in his pocket. He said Jason had trusted me with something…something he shouldn't have, something I couldn't understand."

Rayne gave my hand a thoughtful, comforting, crushing grip. "Wow. You did have fun down here before I crashed the party. It doesn't matter. Have you got some sketch paper, a pencil?"

"Yes. Um… If you want me to get them for you…"

He glanced down at our joined hands and let me go. "Oh. Sorry."

"Don't be. Hang on a minute."

There was a pad in my field satchel. I always carried one about on digs to make drawings of freshly opened sites. I could hardly bring myself to think about what Rayne wanted it for. My mind was awash with images of the past few hours, some horrible, some so good they made my heart turn over. Distractedly I laid the book in front of Rayne, turning back a page for him.

"Pencil?" he said, and I handed him one.

He reproduced Jason's map in a few quick strokes. That was all it took, but he had done it with a draftsman's accuracy, and I smiled in admiration. "Not bad, for a squaddie. Where'd you learn to do that?"

"Thank you. You try carrying a camera into an Iraqi weapons factory, see how far it gets you. Army trained me not to need one. I used to go on inspection tours and then draw up any guns or plans I'd seen, not that they appreciated it."

"Why not?"

"Because they wanted me to come back and draw weapons of mass destruction. Hang on. I'm not finished." He turned the sketch, squinted at it for a moment, and then to my astonishment unhesitatingly reproduced the string of letters and figures we had both seen watermarked into the margin. "So. Dean has a copy, we have a copy. Now. What do you want me to do with it?"

I knew why he was asking. "If you take it, and you find anything out, you'll tell McCade about it, right?"

"Right. That's the deal. Or you can burn this, and we'll both forget it. Let the dean alone with whatever craziness he and Jason concocted between them."

"He said… He said it was a secret Jason should have taken with him to his grave."

Rayne looked up at me. I couldn't read the shadows in his eyes. "You know what?" he said. "At the moment, all I care about is that it doesn't end up taking you to yours."

"What?" Briefly I was too warmed by his words to think further. "You don't think this is serious, do you? Like you said— some kind of academic obsession they got themselves into."

"I don't know. I want to find out more. And—yes, I'll tell McCade, if it's important, but I'll tell you first. All right?"

"All right." I looked at my watch. "Rayne, you're gonna be late now even if you go there by helicopter."

"Shit." He straightened up, folding the sketch. "Look, are you gonna be all right on your own, sunbeam? That old bastard said some hard things to you."

"Yeah. They'll echo." *God knows how far you drove him into it…* I couldn't sidestep that anymore, even if acceptance of the accusation's truth put me into a plain box down at the Ingersoll next. I turned my face into it like a hailstorm, a ferocious headwind, and stepped up to Rayne. "Don't worry. I'll be fine. Just give me a call if you find anything out, or if you want to see me again, or…whatever."

"Okay. We might even get that pint sometime, eh?" I wasn't sure how he would part with me, how much of a parting gesture he would tolerate from me even now. But suddenly he took hold of my face between his hands. "And book me in for another spot of *whatever*." He leaned in and planted on my mouth a kiss of such perfect, passionate simplicity that I began to laugh.

226

Chapter Eleven

I went back to work the next day. I didn't know if there was any time limit on compassionate leave, but I was pretty sure that, in the dean's eyes at least, I'd violated all its other terms. There wasn't anything else I could do at home anyway, not for the moment. My one stab at dealing with Jason's affairs had been driven by personal need, and I'd caught myself out. I'd put a quiet ad in the *Auto Trader* about the DS, and I was going that night to look at an equally inconspicuous Peugeot to replace it. Everything else—his clothes, the house itself—no. Not yet.

You took a new lover, though. You were plenty ready for that. The words danced across the pages of the handout I was trying to prepare for my next lecture. I supposed I would feel better if I could have brought myself to regret Rayne or a single thing that we had done. On the contrary, my mind sought comfort in the replay of each memory. I reached for the feel of his arms closing tight round my back when we'd pounded to conclusion in the spare-room bed. I could still feel, like warm velvet, the press of his last kiss. If even that sensory pleasure had been the end of it, I'd have been more at ease. Could have allowed myself, with a very long leash, a grief-stricken fuck with a stranger. But it hadn't been, and Rayne wasn't a stranger anymore. He had reached something deep inside of me that had been dying. Had made me want passionately to live.

My office door swung wide. I braced myself. I'd left it halfway open, unwilling to hide my presence from the dean, little as I was looking forward to my first encounter with him. He had to pass my door to get to his. I sat up straight behind my desk and waited.

"Are you lecturing this morning, Dr. Logan?"

Ah. Just Susan, the dean's secretary, and that was a new chill. She'd even *Danny*'d me a few times, with an office-party sherry inside her. "Er, yes," I said, wondering if I should add *Miss Bell* by way of return. Wondering if I'd had my licence revoked, or whatever was the academic equivalent of being defrocked. "Yes, the half-nine group, main theatre."

"Then you'll want your handouts and your PowerPoints prepared."

I raised an eyebrow. I hadn't realised that Xeroxing could be used as a threat. "Well—I do, but I've left a note on Elsa's desk…"

"Elsa is off sick again." *You, and all those connected with you— even a shared admin girl—are hopelessly treacherous.* "And, since the dean is unwell too, I've been asked to look after you."

Ordered at gunpoint, my frivolous mind continued the imaginary drama, then I heard her properly, and sobered. "Oh—he's ill?"

"Yes. He won't be in for the next week at least. That's all I know."

My mouth was too dry to speak, and I knew nothing that came out of it would be welcome anyway. I shut up, handed her my lecture notes and transparencies and watched her turn her back on me and leave.

***

The rest of my day was of a piece with this good start. I was relieved to slip into the crowd of my students, who had too many problems of their own to notice staff-level ructions, and who were mostly too young and stupid to pass judgement anyway. There was a lot to be said, I'd concluded by the end of my last class, for youth and stupidity. I'd been so consistently cold-shouldered by so many of my older, wiser friends that I was about ready to chuck my ID card across the doorman's desk and resign. Jesus, what had the old man done—come back here yesterday and broadcast my sins over the tannoy? Then perhaps I was doing him an injustice—perhaps I had really shocked him into a stroke, and Rachel Keats had been at work in his stead.

My friends, I thought bitterly, walking through the green quads to the campus gates. They weren't, were they? They were Jason's. I had never been wildly popular with the mid-life academic circle in which Jase and I had moved. If I achieved anything, they attributed it to his influence, and if I screwed up, because they loved him, they blamed me for it all the more. I hadn't minded—barely noticed—when he was there, his warm wings wrapping me round...

I took a bus out to Laverstock, where, after a cursory glance under the bonnet, I bought the *Auto Trader* Peugeot. I paid cash. Jason's will had passed probate and his funds been transferred to my account, but I hadn't owned a chequebook in years. The vendor looked at me like I was a drug dealer and watched me suspiciously from the kerb all the way down the street as I drove off.

Jase would have had an RAC man with us for a presale check. He'd have got down on his knees with a coin to test the tread and checked the brakes five times before he let me near the thing. Fighting the unfamiliar gearbox, making the Peugeot roar, I let sweep over me the most shaming tide of self-pity yet: *no one to look after me now.*

Christ, when had I forgotten how to look after myself? I'd overheard Rachel Keats: *maybe Dan needed a father figure.* That couldn't really be true, could it? But even Rayne, when I'd pissed him off badly enough, had hit back with much the same thing. Add to that my continuing dreams, where Jase and my dad nightly merged roles, shared every job from fucking me to tucking me up in my bed—

I nearly rear-ended a bus. Swearing violently, I scrabbled for control of the car and of myself. God, when was I going to feel normal again? I'd done everything now, hadn't I? Drunk myself stupid, wept, jumped into bed with a new man and enjoyed afterwards a wild—and, as it was turning out, temporary—sense of rebirth and euphoria. I'd worked through the gamut of reactions.

And, ultimately, there was just me. I pulled up outside the house and checked my mobile. Nothing. What had I expected? Rayne was a busy man. A soldier. He'd said he'd call me when he found something—although, when I came to think about it, wasn't that what *I* had asked him to do? *No strings,* I'd said, and I'd meant it.

I still did. There was no damn sense in transferring my sense of dependency from one man to the next. I got out of the car, looking up at the empty façade of the house I'd shared with Jase. I didn't know how or when I'd become so bloody feeble. It wasn't in my nature. I was proud and independent-minded. I did wilderness-survival courses, climbed mountains. I had lost both parents at an early age and sailed right through it—that was how tough I was.

No. I'd just been numb. Too young to figure out the blow.

My mobile buzzed, and I grabbed for it so hard it clattered to the pavement. But it was just the bloke who wanted to see Jason's car, saying he was on his way.

So half an hour later it was me on the kerb, watching the beautiful old lady's tail lights disappear for the last time. The buyer clearly hadn't seen the handful of reports and articles that had made the local news, and didn't look the type to care if he had. He had been glad to get a bargain, had paid by respectable cheque and shaken my hand.

I went back indoors. Briefly I wondered how the dean was, considered and dismissed the idea of phoning to find out. For an even shorter time, I puzzled over his reaction to the map. But I was suddenly abysmally tired—of the map, of grieving, of having this mountain of bricks and mortar on top of me, of being quilted, padded round, in Jason's wealth, which felt like a fucking satin-lined coffin tonight. If I'd known he really meant me to have it— if I'd known, for God's sake, why he had died…

There were books I hadn't checked. Hundreds of them, actually, lining the living-room walls. I didn't have to give up yet, did I, on the possibility of a note?

Yes, I did. I was building up the thought of one into a cure, a way to lay down my aching load of pain and walk away from it. Even if I found one, that was never going to happen. I looked for a while at the bookshelves, then at the vodka bottles I'd laid in for emergencies. But I'd been there. Done that. Done, as I'd realised on my way home, pretty much everything now.

So I passed an ordinary evening. Not as I had a week or so ago, with reality held back at bargepole length. This time I did it cold. Fixed myself some dinner, put in a couple of hours of marking and prep for the next day. Nothing on TV, so I shoved a DVD of *CSI* into the slot and sat staring at it, taking nothing in, until I heard the end theme and switched off. Bless Jase—he'd bought me the tenth-season box set for my birthday, indulging my childish tastes. But I couldn't bring myself to open it, and it was late enough by now for an ordinary man to go to bed.

Doing it cold was right. I ran the hottest bath I could stand, but could not chase out the chill from my marrow. I stood in the upstairs hallway, equidistant between the main bedroom and spare. I'd washed the linen on both now, so no souvenirs to be found there, olfactory or worse. I could sleep in either. Everything was transient, wasn't it? Nothing, good or bad, left much of a trace. I curled up eventually in my old place in Jason's bed. My mobile remained silent and blank, and after having set the alarm for another cold day in my ordinary world, I shoved it under the pillow and tried to sleep.

Just after I'd succeeded, or so it felt, the damn thing buzzed. I pulled it out, heart sinking. Had I lost the few remaining hours dividing me from tomorrow in one unprofitable nap? I felt sick, and wearier than when I'd gone to bed. I was going to have to get used to this, I supposed—waking up alone, with no enthusiasm for the day ahead. Millions of people did it every morning. I'd been very lucky so far.

But it wasn't the alarm. The sky outside was pitch black. Sitting on the edge of the bed, I stared blankly at the text that had unfolded itself on the screen. No sender's name, just a number. I'd given Rayne mine, but he hadn't offered his in return, another shadow that hadn't fallen on me until I had run out of faith and friends that afternoon. A number, and two words.

I almost laughed. Typical, that some stray signal, some wrong-number prank had found its way into what precious little sleep I was going to get tonight. Then I thought about it. Sleep— in sunlight, in a pile of leaves in woodland, wishing the sweet air would turn to a glass coffin, the trees to thick thorny cables, wrapping us round. *Briar Rose*, the text said. Rayne's smiling name for me when I'd passed out in his arms by the waterfall.

I got up. Clearly I was insane, or one of us was. I got dressed quickly in the dark, choosing not the first things that came to hand but the first dark ones, black jeans and jacket, and the charcoal cashmere sweater I hadn't worn since Jason's death. He had bought it for me, stood with me in this bedroom helping me into it, sliding it over my ribs. A close fit but perfect, and off it had come ten seconds later, Jason shuddering with arousal as he stripped me back down. I had no idea why I was doing any of this, why I slipped downstairs without putting the lights on, why I went out the back way, through the yard and the alley, rather than through the front door. Of course if I'd put the Peugeot in the garage, where there was now space for her, there'd have been no need, but once I'd lowered the rollover door after the Citroën's last exit, that was a sealed unit for me, forbidden ground. No idea why I was playing cloak-and-dagger like a six-year-old, except that something in that bizarre text had set off my alarms. Short acquaintance with Rayne had taught me that this wasn't the way he would choose to pull some kind of sexy tryst. No—for that he'd have kicked my door in, or abseiled through the window, and I need not expect any Milk Tray. Something was wrong.

I stood in the shadows of the alley for a moment. I was listening, though I wasn't sure what for. A premature blackbird offered a couple of phrases, then shot off with an alarm cry as our neighbour's cat slithered over the top of the wall. Other than that there was silence. This far out from the town centre even the murmur of traffic was hushed. I was alone in the cool green night. I waited, my fingers wrapped loosely round the mobile in my pocket, breathing the scents of tomcat and orange blossom, trying to think. I didn't reply to the text. A tiny part of me was still convinced that some random blip of the universe had landed those two words in my inbox. And if not—I didn't want to blow Rayne's game, whatever it might turn out to be.

Cautiously I crossed the kerb and got into the Peugeot. The mechanics of that felt weird to me, now I had time to feel them properly. She was little and cramped after the DS, and her nylon upholstery was a harsh contrast to the old lady's smooth leather. These details struck me with a kind of distant intensity as I toyed with the idea of getting straight back out again, returning to the house and my sensible, desolate bed.

I had nothing to lose. I started up the Peugeot and steered her at a discreet twenty through the sleeping residential streets. Then I got her out onto the main road, and I drove like hell.

***

The woodland car park was deserted. *Of course*, I told myself, jouncing the car to a halt, pulling up the handbrake. *Of course, you fucking idiot.* I was shaking now, with interrupted sleep and the strangeness and stupidity of being out here in the small hours on my own. Absolutely on my own. I'd be lucky if I didn't get arrested for dogging, not that there was anyone to watch. I got out of the car and stood with my hands on my hips, gazing blankly into the moonlit trees. Wow—I'd found for myself a whole new way to feel like a complete bloody loser.

"Christ, Logan." It was barely more than a whisper, and I whipped round, grabbing at the door for balance. "Next time you're gonna buy a new car, bloody tell me first."

One of the trees stepped out from its fellows and became a man. It took my mind a second to patch him together—he was dressed in night camos, and he moved like a slow breeze on water. Then there he was, the pattern completed—Rayne, stunning in the tawny light, holding a gun on me.

"What the fuck…?" I began, and then outrage hit me. I hated guns, didn't I? Guns, the army, and all they represented had shadowed my life since I was six years old. Briefly I wondered how come I was dating a soldier, but I shoved that aside. "You bastard. Put that fucking thing down!"

"Oh. Right." He pushed it into his belt holster, held out his hands placatingly. "But when I saw the strange car…"

"What? You thought you'd shoot the driver?"

"No. I thought I'd been followed. Get back in, and park her over there, down that track. Get her right into the bushes. Squeeze her in by mine."

I obeyed him, my heart thumping. I had been so glad to see him—even from the wrong end of a gun—that I would have parked her in the river if he'd told me to, and I tried to get a grip. I'd parted from him just over twenty-four hours ago. No need for all this teenage inner turmoil. I nosed the Peugeot as deep as I could into the foliage and switched her off.

Rayne was opening his driver's door, gesturing me to join him. "Over here. Quick."

I slid into the passenger seat. I didn't speak. I didn't know what was going on, and I didn't want him to know with what fervour I'd thrown myself out into the night at his summons, if it had even been one. But he shut his door—turned to me, said, "Thank God you're all right," and pressed his mouth to mine as if picking up his last kiss from where we'd left off.

This time it didn't make me laugh. Instead it made me wrap my hands round the back of his skull and hold him, while my whole body shivered in welcome. "Why would I not be?" I asked breathlessly, finally breaking away. "What's going on? That text was straight out of *Spooks*."

"I know. Sorry. It's an army-issue phone. I don't know how much they can monitor. And I didn't want to lead anyone to your house, so I…" He broke off and looked out the window at the Peugeot as if seeing it for the first time. "I called you here. Wow, Dan. Are those your new wheels?"

"Yes." I'd bought the car with perfect indifference, but suddenly I felt a bit defensive. She was mine, after all, the first I'd ever owned. "What's wrong with them?"

"Nothing. She's absolutely…average. Did we not fancy a drop-top baby Merc, then?"

"No. I couldn't have. I…" I shook myself, resisting the temptation to shake him. "Rayne, if you don't tell me what we're doing out here…"

"Yes. Sorry." To my surprise, he took both my hands. His grip was powerful and tender. "Listen," he said, looking straight at me. "If I was to ask you to forget about all this—the map, I mean, and everything you've been wondering about—and just go back to your life…"

I swallowed. "I'd consider it," I said unsteadily. "Because I think you'd be asking me for my own good. But if you've got any answers, about Jason…"

"You need to know."

"Yes. This… This is about him, isn't it?"

"I think so. Partly. How well did you know him?"

"What?" I shrugged, wishing fervently that Rayne and I were back by the waterfall in the sunlight, or anywhere away from this sudden brink. "He was my partner. I lived with him for three years. I thought I knew everything."

"About his family, his…"

"He didn't have any. His parents are dead. No brothers or sisters."

"And his background, his life before the university?"

I almost laughed. Jason *was* the university. He must have had a previous existence, I supposed—a paper round, hobbies—but in my mind he had always been so intimately linked to Salisbury's treasures, her intellectual inheritance, that I'd never thought to look beyond that phase of his existence. "I'm not sure he had one. What are you getting at?"

"I ran a computer archive search on the serial numbers we saw on the map. Almost everything on the system starting with those digits is classified, but—yeah, they're origination codes, to mark up where a document comes from. I didn't recognise them at first because they're old, from back in the seventies. Sunbeam, I don't want to screw with you, but that map was made—or photocopied, anyway—in the Hartcliffe Dean military labs."

I took my hands out of his. I didn't want to, but my grip was closing down, and I was afraid of hurting him. *Hartcliffe Dean.* I'd become quite good at casual mentions of the place over the years. I'd told Jase, right at the very beginning, and I'd told Rayne too, hadn't I, in the middle of one of our fights… Actually that was two mentions in three years. Perhaps I wasn't all that casual yet about that father whose loss I was only beginning now, in my late twenties, to realise and grieve over. The idea of Jason having any connection with that Cold War circus of horrors…

But he didn't. Nothing tangible, anyway—a copy of a useless map, that might or might not have been made there. "So what?" I said weakly. "What has that got to do with Jase?"

Rayne reached a hand to my shoulder. "Dan, stop here. Go home, and I'll sort this out. You don't need to know."

"Yeah, I do. I'm fine." *Because whatever you've found out, it can't be true. Or there'll be some explanation for it, which I'll know as soon as you tell me the rest.*

"There was one article that came up when I ran the search. I don't know why they hadn't classified it—maybe because it had appeared in the press, just a small-circulation academic pamphlet, but… A group of the Hartcliffe Dean scientists being congratulated on a biochemistry breakthrough. They'd synthesised an agent that would—that would bring down the human immune system without the need for chemo. They were billing it as a medical advance, but…"

"Rayne. *What* does this have to do with—?"

"The lead scientist was called Jason Ross."

I choked. Rayne was looking away from me now, out through the windshield. He looked as he had on that night at Stonehenge when I had first seen him, stern and unfathomable.

"All right," I managed, when my throat was clear. "Why *are* you screwing with me? There must be dozens of men with that name in the area. Why…"

"He worked with a biochemist called Lucas Gray. Gray was a computer genius too—did groundbreaking work in gene sequencing. And Ross's partner was called Anderson. Malcolm Anderson."

I got out of the car. I had thought the night air would help but it was just as thick and unbreathable out here. I heard the efforts of my own lungs, and I saw Rayne get out too and come round the bonnet to hold my shoulders. "Dan."

"But you said it was—a medical breakthrough, right? It would be invaluable as a way of treating people for—for leukaemia, and cancer, without using chemo…"

"Yeah, but we don't *have* an invaluable thing for treating leukaemia, do we? You know what happens to medical breakthroughs in military labs." His grip tightened. "Listen. The article was called *The Salisbury Key*. It's not an artefact, or some wonderful theory about stone circles. It's something that keys down human resistance to infection. Any infection. Any bloody biological agent you like."

I tore away from him. The woods and the pale silver sky tried to upend around me, and I grabbed at a tree trunk for support.

"No. Jason would never be involved with something like that. Not even accidentally—if he was working at Hartcliffe, he'd know what it could do."

"You told me a while back you lost your dad because of something that had been done to him there. You said it was connected to a bioweaponry test. How did he die?"

I don't know. I only know what they told me. Christ, I was only six! But that was bollocks, wasn't it? Six or not, I'd spent six years in the same house with him, watching him fade. And I remembered—oh, so much. My head was full of flashing, rewinding images. My ma tried to keep me away, but I adored him, and it was like trying to peel away a baby monkey from his side. She gave up eventually and let me stick around for the doctors' visits, took me with her on hospital visits. *It does no harm. He's too little to understand.* But I did. No one could cure him because no one could work out what was wrong with him. His colds turned into flu and then pneumonia. He'd get a tiny cut and his whole arm would swell up. It was long before AIDS. The doctors would confront my mother in our living room, in hospital corridors, scratching their head. *We can't find any answers, Mrs. Logan. It's as if he has no resistance to infection at all.*

I turned round and, for the third time in my short acquaintance with Rayne, did my best to thump him in the face. This time he didn't block me or resist in any way—he just let me fall into his arms. "I'm sorry," he whispered fiercely into my hair. "I'm sorry."

"Fuck off!" It ripped out of me on a high-pitched sob, and I struggled to free myself, coughing. "What the *hell* do you know? Why should I even believe you, about...about this fucking article?"

"Oh God, why would I make something like that up? But I did try to print it. When I got to the printer it was gone, and ever since then…" He held me through my next hopeless attempt to wrench away. "Ever since then, someone's been following me. That's why we're out here playing spooks in the bloody wood."

"What are you saying—he was only with me because he…did something that helped kill my father?"

"I don't know why he was with you. Because he loved you, I should think." A car engine whispered in the distance. Rayne tensed and clasped me hard, hushing me against his shoulder until the sound died.

***

He gave me time to calm down. He produced a box of tissues from the back of the car and silently handed them to me, and I realised with shame how many times I'd broken down in front of him. As if the times when he was around were the only occasions when I could, as if he earthed the lightning in my storms. Sitting in the passenger seat, I blew my nose and tried to think dispassionately about any part of what he had just said to me. "What… What do you mean, you've been followed?"

"Just that. Fellworth isn't crowded. You can always find empty corridors, rec rooms. Not today. There's been two of the same faces knocking round in all of them." He absently picked a piece of bark off the sleeve of my jacket. "I didn't realise till I set out to come to you earlier. Looked in my rearview, and there they were. So I went to Sainsbury's, let them tail me round the aisles while I bought some apples and a newspaper, then drove straight back to the base."

I almost laughed. He'd looked damn comfortable with a pistol in his hand tonight. I couldn't quite picture him swinging a wire shopping basket. "How did you get out?"

"Dumb luck and stealth. Somebody called an emergency exercise at RAF Norwood up the road. It mobilised half our lot, and I just drove out past the gates in the chaos."

"Jesus. You took a hell of a risk. Why?"

He didn't say anything—just looked at me as if I were a little bit stupid, and after a moment I dropped my gaze. *You took it for me. Like it was obvious; the only thing to do.* "Won't they notice you're gone?"

"Yes. Soon. So what we have to decide is, are we going to drop this, like a pair of sensible men, and go home? I can convince McCade I just went AWOL for a shag. He'd believe that." A tiny smile flickered at the corner of his mouth. "We can redeem that by making it true. Or are we going to run around in the night like idiots, trying to find out what's going on here?"

I shook my head. Option one sounded good. Even with the aftermath of outraged tears making my breath scrape, even with a heart now so full of grief and confusion my rib cage felt too small to hold it, I wanted him. Wanted him the more for those things. "Don't," I said faintly. "Anyway, where would we run?"

He sighed. "Those marker numbers on the map... They were pretty specific. I wish they hadn't been. I wish I could tell you I don't bloody know."

"I wouldn't settle for that. Rayne, I'm asking you, okay?"

"Okay. They indicate one specific lab in the Hartcliffe complex. In the old part—it's all mostly closed down now, but that bit's near derelict. Minimum security. It would be a place to start."

I blew my nose again and sat up straight. "Right. Here it is. Jase wanted to tell me something. Just me. There was nothing in his last instructions about buggering up the lives of nice young soldiers. I'll go on my own. And you can get back to your bunk before they court-martial you, or whatever the punishment is for this kind of thing."

"Oh—firing squad at least, I should think. Dan, you really are a pillock sometimes. Do you think I'd let you go alone?"

"Well, that's flattering—and touching—but how are you going to stop me?"

"By not telling you where the lab is, for a kickoff," he said. I stared at him. Yes, that would do it. He was right—I could be as dumb as gravel. "And I've been trained to withstand torture," he added after a second, dark eyes kindling with mischief, "so don't bother."

Not all forms of it. I flashed back to the sight of him naked on a pale blue sheet, strung out and shuddering, pleading for release. "Great," I said. "Look, it's not that I don't want you there. But all this is my problem. I don't want you taking any shit for it."

"Ah, shut up." He pressed his fingers briefly to my mouth, reinforcing the order, then ran them down the front of my sweater, making my skin tingle, my nipples contract with longing to be touched. "Good. You dressed in dark gear. We'd better get going if we're gonna do this."

***

I kept an eye on my passenger wing mirror, angled so I would notice the headlights of any pursuit. I could see Rayne constantly checking the rearview. My palms damped. This trip would be hard to disguise as a grocery run if we picked up any interested followers. But the road was mostly long straight stretches and remained empty, unspooling itself in the moonlight behind us.

Signs for Hartcliffe Dean appeared. The route was unfamiliar to me. I'd never had reason to go there, and Jason detested the place, giving it a wide berth when our travels took us out in that direction. Nausea stirred in my gut, and I tried to think of something else. Of Rayne, who every second was driving farther from a chance of returning to his barracks unnoticed.

"Listen," I said. "You trust Colonel McCade, right? If you took this to him, wouldn't he help us?"

"He was gonna be my first port of call after you." Rayne glanced at me sideways. "I did tell you. That was the—"

"The deal. I know. I agreed. So…"

"So when I went past his office, his aide said he'd taken emergency leave. He'll be gone for a week at least."

I sat and watched the fields and farms flash by for nearly a minute. I wasn't a suspicious man, I knew. Events of great moment had apparently been transpiring all around me since my early childhood, and I'd never batted an eyelid. I'd taken people's surface, the parts they chose to turn towards me, for the whole thing.

"Rayne," I said, hating my new wariness. "The dean went on sick leave yesterday."

"What, did I grab him by his vintage-tweed collar too hard? Oh." He missed a gear on a corner, and shoved the Audi into second, shooting me a dark look. "Don't even go there. McCade's not your fourth man. He's good all the way through."

"Yeah. Of course. Sorry. I know he's your friend."

"No, he's my CO. It's different. But… You know what the bastard of it is? After I found out he was gone, I couldn't think of a single other person I could trust with this. No one who wouldn't take it to their senior officer, just the way…" He paused, shook his head. "The way I would. Not a single friend. And I've banged on to you about brotherhood, the—the family I chose…"

I took this in, watching him. He had the car running smoothly again, but his hands were tight on the wheel. "Most of your mates are still over in Iraq, then?" I asked cautiously.

"I thought so. But ever since what happened to Reg McCarthy, I'm beginning to think that he had the mates, not me. It's my fault too. I shoved everyone to arm's length after that."

"Reg McCarthy was the name of…"

"The lad I killed when I screwed up that IED disposal, yeah. I know my unit thought I should've taken a demotion, not an easy ride home. It's weird. I…I haven't even said his name, till now."

I took his hand. At first he resisted my attempt to lift it from the wheel, but then he surrendered it. "The bomb killed him," I whispered. "Not you." I turned his hand in mine and kissed its palm.

"You soft bastard," Rayne said, but it wasn't a reproach, and his voice broke lightly over the words.

Chapter Twelve

For me, the weirdest thing about breaking into a military installation was the fact that it felt normal. Standing on the verge with Rayne, looking up assessingly at the wire-topped wall, I had a sense of familiar ground. The road that led past the complex was deserted at this hour, the Audi tucked safely off behind some derelict farm buildings a couple of hundred yards away. Which wasn't to say that the whole scene couldn't break into klaxon-shattered hell any second. What we'd do then, I couldn't imagine. Couldn't imagine running. I felt like a stone that had been picked up and thrown, as if I had only one possible direction left in me.

I hadn't seen any cameras along this stretch, and couldn't hear the low-level hum of electricity from the wires. That was good. I'd been jolted off walls with my hair on end a couple of times in the course of archaeological investigations, and it wasn't any fun. "Doesn't look too bad," I said, and saw Rayne turn to me.

"Oh really, Commando Logan? What would you know?"

"Anti-climb paint. That top wire's barbed but not live. We just need a leg-up, and…" I glanced around. For miles to the south, the peaceful Wiltshire farmlands dreamed in the moonlight. I could hear distant curlews, and owls conversing across the stretches of corn-rippled fields. Nearer at hand, a lay-by on the far side of the road was full of fly-tipped junk. "And something from that lot should do the trick. Come on."

He followed me across to the far verge. "Where did you learn your field skills? SAS boot camp?"

"I learned them from Jason. He never liked me treasure hunting, but he was bloody good at getting us in to find the stuff."

"Treasure hunting?"

"Well. Not that bad. We just sometimes had a difference of opinion over what ought to be rescued and what should stay put. Me, I think if an artefact's about to be buried under a mudslide or blown up in a border war…" I shut up, realising I had started to recall without pain one of my old debates with Jase. I wasn't sure if I was ready for that.

I surveyed the mess of mouldy carpet rolls, bin bags and abandoned fridges. There were a couple of crates too. Rayne saw them at the same time as I did, and we moved in synch to collect them.

"He never did take no for an answer," I found myself continuing. "The search was enough for him, never mind if we found anything or not. He was full of life and curiosity. You know what?" He paused in pulling up a wooden pallet from a ditch and looked at me. "Whatever we find in there, it's going to exonerate him, not incriminate him. He could never be involved in a bioweapons project. He just wasn't capable."

"Okay. Good. Let's go and find that out."

We propped the crates against the wall, where a concrete post ran up to support the wires. They were light, but the pallets, rammed against the base at a diagonal, served as struts on either side. Rayne began tugging at some dried-out undergrowth tangled among the brambles nearby, and I went back to grab another couple of boxes and supports. By the time I got back, he had camouflaged our makeshift ladder neatly and was watching me in what looked like mild amusement.

"What?" I asked, smiling helplessly back at him.

"I was going to try and catch you out, but I don't think it's gonna work."

"Try me."

"What's the last thing we do, before leaping over fences into unknown terrain?"

I dumped the boxes at his feet. "Secure our swift exit, of course. Here. I'll go first. Pass these up to me, and I'll drop them down the other side."

***

We waited for a while once we were over the fence. That was another rule of good trespass—a brief hiatus, listening to the air. If you'd been rumbled, you usually knew about it soon enough, and your best bet was a quick scramble out the same way you came in.

Rayne's shoulder was pressing mine, his warmth as vivid as blood in the cool night. "All right," he said eventually. "I don't think we triggered anything. Come on."

"Do you know your way around this place?"

"They brought us here once during orientation, but they only showed us the bits where the good guys work—the disaster-recovery specialists and the HazMat doctors." He led us to the edge of a long, straight track gleaming coldly in the moonlight. "From the plans I saw, the older labs are laid out in a simple grid, starting from this southeast corner. We should be able to find the right block by counting in."

"Is there much surveillance?"

"Minimal, probably, this far out from the main buildings. But stick to the shadows and the tree line. And if we run into trouble, leg it and let me talk us out of it, okay?"

Bugger that, I thought, but kept it to myself. My pulse was surging, my vision brilliantly clear. No matter how grim a mission this might be, I was at last in motion, forging a track towards answers. To the place, I still believed, where I could lift Jason's memory intact out of all this mess, honour and restore him. And I would no sooner abandon Rayne, this living friend, than my dead one.

I followed him in silence, farther and farther away from the low white structures that looked functional and new, to the part of the complex where the roads began to crack, their verges encroaching. Here the buildings looked more like prefabs or sheds. Between them the trees were making a comeback, heavy dark branches overhanging the roofs, roots lifting up through the old pavements. Rayne was softly counting off the rows as we passed them. The lab we were looking for was H16 on the grid, he'd confided in me once we were safely over the fence and it was too late for me to get rid of him. Soon I grasped the layout, and I tried not to let excitement mount in me as we drew closer.

Row H was a long single building with a corrugated roof, paralleled on both sides by others exactly like it. All were in darkness. Many of their window panes were cracked, others cobwebbed to obscurity. The doors to each unit were numbered, spray-and-stencil, paint faded and peeling. H14, H15...

Rayne stopped by the next door and gestured me to his side. "Okay. One last time—forget this and go home."

"Official army advisory?"

"I'm not sure they'd let me give one anymore, but—yeah, I think it would be."

"I'd like to take it. I can't—not now."

"All right." He pushed the door, and it opened unresisting at his touch.

An empty grey space lay beyond it, and at that moment I felt a corresponding blank open up in my heart. Rayne hadn't needed to worry. This place had been forgotten, and for good reason. It had long ago been stripped of its secrets. Rayne stepped cautiously inside. I saw him move instantly to get his back against the open door, watched his businesslike visual sweep. If he'd been with his comrades, broaching an enemy stronghold, he'd have turned to the next man and said *clear*. He didn't have to. The moon was setting, low enough now in the west to throw a tired pewter light into the room. The only furnishings in it were the ones it would have been more trouble to remove than leave intact—a long bench built into the wall, and a big industrial sink. Both were swathed in cobwebs and dust. There wasn't so much as a test tube left to commemorate Jase, Dean Anderson or their discovery.

I watched Rayne. I thought that it would be good for me now to do so, to pick up, if I could, a little soldierly resolve. If I could view this as a mission gone bust, not the end of the line and my hopes, the pain in my throat might subside. Less easily daunted than I was, he was silently quartering the empty space, crouching by the sink unit, pushing experimentally at the stripped floorboards. Trying to take my cue, I made my way along my own featureless wall, seeing nothing but spiders which shot out of view as my shadow brushed them, but a moment later I heard Rayne sigh, and I turned to see him standing up, dusting off his camos. "Ah, Dan, I'm sorry. Looks like there's fuck-all here."

That was a relief. I could stop being positive. Neutral would do, as he was. I pushed my hands into the pockets of my jeans. "Don't worry. It was a good try."

He made a rueful face at me. "Yeah. A very good try. You're gutted, aren't you?"

"No. I'll be okay. I just—"

He lifted a hand. "Dan. Hush."

I fell silent at once. All I could hear was the suddenly quickened thud of my pulse. I met his eyes. After a moment he shrugged, relaxing. "Sorry. Jumpy, looks like. I thought I…"

A beam of white light strafed the room. Instinctively I flattened myself against the wall behind me. Rayne whispered, succinctly, "Fuck!", and a second later I heard what he had—the soft scrape of oncoming steps. Voices, too, in a low murmur.

Alone, I might have just walked out and met my fate. My insides felt empty and dry. What did it matter if I ended up facing some kind of firing squad? The game, whatever I'd thought I'd been playing, was up.

But I wasn't alone. Rayne was watching me, compassion and alarm mixing in his face, as if he could read my sudden loss of momentum. "Dan, quick. Get down, and come over here to me."

It made sense. He had more cover, deeper shadows. Belatedly it hit me that betraying myself would drop him in it too, and if I had nothing left to lose, he was still a soldier. I listened carefully, wondering if I had time to make the move.

"Dan, now. They're coming."

I had reached out a hand to steady myself. Beneath my fingers was the thin edge of a sheet of board or plywood. More than one—a small stack of them, leaning upright against the wall. Irrelevant, useless as cover or defence, I'd ignored them. But behind them, when I reached farther…

Yes, the frame of a door. The voices and footsteps were closer now. I didn't dare speak, and I wasn't sure if Rayne would see or obey my frantic signal: *no, over here!* Torch beams crisscrossed in the dust-glittered air. I shrank back as far as I could into shadow, then jumped violently as a warm grip closed on my wrist. "Jesus. I never even saw you move."

"Good. Maybe they didn't either. What have you got?"

"A door. Into the next lab, maybe. Help me shift this stuff."

"No. Just ease it forward. If it hid this door from us…"

"It might from them." I leaned to help him. "Reckon we triggered an alarm?"

"Dunno. Might be a routine patrol. If not…"

"We're screwed?"

"Royally," he confirmed, flashing me a brief grin. I saw for an instant a gleam of pure silver in his beautiful lupine eyes, and then he was shoving me gently ahead of him, through the door which mercifully opened at my touch and swallowed us both into darkness.

Christ. Utter black. I bumped into a wall, and on my recoil hit another, barely an arm's length away. For the first time fear boiled up in me, although logically I knew that I must have simply led us through into a cupboard. I hated confined spaces, and the pitch-black wouldn't let me get my bearings or establish in how tight a coffin I was trapped. I turned again, and this time collided with warm flesh and bone.

"Ssh. It's all right."

I clutched at him, as hard as he was holding me then harder. I must have been bruising him, but he didn't flinch. "Sorry," I whispered. "Claustrophobic."

"That's my brave soldier. Fearlessly raids Hartcliffe Dean, then freaks out in the broom closet."

I shook with laughter, pressing my mouth to his shoulder to keep quiet. Through the wall, I could still hear an occasional whisper of movement, but it seemed that the voices and footsteps were fading.

A sharp metallic rasp. I recognised it, having noted it without realising on the way in. The sound the door to lab H16 made when pushed gently from outside. Rayne's hands tightened on my shoulders. I could feel his heart beating, in diametric counterpoint to my own. His breath came and went against my neck. He shifted slightly, turning us, and despite my disorientation I knew that he was moving to shield me, interposing himself between me and door to our refuge.

"No," I breathed, and we locked tight together, a silent, motionless trial of strength to equal strength.

"Nothing in here. Let's go."

The voice came from three feet away, directly beyond the plywood boards. I felt Rayne's tiny, whole-body muscular convulsion, his grasp on me stilling my own helpless jump. The outer door creaked and rasped again, and then there was silence.

This time I did let him bear me back against the wall. I went gladly, a deep exhalation leaving me as my lungs were crushed. I sought him in the blackness, my fingertips brushing his face, guiding his kiss to my mouth. He moaned, and in it I heard all my own shocked prohibitions: *Not here, not now, for God's sake. What the fuck are we doing?* But here and now were all we had. I understood that now. I hadn't found my reasons to explain away a death—I'd found life, rich and real, ready to lay itself down to defend me.

"Don't!" I whispered fiercely. "Don't you dare be my bloody human shield, Rayne."

"Sorry. Instincts."

"Well, next time keep 'em to yourself." I seized his backside. "God, come here."

It didn't take long. Forcing a hand between our bodies, I undid his zip and my own, and felt him fumble my pants down. My arse scraped the woodwork behind me under the impact of his first big thrust, and I stifled a cry. He was caught up in his underwear. I stilled him for long enough to lift his cock free, then let it drive between my thighs. Mine was trapped and getting deliciously crushed against his belly.

"Daniel," he whispered, and I nodded, pulling back the fabric of his T-shirt to kiss his shoulder, as if for the first time I was really finding him, really at last being found.

Our movements were small, tight, silent. We weren't rocking lab H16. The patrol could have come back and stood outside the door, I thought, and heard nothing. I hit the peak first and clung to him, repressing cry after cry against his neck, a second later feeling him jerk and go passionately still.

"Yes," I gasped, clenching my thighs on the wet heat bursting between them. "Yes, love. There." Pushing my hips forward, I ground the rest of it out of him, surging again myself in unexpected, near-painful coda. "Christ…!"

***

Rayne's torch, when we were sure enough of safety to switch it on, revealed a scene of such devastation that we both broke into brief laughter. He had cobwebs in his hair, and a bruise to the side of his mouth. I'd ripped his T-shirt at the shoulder seam. Looking down, I saw that I was no better off, wet with his come and my own, the top button of my jeans popped off and gone God knew where. I remembered that I'd called him *love* and blushed in the torchlight, wondering if I'd crossed a line. But he didn't seem fazed, was smoothing dusty sweat off my face with his fingers, planting unsteady kisses in their wake. "God's sake, Dan. Are you all right?"

I nodded. "Yeah. You?"

"More or less. What do you do to me?"

"Could ask you the same thing. As soon as we stop, I damn well want to start again."

"Well, we can't, you nutcase. That was dangerous enough." His mouth found mine—harsh, almost punitive, then tender, lifting away reluctantly. "Where the hell are we, then? Gay Narnia?"

Our refuge was a storage cupboard, barely tall enough for us both to stand up in, and about three foot by three. Shakily I looked around. At first I thought it barren as the rest of this place, as thoroughly stripped down and abandoned...

"Dan."

I saw it too. In the farthest corner, wedged beneath a shelf. One dust-coated cardboard box.

It was a thing that had been left behind because it didn't matter. It wouldn't have mattered to me, if I'd been clearing this place out years ago with a dozen others like it to finish before the end of my shift. Not a locked filing cabinet or anything else that would draw attention by an air of secrecy. Just a box, open to inspection and so left uninspected. In it were a few sheets of crumpled newspaper, yellowed with age, and underneath those were other papers, folded, inconspicuous.

Rayne and I unpacked these, kneeling on the floor back in the lab. Without a skinful of endorphins, I couldn't bear the cupboard's confines, and we couldn't risk the torch out here, so we did it by moonlight, glancing at and discarding sheet after sheet. They were nothing—unfilled requisition slips, bits of carbon paper. And, carelessly pushed in among them, a sheet with a few lines on it that only a few people in the world would recognise as a map. It was Rayne who found it. He unfolded it and handed it wordlessly to me.

It wasn't the original of Jason's. Just like that one, it looked like it had been lifted and blown up from an OS. It was only a slightly better copy—good enough, even in the cobweb light, to show a tiny circled dot on the moors at the edge of the Bronze Age settlement.

We made our way back to the fence, not through the grid of roads by which we'd come but threading the narrow gaps between buildings, then out into the scrubby woods that lined the perimeter. Typically, now that I had what I wanted, I was far from sure I wanted it anymore. Where would I be if I could have what I wanted right now? Not here, ducking under thick foliage, struggling to keep silent, listening tensely for pursuit. Not between one risk and the next, in this night which surely should be showing signs of dawn by now but remained implacably black around its moonlight. Maybe on a flight with Rayne, heading for somewhere neither of us had ever seen, our only luggage our carry-on rucksacks. Or, more domestically, entwined with him in a warm bed, shagged out and sliding into sleep.

"Hoi, Dan! Here, you dozy git."

I came to a stop. Rayne was no longer at my side. I turned and went to help him pull the camouflaging branches away from our stack of exit crates, mercifully untouched where we'd left them. "Sorry," I said. "A bit distracted."

"Yeah, I bet." Together we built the ladder. It wasn't as good as the one we'd made to come in—had to collapse under a kick from the top, and hopefully look like rubbish, not evidence of an escape. Climbing it was a trickier job. Rayne sent me up ahead of him, and I got a precarious grip on the crossbar and half-hauled him up after me. "You okay?" he asked, getting a handhold. "Still want to go through with this?"

Not at all. Don't want mysteries or even answers anymore. I think I just want you. I made a clumsy job of scrambling down the other side and stepped clear to watch while he smiled at me and dispensed with the boxes to jump the ten-foot drop with easy grace. "Bloody showoff," I observed, and we picked up the crates and pallets and began to carry them back across the road. When I moved, the map rustled faintly in the pocket of my jeans. "That patrol back there wasn't random, was it?"

"No. Pretty specific, I'd say."

"Right. Then someone—whoever took the printout of that article, probably—cares enough about this to try to follow you, and to alert someone here to check on that lab tonight."

"Yeah. Not somebody who could move openly, though, or the whole place would've been on an alert."

I slung the crate into the ditch it had come from. "So what happens, do you reckon, if we just drop it and go home?"

He looked at me. I had once again the restful sensation that it wasn't just *at* but benignly *into*, as if I would seldom have to struggle to explain anything to him. "Maybe nothing," he said. "Or maybe whatever your Jason was so scared of that he had to take his own life."

I nodded. *My Jason*. Hearing him so called set fresh pain in my throat and chest. "He tried to get me out of the country, you know," I said suddenly, the memory surfacing. "His whole career spent here, and then he wanted us to go off to bloody Thailand. It was the night before he died."

"Okay. Worth checking into then, at the very least." Rayne's hand came to rest warmly in the small of my back, steering me into the cover of the roadside trees. We set off towards the car. "He loved the hell out of you, didn't he?"

"Yeah. He did."

"And you're worried about what you called me back there."

I swallowed dryly. I was worried about half a dozen things. But he was right—that was one of them. Just not for the reasons he thought. *Yes, love. There…*

"It's okay," he went on, before I could formulate a response. "Forget it. What goes in the closet stays in the closet. Heat of the moment, that was all."

I watched him slip ahead of me through the shadows of the hawthorns. I was no longer sure of anything of the sort.

***

The plain.

It was where I had started my life with Jase, and the place we had both always returned to. It had stretched, green-gold and implacable, from the very roots of my life. My earliest memory, seen between slats of our garden fence, or unseen rather because always there, a matrix. Tonight I was going to finish something against that backdrop. In sight of that ancient witness.

"Rayne," I said, and he glanced at me questioningly, breaking his watch of the road and the rearview mirror. "When we get through with this, whatever it is…I don't want to come back here."

"Okay." He continued his straight shoot down the Fellworth road. There was no cover here. Anyone who wanted to track us down could do so. The only way to do it was fast. "What do you fancy, then? Sabbatical in the south of France? Egypt?"

He was talking to distract me. Draining adrenaline had taken my sense of reality with it. I sat curled up in the passenger seat, the map held loosely in my grasp. "Don't know. Sounds pathetic, but I never had to decide before."

"He didn't let you?"

"Oh, no. He always did. At least he thought he did, and he convinced me too. I suppose he just swept me up. Don't get me wrong—it was all wonderful."

"Yeah. Yes, I'm sure it was. If you had to choose one place, though…"

I thought about it. Despite our circumstances, the sense of sands running out, I felt as if I finally had time. I could see all the weeks and the months of my life with Jason unfolding, paper flowers in water, translucent and painless. "South Korea," I said. "Kyon Kam, to be exact."

"That's North Korea. Occasionally, anyway. Sounds like a blast."

I stole a glance at him. He was expressionless, but I was starting to be able to read the glimmer of his eyes. "Yeah, right. But that's where I would go. Which is weird, because it was one of the only places me and Jase found anything to fight about."

"I see why you want to go back. What's at Kyon?"

"The most amazing Buddhist artwork and relics you ever saw. They'd be South Korean national treasures, if the government gave a stuff about them. As things stand, any day now Kim Jong-il will disappear them. I'd go back and rescue those, and screw the politics."

"And Jason thought…"

"They should be left on site at any cost, if we couldn't get them to the Seoul museums."

"Whereas you'd just—what? Swing in there on a vine and nick them?"

"Hell, yes. Better culturally appropriated and under glass in the British Museum than rotting in the jungle or melted down for currency by some paramilitary thug."

"I see. The Elgin Marbles aren't going anywhere fast if you have anything to do with it, then."

"No. Nonsense. This is the exact same argument I used to have with Jase. Athens has perfectly good facilities for looking after its treasures—of course the Elgins should go home. All I'm concerned about is preservation, whatever that..."

The sign for the army base whisked past the car, a spectral finger pointing in moonlight. I couldn't believe how quickly we'd got here—or that I'd been drawn into a debate, in these circumstances, on the ethics of conservation. I looked at Rayne to see if he'd deliberately chosen the line of questioning that would most effectively divert me, but he was innocently scanning the road ahead.

I was almost back at my starting point. From here I could see the whole landscape of my first encounter with Jason. With his love and with his madness. "Stop anywhere around here," I said. "I reckon we need to be about ten yards north by northwest of the hut circles I showed you."

"He got close, didn't he?"

I nodded, my mouth dry. "Yeah, poor bastard. He was right on top of it."

Rayne pulled up, by a stand of windbreak conifers this time, without real hope of concealment but taking what was there. I got slowly out into the moonlight. Here the circle closed. Jason wasn't here to protect or drag me with him into the minefield. I could feel a weird strength springing up in me. I didn't need to be sheltered or sacrificed. I could love his memory, but I could stand alone.

I felt a warmth at my shoulder. I didn't have to—not tonight. I turned to smile at Rayne. "Come on. Whatever's here, let's find it. Then we can go home."

Chapter Thirteen

I don't know what I'd thought I'd been going to dig with. I had my satchel with me, automatically grabbed as I left the house, and there was always a small trowel in there, but that was all. Rayne and I stood looking into the Audi's boot for a minute. We picked up and discarded the tyre iron and the sharp-edged plastic case that held the warning triangle. Then I smiled at him, shrugged, and we set out anyway.

Boundary fence, track marked on both sides with fluorescent ping-pong bat circles. A crater of torn-out earth where Rayne's land mine had gone off. We passed these memorials in silence. They had become like bookmarks in my mind, springboards for association, start and end points. A very faint light was gathering in the east. Behind us, the western horizon was beginning to eat the moon. We were able to see, enough to make our way and stay within the safe area, but we stayed close, touching one another often. A steadying hand, a moment's guidance over rough ground, given and received.

And, after all, no digging was going to be required. I stood at the point marked on the old map, and I looked at the land around me as Jason had taught me to do. The hut circles made their ancient raindrop patterns in the turf a short distance behind me. I crouched down. I put my hands on the earth, and I felt rather than saw the barely perceptible line that ran from my fingertips to the northwest hut.

"Here," I said, and Rayne came to kneel beside me. "Surface mark."

"I don't see… Oh, wait a bit. Yes. A mark of what, though?"

"Not sure, but…" I got up, and we made our way carefully along the line, barely little more than a shadow in the turf. I scrambled into the brambles whose growth had half-filled the hut circle. They tore my skin but I didn't feel it, and had to leave it to Rayne to wince for me, call me an idiot and reach to pull them back. Some of the ancient flagstones remained. One of them was unusually large, and the growth of moss around it was not so established as the others. As if a long time ago but within living memory it might have been disturbed. "I think it's a souterrain."

"A what?"

"A tunnel, a crawl-way. In Cornwall they call them fogous. I never heard of one in Wiltshire. Will you help me lift this stone?"

His hands joined mine at the edge of the flag. It wasn't hard to lever up—one corner was hollow, as if designed to be grasped. As if this stone had been chosen and fitted to its purpose. It was bloody heavy, though, and I wondered if the last man to lift it had struggled alone, or if he had been blessed and redeemed as I was by the presence of such a companion as Summer Rayne.

Our eyes met as the packed earth crumbled and the slab came free. He was watching me calmly. "Are you all right then, Indiana Jones?"

We balanced the stone on its edge for a moment, then set it aside. "I have no idea."

"Not surprised." He leaned forward, and we both looked down into the gaping darkness the entry stone had revealed. "Before we go plunging down into that—which is, I assume, what you want—do you feel like telling me what the fuck a fogou was for?"

"Well—that's just the point. No one really knows. Their exits are tiny, easy to block, so they probably weren't for defence, and they're too hard to access as storage space. Maybe they were ritual chambers, places to go to and commune with the spirits of the earth. That's what Jason thought."

"And is that what we're gonna do? Go and commune?"

"*We're* doing nothing. I don't know how sound the roof is. Stay out here and keep watch."

"Right. Because you were so happy in the last tiny space you wedged yourself into. You really want to be down there alone?"

I stared into the pit. I was an archaeologist. I knew the scents and dankness of the earth—no need to be afraid of the hollow, whispering tomb ahead of me now. And, claustrophobe or not, I'd crawled through every souterrain in the Southwest with Jason a couple of summers ago. "No," I said. "But nevertheless, stay put. I'm okay. This is what I do."

He handed me the torch. Playing its beam round the hole, I could see what looked like a narrow chute entry leading into a larger chamber. How large, I couldn't tell, and feet first wouldn't help me if the passage narrowed down again. Doing this in broad daylight in a sunny cornfield, with Jase laughing and bribing me with the prospect of a good pub lunch if I survived, had felt a hell of a lot different. Taking a deep breath, I braced both hands on the sides of the tunnels and lay down on my stomach. Briefly I felt Rayne's grip on my belt, and then he let me go.

The tunnel plunged me down a short slide on skin-peeling gravel, then disgorged me. I dropped fell three or four feet through empty air and landed with a crash on a flat, smooth surface. I nearly broke my elbow in the landing, but better that than damage the torch, and I rolled onto my back, cradling the light. "Ouch! Sod it. Don't worry, I'm…"

But there was no need to tell him. Scrambling up onto my knees, I saw him dropping lithely down into the chamber. Feet first, not arse-over-tit, of course, and as if he did it every day. Torchlight and shadows painted him in tiger stripes. I fought not to let his beauty quench my anger. "Fuck's sake! Don't I do what you tell *me*?"

He appeared to give it thought. I did, too, and realised I'd chosen thin ice from which to reproach him.

"Not so far," he said cheerfully. "Nice place you've got here. Is it a—what did you say? A souterrain?"

I looked around me, rubbing my elbow. The chamber we were standing in—and I *could* stand, I realised to my relief, though I found the ceiling by banging my head off it—was circular, about three yards across. The walls were packed mud, dry and clean, and above us rose an elegantly corbelled roof. I thought of Newgrange and the superbly preserved Stone Age village at Skara Brae.

"Yes. I think so. It's a massive one, though—the biggest I saw outside of Carn Euny in Cornwall." Suddenly the beauty of it, the freshness, made me forget everything else. "Look at it! This isn't Bronze Age. It's Neolithic, five thousand years old if it's a day. It could stand for another five. My God, they built to last!" I turned round, reached up to feel at the corbelling, sealed without mortar to withstand millennia of rain. It was bone dry. "Beautiful…"

"Yes. Gorgeous."

That sounded sincere. Looking back, I smiled at Rayne, glad that he could see it too. But he was looking at me, not the ceiling, and just for a moment I could have melted to my knees on the floor, in the pleasure of being his focus, the relief of having him here, disobedient and steadfast.

"Stop it, soldier," I murmured. "We've got things to do."

"Yeah. This place looks jam-packed with amusements."

"For me it is. It certainly would have been for Jason. God— something like this would almost justify him searching so hard, so close to the Stonehenge complex and Avebury."

"Almost?"

"Yeah." I went to the chamber's perimeter and began to explore its smooth walls, shining the torch beam sideways along them to try and pick out irregularities, any sign of function. I was thinking of sleepless nights, feverish lovemaking. The slow slide into disarray, over the past months, of a strong, sane man. "Not enough. There must be something else here."

Wordlessly we divided the chamber between us. Rayne's experience in his field had made him just as good at a fingertip search as I had learned to be in mine. I eased the torch into a niche in the corbelling, and by its downcast light we worked in silence, taking chamber wall and flooring inch by inch. Touch would often reveal what vision missed—a tiny give in a flagstone, a softness in otherwise hard-packed earth...

Yes. I closed my eyes, held my breath. I was on tiptoe by the chamber's north wall. There had been something, so fleeting I'd brushed straight on over it, but now I reached back, gently urgent, to find the place again.

"Rayne! Here."

He came to stand beside me, unhitching the torch on his way and shining it into the space between the edge of the corbelled roof and the wall, where I had felt the slight roughness, a breaking up of the ancient silky mud. "The wall's a bit softer here. It's been disturbed."

"Really?" he asked. I glanced round and saw him step close to see for himself, eyes bright and intrigued. "Yeah. You're right."

"I can't believe anybody would do this. Anybody with the knowledge to find this place, anyway. They'd have to know the value of keeping it intact, not digging around under the stonework, weakening the structure…"

"All right. Have a fit about it later, sunbeam. What now?"

"I'm going to dig in there myself." He lifted an eyebrow at me, and I said defensively, "Well, I can't do any *more* damage, can I? Will you fetch me the trowel from my bag?"

"You brought your trowel?"

"Yes. Always. You never know."

"No, I don't suppose you do."

It didn't take me long to dislodge enough of the broken earth to find the direction and dimensions of the niche that had been dug here. It was recent, or relatively so. The earth had begun to pack down, but not to bind itself under the pressures that had kept the souterrain walls in one piece. And I didn't understand it. Here was a perfect, watertight chamber beneath the ground, a beautiful hiding place for any treasure or horror you cared to name—and yet someone had violated it, scraped a hollow upwards and outwards, compromised its perfect seal.

I worked as carefully as I could despite the damage, Rayne holding the torch and brushing aside the earth as I trowelled it aside. Something cold and slick touched the back of my hand, and I snatched it back, flinching. "Christ!"

"What's the matter?"

"Shine the beam here. Oh, sorry. It's just roots."

I ignored his faint snort of laughter.

"I don't understand. This goes right out under the edge of the roof stones, almost to surface. It's damp. Why would anyone put anything…" My arm was almost at full stretch inside the hollow now. One last reach and I'd have done all I could without more equipment, without going in from the surface.

The trowel scraped on stone. I pulled back straight away. Probably it was only a rock beneath the turf, but that sound always made us drop the metal in favour of flesh, brushes, whatever would uncover without harming. I shifted back, about to say *give us a leg up*—but he was already there, bending to lift me.

"Ta. There's something here—blocking the passage or ending it, maybe." I could feel a flat surface, a stone, filling the whole space. And what made my heart pound, my spine prickle, was the knowledge shooting up through my fingertips that the stone was carved. A tiny hollow, a circle surrounding it. "Cup and ring," I whispered, and felt Rayne's shrug where his shoulder was pressed to my thigh. Never mind—I'd enjoy explaining to him later the mystic nature of these notations in rock the Neolithic inhabitants of Britain had left behind them, the tantalising hints they gave of maps, constellations, symbols for the cycles of the moon. They had been one of Jason's most beloved mysteries. He'd been running every pattern and arrangement found to date into a custom-designed computer program up until a couple of months before he died.

That was it. Cup-and-ring marks, and under them, around them, short lines in coherent order. Rayne passed the torch up to me without needing to be asked. One quick survey with the beam confirmed what touch was telling me. Not just enigmatic symbols—text, all around the edge of the stone. I thought for a second it was Runic, then recognised the neat dashes and diagonals of Ogham script. The oldest alphabet in the world, designed to be chiselled into rock, used from earliest Bronze Age forward to inscribe boundary markers, monoliths on the graves of chieftains.

"Text," I said. "Text with symbols. Connected to them, translating them maybe."

"What, like a Rosetta stone, or…"

"Exactly. Exactly. Christ—this is what Jason was looking for. I don't know why he got so distraught about it, or what the hell connection there is with Hartcliffe Dean or bloody biochemistry, and I don't care." I could hardly breathe. This would qualify as a key, all right. There was nothing extant in the whole world that linked Stone Age consciousness to the staggeringly different world view that prevailed after the invention of script. "Quick, help me get this out. I've got to see it."

"Okay. I'll have to let you down. You all right? Can you reach?"

"Yeah, with the edge of the trowel. Just…"

The top edge of the stone came free. It almost fell into my hands, and I stretched out my palms for it, pulling muscles in my shoulders and back. I'd have taken any kind of pain to make this catch. When I breathed in, I thought the air brought me a trace of Jason's scent, as if he were here with me, urging me on, teaching and guiding me as he had always done. "He knew exactly what he was after. I don't know why he didn't talk to me about it. This is his key."

"Daniel. Get back."

I froze, the carved slab in my grasp. I had never heard Rayne sound like this before. I tried to work out what was different, and after a moment I realised that it was the note of fear. It sent a cold pang through me. I hadn't thought him capable. Not through bomb blast, near capture by armed guards, overwhelming sexual surrender on a stripped-down bed… He was reaching past me into the hole, shining the torch into the space beyond the carved stone. "What is it?"

"Dan. You know how you never do what I tell you?"

"Yes."

"Fucking do it this time. Take the stone and step back now."

Chapter Fourteen

I knew the symbol, of course. Probably everybody knows it today, in a world where germ warfare is just one slip of the Geneva Convention away, where the first bug smart enough to step-dance round our antibiotics will topple us like dominoes. For a moment—briefly obedient to Rayne, three steps back from the niche in the chamber wall—I couldn't work it out. In the torchlight, my mind was trying to make its three flying arches into some kind of Ogham inscription, or a cup-and-ring I hadn't seen before.

Biohazard. The universal sign for death in a bottle, faded and peeling but still attached to the dully gleaming flask I could see wedged into the far reach of the hole. It was packaged in a layer of plastic sheeting.

Time seemed to stop for me. There hadn't been a photo with the article Rayne had found, but for some reason I was seeing one in my head now. Black and white, in seventies style. Serious, for a scientific publication, but nevertheless its three subjects in their white lab coats grinning, triumphant. *A medical breakthrough*. One of the scientists was Dean Anderson. The second had a blur for a face—I couldn't assign him one. And the third was Jason. *The Salisbury Key.*

It keys down the human immune system. "Rayne," I whispered, and I let the precious relic drop with a crash onto the chamber floor. I needed my hands free. I stepped forward and grabbed him, calmly but with all my strength. "Get away from that. Come away."

He didn't resist me. He wrapped a firm returning embrace around me, never taking his eyes off the flask, and together we edged back towards the far side of the chamber. "Okay," he said. "But I'm not sure distance makes much difference. Not now."

"What?"

"Flasks like that…I recognise the make. We cleared a whole bunch of them out of an old military lab near Mosul. They're not designed to last forever. Even in laboratory conditions, maybe twenty years tops."

Why the hell would you dig a hole in the side of a dry, sealed chamber, then bury your treasure in damp earth? "And in soil?"

"I don't know." His grip on me tightened, and I shuddered and leaned into his warmth. "But that one's past its sell-by date, Dan. It might already be compromised."

"Whoever put it there wanted it to degrade." *Jason tried to get me out of the country. As for his life before the university, I don't think he had one.* But he had, hadn't he? My mind tried to jigsaw-piece decade to decade. In his fifties when I met him. Subtract twenty years from that, and he was still around thirty-five, plenty old enough to have forged a career in biochemistry. I remembered him, bright at first with hope, laying siege to MoD Fellworth's walls for access to this part of the plain. And over the three years that followed, his lights going out one by one, until all he could think of to do was run. "It's a time bomb, isn't it?"

"Which might have gone off. If it's soluble in water, or it can get airborne…"

"It could be out there now."

"And in here."

"Christ." I shifted to look into his face. I don't know what I was expecting—signs of immediate fever, maybe, or whatever happened to someone whose defences to every environmental pathogen had been stripped down. Well, he was pale. I thought I was probably bone-white myself. "Okay. I take your point about distance. But I think I'd rather be struck down by disease in the open air, not this tomb. And we have to report this."

"Who the hell to? I'm not sure who I can trust back at Fellworth."

"Oh, bugger the army. We're not under martial law yet. Come on. Let's just get as far as a mobile signal and call the police."

"Be an interesting conversation, but okay. After you. Er… Dan?"

He'd been pushing me towards the chute exit. I turned and saw that he was looking behind us, to where the symbol stone was lying on the floor. God, I'd dropped it. In the same circumstances—life and death—I'd have done the same again, but it would have to be that bad. I went to scoop it up, turning it over in unsteady hands. It looked undamaged. It fit inside my satchel, and I tucked it there lovingly, making sure nothing could scratch it. It was all the more precious to me now—the Holy Grail and the Ark of the Covenant combined. It was what poor Jase *should* have wanted, the discovery his whole life had been geared to. Instead, for twenty years, he'd had to watch the clock count down. Invisible death lifting up out of this chamber in the earth, dissolving in rain, getting its wings as the sun steamed the turf dry and the sweet wind blew. Shivering, I began to scramble up the tunnel towards surface.

And dropped straight back down. Rayne caught me, steadying me as I regained my balance. "What?"

"We've got company, love."

He coloured faintly. Well, let him hear it when it wasn't pillow talk, though the moment still had plenty of heat in it. My vision was bisected by bright green lines where headlights had seared across my dark-adapted pupils. "There's a car parked just beyond the barricade."

"Shit. Car or jeep?"

"I dunno. I can just see its lights. We should... God, what are you doing?"

"Can't leave this here for them to find."

I followed him back across the chamber. A cold nausea rose in me as I saw his fine hands—so strong, no quiver of fever in them yet—reach up and back into the hole. "Are you nuts? Don't disturb it."

"Think about it. The only people who can possibly know we're here are the ones who nicked that article off the printer, who tried to follow me and nearly cornered us at Hartcliffe. Do you think they're on the side of public health and safety?"

"So, what—a corroded flask containing some kind of bioweapon is gonna be safer with us?"

"No." He flashed an amused, irritated glance at me. "Clearly. But we've got to be better keepers than a bunch of black-ops spooks who've infiltrated the army and are gonna sell it on to the first high-paying terrorists they meet."

"Oh God. You think that's what..."

"I don't know. But I can't risk it. Can you?"

I helped him ease the container out of the back of the niche. Plastic rustled and flaked as we lifted it down. I couldn't see damage or cracks, but the packaging was dirty and clouded with damp. Gingerly we turned the flask around. It would fit, just about, into my satchel, which had a padded folder for delicate instruments. Rayne's eyes met mine for a moment. I knew the irony wasn't lost on either of us, of carrying grim death out of here with us along with a relic that might unravel the mysteries of ancient life.

We slipped out of the souterrain, keeping low. The headlights had gone out, and I hoped to God I had only seen an early-morning jogger or dog-walker parking up. From this distance, in the silvery first light, it was impossible to tell if the vehicle was still there at all. I saw Rayne glancing around, and we shared a silent thought as he turned to me. No way out but the way we'd come in, unless we wanted to spread this toxin—and ourselves—over a wide range of the countryside by stepping on a bomb. And yet it was my instinct too, to head out across the plain, cover distance and find a circuitous route back to the car. He shook his head, and we set off, sitting ducks if anyone cared to cross the fence into the restricted zone and find us, along the route we had cleared.

There was no one. By the time we got to the barricade, I was beginning to wonder if I'd imagined the lights, and I hoped Rayne wasn't thinking so too. One thing, to have dislodged this dragon from its lair in response to a real threat... Carefully I passed the satchel to him over the barbed wire. "Sorry. I could have sworn..."

"Well, don't complain. We've nicked the damn thing now— let's just get back to the car with it. You got a signal on your phone yet?"

"Not a bar."

"Must be the ley lines. Let's keep going. There's often clear patches by the road."

"Okay." I looked at the satchel hanging innocently by its strap from Rayne's strong hands. "Here, give me that back."

"Aw, Dan. Won't you let *me* carry the plague for a bit?"

I shook my head, smiling reluctantly. "Nn-nn. It's my plague. You can carry it later. Hand it back."

He was right—as soon as we were within a few yards of the car, my phone buzzed to tell me it was ready for action. Rayne opened the passenger door, and I eased the satchel inside. I had a good signal now, enough to put a call through to the Salisbury police. I didn't know what their reaction would be. My contacts there had mostly been through Jason, but I thought my name was well enough known to them that they wouldn't dismiss me as a crank caller or lunatic. And if they took me seriously—what? A storm of infection-control specialists, faceless HazMat suits, and the disappearance of this flask into some unmarked van where, if we were all very lucky, it would never be seen or heard of again, along with my last hopes of answers to any of this.

Suddenly and finally, I decided that I didn't want to know. Whatever Jase had been, he had loved me. And I'd loved what I'd known of him and always would. "All right," I said to Rayne, who was watching me closely, as if reading every thought. God, it was something, wasn't it, to be seen like that, not to have to explain. "Let's get this over with. I'll call the Wiltshire HQ."

"Don't worry about that, son. We'll take over from here."

I whirled round. The darkness beyond the car had spoken, the dark between the conifers where no dawn light would penetrate for hours, and where Rayne and I—stupidly, maybe, with hindsight—had not thought to check for pursuit. For a fucking ambush. The shadows hardened into men. For a second, shock multiplied their number in my mind, then I counted three of them as they stepped out of the trees. Three, in army uniform, all carrying weapons. I wondered if they were Rayne's two spooks, the ones who had hunted him—those two and a third, leading them...

"Oh thank God," Rayne said, managing to surprise me more than anything else that had happened on this mind-spinning night. "Colonel McCade."

I looked again. Christ, it was. He was just as dapper, calm and smiling as on the morning when I'd gone to him to get the freedom of his military zone. Of one crucial part of it, anyway. He'd let me. He'd been happy to. I was Jason's heir, his successor, the one who would carry on his search.

"Rayne," I said warningly, and put out a hand to grasp his arm.

"It's okay, Dan. Colonel, I'm sorry. I tried to get to you earlier to tell you about this, but…"

"You couldn't find me. I know." McCade gestured to the two soldiers with him to stop, and he too came to a halt, surveying Rayne and me serenely. No…just Rayne. He looked him up and down. I couldn't fathom his expression. There was no trace of lasciviousness in it—just a kind of cold appreciation, as if Rayne were something he'd created. Something which had pleased him once. "Summer," he said. "You were a good boy. I tried to give you some part of the family you'd lost, you know. I picked you up when you fell. I was very, very fond of you. And in a way, you've done this to yourself. I wasn't even completely sure what you were after, until I saw that article you kindly printed off for me back at the base."

He unshipped the pistol from his belt. He did it so quietly that he might have been taking out a handkerchief, and, for an instant, I paid his movement about that much attention. I couldn't look away from Rayne. I doubted his CO had made a habit of putting his affection into words. I doubted very much he'd ever called him by his name. Rayne's face was a pale, perfect blank. Only his wide, stunned eyes and parted lips told me anything was going on inside. Told me—Christ, that he was too fucking shocked to move.

McCade shot him. It would have been through the heart, except that somewhere back in the seconds preceding the click of the gun's safety catch, I had started moving, for Rayne and for myself. I'd seized him, begun the motion of shoving him out of the way. The bullet went into him anyway, a thud in his flesh that I felt in my own as I tackled him down. I didn't know where he'd been hit. Hot sticky wetness under my right palm, up-leaping earth knocking the breath from me...

I'd landed half on top of him, and I pushed up onto my knees, scrambling round to face McCade. "Don't!" I yelled, thrusting out both hands towards him. I knew all about nonresistance. Jase had taught me. If they had the guns, you didn't even bother—you shielded your fallen as best you could and surrendered. "Jesus fucking Christ, McCade, what are you doing?"

"Clearing up a mess," he said politely, as if I'd asked him in the Fellworth briefing room. His expression hadn't changed. He was looking past me, still watching Rayne. "You just made it harder, son. Not just for me but for him. He could have been at peace by now. Now it's gonna have to be a head shot. Jackson, deal with Dr. Logan, would you? I'll see to the lieutenant."

Deal with and *see to.* I had no trouble understanding. I assumed that McCade and his heavies had decided on their terms in advance, as well, because the soldier he'd referred to as Jackson shifted uneasily and said, "You want me to kill a civilian, sir? Won't he be missed?"

McCade glanced towards him. At last he looked annoyed. "Are you questioning my order? No, sergeant—neither of these two queer bastards is going to be missed. Dr. Logan here ran off with Lieutenant Rayne after starting an affair with him barely a week after Jason Ross died. Isn't that right, Daniel? You were so bloody ashamed, you wanted to vanish. And Rayne—well, Rayne is a soldier. My soldier. No wonder he fucking well crept away."

Rayne made a sound. It was the first that had broken from him, though his ragged breathing had told me he was still alive. Something between a moan and a whimper, fraught with disbelief.

I didn't dare tear my eyes off McCade. I put a hand back blindly, finding his shoulder. "It's all right. It's all right." I meant it too, though how I meant to make it so I'd no idea. Only that I wasn't going to let McCade anywhere near him, whatever that took. In a different world, I'd have minded hearing my misdeeds—my treachery to Jase—rehearsed like this for the soldiers, but now I didn't give a damn. "Back off, McCade," I snarled. "Or if you want to murder somebody in cold blood, start with me. Rayne knows nothing about this. I've just been using him to get access to your records, to get me in."

Another moan from behind me—this time full of protest. I gave him a light slap. Great, that he was conscious and taking enough in to be mad at me, but I needed him to shut up, lay low and let me get on with this. "Yeah, I've been shagging him, but only to get what I wanted."

McCade burst out laughing. Not humourless, villain-style laughter, but genuine amusement. I shut up, more freaked out by this than by the black hole of the gun still trained on me. "You're bloody priceless, Logan," he said. "Ruthlessly slept your way to the top, eh? You look the type." Suddenly he crouched in front of me. The gun was a foot from my chest. He put his head on one side and carried on, almost conversationally, "I can tell by the way you shift every time I do, to get between me and him. But you're missing the point. I'm not trying to choose which one to kill. I'm here to get shot of both of you and bury your bodies so deep in those woods you'll make a nice mystery for some future archaeologist to puzzle over. Then I'll take what I came here to get. What you and this jumped-up squaddie were kind enough to dig up for me."

Rayne jerked beneath my hand. He gave a raw gasp and tried to push up onto his elbows.

"Don't," I said, as the effort forced a cry from him and he began to cough. I'd found the ragged hole in his jacket now, the place where warm wetness was pulsing out. His ribs, I thought. Christ—his lungs... "Stay flat," I rasped, caressing him, pushing him back down.

My hand found his gun belt. Somehow I'd managed to forget that he was armed. I wondered if he'd forgotten too. It would have been one solution, back in the Hartcliffe Dean lab, with the guards closing in on us. Then I thought about Rayne—how loyal he was, how up until yesterday he had considered each one of his comrades a brother. No. He wouldn't pull a gun on a fellow soldier unless his life depended on it. Maybe not even then.

I had no such scruples. I hated guns, but it was squeamishness, not principles. Briefly I wished it had been—that I truly was the thoroughgoing pacifist I'd always believed myself to be. But, like most of my kind, I was turning out only skin deep. It all held good until someone we loved needed guarding. McCade was getting to his feet, gesturing Jackson and the other soldier to close in. To get on with it. I'd amused him, but enough was enough.

Rayne's Browning was heavier than I would've anticipated. It caught in the webbing holster and I made a clumsy move of dragging it free. McCade, I supposed, had been expecting anything but that, because he let me do it—was still turned away, his attention on Jackson, when I surged to my feet and planted the pistol's muzzle in his chest. I felt with my thumb a heavy catch on the Browning. I hoped to God it was the safety. I pushed it and heard the weapon click.

His head whipped round. Peripherally I saw the other two soldiers make a move towards me and stop. "Drop your weapon, you bastard."

Still not wholly convincing, I guessed. McCade's face split once more into a grin. Then perhaps he looked closer and read something in mine, because he let fall the hand holding his pistol, and after a second I heard the weapon drop onto the verge.

"You are pissing me about, aren't you, Logan?" he asked, still smiling. "A little ivory-tower shirt-lifter like you—are you seriously telling me you'd shoot a soldier?"

Suddenly I'd had enough. I was tired, and terrified for Rayne, spilling out his precious life into the larch needles while his boss and I fucked around here. And although I'd left my childhood behind me lock, stock and memories, fragments were boiling up, of school corridors and street corners after I'd finally lain down with my best friend in the barn, because Davie—half proud, half guilty—had talked. *Shirt-lifter. Fudge-packer. Queer.*

"Why the fuck not?" I yelled. "You just shot my bloody boyfriend! Right—you, Jackson, and the other one, whatever you're called…chuck your guns off into the undergrowth, nice and far. Jackson, get McCade's. His too." I glanced across to him, giving the gun muzzle a twist on McCade's khaki-clad breast in case anyone thought my intentions might be faltering. "Then get Rayne up and put him in the car. *Carefully*, or I'll blow Colonel Blimp here back to World War bloody Two."

McCade snorted. He was pale, and he wasn't smiling anymore, but his eyes flashed defiance. "Don't you dare move," he growled at Jackson. "He doesn't mean it."

"You don't understand me, sir." I hardly knew my own voice. It was bitter cold and at the same time shot through with hot fury. "You're right. I'm queer as fuck. I lost one shirt-lifting lover a fortnight ago, and now you've put a bullet into this one.

I'm not even *sane* anymore." That did it. I saw McCade turn from pale to grey. "Tell your men to do as I say."

Jackson and his comrade lifted Rayne between them. They were nearly as gentle as I could have wished, and I saw in their movements a battleground tenderness that made me understand more clearly Rayne's motives for living as he had. They were soldiers, and I didn't think they'd have readily murdered one of their own. Nevertheless they'd have done it under orders, and however comradely they were, they'd thrown in their lot with McCade. I watched them closely as they half-carried Rayne to the car. He was making an effort to walk, but his head was down, and I could hear the anguished scrape of his breathing.

"Right. There's a satchel on the passenger seat. Put it down on the floor, very carefully. Then get him in—like he was made of glass, please, gentlemen. Crystal. That's it. Close the door. Get the keys out of his pocket and start her up, then come back over here."

They obeyed me without a word. I watched them do it, a cold sweat prickling my brow. And suddenly I saw it. I felt it—the power of the gun. I could make them do anything. The thing in my hands was the end to every argument. No more need for sense, negotiation, human kinship. I could kill them.

A hard thrill went through me, then a nausea so terrible I almost threw up. "Don't bloody move, any of you," I said unsteadily, backing off towards the car.

McCade was staring at me intently, as if he could read the cracking of my ice. "Where do you think you're going?" he called. "Where do you think you're going to take him? I can alert every hospital between here and Dover that there's a pair of terrorists on the loose, a rogue soldier with a biological weapon. Every police force. These are paranoid times, son. Who are they gonna believe?" Any second now he would make a move. I got the

Audi's bulk between me and him, and blindly pulled open the driver's door. "Come *on,*" he snarled. "What do you think happens to your lover-boy then? Do you think you'll ever even see him again?"

I knew what I needed to do. It didn't have to be murder—I could kneecap him or put a bullet through his thigh. Disable him and leave the other two occupied with him. It would give me and Rayne a head start. I'd heard about recoil. I planted myself, bracing my shoulders, and took a sight across the roof of the car.

"Dan."

I froze. That was Rayne—one syllable, half-choked with anguish. Rayne, calling me. I dropped back into my own skin, as if I was waking up, becoming real again. I couldn't kill a man—not even this one—in cold blood.

I need have no qualms about shooting a car. McCade's jeep was sitting there among the trees, disguised but not hidden. I could make out enough of it to guess where the tyres were. A long shot in the half-light, but… McCade took a step forward. My time was up. I leaned round out of the Audi's cover long enough to pull the trigger.

The roar and the recoil ripped through me. I thought I saw the jeep sag on one side, but I couldn't be sure. It would have to be enough.

I dropped into the car, slammed her into gear and set off in a squeal of tyres. I still had the gun clutched loosely in one hand. Racking the Audi up to her top speed, I felt a wet, sticky grip cover mine, and glanced across to see Rayne reaching over the handbrake.

"Give it," he rasped, and I let go. He took the gun from me, snapping the safety back on. "Jesus, Dan. Jesus!"

"Just hang on, love. Gonna get you to hospital."

"N-no. You heard him. He'll find us."

"What? That was all just bullshit, wasn't it?"

"Maybe. I dunno. I don't know anything anymore."

I shot him a glance. His eyes were closed, his head tipped back. I couldn't tell in this light which parts of him were most terrifyingly soaked in blood. McCade—Rayne's one good man, the brother-in-arms who was good to the bone—had just put a bullet into him. If that could happen, anything could. Maybe there was no place of safety.

"I should've shot the bastard," I said grimly. The stand of conifers was disappearing in my rearview mirror. No sign of pursuit, but even if I had disabled the jeep, it was only a matter of time. "I should've killed him."

"Nn-nn. Not my Dan. Not you."

So I drove like the devil back to the place where Rayne and I had met that night. It was all I could think of to do. If we transferred to a different car, we might have a ghost of a chance, and I was suddenly glad that fear and indifference had led me to such an anonymous choice. After that, I had no idea. I gunned the Audi, screeching into the riverside car park. Here at least, in the cover of the trees, I could take a look at him, and if he was as bad as I thought, I'd risk him in the city A&E if I had to sit by his bedside with the Browning in my hand. We bumped down the track to where I'd left the Peugeot, the movement jolting a bitten-off cry from him.

"Sorry," I said, grinding to a halt. I got out and dashed round the bonnet, tearing open the passenger door. "Okay. Okay, let me see."

"No. Into yours, now."

"Rayne, this is bad." I knelt on the ground. Clumsily I undid his jacket and pulled up the hem of his T-shirt underneath. His hands fought mine, then clenched tight as a spasm of pain went through him. The bullet had smashed through his rib cage. I retched at the sight of the hole it had left. I could see bone fragments, and he was bleeding fresh with every laboured breath. This was the power of the gun. This was the final argument, my moment's exaltation back in the woods. "Oh, fuck. I'm taking you to hospital."

"No. Not coughing blood, or… Not got my lungs. You just have to pack it, stop it bleeding."

"Just… What the hell with?" I didn't wait for him to answer. I had clean, soft cashmere next to my skin. I'd have given him the skin itself if I could. "Right. Hang on."

He moaned and broke into half-drowned laughter as I tore off my jacket and stripped down. "What the hell…?"

"Shut up." I leaned in and planted a rough kiss on the side of his cod-white, bloodstained face. "Will this do?"

"Deluxe version. Yeah. Bundle it and hold it just there. No. Tighter."

"I'll hurt you. I'll drive it further in."

"Just do it, you soft…" He broke off, face contorting. "Jesus! All right, that'll do. Get my belt off. You have to slide it through the .holster and ammo pouches. Okay. Now wrap it round me over the jumper, hard as you can."

I obeyed him, my fingers slipping on his blood and the complicated buckle. I gave it one final tug when he told me. I thought that he couldn't hang on for much longer, and once he passed out I could ignore him and head for the hospital.

"All right," he rasped when I was done. "Now get me into your car. And put your jacket on, handsome, or you'll catch your death."

He was almost deadweight in my grasp by the time I had supported him over the couple of yards to the Peugeot. "There," I said, shoving open the door with my foot. "Aren't you glad I didn't get the baby Merc now? Nobody's gonna look at this one twice, are they?"

He didn't respond. Relieved, terrified, I eased him into the passenger seat, then ran back to fetch the satchel—the point of this whole exercise, which I'd almost forgotten in the midst of its bloodstained realities. I tucked it down by his feet. "Rayne? You with me?"

Nothing. No flicker of consciousness beneath his closed eyelids. All right—the game was over. If he died here, it wouldn't console me that the secret of the Salisbury key was safe. I didn't think anything would ever bloody well console me. I bumped the Peugeot as softly as I could out from its hiding place in the trees and pulled her up to the main road, indicating—for whose benefit, I didn't know—my intention to head back to the city.

A hand snaked out and grabbed the wheel. "No. Other way."

"Oh, for fuck's sake, Rayne. You need a doctor."

"Please just do it."

"Okay." I yanked up the handbrake, rounded on Rayne in frustration. "Where?"

"Tell you in a minute. I can't talk for a bit. Just set off."

I booted the Peugeot down the dawn-lit road at a grim, steady sixty. The route was a minor one, leading southwest away from the city. I couldn't go far wrong, even with my guide rigid and silent beside me. Dealing with God-knew-what indescribable pain. I tried to imagine the alien burn of metal embedded in my flesh. I put out a hand and gently laid it on his thigh. "Rayne, love…"

"D-Don't!" It was barely audible, a desperate whisper. The road took a twist into thick tree cover, plunging us back into night. By the time I had negotiated the series of bends, flicking the headlights back to full to question the shadows ahead, Rayne was hunched forward in his seat, trying to double over. Afraid he was losing his fight, I began to slow the car down. I had to be able to do *something* for him…

Then he choked out, muffled behind his hands, "Christ! He shot me." His breath was coming fast and unsteady, almost frantic. "He fucking *shot* me!"

Blindly I stroked his hair. "I know. I know what he meant to you. But you'll be okay. You don't need the bastard."

"McCade? Oh bugger him. All those years… My whole life. What was I doing it for?"

"Because you thought it was right. Come on, love. Hang on. And for God's sake give me somewhere to go, before you sodding well bleed to death in my car."

In the brief silence that followed, I could almost hear his world crashing down. I knew how that felt. Securities, certainties, assumptions of a future, all landsliding down into dust. "All right," he rasped out at length. "My brother. Take us to my brother's house."

Chapter Fifteen

The flick of the windscreen wipers had half-hypnotised me. A light summer downpour, sweeping in across the hills, lit up in veils by the rising sun.

"Your brother?" I echoed, bewildered. "The one who lives on pinecones in the wood?"

Rayne chuckled. It was a terrible sound, raw with pain. "Yeah. I might have kept...closer tabs on him than I told you. Anyway, I know which wood."

"Why? I thought you hated him."

"I fucking do. But he's my brother."

My brother. Yes—that would always be the first and last explanation for everything Rayne did. My heart ached, that he'd poured out his loyalty on such desert ground. "Okay," I said. "Where does he live? Will he help us?"

"Cheverton Woods. And...probably not."

"Okay. That's only fifteen minutes away. But what's the point, if he's not gonna..."

"We don't have anywhere else to go."

I thought about arguing. But I hadn't found my brotherhood either, I realised, gripping the wheel tight as we reached the Oldbridge roundabout. My only refuge, and everything I cared to protect, was right here in this car. I swallowed painfully. "How will I find him?"

"I'll direct you. Just drive."

He did, for a while. Then his terse instructions stopped coming, and I twisted round to look at him. "Rayne?"

He was silent and still. His head was tipped back, exposing his beautiful pale throat, and his eyes were shut. Terror burned through me. I put out a hand and felt blindly at his jacket, then at the edge of the seat upholstery. Both were sticky with blood, but I couldn't tell if it was fresh, more than he'd spilled before I'd stopped to pack his wound.

"Rayne!" I yelled, and slapped him as hard as I could on the thigh.

"Ow! Fuck, you little bastard." His eyes flew open. "What was that for?"

"Don't you dare go to sleep. I haven't got bloody sat-nav here, you know, and… Well, just don't go to sleep."

"Wasn't asleep. Where are we—Elsmere Cross? You missed the turning for Cheverton, you pillock."

"Yeah, because you were asleep. I'll take this turning and double back. Now keep bloody talking to me."

He tried. From the corner of my eye I watched his struggle to stay with me, saw him lose it, his head falling back once more. "Rayne!"

"In a couple of miles, look out for a track to your left. It's not signposted, just marked as a private road. Follow it, and…keep following, even when tarmac runs out and it turns to grass. Just keep following…"

"Okay. But you can direct me when we're nearer—"

"Nn-nn. Sorry. No, I can't."

His hand went slack on my thigh. I seized it. "Rayne. Rayne!" But this time he didn't respond, not even when I called him Summer. Not even when I yelled it at him, shouted it at the top of my lungs. Not even when I pleaded.

I slammed the accelerator down. The narrow road began to curve into the leaf-dappled dark of Cheverton Woods. I steered with one hand, clasping his cold fingers with the other. "Summer. Hang on, love. For fuck's sake, hang on!"

Just follow. Keep following. The road narrowed down to a ribbon. Grass sprang up along its median line, just tufts at first then a solid green band. The band spread out and met the verge on both sides, and the tarmac was gone. I gunned the Peugeot hard along the two packed-mud lines that were all that remained to guide her wheels, and I followed.

Deeper and deeper into the trees. I wasn't even sure I'd picked the right fucking track in the first place. This had to be wrong—nobody lived in here. There was no road. Even the wheel ruts were disappearing by the second. There was barely daylight. Oak and ash had given way to solid ranks of conifers, their swooping skirts meeting over the roof of the car. I was bitterly conscious that every yard I drove in this direction was a yard farther away from a hospital, from the rescue I should have insisted on.

The track ran out. I swerved to avoid the bole of a tree growing up in the middle of it and almost slammed broadside into a fence.

A fence. I scrambled out of the car. I hadn't seen the damn thing because it was constructed from timbers and more than half buried in undergrowth. Beyond it, if I stretched, I thought I could see a cabin of some sort. Great—I'd brought my injured lover to an electricity substation.

Which might at least have a landline phone. There was sod-all mobile cover here. Frantically I looked up and down the length of the fence for a gate. None visible, of course. Well, I'd been back and forth over so many barricades tonight that another could hardly matter, and this one looked an easy climb. I reached up and grabbed the top bar.

Light hit my eyes like a fist. The shriek of an alarm tore the deep forest silence in two. Instinctively I leapt back, expecting a jolt of voltage through my hands, though I hadn't seen wires. All along the horizontal timbers hidden spotlights had activated. I raised my arms, trying to block out the white-hot blaze.

"Hoi! Whoever you are, get back behind the wheel and bugger off. This is private property."

There was someone on top of the fence. Half-blinded, eyes streaming, I could only make out a rough shape, but I could see that it was male and included the length of a rifle. Fear and rage shook me. I had gone nearly thirty years of life without catching sight of a gun, and now I couldn't seem to get away from them.

"For Christ's sake!" I yelled across the screech of the alarm. "I've got an injured man here. I need help!"

The alarm stopped. In the ringing silence that followed, I heard my distraught breathing, and I struggled for calm. "I'm serious," I said, shielding my eyes and trying to meet those of whichever mad bastard was defending his Sawney Bean shack out here. "Please."

"Show me him."

"What? He's in the car. Just—"

"I can't see him. Get him out of the car and let me see."

I wanted to roar in frustration. There was a rock on the ground by my feet. I wanted to pick it up and chuck it as hard as I could into this insane fucker's invisible face. Then I wanted to turn the car around and rip out of here as hard as I'd come in. But

I was out of options. End of the road, for me and Rayne, if I didn't get help here.

I ran round to the passenger side and pulled open the door. "Rayne. Rayne. You awake?" I could hardly see him. My vision was blotted by indigo starfish. I shook his shoulder gently, then hard, and then I reached for the pulse in his throat and couldn't find one.

I was back on a driveway in a quiet residential street in Salisbury. Past found present in my head and formed a circle, sinking its teeth into its tail. I burst into tears—noisy, shaming sobs of boyhood, that didn't know and couldn't care who heard. Shuddering under the terrible force of them, I seized Rayne by the armpits and hauled him out, collapsing with him onto the ground beside the car. I struggled to my knees and cradled him, turning his beautiful, blanked-out face towards the light.

"Do you see?" I barked, voice cracking like dry sticks. "Do you fucking see?"

No answer. I didn't care. I hefted Rayne in my arms, cupping the back of his skull. I could smell his blood, the sweet male tang of his body that had before I'd even realised it become as dear as life to me. I buried my face in the crook of his neck and shoulder. He was warm still, not a lump of cold clay as Jason had been when I found him.

A creaking sound a few yards off, as if a heavy gate was being shoved open. Then rapid footsteps, long stride covering ground at a run. A hand closed on my shoulder, and a voice—which, now I heard it again, was eerily familiar—demanded, "Show me him again."

I jerked upright. I couldn't stop the rib-cracking sobs tearing up out of my throat, but I could still kill this bastard who was killing my Rayne with his dumb hostility, his failure to help when I'd begged.

I could kill Winter. I stared up into the light. Now the pale blue blaze was glaring into his face too.

Not so much a brother as a twin, a reflection. Christ, and their parents really had got their names the wrong way round—this shock-blanked angel as fair as mine was dark, hair the colour of pale sand cascading round his shoulders, sea-blue eyes wide, showing all the sapphire ring around their iris. "Summer," he rasped, dropping to his knees, the rifle slack in his grasp. "That's my—that's my brother. What happened to him?"

"He's been shot," I told him tersely. Winter put a hand out—the one not wrapped around the gun barrel—and I slapped it away. "Back off! God, I thought you were meant to be the peace-loving hippie brother."

"What? Look, do you want me to help you or—"

"Get that fucking rifle out of my face."

He frowned. Then he glanced down, expression clearing. "Oh—that? Just a replica." He chucked it aside, and I watched in disbelief while it skittered away across the ground. "A deterrent, against..." His eyes clouded, suspicion creasing his brow. "Against trespassers. Why have you brought him here? He's nothing to me. He's a stranger."

"And you'd leave a stranger out here to die?" Another sob shook me. Mortified, I wiped my eyes. I could hardly speak. "Look. An army officer shot him. We've got something they want, and...they're after us. He told me to come here."

"The army?" Winter lurched to his feet. He ran to the fence, hit a hidden switch, and the floodlights snapped off, leaving me dazed and half-blinded. A wide, crazy smile had cracked across his face. "The fucking army?" His grin broadened, sea-blue gaze hardening to a kind of grim delight. "The bastards!"

"Yeah," I managed. I was nearly at the end of my rope. "They're bastards, and this is your brother. There's something in the car—I can't explain, but it's a bioweapon, a chemical, and I don't know if it's active or not. So…" I broke off, coughing, tasting the coppery salt of my tears. "So I don't want you to take me in, or that, but…Christ, if you're human, help Rayne."

Winter crouched beside us. This time when he reached for Rayne I didn't stop him. There was something cool and unfazed in the way he pulled up the edge of his T-shirt and examined the blood-soaked padding underneath. "Exit wound?"

"What?"

"Did the bullet lodge or go straight through?"

"God, I don't know." That had never occurred to me. I'd been so busy staunching the first hole, I hadn't thought to look for another. "I never…"

"Right. Lift him up a bit. That's it. Oh yeah. He's in luck today."

I shuddered. "You have to be fucking kidding."

Winter raised red-daubed fingertips and showed them to me. "Not at all," he said cheerfully. "A bullet stuck in there, he'd probably die of the infection. This I can more or less treat, if he doesn't peg out from blood loss. Okay, help me get him in."

Silently I obeyed him. The forest and the overhead canopy of sun-prickled conifers were beginning a slow waltz around me, and the damn tears wouldn't stop, although I'd got them muffled down to the odd harsh gasp. I'd begun to mourn, I realised with horror. I'd fought death before, and lost before I'd got in my first blow. I'd taken the absence of pulse in Rayne's throat as the end of things, not a mistake of my own clumsy fingers. And Winter—this double, this wrong-side-of-the-mirror twin—didn't look like he was tending a corpse. He was bending to lift Rayne by the knees at the same time as I raised his shoulders. I'd been picturing some skinny, drug-addled kid. But he was as athletically built as his brother, muscles cording in his bare arms as he stood upright.

I noticed belatedly that he was wearing just a white cotton vest over pyjama bottoms, that his feet were bare. "We woke you up."

"Yeah. It's six in the morning, in case you hadn't noticed, you nutcase. Right, bring him this way, through the gate. Who the hell are you, anyway?"

I didn't know where to start. *Boyfriend* didn't even start to cover it, and *lover* was too wildly dramatic for this place—this garden path, or a strip at least of concrete flags leading from the fence to the cabin I'd seen beyond it. "Dan," I said eventually, concentrating fiercely on the warm weight in my arms. "His friend."

Winter glanced up at me. There was a rough-built wooden porch with elaborately carved support posts—dragons and serpents, I noticed with a dreamer's distraction, coiling round and round.

"His friend who cries over him," he said, pushing open the door with his foot and backing in. "My God. After all the grief he gave me over every little joint and handful of pills, all that right-wing establishmentarian crap, the bastard turns out to be gay."

I opened my mouth to deny it. After all, until three weeks ago, he hadn't been, had he? It was just me. Then it struck me that I was about to start defending him, as if because Winter had mentioned his sexuality in the same breath as his own bloody drug habit, the two things were the same. "Do you have some kind of problem with that, you paranoid backwoods junkie?"

We were standing in a sunlit room. Whoever had built this cabin had aligned it so that its window looked southeast along a firebreak. The walls were painted every colour imaginable, in streaks and spirals, as if a star had exploded in a fruit basket. I noted these things peripherally, my gaze deadlocked to Winter's. To my astonishment, he broke into laughter. "All right. Calm down, Conan. Bring him through here."

***

I sat with my head in my hands, in a room barely large enough to accommodate the bunk where Rayne was sleeping, his wounds clean and dressed, his face bloodless but serene. There was a stool by the bunk, which Winter had swept clear of books and the torch that served him as a bedside lamp and sat me forcibly down when it became clear to both of us that I was only getting in his way.

I'd tried to help. I didn't know where all the bandages and antiseptic were coming from, but my relief at the sight of them had killed my curiosity stone dead. My host's mysterious expertise with them had unstrung that and the last of my resistance too. Twenty-four hours ago, I had been crawling out of bed at around this time, with only the dull, slow-grinding cares of daily life to crush me down. Wondering how to deal with Dean Anderson, who back then had been a source of paternal disapproval, not one member of a triad who had held the fate of a world in their hands. I was paid out, lost.

Winter Rayne had let me hold his brother on his side while he swabbed out first the exit wound—the one I hadn't noticed, bleeding silently into the car upholstery all the way out here—then the ragged hole between his ribs. Then he'd observed that I wasn't much of a soldier, was I, going green as a primrose at the sight of a bit of first aid, and I'd told him faintly that I was an archaeologist, at which point he had broken into another incredulous laugh and put me aside.

I'd sat and waited. Winter had run back and forth with basins of hot water—packed the wounds, dressed them, watched critically while one spot of blood appeared in the cotton wool but no more than that. Had done, as far as I could see, everything possible for his brother. It was all good. But Rayne had not woken up, and I was waiting still.

I held his hand. I looked blindly round the insane little room, noting without comprehension that it was papered with every imaginable poster from the golden years of the counterculture. All the classics—Che Guevara, black on red; the iconic fist with upraised middle finger flipping the bird at society. Even one I'd had myself as a preteen, thinking it wildly risqué—those feet, just soles seen from the end of the bed, one pair pointing up and bracketing the pair between them pointing down. In another world, I'd have laughed till I cried at this shrine to a long-dead revolution. What had I done, bringing Rayne to this poor nutter's lair?

The bedroom door swung open. I jolted upright. Winter was there in the doorway, his lovely mane alight with sunshine behind him. My satchel was swinging from his fist. "Is this it?"

"Yes. For Christ's sake be careful."

"Right. Tell me everything you know about it, right now. Don't bother lying."

I shrugged. I didn't think I had a lie left in me. "There's not much. A group of scientists at Hartcliffe Dean cooked it up in the seventies. It's some kind of chemical weapon—not a disease, something that strips out the human immune system and—"

"Makes the whole world a disease." Winter was nodding frantically. "Yeah. The ultimate pathogen. Thought it was just an internet legend or another Hartcliffe Dean conspiracy theory."

"You've *heard* of it?"

"Course. We all have. They call it the Key. Thanks very much, Dan. That'll do."

He was gone. I sat for a while, staring at the doorframe which had contained him. From here, looking through to the living room, I could see that what Winter lacked in basics he more than made up for in technology. The far wall was stacked with TV and computer screens, some blank, some showing static-swept broadcasts, others ticking over with equations. None of this was real, I decided. McCade had shot both of us back there, and I was working through some kind of abstract purgatory before my soul could move on.

The limp hand in mine suddenly tightened. I jumped so hard I almost fell off my stool. Turning, I saw Rayne, eyes wide, staring at the open doorway too. "Dan," he whispered. "Was that my brother?"

I couldn't speak. I knelt carefully on the edge of the bunk and felt his brow, then turned down the blankets Winter had laid over him and checked both sets of dressings. He hadn't bled any more. "Yeah," I managed finally. "That was him."

"You found him. Did he help?"

"Mm. First he held me up with a plastic rifle, then he helped us, yes. Quite a bit."

Rayne nodded. He seemed satisfied with this. He lifted a hand and gently ran its palm down the side of my face. "You've been crying."

"No. You stupid sod. You had two bloody holes in you. You passed out cold and then I couldn't get you to... You wouldn't wake up."

The hand went still. Only the thumb continued its caress, a velvety brush against my jaw. "Two? It went straight through?"

"Yes. So you just kept bleeding. Why didn't you tell me?"

"Didn't know. Didn't notice. Dan, sweetheart, you look like you haven't slept in a week. Come here."

There wasn't really room. The door was still wide open, Winter bustling back and forth in the living room, tapping first at this keyboard then at that. And I would hurt Rayne if I lay down beside him. But when he put out his arms for me, I couldn't do anything else. My bones and skull were made of lead, gravity pulling with ten times normal force, *sweetheart* resounding in my head like a beautiful bell.

He lifted the blankets for me, and I stretched out gingerly, wincing for him when my hands brushed his bandages. He kissed me as I lay down, clumsy, loving kisses to my eyelids and the corners of my mouth. He got an arm round me—scooped me into an embrace that turned my joints to sunlit water, and guided my head to his shoulder. "It's all right. You can sleep. I've got you now."

Chapter Sixteen

When I woke up, there was an altercation going on. It had started deep in my dreams, when a voice which was one shade off the one I now loved and recognised better than any other in the world had announced mockingly, "Oh, babes in the bloody wood," and the real voice—the one I *did* love, the authentic version—had replied, "Winter, you bastard. Don't you ever knock?"

"On an open door? In, incidentally, my own home?"

I lifted my head. Rayne was sitting half-upright in the bunk, both arms still wrapped round me. He was propping me up. That would never do. Pulling out of his embrace, I scrambled round behind him and offered him one of my own. He subsided gratefully against me, never taking his eyes off his brother, who was back in the doorway, arms folded, grinning sardonically. "I can't believe it. My hardarse soldier brother, gone to the other side. What *will* the generals say?"

"I'm more concerned with what they'll say when they find out I gave a chemical weapon to you, you hippie freak. What have you done with it?"

"Sold it on eBay. What do you think? I've contacted some people. They're working on it now."

"Oh great." Rayne stifled a grunt of discomfort, and I shifted to support him. "So you've emailed your network of imaginary friends. Tell me, Win—did you *ever* talk to anybody, any living person, outside of a chatroom? I honestly can't remember."

"Probably you can't. Too busy hanging round the army recruitment office, whining like a pup to get in. I see they let you."

"Yeah. Looks like you fulfilled all *your* golden promise too."

Winter turned away. I heard Rayne swallow, as if even he regretted that last thrust.

"Go easy," I murmured to him, rubbing my chin on the top of his head. "I told him what that flask could do. He didn't have to take us in."

"Oh, you've no idea. Probably he thinks it's some kind of role-playing game, diseases and dragons, or…" He shut up. I was still two-thirds asleep and lost in the pleasure of holding him. "Dan," he said. "Who the hell are all those people?"

I looked up. Beyond the open door, I could see that Winter's living room had acquired a small crowd. Men and women of various ages, some dressed smartly, some the tie-dyed stereotype. All were chatting animatedly, going from screen to screen, leaning over keyboards.

"Well," I said. "P perhaps they're his imaginary friends."

Winter leaned back round the door. He had two mugs of tea in his hands. If he was upset by his exchange of pleasantries with Rayne, it didn't show. "That's right," he said equably, setting the tea down on the stool by the bed. "One of them's a molecular biologist, and a couple of the others are professors on sabbatical from MIT. Granted, the rest are wild-eyed conspiracy theorists, but I reckoned we needed them too." He rested one shoulder on the wall and looked down at us. "You're right. I did email my network, and the ones who live close enough turned up."

"Winter…"

"No. Listen for a second. You're always so damn quick to judge. When I first came out here, I wanted to be a survivalist. So I set myself up with the fence and the computers, and I planned to watch the end of the world on TV. And you're right, brother— I was a bloody junkie. I'd just got a gorilla of a habit off my back. I wanted to be out of temptation's way. But now… Now I live out here because I like my privacy, not because I'm a sociopath. I like to grow dope for my own use in my own greenhouse, and after six years in foster care I like to know who's coming through my door. Other than that—I'm a paramedic with Lymington hospital. I work shifts. I pay my taxes."

Rayne rubbed a hand over his eyes. "Okay," he said. "I'm sorry. But your friends—you've got to get them out of here. It's some kind of biological agent. It's lethal, and—"

"I told them. They know the score. Just like…" He paused and flickered me a smile. "Just like your good friend Daniel here."

"Well, he should go too. So should you." He twisted round in the bed to face me. "Dan, we've fucked up. Too many civilians here. I'm gonna call Fellworth. Let them do what they like with this shit—at least they might know how to destroy it."

I seized him gently by the jaw. "Do me a big favour, love, and just shut up. Winter, they haven't opened that flask, have they?"

"God, no. A shame, because the MIT guys brought a kit that tests for every military pathogen ever invented, if we could just get a sample. No, it's in the kitchen, boxed up in Tupperware."

I snorted. "Tupperware. Great. That ought to do it."

"Oh, you'd be surprised what you can do with—"

He broke off. A moment later I heard what had caught his attention. The muted babble from the living room had faded out. The half-dozen people scattered at the various keyboards and monitors had gathered round just one of them. Winter turned to look, and Rayne sat up, swinging his feet to the floor. I knelt behind him, keeping a restraining arm around his waist.

"Microwave," a woman was saying. She was peering into a screen, and from here I could just see that she was surfing rapidly from one site to another, chasing down link after link. She had a strong Wiltshire accent, and her small, tense body was giving off a near-visible aura of excitement. "If this is the derivative of *Trisinia mactabilis* like you say, Andrew, the one that came out of the MoD labs in the seventies, it's easy enough to destroy. You just bloody stick it in the microwave."

Rayne made a choked sound. It wasn't quite laughter, and I held him tighter. He said hoarsely, "You can *microwave* it."

The group in the living room finally seemed to register our presence. Winter Rayne's home was apparently a place where two men could lie tangled on one narrow bunk and attract no attention at all. I could think of worse situations. Even now no one looked fazed, though Winter and I had stripped Rayne to the waist to treat him, and I'd taken off my bloodstained jacket before I'd lain down with him.

The woman turned round in her chair. "That's right. I think it probably didn't occur to them because there weren't that many microwaves around back then. But that's all it would take. Hey," she said, brightening, focussing on me. "Did you get into Hartcliffe Dean? They took aliens there after a UFO went down in Rendlesham Forest, you know. Don't suppose you *saw* anything?"

***

Rayne sat back. I went with him, helping him lean against the cabin's timber wall. He met my eyes, and in the tired darkness of his gaze I saw that we were thinking exactly the same thing. As for Winter, he hadn't gone to join the celebratory chatter in the front room. Problem solved, a neat intellectual puzzle unlocked by brilliant teamwork. Instead he opened a cabinet drawer and pulled out a T-shirt, which he handed to me. It had, predictably, a Weird Fish emblazoned on it, but I took it without comment and pulled it on.

"None for you at the moment," he said to his brother, coming thoughtfully to sit on the bunk. "You need to stay put." He leaned his elbows on his knees and laced his hands together. "They're scientists, you know. Brilliant minds. They just...don't get out much. They're not practical."

"That's fair enough," I said. "Don't suppose we'd get away with microwaving the flask in your Tupperware, would we?"

"I don't know. Maybe, but..."

Rayne shook his head. "Those flasks are designed to withstand a broad spectrum of radiation. We couldn't be sure."

"Right. That's easy, then," I said. "Jason brought this into my life, and I brought it into both of yours. That makes it my problem."

I began to get up. Then I realised that I was sandwiched neatly between Summer and Winter Rayne—brothers divided, at war with one another, but still essentially two sides of the same formidable coin. Two pairs of eyes, the irises circled with their extraordinary dark blue and grey, fixed on me in outrage.

"Don't you bloody dare," Rayne said, grasping my arm. "Winter, stop him."

"Too bloody right." Winter rose smoothly to his feet, blocking my route to the door. "Nobody uses a microwave in this house without my say-so."

"Ah, come on—what are you gonna do, pull your plastic gun on me again?"

"No, but I'll happily clobber you with the end of this torch..." He tailed off, glancing behind him. "Look, let's argue about it in a minute. Whoever ends up doing this, I've got to clear the house."

That was a fair point. I watched him cautiously. He went into the living room, clapping his hands. A couple of his guests clapped back, beaming at him, then fell silent along with the rest. "Hoi," he said. "We forgot something. You all know the story of the mice who had the bright idea of tying a bell on the tail of the cat, right?"

I wasn't sure the MIT boys knew it. Rayne, his hand still wrapped firmly round my wrist, gave a pained chuckle, and the girl who'd come up with the microwave idea sat bolt upright, delighted to be first with the answer again. "Yes! So they all know he's coming. Then one of the mice says, 'But who's going to bell the'... Oh."

Winter saw them out. They left in sober silence. I heard him tell them not to worry—that he'd call them when everything was over. He thanked them sincerely and told them to help themselves from the cellar where he kept his home-brew on the way out. Then he went and leaned casually over the chair by the bedroom door, where we'd thrown Rayne's clothes in our haste to treat him.

I should have known. But I was occupied with Rayne, who had been sitting up for too long and was paying for it, coughing and shivering. I bundled a blanket around him, rubbing his back and bracing him until the spasm eased. Distractedly I saw Winter take something out of the pile of discarded clothing and slip away quietly through another door. "Rayne," I said. "Stay here for a minute, will you?"

I followed Winter out across a small paved yard. The cabin was living quarters only—his bathroom and kitchen were in a separate concrete block. When I pushed the kitchen door open, he turned to me, the flask in one hand, Rayne's service revolver casually held in the other.

"I don't want to hurt you," he told me calmly. "You seem like a nice bloke. I'm glad Summer's found you."

"He's just found you too. Why are you doing this?"

He shrugged. His smile was very sweet. He was so like his brother that I wanted to cry. "I talk a good game, don't I. Most of it was even true. I am a paramedic. I don't mainline crack anymore. But the truth is—well, just what he's told you, probably. I am the fuck-up brother. I ruined everything for him. Which is stupid, because I loved him, admired him so much it drove me crazy. I wanted to be like him, but I couldn't, so I went the other way."

"Winter, don't. He doesn't see it like that."

"Ah, come on. He does. I don't even mind, you know? I've tried to cobble some sort of life together. But it's hard. A lot of the time I feel like I'm just stringing one day to the next. If I do this, at least I was good for something. At least I did something good for him in the end."

"Christ." I looked frantically around the shadowed yard. Somewhere above the forest canopy a beautiful July day was unfolding. I didn't want it to be anybody's last. "Let me come in there with you."

"Not a chance. If this bug doesn't kill me, he will. Back off." He reinforced the order with a movement of Rayne's pistol, and I took an involuntary step away. "Hey, I like this better than my plastic gun. Here's what we do. I go microwave the superweapon, and you and my brother stay the fuck away from here for the next six hours or so. It's a good, nasty, dirty kitchen, so that should be long enough to let us know. I'll be locking the door and the window, and you'd better believe I'll put a bullet through the first have-a-go hero that tries to bust in."

"I don't believe that, Winter."

"Risk it and see. Did he tell you about me? About our family?"

"A bit. The bare minimum. *You* tell me."

He pulled a face, acknowledging my effort. "Oh, you're not getting the life story—the one where I hand you the gun at the end because you've been so sweet and understanding. Do you know what I did in our last foster home? He liked it there, Summer did. The dad was a geologist, took him on all sorts of field trips with him. It was great until I left a baggie of dope stuck under a sofa cushion and one of their own kids found it. I went to Young Offenders for that. The kid was in hospital for a month. And Summer…"

"Went into the army."

"Yeah. By the time I got out, he was on a cadet programme in the Grampians. I never saw him again."

"Jesus… But he'd have joined up anyway, Winter. You know he would. It was all he wanted."

"Maybe. Or maybe I was just such a force of bloody chaos that was the only place he felt safe. And now it's screwed him over. Hasn't it? I've got to do something. Something to make it up."

He began to push the kitchen door closed. It was solid. These looked like old outbuildings, storehouses. Thick walls, small windows. I wouldn't stand a chance. "Please," I said, having one last try. "You didn't bring this down on him. Not this last part. I did."

"Summer must have thought you were worth it." His face became a shadow among shadows as he edged the door shut. "I never saw him look at anyone the way he looks at you. I didn't think he could. No matter what happens, take care of him."

The lock clicked once. "Winter!" I yelled, banging my hands off the door in frustration. I darted round to the side of the outhouse block, but before I could get to the window, he pulled the blind down.

Rayne intercepted me in the doorway back to the cabin. He was naked but for his bandages and combat trousers, and barely on his feet. His face was a white mask of horror. I caught him the instant before his legs buckled. "Dan! Dan, what has he done?"

"I'm sorry." I clutched him tight, easing him down to his knees on the scuffed lino. "He's locked himself into the kitchen. I couldn't stop him."

"Well, let's go and *unlock* him, for fuck's sake."

"He took your gun. I think it's too late. Oh, Jesus, this is all my fault."

"Ssh. No. Just get me out there. He'll do as I say."

But all that came out of the kitchen in response to Rayne's barked orders and pounding on the door was an unfathomable silence. The birdsong that wove through it, the voice of the wind in the trees, deepened it to a drowning pool here in this sunken yard. I held Rayne's shoulders. Bloodstains were opening like roses under his dressings. A painful tremor had seized him with the effort to stay upright.

"He's just keeping quiet," I said. "Whatever it is, it doesn't work this fast."

"No. Bastard's probably listening to his iPod. Winter, let me in. You don't even know how to use that gun."

"I worked out how, didn't I? Listen, love—he thinks the sun shines out of your arse. Stop yelling at him. Just… Just ask."

"Oh, right. Dozens of foster parents tried that—the gentle approach. All he bloody understands is being yelled at."

"Rayne."

"Okay. Okay, fine." His voice cracked. He leaned his brow on the door, flattening his hands to its surface. "Dan here thinks you're just misunderstood. All right. I'm asking you nicely, then. Come the fuck out of there, Winter. Please."

An ongoing silence, deep as ocean now. After almost a minute of it, I felt the tensions in Rayne's shoulders dissolve. He turned to me. I wished that Winter could have seen the hollow desperation in his eyes. "Oh, Dan. What the hell am I going to do?"

I put my arms around him. "Come inside. You're bleeding again. Come and lie down, and I'll stay out here and work on him. Come on."

I could only get him as far as the cabin's back door. Once there, he planted both hands on the frame, bracing up rigid when I tried to move him on. "Not leaving him like this. I'll stay here."

"Rayne, for God's sake. You can't help him."

"I know. But I'm not going in."

I eased him down onto the concrete steps. I strode into the cabin, pulled the blankets off the bunk and came back. I understood. He wanted to keep vigil. I did too—over him and his strange other half, for all the good it would do. "Here," I said, settling beside him on the back step, wrapping him up in the blankets. "Come here. At least let me keep you warm."

After a long while I felt him lose his battle against sleep. He was half-sitting, half-lying over my lap. His head went down into the crook of my elbow, and he twitched and cried out before going under. I stroked his shoulder, trying to ease the transition, and kept up the caress until he was limp and heavy in my arms.

My backside went numb against the step. Leaning my head against the wall, I gazed blindly up into the apricot afternoon sky beyond the trees, remembering the waterfall and that awkward, transcendent hour among the leaves. Remembering how he'd held me afterwards, letting me have my sleep out while he lost feeling from the waist down. Silent laughter rippled through me. I ran a hand over his hair. *Look after him*, Winter had said. *Whatever happens*. The apricot light turned to bronze, and then the tender blue-green of day's ending. I cradled him and kept the watch.

***

Just before dark, a scrape of metal made me jump. Rayne gasped and jerked his head up. The scraping came again, cutting across the still air. The sound of bolts being drawn back from inside the storehouse. Rayne and I watched, motionless, as the kitchen door swung open.

Winter stepped out into the yard. His clothes were rumpled, and he was blinking sleepily. He pushed back his tangle of hair. "Sorry," he said. "I put some music on to listen to, and…I think I nodded off. You two look like a Caravaggio pietà. What are you doing out here?"

"He wouldn't go in," I said. "Winter—are you all right?"

"Um… Yeah. I feel a bit stupid, but otherwise fine." He grinned. It was Rayne's own smile, turned up to madman's intensity. "And trust me, you could get botulism in that kitchen without any bloody help from Hartcliffe Dean at all."

Rayne drew a breath. He started to say something, but it died in his throat. He planted a hand on my thigh, and I aided his struggle upright. He made his way unsteadily across the yard, the blanket falling to the ground behind him.

Winter watched his approach with wide, wary eyes. "Look," he said nervously. "I'm sorry, all right? I just wanted to…"

But Rayne had closed the final gap between them. I waited— I wanted to be sure that Winter's shocked paralysis would melt in time to catch Rayne when he walked, blind and lost, into his arms. It did. I heard his faint, astonished cry, and saw him grab hold, awkward at first and then fierce, as tight as if both their lives depended on it. I picked up the blanket and made my way quietly back into the house.

***

Engine noise in the distance. I found that I wasn't afraid. The only thing that surprised me was that it hadn't come sooner. Dropping the blanket on the sofa, I slipped out into the garden. The night smelled sweet, resinous with conifers after a long hot day. I wondered if Winter had taken the time to reset his alarms and floodlights. Pushing open the heavy wooden gate, I wondered if I could reach his plastic rifle in time—I could see it there by my car, where he'd dropped it—and look halfway convincing with it in my hands.

I decided not to try. I had my flesh and bone, and these I could legitimately use. Whatever was on its way here now would have to go through me.

A jeep pulled up first, closely followed by a grim-looking unmarked van with blacked-out windows. Both vehicles ground to a halt on the dusty, rutted track, and the jeep's door swung open. A tall, rangy man in an army colonel's uniform got out. He turned and made a gesture at the faceless creatures in white HazMat suits already spilling out of the van. "Wait a moment, please."

They stopped. He looked a little surprised to be obeyed, as if something in this game was new to him. He turned to me, his odd air of uncertainty increasing. "Are you Dr. Daniel Logan?"

"That's right. Can I ask who wants to know?"

"Lieutenant Commander George Davis, of… That is, acting Colonel Davis, Fellworth MoD. Dr. Logan, are you—may I ask if you're feeling quite well?"

"Not bad at all, considering. What happened to McCade?"

"Two of his own men turned him in early this morning. With an unbelievable bloody story which I assume you're about to corroborate. We've been looking for you and Lieutenant Rayne ever since. I gather he got hurt."

He got hurt. A shiver ran through me. I still had his blood on my jeans. I remembered the look in his eyes when his shock had cleared enough for him to realise who had hurt him. "Yes," I said harshly. "He was helping me defend whatever biological filth you've brought that team of spooks along to deal with, and your Colonel McCade put a bullet through him."

"I know. Is Rayne here? Does he need medical treatment?"

I couldn't work out why Davis hadn't simply mowed me down, except that he looked like someone had just shaken him out of bed and told him he was now the boss of Fellworth. "Of course he does. But that lot don't look like doctors. If you expect me to just hand him over, after what I've seen of army camaraderie tonight—"

The gate creaked. I spun round and saw Winter emerging into the headlights, a supporting arm tight around Rayne. "All right, Daniel," he said. "You can stop holding the fort." He glanced at his brother. "Lairy, isn't he, for a bloody archaeologist?"

"You don't know the half of it," Rayne agreed tiredly, reaching for me. "Stand down, Dan. I know Davis."

"Oh good! You knew McCade," I reminded him. I pulled him close. "You should've stayed in the house. I wouldn't have let them past."

"No, I don't think you would... Hello, George. I thought you were still out in Iraq."

Davis ran a hand into his hair, dislodging his beret. He was looking from Rayne to his brother with a disbelief I recognised. Next time he spoke, it was in a thick Shires accent that made him sound more like a farmer than military brass. "I was until last week, mate. I was just settling in at Larkhill. Then I get a phone call from Fellworth this morning saying they were minus a CO, and could I cover, because Roy McCade's own men just frog-marched him in, telling some tale about a biological superweapon stolen from Hartcliffe Dean in the seventies."

"Deactivated," Winter said cheerfully. He was looking at the jeep and the HazMat team as if this was what he'd been expecting all his life. "A derivative of *Trisinia*, easily destroyed by microwaving. Quarantine period about six hours—we've tested it."

"Tested it? What the hell with?"

"The only equipment available. I suppose your boys want to go and have a look for themselves. It's in the kitchen in the storehouse out the back. Tell them not to touch anything else, please."

"All right." Davis looked dazed. He turned to the HazMat men waiting by the truck. "Standard containment procedure, gentlemen. Keep it low-key, and respect the civilian assistance. Rayne, I've got a doctor here too, if you want to let him..."

I watched the faceless men march past us into the house. I glanced at the van, with its heavy doors and air of total anonymity. "Rayne, no."

"Okay." My restraining grip on him was far from soldierly, I knew. I wondered if I was embarrassing him. But when I shifted, he reached and put my hand back where it had been. "Sorry,

George. Dan here's a bit disinclined to trust the military. I can't say I disagree with him, after today."

Davis sighed. "I'm beginning to wonder if I trust them myself. *McCade*, for God's sake. I served with him for ten years. There's an ambulance on its way from Lymington A&E—will that do?"

"Maybe." That was Winter, who had finished scrutinising the van and Davis's jeep, clearly taking note of their number plates for his inner record. He came to stand casually in front of me and his brother. I realised that, if I was shielding Rayne, Winter was shielding both of us. "I work at Lymington, mind, George. So I'll know if your paramedics are real or fake. By the way, how did you find me?"

"We checked Rayne's records for anyone he might have taken refuge with, and tracked you down to the hospital. It's…an unusual name. Then they gave us this address. Sorry—was it meant to be harder? It took us all day to work out which shack down which forest clearing, if that's any consolation."

Chapter Seventeen

Jason's lovely house was almost empty now. Standing in the living room, I listened to the gentle thuds and footsteps coming from the floor above, the dining room and kitchen. Outside, eclipsing all light from the street-level window, a huge removals van was waiting, causing the genteel kind of chaos you'd expect in this kind of Salisbury suburb, where people who could not squeeze their Daimlers past would simply sit and wait with pained expressions, rather than honking and revving and muscling by on the pavement. The van was from Harlowe's, a specialist auction house. There had been things in Jason's house which, even as an archaeologist, I wouldn't have dared put a price on, and I'd instructed the valuer to tell me what could reasonably be sold and what belonged more rightly in a museum.

Closing up the house had been in some ways easier than I'd expected. I'd had so much more help. Winter Rayne's imaginary friends, who'd turned out quite handy with tea chests and packing foam as well as conspiracy theories, and a few friends of my own, whom I'd neglected for so long they must have thought that they'd imagined me. Michael was here today, my postgrad flatmate, and a handful of others who'd cautiously texted or phoned me over the course of the last two weeks. People were forgiving. I was grateful and touched.

Other vans had been and gone, bearing off the ordinary stuff of daily life. One of them had gone to a flat down a quiet street round the corner from the university. The flat wasn't anything special, just convenient for work, with plenty of room for my books. It was temporary. I didn't know what I wanted to do with the rest of my life. Not in career terms, anyway, and the uncertainty had ceased to bother me. I had some ideas about the first part of it, that was all.

I heard my name called softly, and turned to see Rayne jog down the steps into the living room. His face and clothes were dusty, and he'd tied a red handkerchief around his head bandanna-style. He looked so handsome and so absurd that I broke into laughter. "God almighty. Take that thing off."

"Why? Does it not suit me?"

"It does, but…" He had been working hard. He smelled of army-issue soap and fresh sweat, and his T-shirt was clinging to him. "You look like the Karate Kid grew up and made a porn movie."

He made a face. "What a thought. They're nearly finished up there, sunbeam. How are you doing?"

I gave it thought. Though easier in many ways, this job had been in others just exactly the heartbreaking bitch I'd imagined. I'd been at it for hours, and I was sickened and exhausted. "I've done better," I admitted. "It's just the last of these books. I can't keep all of them, but the ones he kept in here were his favourites, and…"

A warm embrace wrapped round me from behind. I let the rest of what I'd been saying fade off into a moan, and I leaned back, closing my eyes. My aching muscles seemed to give up their pain the instant he touched me. He was like sunlight, inside and out. He said, brushing kisses down the side of my neck, "Come on. I'll help you choose. Let's get it done."

We worked methodically for half an hour or so. The furniture-removal men finished up, and I went to see them out. Winter appeared on the stairs to say that he and his mates were about done too. I shook his hand and offered for the tenth time to pay them, receiving in return only a haughty look I had come to know well before I'd even met him. "Not a chance," he said. "We'll be down the Regency if you two want to join us later. If not...give him a kiss for me, or whatever the pair of you do. And remember what I told you—I'll be around."

"Yes. Thank you. Look, he's just in here. Don't you want to..."

He shook his head. "Sorry. It's too hard. Can you understand?"

I understood. I said goodbye to Mike and the others, closed the door and leaned my brow briefly on the old woodwork. My understanding could not have been more complete or more painful. Well, I had things I needed to do too. Circles to complete, ends to tie. The new dean of the university was a smart young career academic who couldn't give a toss about college politics or who had slept with or betrayed whom before his arrival. He'd offered me a three-month assignment to supervise and write up the excavation of the newly discovered Salisbury Plain souterrain. Dean Anderson's sudden illness had obliged him to retire to his second home in Madeira, where it had been decided—by whom, I never knew—not to pursue him further. His replacement only wanted me to do a job of work, and I was happy to accept. It was a good one, a dignified end to an academic career.

And a hell of a lot easier than a third tour of duty in Iraq. I straightened up from the door. That was the closing of Rayne's circle—what he felt he owed to his old life, to the man who'd died on his watch last time out. He'd told me the night before. I'd had my reaction then, though not in front of him—taking my tears, and the hot flash of rage that had made me punch a hole through Jason's wisteria trellis, out into the yard. I had to be calm for him now.

He looked up as I came into the living room. "Was that my affectionate brother on his way out? Nice of him to say goodbye."

"You know why he couldn't." I flickered him a quick smile, then turned away and began lifting books down from their shelves.

Rayne was watching me. I could feel it in the prickle of hairs at the back of my neck. I kept my shoulders straight, my expression neutral. We had had a fortnight together. I'd spent the first week of it by his hospital bed in Lymington, pushing the rules on visiting hours until the staff gave up and started working round me. He'd healed fast, and we'd spent almost all of the second week upstairs in this now-vacant house, doing everything his stitches permitted. Not much time, but enough for me to know I wanted a lifetime more of it. Tomorrow his sick leave would be up. I'd see little of him for the next couple of weeks, while the physios and sergeants at Fellworth MoD knocked him back into good enough shape to be sent back out. "Dan," he said, quietly. "You're being very good."

A bit too good, I read between the lines. He'd spent enough time with me by now to know that I wasn't renowned for my stoical silences. "If you knew how I wanted to be, you wouldn't be so impressed."

"The army isn't all McCade, or secret labs at Hartcliffe Dean. It took me about a week to work that out myself. I was ready to walk away—you know I was. But they're not, and I owe them—"

"Rayne. Have I argued?"

A silence fell. I kept my back to him, kept working. There were about sixty books left. I thought I'd perfected my technique of subtly fanning the pages of each for inserts without being noticed, but a few minutes later Rayne said, "Sorry. Getting to the end, aren't we? I've been checking too."

I closed my eyes. I was so tired I could have folded up by the bookshelves and dropped into a coma. Those few days of Rayne's disillusionment had been among the happiest of my life. We'd started to make wild, stupid plans. "It's okay," I said. "The one thing I've learned out of all this is that you can't hang on to anybody. And you never really do get any answers." I rubbed my brow. "Stick something on the TV, will you? Just to distract us while we finish up here."

He didn't move for a while. I ignored his stillness, my awareness of his warm grey gaze upon me—if I looked at him, I was lost. Then I heard him get up and switch on the TV. "What do you want? You've got the last season of *CSI* here."

"Fine. You'll have to open it. I never got around to watching it, after…" I shut up. There would never be an end to *after he died* unless I stopped myself from saying it. I'd been learning, getting better, but today, clearing out his home with what felt like ruthless efforts of decision, it had been hard.

"No. It's open." I heard the click of the DVD case. "Don't tell me someone pirated the first disc for you."

"Are you kidding?" *That was his last gift to me. He loved me. He liked to keep me amused.* "Jason's idea of piracy was Captain Hook and his crocodile."

Rayne snorted. "Okay. It's just that it's blank, that's all."

I heard the slither of the disc going in, then the background hum of activating soundtrack. There was a crackle on it, a muted hiss I associated with the playback on my videocam when I'd been recording the progress of a dig. I wasn't paying much attention, and I didn't turn around. Only forty books left now, and Rayne was going back to war.

There were two people saying my name. The first voice, hushed and startled, I could deal with—just Rayne, who still never let me call him Summer out of bed, and who still used my *Daniel* as if it were something tender and holy. The second—the second, drifting from the TV speakers and vibrating in the air, froze me where I stood.

"Daniel? Danny, my beautiful boy…"

I turned round. I made two steps towards the TV before my legs gave and I crashed to my knees on the carpet. Rayne was diving for the remote, running a finger down it to find the pause. The screen image jolted, skipped a frame or two and stopped. Rayne said fervently, "Jesus fucking Christ," and dropped down beside me.

I'd started to forget how he looked. I'd read somewhere that it's easier to conjure the face of an acquaintance than a lover. The loving mind sees past the mask, dismantles it in favour of shared time, experience, feeling. When it's gone, it can leave you with nothing. A blur. I'd started to forget. "Rayne," I said. "That's Jason."

His arm was locked around me. "I know. I saw him once, remember? At Stonehenge. God almighty. Do you want me to stop it? Do you want me to go?"

"No. Not either." My voice was a rasp. "Please. Play it."

I'd forgotten how lovely he was. He could scare the crap out of people, and I'd never known why, because his leonine features had always turned on me benignly. Here on this video frame, I could finally see it—the severity that frightened essays out of students overnight, that swept aside Ofsted inspectors and other petty wasps and pests attendant on college life. He had never once looked like that at me. He had never once been angry with me. Finally I recognised that that was superhuman.

I pissed Rayne off all the time.

Rayne hit play, and the image resolved into motion. The stern look had been for the camera, not me. Jason leaned in, touched a button, then sat back. His eyes met mine through the screen. There it was—that look of absolute, unalterable affection. No, it wasn't superhuman, was it? Just bloody unlikely in a relationship between two adults. Almost normal, from a father to a favourite son. "There," Jason said. "I think it's running. I bet you're surprised I can work this. Sorry to do it to you this way, Dan, but I reckon if you're watching your dreadful shows again maybe the worst is over. I can't risk a letter or anything else Malcolm might find."

He was in the kitchen, sitting at the table. Behind him I could see my world as it had once been—the door to the garage sealed shut, the DS quiescent behind it. He wasn't—oh, thank Christ he wasn't wearing the clothes I'd found him in. I'd been so afraid that my reluctance to leave with him had been the last straw. My head spun with shock and relief, and I let myself subside against Rayne.

"So," Jase was continuing, folding his hands on the tabletop. "There are things you should know. If you're watching this, and the whole bloody world hasn't come to an end, you disentangled the mess I left you to deal with. I'd have put good money on that, sweetheart. You're so bright, and you know how to get help too, which is just as important. People love you. I'm sure you found someone." Pain tightened his brow. "You know, I've often thought about ditching and running, taking you with me. I'll probably ask you. I know what you'll say, and damn right, too. It would have been wrong. What I'm going to do is wrong, the worst of all, but I just can't live with this anymore."

The image froze again. I jumped as if I'd been in the passenger seat of a car whose driver had suddenly slammed on the brakes. I looked up at Rayne. "What is it?" I asked hoarsely. "Why'd you stop it?"

He put down the remote and ran his fingertips over my cheekbones. "Because it just about kills me to see you cry. Are you sure you want this?"

"Not crying," I said, making inelegant use of my sleeve. "No, I don't. I have to, though, love. Please."

His grip on me tightened. "I want you to know," the screen-ghost said, "that if anything could save me, Dan, it would be you. I never had a hope of loving anyone again. You made me try, made me stay, much longer than I would have done otherwise. You told me a long time ago that you'd had three lovers in your life. I only had one before you. His name was Lucas Gray. You might know by now that he was one of my scientific partners in my lab at Hartcliffe Dean. The other was Malcolm, the dean." He shook his head, ran one hand across his mouth. "The man who became the dean. Christ. That was the deal they made for us—a new life, a new start in our earlier degree fields, if we finished the work on the *Trisinia mactabilis* formula. I'm not going to excuse the fact that we'd started it. That we were damn well working there in the first place. Can you believe that it was all exciting at first? That I was naïve enough to believe they would turn it to medical use?"

He shifted, and the screen flicked to black. But this time it came straight back on, and I realised he'd paused the camera. When the playback resumed, his eyes were bloodshot, his lashes caught together with tears. A great pang of pity and love went through me. I put a shaking hand out to the screen. "Sorry," he said. "Ah, I wish I *could* say sorry, to all the people I've hurt... All right. Luc and I were lovers, but it was Malcolm I had the real partnership with. I'd known him since childhood. He was on my level, my wavelength as a scientist, and between us we...we treated Luc as a lab technician. It was unjustifiable. Luc understood the process better than either of us. He was an early computer genius. He gave us the basics for the formula in terms of DNA sequencing. But he was a good chemist too, and at the time I didn't realise what he'd achieved. He just cooked up what we told him to. I got wrapped up in creating the *Trisinia* formula with Malcolm, and..."

He fell silent for so long that I thought the playback had stopped. Then I realised, with a deep ache in my own lungs, that I could see him breathing. "We finished it. The formula. We did it. God forgive us, we were pleased with ourselves. We called it *the key*. No harm was going to come of it. It would never exist except on paper. But Lucas got hold of it, and he went to his lab, and...he made that up too, just like he did all the rest of our kitchen-work for us. Then he blackmailed me. He told a young sergeant who was supervising our work that the key had been created. The man's name was McCade—I've watched him come up through the ranks at Fellworth. He's about to make colonel, and you can bet we'll get our access to the SPTA then. Anyway, Luc said he'd hand a sample of the formula to McCade if I didn't cut ties with Malcolm and leave Hartcliffe Dean."

Jason sighed and gave a wry, weary smile so real that he could have been in the room with me. "I should have just been gentle, shouldn't I? He was only acting out of love. Instead I blew him out of the water, I suppose you'd say. I was so angry that he'd made the damn stuff—angry because he'd done what I'd shown him how to do. My hypocrisy was punished. Luc told me he was going to hide the batch he'd made. Even then I didn't take him seriously. But he disappeared overnight, and in the morning the early-shift staff found him back in the lab, where he'd killed himself. Hanged himself. And I searched and searched, but the sample was gone. Oh, sorry, Daniel. Give me a minute."

For me it was only a second—the glitch in the recording that showed where Jase had paused it. I could feel that Rayne was shaking a little, and, mindful of his healing scars, his still-fresh shock over McCade, I moved to kneel beside him and return the comfort he was giving me.

Jason reappeared on the screen, terribly pale but composed. "Maybe you already know a lot of what I just told you, but I wanted you to be sure, absolutely certain, that no part of what I'm going to do is your fault. Lucas left me a map. I don't know if he was just in a hurry or if he meant it to be virtually useless. There were no instructions with it, and all I could assume was that it was meant to give me some idea of where he'd hidden the formula. He sent the same thing to Malcolm, who was so freaked out by the whole thing that he destroyed his straight away. Malcolm said we should just forget it. The MoD were willing to wipe our records clean, set us up in new lives. I suppose we were a blackmail risk to them, not that that ever occurred to me. So that's what I did. Even though I knew the containment flasks we had in the labs at that time became unsafe after about twenty years, I let them wipe my slate. I took my doctorate in archaeology, and...I lived alone. Malcolm got married. I envied him his ability to forget. For myself, I was afraid of imposing who I was, what I'd done, on anyone else. I buried myself in my career, and I pretended to myself that there was some archaeological treasure hidden on the plain that would solve all my problems if only I could get access to the military zone. The annoying thing is, I'm pretty sure there *is* something. All the clues are there—you saw them straight away on the day of our field trip, my beautiful boy."

He smiled, and his eyes kindled. "Which brings me to you. Ah, Dan—what must you think? If you've found out some part of the truth, God knows what's been going through your head. Yes, when you told me your father had been a test subject at Hartcliffe Dean, and that he'd died—that was a horror to me, and I won't deny that I treated you differently because of it. I'd have given anything to have a son, and—well, you're everything any father could want. But you've got to believe, my love—long before we went out together to Salisbury Plain, I'd fallen for you. Head over bloody heels. I was just about dying of it. You were my student— a dream I could never have. Then you turned around and knocked my whole world off its axis by making it true."

Rayne kissed me. It was the gentlest of gestures, only the brush of his lips to my brow. But it held me down, kept me warm, in a time-slip whirlwind threatening to demolish the frail reality I'd constructed since Jason's death. I felt his fingers tugging gently at my hair. "It's all right. Hang on."

On the screen, Jason had lowered his head. He was looking at his hands clenched together on the tabletop. Then he raised his eyes, and it was as if the screen, the fourth wall, burst and melted off to nothing. "One more thing. Well, a couple. Sell this mausoleum of a house. You gave it life for a while, but you mustn't get buried here in my dust and antiquities. And..." His dear familiar smile appeared, crinkling at the corners, almost mischievous. "You were wrong about two things—first, that I didn't notice when you looked at other men, and second, that I'd mind if I did. For God's sake, love. You were completely, sweetly faithful to me for all our time together. You know, it's stupid, but I feel jealous of you now—for the first time—because I know you'll find someone else, and I won't be there. I...I mind that, for the first time. But you're too good to waste. I hope there *will* be someone there to love and help you, the way I know you'll love and help him. The way you always did for me."

He didn't say goodbye. He just leaned forward for the last time and switched off. I saw for one instant his expression of concentrated mistrust for small, fiddly machinery, and then he was gone.

Rayne was getting up. *He'll go too,* my shocked brain informed me numbly. I waited for retreating footsteps, the gentle closing of a door. Instead warm hands closed on my shoulders, lifting, and I scrambled up to stand beside him. He was looking at me as if he'd never seen me before. "Dan," he said roughly. "Come here. Come with me."

Apart from the bookshelves, there was one piece of furniture left in the room—the massive sofa, still in place, solid on its carved wooden feet. The removal men had tried and failed to get it through the door. Probably it would have to be sold with the house, or the windows taken out to extract it. Vaguely I wondered how it had ever got in. Then it was just a place for me and Rayne to crash down together. The dust sheet billowed around us as we landed. I seized him, dragging him down on top of me, and we tussled fiercely. I wanted to be crushed, bruised, hurt—wanted to do those things in my turn, to grasp and merge myself with another living body. With this one—this one only, always.

"Rayne," I snarled, driving my fingertips into the muscle of his lovely backside, gasping in wild relief as he bit me through the cotton of my shirt.

"God, Dan. He loved you so much."

"I loved him. I…I love you." The truth of it blazed through me. Both truths—the lover I'd lost, and the one here in my arms, shuddering and lifting me so hard against him I thought my ribs would break. Distance couldn't change it. Death couldn't. *Death, be not proud…* "I understand about Iraq, okay? I understand. I'll wait."

"That's just it. I bloody love you too—way too much to leave you."

I seized his face between my hands. I had to be able to see into his eyes. "But...you will anyway? You have to?"

"No," he ground out, looking straight at me. "Not if I can help it. I don't know if they still shoot deserters, but..."

"They already shot you, love."

He broke into soft, pained laughter. "Yeah, they did. Oh, Dan, I can't leave you. I don't want to go."

We moved together like small waves in water, sea's-edge waves with the whole waiting power of a tide in their wake. Both of us still fully dressed, unwilling to relinquish our grip, our bruising mutual embrace, even that long. My arms were wrapped tight round his shoulders. I pushed up again and again with my hips to meet the slow, forceful down-thrust of his.

Something opened inside me, a barricade I hadn't known was there until it fell. "Summer," I gasped, and writhed away from him, awkwardly over onto my stomach. "Summer, yes."

"God." He grabbed me, stopped me falling off the sofa. "Short notice, isn't it? Don't we need..."

"Yes. Probably. But...I can't wait. Please just try."

He took my jeans down. His hands on my naked backside were hot and dry. I squeezed my eyes shut tight while he explored me, assessing his task, his unexploded bomb. His thumb pressed into the crack of my arse, making me groan with need. "Everything looks so small," he whispered. "I know you've showed me how, but I've never—"

"'S okay. Break your duck on me."

"I'll hurt you."

"A bit. Maybe I need you to. A bit of spit'll help."

I felt him wriggle far enough out of his jeans. Those beautiful old Levis again, the movement of his knuckles as he unfastened button after button, then the hot length of his cock, squeezing tight against me, up into my cleft. My whole body responded, clambering up into desperate readiness. My heart raced. My shaft ground hard against the dust sheet. I could take him...

But the reaction went too far, and I clenched up. "Sunbeam," Rayne breathed against my ear, gently tonguing beneath it. God, his instincts were good—he thrust a hand between my buttocks and waited until the muscle ring guarding my entrance twitched at the stimulation. "That's it. All right, open up for me." Firmly he massaged the taut little diameter, drawing it apart with his fingers.

I made a sound somewhere between lust and despair and spread my thighs as wide as my imprisoning clothing would let me, gasped and sank my face into the sofa as his cock pushed in.

It was one breath off impossible. We lay in rigid stillness, clinging together for dear life. I shot out one hand to the edge of the sofa and clutched it, a dragging tension all down my arm, fingers digging deep into the leather. My other hand, crushed between the cushions, suddenly felt the shape of one of Jason's little pots of fragrant lube, and I choked on laughter—it was way too late for that. Rayne was poised above me, breathing in forced gasps. But the only thing I could imagine less clearly than going on was the possibility of stopping, and with a terrible effort I let go the clench my spasming muscles had wrapped round his penetration, groaned and pushed up halfway onto my knees.

Enough. It gave him the leeway to shove half an inch farther in. Propped on one hand, he used the other to draw me to him, running his palm over my labouring chest, down my belly and down again to seize my cock. There he began a brief, forceful rhythm, so hard it distracted me from what was happening inside me and sent a ripple of pleasure through my struggling flesh. Again, and again, the pulses blossoming out...

I gave up the unequal fight not to yell, and that helped too, unlocking me in shock waves. *Neighbours'll think he's murdering me,* I thought detachedly, then realised more than half the racket was his own. I heaved in great draughts of dusty air and felt the boundaries dissolve, between myself and the world, as if the doors and windows of Jason's house had flown wide to release me, had become my mouth and lungs…

I opened up like a peach. I heard his groan as my resistance gave. He seized the advantage, thrust by thrust, with tender power. He shoved so far inside me that I thought I'd tear apart, and I struggled beneath him, unable to bear the mounting tide of pleasure. With Jason I could wait for it. With Jase it had been like a symphony—the build-up, our orchestrated climax… Now all I could hear was the roar of my blood, my own near-bestial grunts, and my oncoming orgasm would brook no delay. Would rip out of me when it wanted. Too much for me—I writhed and clawed to be away, off this knife-point of ecstasy. He dragged me back against him, his arms tight round me, bracing me against his own force. "Lover," I begged him. "Get me off. Finish it."

He cried out. The white-hot purity of passion in the sound bladed up through my heart. I went down under him, and he landed on me hard, fucking me halfway off the sofa before we found the place where at last we could meet, burn out of our flesh and become briefly one in the crucible of orgasm. My arse was near numbed out by the pounding he was giving me but I felt him shoot deep inside me, and that made me come—my arms braced and rigid to the floor, my head snapping back—so wild and incandescent that I almost broke my spine in my efforts to heave up violently enough against him, to give myself to him ardently enough and take him far enough in. We lost our balance, my arms gave, tumbling us onto the floor in a tangle of limbs.

His cock tore out of me. The pain was incredible. I heard his fractured yell—the exit must have nearly killed him too, and neither of us was quite done. We scrambled back together. The jewelled and priceless rugs were gone—it was just flesh and floorboards here now. We clung to one another, rolling, picking up splinters, thrusting through and past the ending. A shaft of evening light came through the stripped-down window, and there he was, my angel, from the only painting I was keeping from this house, live and real in my arms, stern ecstatic mask melting to a grin as he gazed down at me.

Epilogue
Salisbury, October 2010

Another empty house—this one only the few bare rooms of the flat where Rayne and I had been living since July. The army hadn't played hardball once he'd declared his intention to get out—too grateful, I thought, for his ongoing silence over McCade to make a fuss—and he'd worked his notice quietly at Fellworth, coming home to me here every night. I'd finished my work on the souterrain, and so our obligations were discharged.

I'd finished with the books. With these books, anyway, for now. They had been my last bulky possession. Rayne held the last box closed while I taped it down. "Are you okay, love?"

"I will be. I'll be better once we're on the road. Mike's got the key—he'll see that this lot goes to Harlowe's."

Rayne got up. He gave my hair a gentle ruffle and turned to the window. "Well, you won't have long to wait."

The street was a quiet one—almost deserted at this hour of an autumn morning, only a few bright leaves drifting down over the cobbles to disturb it. I listened, a smile beginning to tug at my mouth. The oncoming noise was quite distinct.

Volkswagen beetles and buses—they all sang the same song, a high, vibrant purr from their near-indestructible engines. I went to stand beside Rayne in the window. I leaned my shoulder against his. "Here he comes, then."

"Yeah. Oh my God—look at the state of that. What the bloody hell have we done?"

"Oh, I dunno. I think she's a beauty, in her own way."

"I'll kill him if I'm stuck with him in that. I'll put a pillow over his head the first time his friggin' *Close Encounters* alarm clock goes off."

I grinned and slipped an arm around his waist. The VW bus that had just sailed into our side street was fresh from somebody's LSD dream. It was partly my own fault—I'd financed this stage of the enterprise, and instead of going with Winter to look at prospective vehicles, I'd told him to knock himself out. He'd said he had a friend who, despising the facile ease of daisy decals and peace signs, stripped buses down and repainted them according to the dictates of his crazed imagination. The result—somewhere between HR Giger and Marc Chagall—was now parked outside my flat, emitting a rumble of Genesis prog-rock.

"You'll be fine," I said. "It's only as far as Luang Prabang, then he's gonna hippie-trail off to Thailand like he always should have done, and you and I will hire something more dignified for our onward journey." I didn't take Rayne's bitching about his brother too seriously. Over the past months, I'd watched them grow back together like saplings of the same stock, meshing in a green arch over a road. Rayne had let his army prejudices grow out with the haircut, and Winter was clean, even of the home-grown dope from his backyard, though he'd have died before admitting he'd done it to impress Rayne.

"He wants to pay you back, you know," Rayne said.

"For the van? Yeah, I know. I'll tie a ribbon on it for him the night before we ditch him in Luang. It's the least I owe him." Rayne's arm stole gently around me, completing our circuit, and I knew that he too was remembering a night in Cheverton Woods, of pain and blood and unimaginable fear. Distractedly I watched Winter swing out of the driver's door, look up to our window and give us a wild, beaming wave. *It's time to go...* "We'll need something a lot tougher to get to Kyon Kam anyway."

Rayne turned to me. His dark gaze kindled, as it always did when we talked about our plans for Korea. I'd made contact with Ryu Mok, a postgrad student I'd met out there the year before. A tricky character, Mok, with as many wrong-side contacts among the hinterland banditti as academic friends at Seoul University. He wanted his nation's treasures pulled out of the Kyon swamps— whether for love or for gold I didn't know, but I was certain he and his comrades could get us there, if we survived the troops of mercenary snipers who emerged from the rainforest and faded back as silently as they had come. Dangerous work—I would need a friend out there. A soldier by my side.

A comrade and a brother, who would light up with pleasure at the thought of a dangerous life. Rayne, who had settled with himself the terms of his personal peacetime over the last three months, was at heart a soldier still and always would be. Beyond Kyon Kam, I had no idea where our roads would take us. Rayne had suggested, smiling wickedly, that since I'd saved my nation's future, maybe I'd paid my debt to the past. I didn't know. Once I'd lifted the temple sculptures out into the light, held them in my hands and devoured their fine-wrought beauty, admired for the last time their gems and high-relief carving and seen them safely back to Seoul, what would I want?

331

Not knowing was a luxury. I had only one cherished certainty left to me. I turned passionately into his kiss, hearing from outside his brother's mocking howls and wolf-whistles. Winter would have something to put up with too, in that little bus, between here and Luang.

"Come on," he said to me, hands clasping firm on my shoulders. "It's time to go."

Our two rucksacks were propped by the door. That was what my material world had boiled down to—and, I thought, bending to pick up mine and sling it over my shoulder, probably as much as a man my age ought to have to weigh him down. Matters of the heart—those sacred burdens—were different. They were infinite; they felt like angel's wings. The little mediaeval painting remained on the living room wall, the only thing I'd left behind. It looked right there. The next occupant might like it, or maybe Mike would take it when he came by for the books. Either way, I thought I would leave it to make its own way in the world from now on. I gave it one last glance over my shoulder, and then I followed Rayne out through the door.

***

We made one stop on our route towards Folkestone. All three of us had spent our lives within sight or sound, or at least within a summer's-wind breath, of Salisbury Plain, and by silent common consent, we detoured off the A303 to take a last run through her vast spaces, her brilliant autumn veils. Past Stonehenge, past the signs for Fellworth MoD... Winter, reluctantly taking first spell in the back while I drove, reached to ruffle Rayne's hair across the back of the passenger seat, and I saw him frown and slap his hand away, but with a hidden smile.

"Mind if I stop for a minute, gentlemen?"

"You're kidding me, Dr. Logan. I bet Indiana Jones doesn't need to stop to pee half an hour after he's left home."

"Shut up, Winter, and pass me my backpack."

I pulled to a halt on the verge. We were within sight of the souterrain, though I'd taken care not to park by the conifer stand where McCade and his men had ambushed us. Rayne still woke up at night shuddering, rasping out his name. The whole area had been cleared of ordnance now. It was considered a site of great archaeological importance and needed only one thing to make it complete. Unzipping my rucksack, I drew out from the top of it the inscribed stone I'd found in the womb of the earth. The true Salisbury key. "If you'll excuse me for five minutes, I think I'm going to put this back."

Rayne stared at me. "Are you serious? You're letting it go?"

The stone had sat on a shelf in our bedroom for the last few months. We'd both looked at it from time to time, tried to interpret its message, but despite my hopes for it, I hadn't been able to make its separate sets of symbols—the Ogham, the cups and rings—relate to one another. I should have handed it to the university's archaeology department and let greater minds than mine have a go at unravelling its secrets. Rachel Keats was in charge there now though, and somehow I hadn't felt like laying such a treasure into her lap.

"Well," I said, watching in amusement while Winter pulled the stone from my hands with his usual unceremonious hunger for anything strange or new. "We haven't been able to make anything of it, have we? There's a bunch of first-year students booked to start work on the souterrain next week. I'd almost like to stick around and see the look on Rachel's face when one of them digs that up."

"Mmm. Nasty." Rayne gave me a considering look, then grinned. "I like it."

"What is this?"

With difficulty I dragged my attention off my lover, whose new uninhibited smiles had the power to transfix me indefinitely. I turned to Winter. He was holding the stone like his firstborn baby, angling it gently to the light.

"We found it in the souterrain," I told him. "It was blocking the passage where the flask had been hidden."

"Do you know why it was there?"

"Not really. Lucas Gray must have put it there, maybe to…" I hesitated. I was getting there, but it still cost me to talk calmly about Jason and the circumstances surrounding his death. "Maybe to *give* Jason something, make up to him in some crazy way for everything he'd done to him. For making him search all that time."

"Dan," Rayne said. He brushed a swift, comforting touch to the side of my face. "You don't have to think about this anymore. Winter, leave it."

"Sorry, Dan. Don't mean to bum you out. But why didn't you let me see it?"

I shrugged. "I don't know. After everything that happened—after nearly getting both of you killed over that damn flask—it didn't seem important anymore."

"Well, that's just where you're wrong, Dr. Logan." Winter ran one appreciative finger over the stone, tracing its spirals, hollows and enigmatic script. "This is important. These marks around the edges—"

"They're Ogham writing. It's an ancient alphabet, based on…"

"Yes. Thank you." Winter gave me a look of friendly weariness, very like his brother's when I was pointing out the obvious to him. "I know what Ogham is. But this isn't. If it was Ogham, you'd be able to read it, right?"

I frowned. "Not necessarily. I can pick out bits, if it's transliterated Latin or one of the Brythonic languages, but..."

"But you'd get the sense of it being a language of some sort, wouldn't you? Coherent words."

"Give me that back." I seized the relic as brusquely as he'd taken it from me. That had been the problem, the reason—apart from all the pain of its associations—that I'd let the thing lie. The Ogham *had* been incomprehensible to me. Not just difficult but nonsensical. "I thought... I thought maybe it was someone's practice-piece," I said. "An exercise in carving, because they don't use the full alphabet. Far from it—just a couple of the letters, repeated along the edge, like..."

Winter was nodding frantically. "Yes. Like binary."

"Like *binary*?" Rayne shook his head, gently extricating the stone from my grasp in his turn. "Computer binary? Don't be daft, Win. This thing's thousands of years old."

I folded my hands on top of the steering wheel and stared out across the plain. Around me in the VW's confined space, I heard arising the sound of Summer and Winter arguing black from white, a background music I'd grown very used to in the last few months. Not everything was down to aliens and conspiracy theories, Rayne was telling his brother. Human beings were capable of building pyramids and stone circles—bloody crop circles too—without the intervention of spacemen. And Winter was countering him, passion for passion, that not every damn thing on earth could or should have an earthly explanation forced upon it.

I looked into the blue skies over the site of the souterrain, where a pair of stone-curlews were wheeling. They were migrants, I remembered. Soon they would be gone. "Lucas Gray," I said quietly. "He was a computer programmer."

Rayne turned to me. "What? Are you saying Lucas did this?"

"Made the marks? No, not at all. They're the same age as the other inscriptions. But Lucas would have recognised it—if it was binary, I mean. He'd have known it was…" I hesitated, searching for a word. *Significant* hardly covered it.

"He'd have known it was fucking incredible," Winter finished for me reverently. "It would overturn every moribund bit of received bloody wisdom about what ancient people knew, and how they knew it, and if it translates the other marks on this stone…"

His mouth dropped open. Galactic distances were opening in his blue eyes. "Jesus, Rayne," I said dryly. "Quick, grab his ankle before he floats off."

"It's your fault if he does. You should know better by now than to encourage him. It can't be binary—can it? That would be absurd."

I looked in pleasure at his flushed, indignant face. Rayne liked his world to make sense. I liked how mine made sense to me when he was around. "I don't know," I said, not taking my eyes off him. "If it was, could you read it, Winter?"

"Me? God, no. But I know some people who could."

I smiled. "Like you knew some people who could disarm a chemical weapon." I hooked my arm over the back of the seat and turned to face him. "You were ready to die for that. For your brother, and for…for me, although you'd barely known me ten minutes. Did I ever thank you?" He just gawped at me in bewilderment, and I pressed on. "Listen. This stone, this artefact… Whatever it is, it's not mine to keep or give away. But if you think you and your global family could work out what it means—take it. Have a try."

"Me? Christ, Dan. I'm not qualified to do something like that. I'm not—"

"Who is? Who else would even have thought far enough outside the box to read those marks as binary?"

"Well, that is the problem with you academics," Winter said unsteadily. "You do have monorail minds."

"Sometimes, yes." I took the stone from Rayne's hands and passed it over to Winter, who hesitated now before touching it. "Not Jason. While he was looking for his key—this one, the real one—he never thought it would be found by any one scientist, anyone working in isolation. He was always looking for ideas from other people—establishment intellects, yes, but radicals too, pioneers like Paul Devereux. People like you."

"Dan, are you sure about this?" That was Rayne, who'd been watching me quietly while I found my way to these conclusions. "I thought you'd have given your arm and six pints of blood for this kind of discovery."

"I would have." It came out hoarsely, and I swallowed. A weird anguish was rising inside me. "If it was my discovery, and— and five months back, I would have. But I don't want this now. Not something that's gonna tie me to Salisbury, and memories of Jason—oh, not of *him*, but the way he died—forever, for all I know. I want to get away from everything here, go and bugger about in a jungle and get shot at, and after that I don't know what I want." I stopped, long enough to snatch a breath. "Except you. Except you."

Rayne kissed me. For once Winter had nothing to say about it. He was oblivious to us, his whole attention fixed on the relic. I heard him comment softly, through the thunder of blood in my ears. "This stone's a miracle, you know."

After a long moment, Rayne let me go. He put both hands to my face and looked into it as if, for him, as many answers lay there as Winter would find in his stone. "Yes," he said, brushing my fringe back from my brow. "A bloody miracle."

Harper Fox

About the Author

Harper Fox has become a well-loved go-to author for fans of M/M romance. Here you'll find immersive tales of excitement, magic, drama, all underpinned by the ordinary processes of love, hope and loss in an imperfect world.

Harper has garnered critical acclaim for novels such as *Scrap Metal*, *Brothers of the Wild North Sea*, *Seven Summer Nights* and *The Salisbury Key*. She is also creator of the enduringly popular *Tyack & Frayne* mystery series. Many of her ebooks are also available in paperback and audio format. You can find news of her current projects and full backlist at her website, www.harperfox.net.

A northerner at heart, Harper has returned to her native Northumberland after a spell in Cornwall. She travels between the two as often as she can, and feels she has a home in both magical kingdoms. She is married to Jane, and enslaved by three cats.

Made in the USA
Las Vegas, NV
05 February 2025